OTHER TITLES BY PATRICK KENDRICK
Papa's Problem, a Florida Book Award Winner

D1469122

BAYVILLE FREE LIBRARY

EXTENDED FAMILY

The characters and events portrayed in this book are fictitious. Any similarity to real persons, living or dead, is coincidental and not intended by the author.

Text copyright ©2012 by Patrick Kendrick
All rights reserved.
Printed in the United States of America.

No part of this book may be reproduced, or stored in a retrieval system, or transmitted in any form or by any means, electronic, mechanical, photocopying, recording, or otherwise, without express written permission of the publisher.

Published by Thomas & Mercer
P.O. Box 400818
Las Vegas, NV 89140

ISBN-13: 9781612183107
ISBN-10: 1612183107

EXTENDED FAMILY

by Patrick Kendrick

THOMAS & MERCER

For Millie

Epigraph:

Our greatest evils flow from ourselves.
Jean-Jacques Rousseau

Now I am become death, the destroyer of worlds.
J. Robert Oppenheimer, quoting from *Bhagavad Gita*

ACKNOWLEDGMENTS

I'd like to thank my wonderful, hardworking agent, Jill Marsal, for never giving up on me. Thanks to my editors: Andy Bartlett for his good taste, David Downing for making it taste better. I owe deep gratitude to my initial readers: Lisa, Bill, Cathy, and Paul for their opinions and encouragement. Thanks to Joe and Ardis Clark for getting me started. A special thanks to: Kim, Jay, Jane, and Rocky for believing in me. God bless you all.

PROLOGUE

He entered the Future-Gen clinic wearing his considerable and practiced charm like an expensive blazer. The receptionist thought she had her radio's volume turned down so only she could hear it—that was the deal she'd struck with her boss—but just a couple of steps inside the door, the man turned his thousand-megawatt smile on her and began bobbing his head to the beat, mouthing along, "That's the way, uh-huh, uh-huh, I *like* it, uh-huh, uh-huh." Just like that, he had her laughing. He was remarkably attractive, with piercing dark-brown, almost black, eyes; full, succulent lips; a regal nose; angular cheekbones; and a deeply dimpled chin. Put him in a white suit and he'd be John Travolta in *Saturday Night Fever*; she just knew this man could dance.

His hair was as thick as a bear's and displayed his only apparent physical flaw—some premature graying on his temples. One could argue if it was a flaw at all, as it lent him a distinguished look—put him in a classroom instead of a disco, and he'd be the professor making his coeds melt. He was tall, wide-shouldered, narrow-waisted, and carried himself like an athlete. His high school yearbook contained pictures of him as the star golf, baseball, and tennis player, as well as debate champion, member of the drama club, editor of the student newspaper, the student "most likely to succeed." His college years, including graduate school and on, were a continuation of his academic and athletic prowess.

It would have been difficult to construct a more perfect candidate for sperm donation. Indeed, after a careful evaluation of his family medical history (no cancer, cardiac, gastrointestinal, or skeletal myopathy, good longevity on mother's and father's sides), DNA makeup, and physical characteristics (no one did psychological testing in the early days of donor programs, other than a perfunctory IQ test, which showed his to be well into the MENSA range), he was found to be the perfect donor, willing and able to provide the perfect specimen. In fact, he became sought after by numerous cryogenic storage facilities in that era before HIPAA medical information regulations, when doctors bought and sold medical data like postal addresses. These businesses actually charged a premium for his donated and abundant sperm.

Women went to sperm banks and filled out questionnaires about why they wanted or needed artificial insemination and, almost as an afterthought, listed the physical and mental qualities they desired in their mate. Our man's concentration of those qualities made his sperm and its potential offspring the number one choice of 93 percent of all women who sought artificial insemination.

The receptionist behind the granite-topped counter at Future-Gen was immediately smitten with this man. Having worked at FG for over two years now and played the field sexually, but with no serious prospects, she began to see the benefits of having a choice in the genetic makeup of one's progeny. She had seen all types of men come in to make their donations, all shapes and sizes, but this man was, well, perfect. A typical sample of the "me generation," the receptionist was attractive in that over-the-top, big-hair, go-to-nightclub, sniff-a-little-coke, and fuck-the-night-away fashion. Still, it was hard to find a good man, or like she used to joke with her gal pals, "a hard man was good to find."

The man identified himself, and the receptionist—after cross-checking his identification against his FG-assigned number (56QAH)—led him past her reception area, through a door, and into the hallway flanked by the donor rooms.

"Do you…would you care for some…uh…reading material?"

His warm smile showed his perfectly aligned teeth, framed with the cutest dimples. "No, thank you…uh…Susan," noting her name tag. "I've brought my own reading material." He held up a smart leather portfolio—such as any savvy business executive would carry—and grinned again. He laughed, inviting Susan to do the same.

"Very well," she said. "If you need anything else…" She cut herself off, feeling her cheeks go red, and showed him into a tastefully decorated room. "There is the container for your donation and a wash area," she said, pointing to the specimen container in its sealed plastic bag on a marble sink against the far wall. Take your time."

Susan closed the door behind her and fanned her flushed face all the way back to her desk. She had never been embarrassed by her job or by the men who came in to do what they had to do to make a donation—in some cases, just the thickness of a wall away. But this guy—God was he good looking! She wondered if she could be bold enough to ask him out.

The man undressed himself, carefully hanging his clothes in a thoughtfully provided and handsome mahogany armoire. There was a full-length mirror on the door of the armoire and the man stood in front of it admiring his nude form. Wide, powerful chest and narrow hips. Strong, muscular arms, thighs, and calves. With less than 4 percent body fat, he was toned and taut. He ran his hands over himself, from nipples to groin, feeling his hardness. He took a towel from the armoire and spread it out on the leather couch against the opposite wall of the room. The climate in the room was cool, perfect for him; he was very comfortable and easily aroused. He sat down, his manhood fully erect.

He opened his attaché and withdrew his reading material. The material was not *Playboy*, *Penthouse*, or any of the countless other men's magazines. Nor was it *Blueboy* or any of the gay publications. It was a collection of photos he had taken just the night before, then developed himself in the state-of-the-art darkroom in the considerable manse he called home.

In the photos was a woman, lying on a bed, provocatively dressed in select Victoria's Secret lingerie, including stockings and a corset. The man let his eyes roam over her long, sculpted legs, remembering how they'd felt, how they'd smelled and tasted. He moved to the next photo—her flat and inviting abdomen, the nicely trimmed mons—noting that, yes, the carpet matched the drapes, a true redhead, top and bottom. He began stroking himself.

Now his eyes moved to the next photo, this one showing her breasts, perfect Cs, the nipples that soft petal pink that redheads possess, which were his personal favorite. He felt himself grow even more and vigorously alternated between twisting his penis and cupping his testicles. His sphincter began to tighten, rhythmically, matching his increasing pulse, and he massaged his prostate to stoke his internal engine to maximum production.

Finally, he came to the photo of the redhead's face. She'd been beautiful, with tangerine-colored tassels of curly hair and eyes the color of spring water, the photo so clear you could easily see their crystalline green color, her pale skin flawless, her pores almost imperceptible. Full, luscious, naturally plump lips, with just the tiniest stream of blood escaping the corner of her exquisite mouth that had held his cock so lovingly, sucking the cum from it like an infant seeking nourishment. The blood ran down her chin and joined the rest of the blood puddled around her severed head. The head sat atop the television, a big-screen, projection-type Magnavox that displayed a grainy picture caught on his camera—a scene from *Hawaii Five-O*. Blood trickled down the screen, dissecting the picture with vertical crimson lines, but Jack Lord didn't notice.

The man reached orgasm and collected his deposit into the specimen cup that had been left for him in the room—prelabeled with his assigned identification number (56QAH) and this session's lot number (Lot 900)—then placed the cup in the resealable plastic bag.

The chances of any woman getting pregnant from his sperm, even a woman plagued with low fertility factors, were very high. Incredibly, our man not only produced nearly double the ejaculate of most men, but double the concentration of spermatozoa—some fifty million per milliliter, all of them highly mobile. If the woman could produce an ovum, one of the millions of sperms was sure to penetrate that egg like a voracious rapist and produce in the willing receptacle's womb an offspring of this man—this perfect man—carrying many, perhaps most, of his dominant characteristics. Like a proven herd sire, indeed, he had "progeny on the ground," as the ranchers say, and most of them were male, promising to grow into highly intelligent, devastatingly handsome mesomorphs, with many of their biological father's physical traits and many of his unspeakable psychological characteristics.

He put his photos back in his portfolio case. They were all that remained of the girl, or the memory of her. After photographing her remains, he had poured gasoline throughout her home and incinerated all of it, eliminating any evidence of himself at the scene and any trace of her, save the memory of her exquisite suffering and death. He washed his hands and got dressed, admiring himself one last time before leaving the room. He went back to the reception area and placed the specimen on the counter.

Susan, the receptionist, looked up and noted the considerable volume in the specimen cup. Her eyes went wide and dirty thoughts went through her head like images of a pornographic film. Again, she felt her cheeks go hot.

"This is a little…awkward, Susan," he said. "But I'm here for a physician's conference and don't know the town that well. Can you recommend a really nice place for dinner?"

"Sure," said Susan. "Expensive?"

"Yes," he said, flashing his movie-star smile. "And something with a little atmosphere. Low lighting."

"Edouardo's. The steaks are prime and melt in your mouth. Dark, paneled walls, brass rails, a guy in a tuxedo softly tinkling the ivories…"

"And you and me?"

Susan glanced clumsily back at the specimen cup, then back to the donor's handsome face. She felt her heartbeat in her throat. "Are you sure you're…up to it?" she said, trying to suppress a giggle.

He laughed. "Smart-ass. Don't worry, I'll be fine. Come on. Join me."

"Well…okay. About seven? Meet me there?"

"Perfect," he said, then came around the end of the reception counter. Susan looked up at him—his eyes were so dark, so deep. He pushed her hair away from her check and gave her a light kiss. He inhaled heavily and she could tell he was *smelling* her.

"That's nice," he said, and strolled to the door. He turned there. "At seven, then," he said, giving her that toothy grin again. "Don't be late."

Susan gave him a cutesy wave and, after the door closed, turned up the radio on her desk. The Boss was singing, "Baby this town rips the bones from your back. It's a death trap. It's a suicide rap. We gotta get out while we're young 'cause tramps like us, baby, we were born to run."

ONE

ONE GENERATION LATER

Journal: The Work Begins

When you read this, sir, you will undoubtedly believe this journal to be the work of a sick mind fueled by a fevered imagination, but it is not. Some of it comes from my direct observation of these crimes and these demented people, most of whom exist in your neighborhood, invisible to all except those of us who know what to look for and where to look. It helps to have a sensitized mind—that which some people call "clairvoyance," though I avoid that term and the images of cheap carnies and hucksters associated with it. Having access to government databases—classified files, medical records, credit histories (which can be very telling, I assure you)—most definitely is an advantage. That, coupled with my knowledge of coded identifiers for the subjects, has made finding these subjects easier than I would have thought. Once located, I assess them and determine their qualities, their capabilities, their potential. In some cases, such as Subject 56QAH/Lot 1100, they might need a little push, a little on-the-job training, if you will. That's the fun part, though. It's like shooting fish in a barrel—or should I say, children on a playground…

• • •

The parking lot belonged to a small church that barely subsisted on the meager tithings of its dwindling congregation. Its gravel surface was pocked with potholes and lined with tufts of weeds. The lot's curbs were old, rotting railroad ties.

That's what Pastor Wilton thought was burning as he got out of his rusted and faded maroon Mercury Marquis and approached his modest church. It was just after five a.m., and one of those railroad ties along the far side of the lot was somehow on fire. The aging clergyman looked around for a hose, then remembered the bib was on the other side of the building and the hose was brittle and split anyway. He unlocked the front doors, found his way to the office through the dark, and called 911. He reported the fire, making it clear that it was not threatening the building. As he waited for the fire department to arrive, he pondered the situation. Kids probably started the fire. This is why they needed a bigger building, one with a community center where kids could gather and stay out of trouble.

Then Pastor Wilton remembered the fire extinguisher in the church's kitchen. It was old, maybe didn't work anymore, like everything else around here, but what could it hurt? He went to the kitchen, brushed off the cobwebs, and pulled it from the wall. He stepped back into the dim morning light and shuffled out to the fire. As he got close to the flames, he noticed a purse lying near the blaze, its contents spilled out like a cornucopia: a hairbrush, car keys, wallet-sized photos, a tampon, cigarettes, and several lipsticks whose gold cases reflected the light of the fire like spent bullet cases. The old reverend thought, *Oh no, these troublemaking kids probably stole one of the parishioner's purses, grabbed the money out of it, found a lighter, and set the fire.*

Pastor Wilton pulled the pin on the extinguisher and aimed it at the fire. Then he saw the shoes. Strange. There wouldn't have been shoes *in* the purse. He looked closer and saw something else, something that made his heart begin to fibrillate and invoked images of old horror magazines he used to read when he was a child: the fleshless and charred skeleton of a hand reaching up through the flames toward heaven.

TWO

I was kitesurfing when I got the call. Trying to, anyway. I'm not very good at it, but I keep trying. Those few moments when the wind fills my sail and I'm skimming the ocean's surface like a skipping stone, feeling like I've caught a piece of the sky and the sea at the same time, it's as close to God as any of us can come.

I went in to take a breather on the beach, my lats, pecs, and triceps throbbing from exertion. I'd brought a Sun Shower with me and rinsed off with fresh water, noting the pattern of sea louse stings on my legs and chest where they got caught in the hair. Skeptics question whether global warming is real. All I know is I grew up swimming in the Atlantic, and in my roughly three decades here, I've seen the reefs go barren, the color washed out of the coral like overlaundered clothes. Sea lice, the larvae of jellyfish that thrive in warmer waters, have increased exponentially. As a kid, I might have gotten a sting or two while swimming in the summer waters. Now, the sea lice are here year round, so thick that, at times, diving in the ocean is like jumping into a vat of acid, then coating yourself with itching powder.

I finished rinsing off and was reaching for a towel when I heard the muffled ringtone—a tinny version of Copland's *Fanfare for the Common Man*—coming from the bottom of my beach bag. I touched the screen of my iPhone where it said *Answer*. It was Leonard Cotton, a smartassed ne'er-do-well with a gift for making you want to strangle him one minute, then hug him the next.

"'Lo," I said.

"Hey, dude. What's up?" he began.

"Just the wind and the waves, bud."

"You kitesurfin', man?"

"Trying."

"Cool. Wish I was there."

"You could be if they ever make a kite big enough to lift your huge ass."

Leonard was a linebacker for the University of Florida Gator football team. A blown knee kept him from going pro, but he never gave up on the weights and steaks and keeps his six-foot-five frame at a svelte 285 pounds. He has a black belt in jujitsu and is one tough mother with a little prankish boy living inside his tender soul. On those rare but wonderful occasions when we get out together, we joke around, telling people we're brothers even though he is big, black, bold, and bald, and I'm six feet even and 170 pounds, with sun-lightened, sandy-brown hair sitting atop my white-bread head.

"You still coverin' my zone for me?" he asked.

"Yeah. You still in Wally World?"

"Oh yeah. Me and duh fam gettin' it on with Goofy, Minnie, and Mickey."

"Where's Donald Duck?"

"Fuck the duck, man. I don't need feathers stuck up my ass, bro."

"Why not? You've had everything else stuck up there."

"Oh, man! That ain't right. That just ain't right. You still luh me, though, right?"

"Like chocolate, man."

"All right, all right. I was just checkin' on you. Makin' sure you're coverin' my ass."

"It's a big job, but somebody has to do it."

"That's cool. I owe you, man. See you when I get back."

"You bet. Give the kids a hug and tell 'Nessie I'm still here when she wants me."

"I'll give her your love, like only I can. Later, Grey."

"Bye-bye, Superfly."

I clicked off and was reaching for the towel when the cell started ringing again. I wasn't expecting a call, though I suppose I should've been. Covering Leonard's assigned area, which was Broward County, in addition to my own, gave me about half of the Sunshine State. There are only thirteen state fire marshal offices throughout Florida and not all of them have investigators. I work out of the West Palm Beach office, one of the busier ones. Still, most calls come in at night, when people are at home to set a fire by spilling a pan of hot grease, or leaving a candle lit in the bedroom, or falling asleep on the couch while smoking a cigarette. And most arsonists work at night, naturally.

Usually, the fire command officer on the scene can make the call as to the fire's origin and be done with it. But if the fire officer is too green and can't make that determination, or if the property damage is over one hundred grand, or if he suspects arson, smells an accelerant, or finds a can of gas sitting where it shouldn't be, or just finds a big sign pointing to the fire scene saying, "ARSONIST AT WORK," then the state fire marshal has to be called out to investigate.

One other criterion makes it mandatory that we respond to a fire: when there is a fatality.

I looked at the phone and saw it was the number of our South Florida dispatch office. It was eight o'clock in the morning, shift change for the dispatchers. I was hoping the dispatcher was calling just to see if I was still covering my buddy's area. The sun was shining and bits of bright-silver light were glinting off the sea like warning signals from a league of lost souls. The wind was building, promising to lend me some awesome rides. It could have been a perfect day, but it wasn't going to be now. I answered the call.

"Officer Gift?" A woman with a musical voice.

"Speaking."

"You're being requested to respond to the City of Tamarac, in Broward County. There's been a fire fatality."

"Commercial or residential structure?"

"Uh, let me look at my notes, here. Hmm. It's not a structure fire at all."

"Then how was there a fire fatality?"

"It appears someone set somebody on fire in a church parking lot. It's at the Eliathah Seventh Day Adventist Church at seventy-five fifty University Drive."

"When did they get the call?"

"The CAD system shows it came in at five eleven this morning."

"What took them so long to call for us?"

"That, I can't tell you. But it says the FBI requested the state fire marshal."

"FBI? What the hell are they doing there?"

"Don't know, hon. Sorry."

"'S okay. Ask them to keep the scene secure. Tell them I'll be there in about an hour."

• • •

I took the turnpike to just south of Boca Raton, then got onto the Sawgrass Expressway, continuing south with the Everglades to the west, stretching out as far as I could see. Blue herons stood knee-deep in the canals, patiently looking for fish. Ospreys swooped down and plucked bluegills out of the dark water. Anhingas—snake birds—dotted the banks, wings spread to dry.

I took in the beauty while I could, anticipating the ugliness I would have to encounter shortly. Burn victims are terrible to see; you never really get used to it. Sometimes I awake at night, tangled in sweat-soaked sheets, my heart racing and body trembling, fighting to regain consciousness so I can get the images out of my head. I gulp the water I keep next to the bed and dare not close my eyes again, lest that slide show of horror pop up again on the inside of my eyelids.

I was about eight months on the job as a firefighter and we responded to a blaze at a pawnshop. We saw smoke billowing up from a few blocks out, so we caught the hydrant going in and stretched the hose lines up to the front door. But flames were shooting out the entrance, so we rounded the corner of the shop, where we came across a man leaning up against the wall. My first impression of him was that he was a homeless guy taking a break from the streets. His clothes and skin appeared dirty and unkempt. But as we got closer I could hear him moaning, and when he heard us dragging the hose around, he startled me by opening up and wailing. He reached out blindly toward us, and then I saw. His eyelids had been burned away, as had all the hair on his body. The fire had blinded him, searing his eyes a bluish white. What I had mistaken for dirt on him was his sooty skin, which began to drip off of him like tallow. He begged for us to kill him. I stood there aghast, my fire axe suddenly heavy in my hands. For a brief moment, I saw myself swinging the blade into his head and taking him out of his misery, but the squawk of my lieutenant's call for the medics on his radio snapped me out of it and I returned to the task of pulling the hose past the burned man to the rear entrance of the building.

Once inside, the lieutenant and I found ourselves inside a blast furnace, with stored ammunition igniting and zipping around the pawnshop, tearing out chunks of the walls and exploding hocked televisions like grenades. Still, I found that I would rather be inside that living hell than back outside, looking into the blind eyes of the man who had brought forth that homicidal notion in me, its message come aborning from some dark place in my mind I would forever fight to avoid revisiting, but whose tenacious nature would cling to me like a malevolent shadow.

I shoved it all away again and pulled my unmarked cruiser into Eliathah's parking lot. I had to park outside the ring of dozens of Broward County Sheriff cars, and I could see the fire department's engine company was still there, the crew looking fatigued. A crowd had started to gather and gawk, and as I got out of my car I saw an old man trip in a pothole and go down. I walked over to him and helped him up. He found his feet more easily than I would've expected, and his grip on my arm had steel in it. He brushed off his pants and thanked me, telling me I was a gentleman and a scholar, so I had that going for me. He wore khaki trousers and a pressed white shirt buttoned all the way up to his Adam's apple. He was a startlingly handsome old guy, with the softened but still recognizable build of a former athlete. His hair was white but thick, and his eyes looked into mine with paternal concern as he shook my hand with both of his. I watched him amble slowly down the sidewalk and pass the sign in front of the church that read, "God's Love Is The Eternal Flame That Will Save Your Soul."

I looked beyond the yellow crime scene tape. Some Broward County Sheriff detectives were there, as was a tall, beautiful woman I didn't recognize. She wore a blue blazer and sipped coffee out of a paper cup with her pinky finger extended like a feminine flag of defiance in an all-male world. Her hair held the color and sheen of a raven's feathers and looked liked she ironed it every morning before she went out. Her skin was pale porcelain, her face expressionless except for a slight crease in the brow. She appeared to be looking for something, which turned out to be me. She had to be FBI.

The Broward Sheriff's Office's district chief, Hank Dugger, was standing in the group, too, looking perturbed. I'd only been on a few investigations in Broward, back when I was still in training and doing ride time with Leonard to learn the job, but I remembered Dugger as an impatient, no-bullshit kind of guy. He saw me coming and came at me like a tank, bumping people out of his way with his barrel chest. He wore a jacket and a tie that looked like it was too tight, and his round, brown face shone with perspiration.

"Gift, right?" he said. "Out of Palm Beach?"

"Yes, sir."

"Where's Cotton?"

"Vacation."

He nodded. "Wish I was on vacation," he mumbled.

"Heard the FBI was here."

"Yeah. What's with that? We had our guys out here, you know, going over the scene. We would've called you, but when she showed up, she just about bitch-slapped us away from the scene. Like we didn't know to preserve the scene. That's why it took so long to call you out. She had to go over the body herself before she let us get into it. Says she's out of Miami and they think this case might be related to some other cases with similar MOs. I haven't heard about anything like this, have you?"

He'd followed me around to the back of my car. I'd opened the trunk and reached in for my evidence kit. It's a canvas bag with a shoulder strap so I can keep my hands free as I approach a scene. When I first started doing investigations I was attacked by some nut who came flying out of the bushes like a banshee. I broke the department-issued tackle box (and my wrist) beating the guy over the head with it.

I hefted out the bag and swung it over my shoulder. I like my bag. It holds everything I need, including a second backup gun. Like most law enforcement officers, I carry a 9 mm Glock on my waist, a twelve-round clip, and a smaller backup, a .38 Special Smith & Wesson, on my ankle. But I keep the cannon, a .44 Magnum Ruger Super Blackhawk, in the evidence kit in case I need a heavy hitter.

"What do you have here, exactly?" I asked.

"Oh, sorry, I thought you knew. It looks like someone poured gas, or some flammable liquid, all over the vic and lit her up. She must have been dead first. She wasn't tied up and it doesn't look like she was flailing around or anything. You *know* you would be moving around if someone set your ass on fire."

We talked as we walked, moving through the crowd as I pulled on some latex gloves.

"Maybe the perp was trying to hide evidence or the victim's identity?"

"Evidence, maybe. But whoever did it wasn't trying to keep her identity secret. Her ID was in her purse. Name is Jolie Matarese. She works in a doctor's office in Ft. Lauderdale but does a little hooking on the side. Keeps an ad on Backpage.com and the Erotic Review under the name Chloe. Has a thin jacket in Broward, picked up for soliciting about three years ago."

"You tell the FBI lady that?"

"No. She told me," he said. He seemed exasperated. "I'm getting old. Why don't you introduce yourself? I've got a budget roll-out meeting with the city commission this morning. I'm not a cop anymore. Just a fucking politician." He pulled out a card and handed it to me. "Give me a call and keep me in the loop, okay?"

"You bet, Chief."

"And tell Leonard I said hello."

"Yep," I said, and approached the scene and the pretty agent in the blazer.

I introduced myself and she gave a lift of her chin. "Special Agent Rose Cleary." Then, under her breath, "I hope you're a little sharper than these yahoos."

I thought she was being too hard and said so. "They're not bad guys."

"No, I suppose not, for fishing buddies." Her eyes were lapis blue, but so dark you could only make out their color when she looked up and the sun caught them. She held her hand up and shielded her face, and they turned black. She narrowed them at me. "Is that seaweed in your hair?"

I laughed. "Probably so. I was at the beach when I got the call."

"Okay, then." A hint of a smile. "Come here, I want to show you something."

We moved past the yellow crime scene tape and I saw a lump covered with more yellow plastic. There was a black zippered bag, the type used by the medical examiner's office, stretched out next to the body.

"They almost had her in the bag when I got here. They've walked all over the scene. See that cigarette butt over there? It's from that BSO shift supervisor over there. When I asked what they thought they were doing, they looked at me like deer in headlights and said, 'Well, there's not much here. She's all burned up.' Thought I'd stumbled into Mayberry somehow."

"I don't think they get a lot of homicides here."

"I don't think they get a lot of education, either."

"You always so pleasant?"

"No. Sometimes I'm a real bitch." She stared at my bag. "Is that an elephant gun in your canvas bag, or are you just happy to see me?"

I felt my face flush.

"What are you expecting—an invasion? You have, what, thirty pounds of weapons on you?"

A puff of wind blew through the scene and I could feel it cool the perspiration on my neck. "It's a forty-four Magnum. In case I need some stopping power."

She smiled—perfect teeth and wide dimples on either side of her full-lipped mouth. "Forty-four Magnum. That's for candy-asses."

"I…why? What?" I stammered. "What do you carry?"

She lifted her jacket, showing me the distinctive handle—one with a red plastic insert—of a .454 Casull Magnum, the most powerful handgun made.

"That only holds five shots, though," I said, trying to redeem myself with my worldly gun knowledge.

"Only need one." She looked at me with the most devilish gleam in her eyes. "Don't mind me, I'm just ragging on you. You haven't been doing this very long, have you?"

"I was hoping it wouldn't show. Three years with the state office, a couple more before that with West Palm."

"Why the career change?"

She was walking away from me, over to the body, and I was following her. I was wondering who she was investigating here—me or the dead woman. But I couldn't say I minded the attention.

"I was with the fire department in West Palm Beach for about ten years when I got hurt. They wouldn't let me be a firefighter after that."

She looked back at me over her shoulder. "I'm sorry."

"'S okay."

We were approaching the body, and my stomach was tightening. You'd think I would be accustomed to it by now; though, in a way, I guess I'm glad I'm not. When you get so burned-out that looking at a dead human being moves you no more than looking into a garbage can, then you've lost the reason you got into this business in the first place.

"No, really," the lady agent said. "I'm sorry I'm being a tool. It's just…ah, shit, you'd think I'd get used to it. But I don't. I can't. When I got here this morning, these bozos were treating me like I was just some chick that rolled up to ask directions. Put me in a bad mood. Let's you and I start over."

"Fair enough."

"We're going to need some lab work and I don't have time to wait for a Quantico report. Your guys do chemical analysis, don't they?"

"Sure do. Pretty good at it, too."

"I've heard that." We knelt by the body and she reached for the yellow plastic covering it. Agent Cleary's hands were still feminine, nails manicured, painted with clear polish, no color, and no wedding band or engagement ring, either. I decided she could give me as hard a time as she liked. She was the best kind of distraction.

She didn't immediately uncover the body. "Like I said, when I got here, the cops had the ME's office getting ready to do a pickup. I told them to wait until I could have a state fire marshal respond out.

I suppose the road patrols thought the victim was too far scorched to give us any evidence. Maybe that's why they didn't call you.

"Now, burn victims are not my specialty; serial killers are. I've only seen two immolation deaths—and both of those have been in the past week. Both murders. There are some other similarities, but I don't want to tell you everything just yet. I think there's value in hearing another investigator's first impressions. Give it a shot?"

I was crouching down next to her, so close I could feel her breath when she talked to me. I nodded like a bobble-head doll, swallowed a cottony wad of spit, and she peeled back the yellow plastic.

Some pearls of wisdom from one of my college professors drifted into my memory. Statements like, "Transient evidence may be gone before the investigation begins…" or "Artifact is less important than the evidence left on it…" So I kept my eyes peeled and my mouth shut as I looked the scene over and took notes. I always take lots of notes. When I get back to my office, or a quiet place I can work, I try to see what's in my notes that I can tie to the National Fire Protection Association's standards, particularly No. 921, which dictates how fire investigators have to work. If you can't make the logical connection between what you find and the NFPA 921, you probably are not going to get a conviction if you ever find the person responsible for the crime.

There was nothing to tell by looking at the burn pattern, which was mostly on her upper body and face, so I looked around the scorched area for any and every thing I could find. An accelerant had been poured over the body and had spread out onto the pavement around her. It had a petroleum base, because it had stained the asphalt. If it had been an alcohol base, it would have burned away quickly and would not have left the deep burn pattern.

The victim was wearing a light sweater on top of a blood-stained red plaid skirt, and there was some of the material left from both. I pulled at some of the cloth on the sweater and it pulled away easily. I smelled the swatch and could easily detect gasoline. I withdrew a stainless steel can, like a small paint can, out of my evidence bag and placed the sample in it, then tapped the lid on it.

"Gasoline, right?" said Rose.

"Yes," I confirmed and pulled out the forms I would have to use for every piece of evidence I was going to submit to the lab. Last year alone, the bureau analyzed over 2,300 cases containing almost 4,600 samples. Some of them came from explosions, chemical bombs, or clandestine laboratories. A lot of them came from day-to-day arson investigations: pieces of wood, or other building products, and a whole bunch of carpet, because carpet is often the medium in which the amateur arsonist places his accelerant to get a building burning. The state fire marshal's office does over 4,200 investigations a year, and of those, about 45 percent are arson. Unfortunately, because so much of the evidence is burned up in the fire, only about 18 percent lead to arrests in Florida, which is about 2 percent higher than the national average, so we pride ourselves on being as good as we can be.

I used several of the small metal epoxy-lined evidence cans. Typically, we don't use plastic bags for collection, as the plastic can break down and ruin the sample or throw off the lab results, particularly with petroleum distillates. Besides, if you want to determine what kind of ignitable fluid a perpetrator used, the guys at the lab will use the same collection can to begin their gas chromatography. Gasoline has over four hundred chemicals in it and they can often pinpoint where in the country the gas came from based on the chemical analysis, so it's useful information. To collect samples, I used large tweezers and a pair of trauma scissors that cut through anything, including leather, both decontaminated after every use so as not to cross-contaminate the evidence. I took photos of every sample area and labeled each corresponding can. I did not take any body tissue samples for a couple of reasons: one, I could make the assumption that whatever flammable liquid that was still in her clothes was the same as that which burned her flesh, and two, you have to freeze every human tissue sample you send into the lab and I did not want to go through all that. The medical examiner could do that for me if I requested him to do so.

I handed Agent Cleary the Evidence Submission Form DFS-K5-1096 attached to a clipboard.

"Can you fill this out while I look for more samples? It's self-explanatory. There, where it says, 'List of Laboratory Tests,' mark 'A—Determine presence and/or identity of ignitable liquid residues.' I'll put in the agency number and address."

"Sure," she said. "It's gonna cost you lunch, though." That devilish look again. Like I was going to want lunch after looking at a young lady who had been set on fire. My mother, a no-nonsense nurse from Missouri, the "Show Me State," would have called her "a real pistol."

"Did you take photos before I got here?"

"Bear poop in the woods?"

I laughed in spite of myself. "Classy."

"Oh yeah. Classy broad." She laughed. I love a beautiful woman with a dirty laugh. "I can download the photos. I'll give you a set."

"If you let me send them to the lab boys, they'll do forensics on them, too. Get a closer look, put them on the web to other agencies...save you a lot of work."

"Okay, okay. I'm buying. Jeez, did you used to sell vacuum cleaners door-to-door?"

"No. But you'll have to fill out this form, too." I handed her a Photo Laboratory Request Form DFS-K5-1112.

She looked at it and shook her head. "What a friggin' Boy Scout you are."

"I even help little old ladies cross the street." I took another swatch of cloth, this one from the skirt. It was damp, too, but I didn't smell gas or any other petroleum on it.

Without me saying anything, Cleary said, "I noticed that, too. It's damp, but I don't think it was from the accelerant. What do you think it is?"

"If I had to guess…I think it's urine."

"Me, too."

"Maybe she was tied up in a trunk, or something, for a while. That, or maybe she was scared to death and couldn't hold it."

"Yeah," she said, but I could tell she was still thinking it over. So was I. "Or the perpetrator pissed on her. You know, like disrespect?"

"I thought of that, too." This time, there were no flip words from her. "On the evidence form, mark 'O,' if you will, where it says, 'Other Tests,' and write in 'bodily fluids.' That way, they'll test for blood and urine."

"Okay. What else do you see, Inspector Gift? By the way, what's your first name, if you don't mind?"

"Call me Grey."

"Okay, Grey, what else do you see?"

"Well, her abdominal cavity is hollowed out. It didn't get that way just from being burned. I think the guy who did this took her organs out."

Cleary winced and shook her head.

I noted some of the unburned and beautiful hair tousled around the victim's head—long and blonde. I bet she was pretty when she had a face. I thought I would have to pry her mouth open because there was so much accelerant poured on her face,

18

but the tissues and ligaments that would have kept her mouth shut were burned away and the jaw opened easily. Inside, I noted the back of her throat was not burned, which meant she was dead before he torched her; otherwise, she would have inhaled some of the soot and her throat would have been blackened. I also noticed that her throat had been cut away from just behind the tongue.

A mixed feeling of rage and depression rushed over me like a wave. "I think this was done by somebody who has done some hunting before. Someone who is used to field dressing an animal and removing its organs. Also, I'm only a dumb fireman, but I think the guy might have done that because he wanted to hide something. Maybe he forced her to have oral sex with him and his semen was inside her stomach, so he took it out to minimize evidence."

When I looked to her for her reaction, she was on the phone looking at a text message. Then she looked up, smiling benignly.

"I was listening," she assured me. "And I think you're going to win the prize today, Grey-man. Guess what was just found up in Palm Beach County by a guy fishing?"

I thought for just a second before answering. "Some human organs? Maybe in a plastic bag?"

"Why a plastic bag?"

"Because if someone would have just thrown them in the water, the fish would have eaten them."

"Bingo," she said. "But not just any plastic bag. This one was a red biohazard bag. Know anyone who uses something like that?"

I could think of a few places—hospitals and doctors' offices—that have to discard any bodily wastes in a designated red biohazard bag by law, but I knew she was thinking the same thing I was thinking: paramedics at every fire station also have to use red biohazard bags to discard human waste. That wave ran over me again and I looked up at the sky. It was bright and blue-white, like the blinded eyes of a man I once saw who had been set afire with gasoline.

THREE

Journal: Failures

I label this particular group "Failures" because, rather than use the gift they've been given as they reach its "ripening," as I like to call it, they lose it all. They lack the cool objectivity and sense of purpose necessary to thrive, as well as the ability to remain hidden in plain sight and continue the mayhem that is the very lifeblood of who we are.

Still, they are worth studying, if for nothing else, to see what you should not do.

• • •

One Month Ago

In Alpharetta, Georgia, a middle-class suburb of Atlanta, a twenty-eight-year-old man named Carl Oatmeyer drove himself to work at Walmart rather than carpool with his coworkers. This, in itself, should have been a telling sign, as no one in their right mind would want to drive in Atlanta's morning rush hour traffic.

Oatmeyer was a handsome man with dark hair, the temples graying prematurely, and intensely dark eyes, whose brightness was only slightly diminished by the violet circles that had appeared this last week as a result of his recent sleeplessness. He got out of the car and went around to the trunk. Inside it was a long black canvas duffel bag. Oatmeyer unzipped the bag and removed one of the many guns from inside the bag, then threw the bag's strap over his shoulder and took its weight. He slammed the trunk of the car down so hard it caused the envelope to fall out of the visor over the driver's seat in the cab—the one that held the letter telling Carl Oatmeyer that he no longer worked at the Walmart. Due to the "ongoing economic downturn," his position, that of head stock clerk, had been eliminated.

As Oatmeyer approached the retail store, a greeter, an old fellow who remembered everyone's name who worked there, said, "Mornin', Carl."

Carl raised the pistol, said, "Morning, Mr. Sykes," and shot him through the head. He emptied the pistol at anything that appeared to be an appropriate target: a row of jarred foods, a sign advertising Walmart's "Rollback Prices," a checkout clerk who stared at him with her mouth hanging open cartoonishly. Then, out of his bag, he removed one of the automatic rifles he'd purchased right there in the sporting goods section and really cranked up the fun. Shoppers hearing the gunfire began to scream, then ran right at him on their way out. Like fish in a barrel. Talk about a blue-light special! Blood flowed through the aisles. Oatmeyer stared down at it, noticing the reflection of the florescent overhead lights in the spreading redness and the pink Play-Doh blobs of brain and organ tissues splayed about like scattered marbles. It was beautiful in some surreal way, and he wondered why he'd waited so long to enjoy this…*sensation*.

Oatmeyer continued through the store, drawn like a salmon to its nesting place, to women's wear and particularly to maternity wear. There, he found the cashier hiding behind the counter and shot her. After the *slam* of the gunfire stopped resounding, he heard a whimpering, almost like a puppy's, and a whispered *shhh*. Oatmeyer found two women, both very pregnant, their bellies extending impossibly over their stretch pants, and smiled benevolently at them, though sweat was running down his face in rivulets. He shot both of them and watched them try to crawl away, their maternal instincts to protect their unborn babies giving them inhuman strength. Then he shot them in their heads, "execution style," the term newspapers would later use to describe the attack.

A security guard managed to sneak up behind him and drew down on Oatmeyer with his firearm. "Drop your weapon!" he yelled from behind the protective cover of some shelved electronic toys. Oatmeyer turned around and looked at the man.

"Carl?" said the security guard, and Oatmeyer shot him, too.

Oatmeyer took a Bic lighter out of his pants pocket and another automatic rifle from his duffel bag. He walked around the store, lighting whatever would catch fire and shooting anything that moved before, finally, stopping in front of a full-length mirror attached to a support column. Staring at his own image as if seeing himself for the first time, he dropped the rifle and took out another handgun. He placed the barrel of the pistol in his mouth, noting its cold hardness and oily taste against his palate, and pulled the trigger.

• • •

Two Weeks Ago

In Denton, Texas, a woman named Shannon Burkhalter stared at her children in disbelief. They were so beautiful it was impossible to her that she'd brought them into this world. Surely, God must have brought them there. They didn't really seem like a part of her.

There were three of them, each two years apart. And God had now placed one more inside her. Every day she felt it grow in her, and she knew this one would be even more beautiful than the others.

She watched them, transfixed. The two older boys watched television, a Nickelodeon program, and giggled so hard that, when they stopped, they leaned into each other, worn out, like puppies in a litter taking comfort from each other. She continued to observe them, their breath causing their small chests to rise and fall, their round eyes blinking, taking in everything, the glow of the television set flashing in them. The younger of the two sucked his thumb.

Shannon looked at her daughter, the two-year-old. She bounced around the room like a pinball, picking things up, putting them somewhere else, occasionally coming over to Mommy and smiling up at her, gaps where some of the teeth had not grown in yet, then running away, wanting to be chased. But Mommy did not chase the children like Daddy did. It didn't seem proper.

Shannon felt her mood begin to darken and she got up and went to the bathroom where she kept her prescriptions. She opened the medicine cabinet and looked at the assortment of drugs. She wasn't even sure which ones did what anymore, but she knew if she took one without the other, her mood could worsen. She opened the Clozaril, the Risperdal, the Zoloft, and the Xanax and took one of each, then cupped her hands under the sink, filled them with water, and slurped, washing down the pills.

She called her husband at work. When he got on the phone, she said, "Wayne, I'm not feeling well."

"Ah, hon, what is it? Your stomach again?"

"No, Wayne. It's not my stomach. I just, you know, I'm feeling...like everything is unreal, like I just don't...I don't know. Like there is a blackness around my head and it wants to close in."

She could hear Wayne breathing on the phone. "Did you call your doctor?"

"No, Wayne. What's he going to do? Give me another pill?"

"Maybe the other ones aren't working. I don't think they're working. Do you?"

"Sometimes. But I just want...I need to talk to God. I think I should go to church."

"That's good, honey. We should all talk to God more. I could use his help right now at work," he said, trying to inject some humor. When he heard she wasn't laughing, he said, "You can go to church when I get home, okay? How's that?"

She had started to cry but tried to hold it together so Wayne wouldn't know.

"O...kay. Wh...when is that going to be?"

"Same as always, hon. About seven o'clock. Will you be all right until then?"

"I suppose," she said, and hung up the phone. Waiting until seven seemed like an eternity to her right then; it was only four thirty.

She went outside and walked around the house thirty-two times, which was how old she was. Then she walked around the house sixty-two times, which was how old her mother was when she died. As she did this, she noticed their dog, a pug named Frasier, walking alongside her, as if it sensed her pain and was offering solace. She looked down into its watery eyes and picked it up. It was an overcast day but not raining, and a cool breeze ruffled the long green grass of their yard. Tulips were beginning to emerge from their bulbs as spring nudged out the last of the winter gray. She scratched the dog's ears and its curled tail wagged.

There was a large cistern that caught water coming from the gutters via a downspout. Shannon liked to use the rainwater to wash her hair, which was still a luxurious, shining black, with only an occasional white hair here and there. She took the heavy wooden lid off and looked into the cistern. She could see her reflection as if it were a mirror she was looking into. Her dark-brown eyes looked back at her and she remembered all the boys telling her what incredible eyes she had when she was single. Now her eyes looked haunted to her. She stared into the water for at least fifteen minutes, even though one of the children had started to cry in the house. The answer finally came to her: *God wants them back.*

Shannon placed Frasier into the cistern. The pug struggled to keep its head above the water but did not have the room to swim out of it, nor could it find a purchase with its now flailing legs in order to jump out. The dog's buggy eyes seemed to bulge out of its head. Shannon placed the heavy lid back on the cistern and locked her elbows down. She heard the dog's yelps and its head hitting the bottom of the lid, but the sounds subsided quickly, and to her surprise, she felt relief. Now God had a pet.

She went into the house and began to fill the tub for her children.

• • •

Last Week

In Covino, California, a man dressed like the Easter Bunny knocked on the door of his estranged wife. Lloyd Regan knew his soon-to-be-ex-wife always had her family over for brunch on this holiest of holidays. The car-crowded driveway confirmed this to be true. Lloyd wanted to be a part of the party, too. So he brought some special gifts for them. Under his white furry rabbit suit and strapped to his back was a garden sprayer, such as would be used to atomize pesticides or weed killer. The sprayer had a pump handle to create pressure within the container and a long plastic hose with a nozzle at the end of it that was activated by a trigger on the handle. But instead of being filled with a garden-friendly concoction, Regan had filled the sprayer with gasoline. In the waistband of his costume, he had a small .380 automatic handgun, which he hid behind the bouquet of flowers he held as he knocked on the door.

As luck would have it, his mother-in-law answered the door. Lloyd dropped the bouquet, revealing the handgun, and shot the woman in the face.

A sixteen-year-old girl, one of Lloyd's in-laws' daughters, had walked into the kitchen and witnessed the shooting. She stared in disbelief at the six-foot-tall white rabbit spattered with blood. She screamed and turned to run and Lloyd shot her in the back. Then he marched through the home, seeking out his wife like a guided missile. He shot her twice, first in the heart, then in her face. He then summarily shot her father, her sister, and one of her brothers, as well as the visiting neighbors.

Doffing the clumsy rabbit head, Lloyd produced the nozzle tip of his homemade flamethrower, held a flame to the tip, and squeezed the trigger. There was a *whoosh* and a comet of fire shot out, igniting curtains, upholstery, carpets, and former family members. The sixteen-year-old girl was still alive, but her spine was severed from the gunshot wound and she could not move, though she tried to after Lloyd set her afire.

As he searched for more things to shoot, burn, or kill, he did not notice the plastic hose of his flamethrower leaking gasoline onto his rabbit-fur sleeve. Suddenly, his arm was on fire, and then the other one was, too. He tried to get the suit off, but when he grasped for the zipper in the back of the costume, he set his back on fire, then his hair. Screaming, he ran out of the house, a burning bunny hopping down the street until, finally, he was overcome by smoke and heat and fell onto a neighbor's manicured lawn, smoldering.

• • •

Yesterday

Ellen Trotsky opened her eyes, slowly, and immediately regretted doing so. She was still tied up in the woods, her wrists bound by the plastic cinches that the cops used for handcuffs now. A nylon rope was looped through her restrained wrists and thrown over a thick pine bough overhead, her arms stretched up toward heaven, her feet barely touching the ground. Her skin was covered with insect bites, scratches, and bruises she had sustained during both her abduction and her subsequent attempts at escape. She could smell the scent of her exertions coming from her armpits, which were ringed with dirt and sprouting two days of stubble. She could smell her urine-stained clothing and the smoky, burned wood of the campfire, and images of what she'd witnessed by the light of that fire popped into her head like a fright film directed by Charles Manson. The thoughts sent icy adrenaline through her exhausted body, goose bumps spread like a rash across her skin, and she renewed her attempts at escape. She pulled at the tough plastic binds though they bit into her wrists and blood began to trickle down her arms. Gratefully, after she had passed out, she had twisted around in the night and was no longer facing the scene of carnage that was so terrifying that she had lost consciousness from witnessing it.

As she struggled to free herself, inevitably, she turned and could not keep herself from looking at the still-smoldering campfire and tableau of surreal torture. All that was left of her friend, Nancy Placid, were some blackened bones in a campfire pit.

She remembered the sounds of flesh smacking on flesh as the killer sexually assaulted and beat her friend, then the screaming turned to whimpering, and finally a choking gasp as he strangled her, followed by a deafening silence. After a few minutes that seemed like hours, he doused her friend's body with gasoline and rolled her into the fire like so much refuse. She had burst into flames like a wax mannequin. Then Officer Bobby had come up from behind Ellen, brushed a clump of hair away from her sweaty face, and whispered, "You're next." That was when Ellen had passed out. Now, as those memories flooded her fractured mind, her stomach lurched and she vomited an acidic bile—all she could manage, not having eaten for two days.

Ellen heard a car coming through the woods. She knew they were somewhere deep in the woods of eastern Pennsylvania, perhaps near Gettysburg, and no one else would be coming out there but the killer. Fear gripped her even as the memory of meeting the killer, a nice-looking charmer with the most intense eyes and dimpled chin, came back to her. He had approached her and Nancy while they played pool at Ott's Tavern in Emmitsburg, Maryland. He had asked them if he could partner up with them so they could team up against some of the firefighters who had come over from the National Fire Academy for the Thursday-night Ladies' Night at the popular bar. Ellen and Nancy enthusiastically said yes right away, then excused themselves to the rest-room, where they bickered over which one would sleep with him, then giggled like schoolgirls, though they had graduated from high school over five years ago.

Nancy had the boobs and typically drew the initial attention of the ever-changing cadre of firefighters who came from all over the world to the academy. She would bend over the pool table with her low-cut blouse and sway those things around like udders, dis-tracting their opponents until, the next thing you knew, she was walking away with some beer money. But Ellen had an ass like Beyonce Knowles that protruded so far out the firefighters often joked with her, asking if they could set their beer on it while they took their shots.

They were, in the local nomenclature, "beef-a-loes," and they knew it but considered themselves a cut above the rest of the resi-dent women, most of whom had not aged so gracefully after high school. Some had too much "junk in the trunk," as Nancy would say, and bore faces prematurely lined from working on the area's farms. Ellen worked as a clerk at the Learning Resource Center at the academy and Nancy worked in the cafeteria on campus, so their skin escaped the ravages of weather and wind. Of course, working on campus also gave them first look at the fresh meat that rotated in and out of the academy every two weeks.

The man who had approached them in the bar was not from the campus. They would have noticed him, with his distinctive movie-star looks. Nancy thought he looked like George Cloo-ney, while Ellen thought he favored Patrick Dempsey, but both declared, while huddled in the bathroom touching up makeup and perfume, that he was definitely "McDreamy." When Bob—"Officer Bobby," he'd insisted—offered them a ride home in his police cruiser, it sealed the deal: they would *both* do him, and they shook pinkies on it, just like in the good ol' high school days, the pinnacle of their short lives.

Now, as Ellen remembered how his face had morphed by the campfire into this countenance of pure evil and insanity as he'd butchered her BFF, she could not make herself imagine anything attractive about him.

The car was so close now, and Ellen so terrified, she would have peed her pants again, but she was so dehydrated it couldn't happen. She would have screamed, but she knew no one would hear her way out here, wherever they were.

Ellen resolved to get away if she had to pull her own hands off, and an idea came to her. With the resolve that only terror can produce, she summoned her strength and jumped as high as she could and did not even try to land on her feet. Instead, she allowed herself to fall straight back, and as she did so she increased the distance between her body and initial contact with the ground to some three feet. It was enough. She came down hard on her back, knocking the breath out of her lungs and smacking her head against the ground so hard she almost lost consciousness. But it only took one glance at what was left of Nancy to pull her back to reality and she sprang up, hardly noticing her hands had been degloved, the flesh completely ripped off of them from wrists to fingertips, the meat still hanging in the plastic loop that had held her prisoner. She heard the car stop behind some bushes, just beyond the clearing that held the campsite and its captives, and she took off in the opposite direction.

Though her legs were still shaking from fear, pain, exhaustion, and malnutrition, Ellen ran like the track star she used to be in school. She hadn't gotten that butt from just sitting on it, and the muscle memory in those powerful thighs kicked back, empowering her flight. She ran unfettered, reckless, branches and thorns scratching her face, legs, and arms, her mouth as dry as a canyon, her heart racing so fast she was sure it would burst. Her hands stung as the wind touched their fleshless surfaces, burning like hell, but nothing was going to stop her.

The topography began to run downhill and ended up at a small creek before going back uphill on the other side. The water was so clear and cold Ellen stopped in the creek and let it run over her cut feet. She stopped and listened for sounds of her pursuer, holding her breath, but her heart was beating so hard she could only hear its *thump-thump-thump* pounding blood up to her ears. She squatted down and was going to cup some water in her hands to drink, but the water burned her wounded hands, so she went to her knees and sipped directly from the stream with her mouth, like a deer. The cool water felt like heaven on her dried, cracked lips, and she slurped it down until she almost drowned in it. As she was bent over, she heard a *thwack*, and some mud flew up from the creek bed. A second later, the distant crack of a firearm. Ellen looked up and saw him, the monster who'd killed her friend, now dressed in his patrolman uniform, sunlight reflecting off of his badge and sunglasses as he aimed down at her with his pistol.

Ellen had no choice but to run up the hill, though she knew she would be an easy target. But she would rather be shot than allow him to catch her, and he would have to stop each time to fire a shot, and by doing so, she could regain a lead and distance herself from him. She zigzagged up the hill, dodging behind trees when she could. Bullets ripped patches of bark out of the trees and kicked up dirt from the ground as she ran. She refused to stop and look back again until she got to the top of the hill and found cover among some thick bushes. He was already to the creek now, splashing through it with his gleaming patrolman boots, perhaps only twenty yards away.

Ellen turned and poured it on, fighting to put some distance between them, but her legs were so tired she began to stumble from fatigue. Each time she stumbled it was more and more difficult to get back up and run again. She was slowing down and her lungs wheezed. The brush was thicker, too, slowing her even more, and she heard him coming, right behind her, grunting like a rutting moose as he smashed at the undergrowth with his billy club.

When he was only an arm's length behind her, he whispered, mockingly, "Gonna get you, gonna get you." Ellen summoned her last ounce of strength and threw herself forward, only to find the brush opened onto an open road, a highway, and she bolted across it without looking in either direction. A sound like the air horn of a train ripped through the air; she felt the earth rumble under her feet, and a suction of wind almost pulled her back into the road as a giant tractor-trailer narrowly missed her. Then there was an ungodly sound, like a side of beef falling from a fifty-story building and smacking the pavement, as the demented patrolman, "Officer Bobby," met the grille of the massive Mack truck. He was hit with such force, he splattered in all directions. The driver locked up the truck's brakes, and, blue smoke billowing from its tires, the truck slid sideways down the road ahead, finally coming to a halt one hundred yards away from where Ellen had sunk to her knees on the shoulder. In the sudden quiet that followed, Ellen searched the highway for what was left of the man who would have killed her in some unfathomable way, but could find only a smear of red on the asphalt.

• • •

My task has been to locate and identify those people with that "special something." At last my value has been recognized. No one else has the knowledge, skills, or abilities (KSAs in federal government jargon) that enable me to take on this task. I'm looking for the ones who can be trained to reach their full potential or perhaps "harvested" for future needs. Other than the one subject, 56QAH/ Lot 656, who shows great promise, my search has been dismally regrettable. I would even go so far as to say embarrassing.

FOUR

Agent Cleary left her car at the church and rode back north with me in my patrol car. I radioed ahead to have a special-delivery courier meet me at the Broward SFM office, where I dropped our collected evidence, forms, and contact information, to be delivered to the state office in Havana, just outside of Tallahassee. The lab boys there would be able to make a determination on the accelerant by late that night, or certainly by early the next day. The report on DNA, if they could find some in the urine, would take a little longer; they don't usually do forensics on biological evidence, but I had a nutty professor buddy in the lab who I knew I could count on to get it into the right hands.

I called my supervisor, Captain Sam Brandsma, or "Bland Sam," as he was more commonly known, and filled him in on current events. I was covering Leonard Cotton's on-call duty in Broward County, on my day off, and was now committed to a mutilation/immolation murder case with an FBI serial killer specialist. He would be getting a call from her supervisor requesting me on an "expert officer" loan. I was officially on the clock but on the federal government's dime *if* we completed and returned the proper paperwork. I waited for his subtle but sure ass-chewing, but heard only silence.

"You still there?" I asked.

"Let me get this straight," he said in the deadpan tone that had earned him his nickname. "One of the *four* investigators I've got assigned to my West Palm office covers for the Broward office that has *nine* assigned investigators and then is shanghaied by the Feds, and I get what out of this?"

"The FBI's undying gratitude?"

"I better get my money, or my man, back pretty quick," he said, his voice raising a little. "I know you're one of the generation X kids who lived at home until he was thirty and thinks money grows on trees, but it really doesn't. You know we have a six-billion-dollar budget deficit in the State of Florida, where we get our paychecks from, right?"

"Think I heard something about that."

Then he said what he always says to me, which I believe is his attempt at humor.

"Gift?"

"Yes, sir?"

"You are anything but." Then he hung up the phone.

• • •

It was late spring in Florida and the tabebuia tree's tiny yellow flowers had burst open and begun sprinkling their petals on the ground with an impossible beauty. They would only bloom for four to six weeks, which made that beauty even more precious. The jacarandas offered their purple flowers but remained in bloom a bit longer, followed by the royal poincianas, whose flame-colored flowers might last all summer if they weren't blown off by hurricanes. Lawns were covered with short-seasoned impatiens and hibiscus flowers of every color, from cream with red centers to salmon, pink, white, and purple. Blue sage and lavender lantana lined driveways, and scarlet cardinals and mockingbirds flew in and out of mango and avocado trees like feathered dive-bombers, building and fiercely protecting their nests. It was lovely and I consciously tried to observe the beauty to get through the rest of the day and the morbid reality we would have to deal with. Picking up a bag of human organs from a murder victim could present very few elevating moments.

"You said you got hurt while you were in the fire service," Cleary said. She was just making conversation.

"Yes, I did," I answered.

"Mind if I ask what happened? You seem like you're still pretty fit. What are you—about eight or ten percent body fat?"

"Closer to five."

"Wow, that's lean. You work out a lot?"

"I do. Some weights and cardio. Watch my fat intake. But I like to keep active with outdoor sports, board and kitesurfing, in the winter or spring when the waves kick up and I can find the time."

We were silent for a time after that.

"So, you going to tell me what happened, or do I have to do a public records search on you?" Again, the devilish smile.

"Okay, nosey. I got caught in a fire. I was in an attic that had been converted into a small upstairs bedroom for a little boy. The family called it in and the house was smoking like a chimney, but we didn't see any flames coming out the windows or anywhere. The family was out in the front yard when we arrived and they'd just noticed the boy wasn't with them. I was a lieutenant by then and I didn't want to put my guys at risk, so I made the decision to go into the attic myself while they stayed below with a thermal imager and tried to locate the fire."

"Thermal imager?"

"It's an infrared device that shows relative heat in a dark or smoky environment. The warmer something is in relation to its environment, the whiter it shows on the imager. Pretty cool tool, actually. Saves us from having to pull the ceilings in buildings to locate a fire. I keep one in the trunk. They're handy."

"Okay, so you're in the attic with your hose…"

"Well, that's where it gets a little hinky. See, I didn't have a hose—that's why I didn't want the guys going up. But I thought I was okay. We looked at the attic with the thermal imager from underneath and didn't see any hot spots. I thought we just had to worry about smoke, and if the kid was going to survive, one of us had to get up there quick. It's what we were hired for, after all, even though there are a bunch of risk managers out there who would have us stand outside, spray a little water, and call ourselves firefighters just so we don't invoke the wrath of the workman's comp gods. That's a whole other conversation I could talk your ears off about."

"Get to the punch line, Mark Twain."

"Well, long story short, I got into the attic, but it was tighter than I thought. And hotter. I realized that the fire was probably in the attic's crawl space just above me. I could hear the kid coughing, so I didn't have time to go back down and get the hose or any help. The boy wouldn't have lasted that long. So I went to him and gave him my air mask, which is against the rules, according to risk management."

"Yeah. The lawyers and federal laws have turned us all into wusses."

"Exactly. Anyway, I put my mask on the boy and was on my way out when the ceiling, roof and all, came down on us."

"Did you get burned?"

"Not so much. I had a good crew and they got water on us right away. But my head got trapped in some broken trusses for a long time. I didn't have any air. They got me out, but I was in a coma for a few days. Woke up, finally, and they told me I had a cracked skull and would need therapy, rehab, et cetera. Went back to work a couple months later and the first fire I went into I got really hot again, blacked out, and had a seizure. Florida statutes say you can't be a firefighter if you have seizures, so they were going to retire me out on a medical. But we found a loophole that allowed me to work in the Fire Prevention Bureau so I didn't have to retire. I didn't want to go around doing Pub Ed programs—slip and fall prevention, home and school fire drills, escape planning, stop, drop, and roll, and all that—so I went into investigations. I liked arson, particularly, and found out I was pretty decent at finding how the fires started and who started them."

"What about the boy? Did he make it?"

"Yes. He did. But he got hurt, too, when the roof collapsed."

"Bad?"

After all these years, I still find it hard to talk about. I keep thinking if I would have done something different, brought that hose with me, or got more help...

"He...he's in a wheelchair."

"Oh, I'm sorry," she said, and I knew she meant it. "But, at least he..."

"Lived?"

"I...I'm...sure...well...his parents must be very grateful."

There was nothing for me to say. I remember the parents came to see me while I was rehabilitating. They thanked me, the words came out of their mouths, but I saw something else in their eyes, something that made their words sound hollow, their gratitude disingenuous.

39

Cleary moved on. "So, why didn't you stay with West Palm Beach FD?"

I was hesitant to tell her because the more people know about your business, the more they can hurt you, whether they mean to or not, but I felt like she was a solid person. One maybe who had her own secrets and stories and she knew how to keep her cards close to her vest because of that, so I told her.

"I…need to ask you to keep what I tell you confidential."

"Who am I going to tell?"

"Don't know. But if it got out, I might not be able to keep my job with the state."

"My lips are sealed."

"Okay…I had more seizures. They are what you call *petite mal*, or *absence* seizures, not *grand mal*. I haven't had one in a few years, and you wouldn't notice even if I did, probably. I just kind of go off into la-la land. Get the stares, maybe my cheek twitches, or a finger. My brain's a mess of short-circuited synapses and it sure isn't good for you, but for the most part, no one notices. Unless, of course, you're driving a car…"

"Do you miss being a firefighter?"

"Like a mother's love."

"That's too bad. But you still like doing investigations?"

"You bet. And I'm grateful they let me do my job. Makes me feel…useful, still."

"So, it's okay to have your…uh…medical condition and be a fire marshal?"

"Uh…no. But I got two things going for me. One, I haven't had a seizure in years, and two, they don't know about it. And I'd like to keep it that way. Understand?"

"Gotcha. I've got secrets, too."

"Such as?"

"I used to be a man."

I should have known she was joking, but I jerked around to look at her so fast I swerved the car a little. Then I saw she was trying to keep a straight face but couldn't, and we both laughed. Gallows humor, I knew. It's common in the fire service and I supposed it must be with the FBI as well. We joke about the weird stuff, the accidents and sicknesses, the murders and suicides, because if we didn't, we'd go crazy.

"So, what about you? What's your story?" I asked.

"Oh, God. Do we have to?"

"Quid pro quo, lady."

"Oh, all right. If you're going to speak Latin to me, then I just get all soft and have to tell you my life story. So here it is: born and raised in Boston, nice little Irish-Catholic girl. Dorky, gangly, Coke-bottle glasses, but brainy. Went to college to study engineering. Lost the glasses, filled out my bra, found a husband—one of my professors—and we got married. We started our own consulting company specializing in motion and impact analysis, which you probably never heard of. It's where you study things to see how they'll come apart, what their weak spots are, et cetera. Pretty boring to most people, but it was my thing. I still can't look at something without trying to figure out how it works, how it'll come apart."

"Sounds like the FBI was perfect for you."

"Well, it turned out that way. See, while I was out securing contracts for our consulting company, my professor hubby was trying to secure more coeds. He finally knocked one up, which is something he didn't want to do for me, and we got divorced. We sold the company and made a little profit, but because I was listed as the CEO and he was just a consultant, the courts figured his income was less than mine, so I could either pay him alimony or pay him off, which is what I did."

"Oh, man. That's just not fair."

"Tell me about it. Anyway, I had to start over. I'd met some people while doing the analysis consulting, including a lot of federal people. One man I knew suggested going into the FBI, do research work for them. But once I got in, I had to do some field work and found out that, lo and behold, I really liked it."

"Hmmm. I suppose we all find our way."

"Yep."

I could have talked to her all day, but we were nearing the place where the fisherman had found the discarded bio-bag, and we fell silent. We exited the turnpike and could see the flashing blue lights after heading west on Southern Boulevard. Another plethora of cop cars, this time Palm Beach County Sheriff units, as well as some plainclothes cops in their unmarked cars, probably trying to make their bones on a real-life serial killer case.

I parked the car and Special Agent Rose Cleary adjusted that big gun under her proper blue blazer and got out of the car, radiating a sense of authority. Nobody was going to be telling her her business today.

FIVE

I walked along the canal bank, the muck sucking at my boots, feeling the day begin to heat, the humidity rising off the brown water. I knew the Palm Beach Canal well. I lived just around the corner then and had lived near it most of my life. The canal served as the east-west line of irrigation for the western fringe's farm country, Belle Glade and Pahokee and the other small agrarian towns whose only hope of survival was the "black gold" soil and the allure of high school football. They could grow anything out there—tomatoes, cucumbers, sugar cane, and tough young athletes with dreams of making it into the NFL. Dreams snuffed out for all but a few by the reality of growing up in poverty and gang warfare, whose carnage claimed so many of them before they could even get to college.

My mother used to take my sister Grace and me out there when we were children to the U-pick-'em farms to harvest our own fruit and vegetables, back when gasoline was less than a buck a gallon and it paid to do so. Maureen "Mo" Gift would promise her kids a big prize to whoever picked the biggest strawberry and it was, inevitably, that you would be allowed to eat it. We were fine with that. She would clean and top the berries and put them in bowls with canned milk and sprinkled with a little sugar. Heaven.

That was after my father had left to pursue the allure of open ranges, free-flowing whiskey, wild horses, and the women who are attracted to rootless men who have no compunctions about leaving their children behind like orphans. Our first home was out west of the "twenty-mile bend" where the Palm Beach Canal turned and sliced into the heart of Belle Glade farmland like a giant hook. Migrant workers lived along the bend, most of them poor black people then, not the hordes of Hispanic and illegal immigrants who toil in the fields now, subjecting themselves to pesticides and their offspring to birth defects—cleft palates, armless and legless torsos, blindness, and retardation—often birthing them in the same windowless clapboard homes I grew up in.

My first memory was being invited to our neighbor's home— we were white in an all-black migrant camp—for a rabbit dinner. Tired men sat on the porch in overalls, smoking hand-rolled cigarettes, their skins still slick from the day's exertions, their hands red and shining from the dried blood of skinning rabbits, impervious to huge green flies crawling on their faces and in and around the rim of the galvanized steel tub filled with the fur and organs of the night's meal.

Later, as a teen living east of that place in West Palm, young and stupid and full of testosterone and the innate desire to show off for the opposite sex, we swam in the canal at a place we called "the cable" because of the long braided steel cable with a handle bolted onto it that hung out over the dark-water stream from the branch of a giant Australian pine. We never thought about the cottonmouth moccasins and enormous alligators that lurked within a stone's throw of the cable; it was our swimming hole, our place of initiation, and a place of wooing girls without seeming to do so, their thighs, still swollen with baby fat, sticking out of their torn jean shorts, their budding breasts peeking through their wet T-shirts.

Now I was standing maybe a couple hundred yards from that place of adolescent adventure and promise, staring into water now filled with feces and nitrates. The canal served more as a drainage ditch than a source of irrigation water now that farming was run by corporations rather than families. I was wondering why someone would choose to remove a woman's organs and deposit them here, after burning her corpse in a county forty miles away. If, indeed, they were hers.

Right now, we didn't know anything for certain. The red biohazard bag that contained the remains had been whisked off to the medical examiner's office and a group of irritated-looking Palm Beach County Sheriff patrolmen stood along the bank in their green polyester uniforms, looking hot and probably trying to remind themselves that they got paid the same whether they were standing guard on a crime scene or sitting surveillance at a county park watching the men's rooms for perverts who proposition young boys while their parents are making Kool-Aid and turning burgers on the grill.

Cleary had been talking to a group of plainclothes cops near the bridge from which, it was assumed, the killer had thrown the bag. I was out of earshot, but there was a lot of hand movement and she came back down the canal bank toward me, doing a pretty good balancing act with her high-heeled shoes in the soft sand. Her pale face was now red, and I didn't think it was from the heat. I could smell my own body's scent. My black department-issued T-shirt reading *STATE FIRE MARSHAL* in gold silkscreen letters stuck to my skin under the noon sun. In spite of still wearing her dark-blue blazer, Cleary had only a little dampness on her temples when she reached me.

"Am I from friggin' Mars?" she inquired.

I didn't answer.

"Did you hear me on the phone when I asked them to block off the area and stay back? So, like, maybe we could see *something* before they trampled in here like a bunch of water buffaloes in heat."

"Wow," I said. "Vivid picture. I can almost smell them."

She shook her head. "When this shit happens, I always think, if I were a man and asked them the same thing, would it have been different?"

I understood where she was coming from and said so. "Don't take it personally. Us fire marshals are sometimes treated like red-headed stepchildren, too. It's customary for the local gendarme to feel they have squatter's rights. Who were the plainclothes guys?"

"Two of them were detectives from the sheriff's office—the two in the too-tight Greg Norman polos doing their best to look hetero. That other one—the one in the black suit and designer sunglasses? I have no idea. I think he's state, or federal, maybe FDLE or Justice Department. All I know is he's not with my agency. He didn't offer and I didn't ask, and his local butt-buddies didn't make introductions. Doesn't matter, they've been up and down the canal bank so much it looks like a track team ran through here. They gave me the name of the fisherman who found the bag, though."

I looked over her shoulder and saw the man with the incongruous suit and tortoise-framed glasses staring at us, his face expressionless, angular, the flesh surgically taut. His dark-skinned hands showed signs of wear, toughness, and age, like well-used tools. I was about to say something to Cleary when I noticed a couple of the patrolmen listening to us as well and looking short-tempered. Everyone's wanting to grab the headlines on something like this. Believe it. I nodded sideways with my head, indicating it was time to leave, and she followed my lead.

When we got to the car at the top of the canal bank, I said, "Don't jerk around and look, but glance back at the bridge when you get a chance."

She was cool. She threw her hair back out of her face nonchalantly and looked back at the bridge at the same time. "Yeah?"

"You see how high that rail is?"

She reached into the car and pulled a compact out of her purse and used its mirror to look over her shoulder while sprucing up her hair. "Uh-huh."

"If you were in a car and you tried to throw something out the window, it would probably hit that rail. Even if you were in a jacked-up pickup truck, you probably wouldn't make it over that rail. If you were wanting to hide something, you'd want to be sure it was gone, right?"

"I'm following you. So, you think whoever threw it off the bridge had to stop their vehicle?"

"Yes, ma'am. And I haven't seen one officer up on that bridge the whole time we've been here."

"You're right. But they might have been up there before we got here."

"Maybe. But I'll tell you something else."

"What's that?"

"They were looking on the wrong side of the canal, too."

"What do you mean?"

"I mean, the whole time we were here, I was watching the canal, then watching the cops, then watching you—the best part, by the way."

"Finish your story, Slick."

"Well, I grew up around here. When you fish here in the evening, you want to be on this side, the north side, because you get a shadow from the bridge on the water and the fish won't bite in the sunlight." I could see a smile emerge on her face already. I continued. "But when you fish here in the morning, you get the shade of the pines on the other side of the canal, so that's where you fish—*in the morning*. And I didn't see one person on that side of the canal. Did you?"

She grinned at me like it was Christmas, and she was lovely. "Should we go take a look now?"

"It looks like these guys will be wrapping it up here soon. Why don't we get some lunch, then come back when it's not so crowded? I didn't get breakfast and I'm hungry enough to eat a dirty diaper through a park bench."

She winced at that silly old Southern colloquialism, but the smile never faded. "You sure know how to sweet-talk a girl."

SIX

It was a straight shot down Southern Boulevard to A1A. I could have taken I-95, but I thought Rose would enjoy the ride by the beach; I knew I would. We drove past Trump's Mar-A-Lago estate—the one that was once owned by the Post cereal family—its high walls crowned with broken glass as if to thwart attacking brigands from the sea. The ocean was turquoise and blended into lavender over the reefs. The sky was cloudless and a light breeze held pelicans aloft while they scanned the surf for baitfish that dotted the waves like green darts. I wished I could have stopped, pulled my surf kite out, and continued what I'd been doing earlier that morning before getting drawn into this horror.

"Did they say if the fisherman who found the bio-bag was any help?" I asked.

Rose Cleary was looking out the window at the ocean, its calming effect working on her, her chest rising slowly now with each breath, her face placid, serene, her perpetual frown gone, at least momentarily. She was beautiful, but there was something sad, if not tragic about her. Maybe it was the divorce she'd mentioned. Maybe something else. I couldn't put my finger on it and I didn't want to pry; I'd just met her that morning.

"God, it's beautiful here," she said. "I'm sorry. What did you say?"

I turned the radio down.

"I asked about the fisherman. You know, the guy who found the bag with the guts in it?"

"Oh, yes. He's a groundskeeper in Palm Beach. Name's Jesse Francois. Stops off to fish every day before coming to work. They said he found the bag and called them to report it because he knew it was a biohazard bag and he wondered why someone would throw it in the canal."

"Did they say if he looked inside the bag?"

"They said no."

"Hmmm. Wonder why he recognized it as a biohazard bag? Doesn't seem likely that a guy who cuts grass for a living would know or care about that."

"Don't know. Maybe he was a doctor before the earthquake reduced his country to rubble."

"Well, since we're right here in Palm Beach, land of the rich and famous, maybe we should go talk to him after lunch. I thought we'd grab a bite at E. R. Bradley's in West Palm. It's just across the intracoastal. We could come back this way."

She nodded and I could see the frown coming back. We drove without words the rest of the way, turning back west on Royal Poinciana Way, crossing the Flagler Memorial Bridge, then going south again along the waterway until we came to where Clematis Street split, and parked behind Bradley's.

We hesitated before stepping out into the heat.

"So," I asked her, "how many serial killer cases have you worked?"

She looked at the headliner in the car as if it were a chalkboard on which she was doing calculations, her fingers dancing along her thumb as she counted.

"Over thirty now," she said, as if we were talking about measurements for drapes.

"Good Lord. I guess there's a lot of sick people out there."

She looked at me, then past me, as if she were seeing something out my window. I almost turned to look; then her eyes refocused and she said, "More than you could ever imagine."

"Does it ever get to you?"

She repeated, "More than you could ever imagine."

"I'm sorry," I said, sensing I had intruded on some guarded knowledge. I felt like a kid blundering on with obvious questions in spite of the memories they might dredge up. I wondered why a woman, especially one with her gifts—intelligence, beauty, and, I thought, sensitivity, too—would want to work in a field that even most men would find distasteful and harmful to the soul. I looked for a positive spin to put on the subject but couldn't find it. Finally, I just said, "At least there's people like you who put these monsters in jail."

The way she looked at me made it hard not to look away. "Most of them don't end up in jail, to tell the truth," she said. "They either go on one more rampage, then kill themselves, or sometimes we never find them. Sometimes they quit or take long periods off without killing anyone, like the BTK killer. Those are the hardest to find. Sometimes another wacko kills someone, gets caught, and takes credit for the real serial killer's murders. Or they slide across the border into Canada, or worse, into Mexico, where killing is as common as tortillas and another murder is chalked up to one of the drug cartels. But every now and then..." she hesitated, as if wondering whether she should say it or not. "Every now and then, I get to kill one."

I was stunned but tried not to show it. "That's got to be rough."

She looked at me and smirked at my naïveté. "You kidding? It's the best part of the job."

I felt the skin on the back of my neck tighten and a chill went through me as if I'd stumbled into a walk-in freezer. She noticed.

"Don't worry, Mr. Gift. I'm not mental. The first time I killed one was after he'd kindly placed a knife in my abdomen. Right across here," she said, indicating an area just south of where her navel would be. "After that, I got a bigger gun and was quicker to use it."

"Can't say I blame you," I said. "Is that why you don't wear the traditional blue windbreaker with huge FBI letters on the back?"

"Good call, Inspector. Why make yourself a more obvious target?"

Looking into her face so she knew I meant it, I said, "I think you're a brave woman, Agent Cleary."

She smiled wanly at me and said, "Let's get something to eat."

Inside the restaurant, we were seated at a table that gave us a clear view of the intracoastal. Throaty motorboats and elegant yachts cruised up and down the waterway, their owners enjoying the day's pristine beauty, immune to the nightmarish visions that regurgitate into your mind and astonish you with the horror of what man is capable of doing to his fellow man.

You don't have to be an FBI profiler to witness those atrocities, either. I used to see them when I was a firefighter working the streets. The children whose necks are snapped when their mother's minivan is ripped apart by a drunk driver as they're returning from a soccer practice. The public defender who dives out of a nine-story window because the self-loathing he harbors from excavating his guilty clients from jail has consumed him. The burned husk of the amateur arsonist who dumps five full jerry cans of gasoline around the floor of a beauty parlor and forgets about the pilot light on the water heater. The broken teeth, hematomas, angulated extremities, even death brought about from Friday-night barroom brawls, or the johns' lacerations resulting from their refusal to pay the hookers that just fellated them on their way to pick up their kids from daycare, or the Guatemalans who get their throats cut for the payday wad of money they keep in their front pants pocket because they don't trust institutionalized banking.

All reasons I remind myself to look for the beauty of a sunset, a row of flowers in bloom, a bird in flight, a dolphin playing in the surf. For all the things I'd witnessed as a firefighter and paramedic, and for things I've tried to forget from a terrible time in an almost-forgotten place in Somalia when I thought the role of an Army Ranger could fulfill my need to help the world. What did I know? I was just a kid, not even of legal drinking age, when we touched down in Mogadishu and walked into hell. I sold my soul, helped kill over a thousand people, and saw dozens of my own brothers-in-arms torn to ribbons.

"What's good here?" Cleary asked.

"They've got chicken salad on a pita that never disappoints. It's light."

"Sounds good to me."

There was an uncomfortable silence while we waited for our lunch. You can only look out at the boats so long.

"You okay?" I asked, trying to draw my lunch companion back to the present.

"Yeah," she said weakly. "I'm just irritated."

"From how you were treated by the cops this morning?"

"No. Not from their attitude toward me. It's the overall lack of professionalism. The supervisor dropping a cigarette in the crime scene. The Hardy Boys at the canal scene tramping around and turf-protecting."

"You know, so what? Let it go. We can work together and we'll get past all that. The evidence we gather will have the same significance and we'll get a direction from that. Don't let personalities get in the way of your thinking."

"I know. You're right. But all that crap—it's distracting to me. That's my biggest problem with it all. All these little things are distracting me from what I should be concentrating on." She shook her head as if to affirm this truth to herself. "Thanks, Inspector Gift."

"Call me Grey. And there's no need to thank me. This is a collaborative assignment, right?"

"Right. And it's Rose."

Rose managed to pick through half of her sandwich. She was constantly interrupted by her BlackBerry. She'd take a bite, text something into the device, get another message, shake her head, text again, then turn back to her lunch.

"Need to be somewhere?" I asked, noting her increasing stress level.

"Yes. Everywhere," she said. "We have a new—or newer, I should say—computer system that collates information from our database with other law enforcement agencies and like cases within our own system. One thing positive that came from nine/eleven. A lot of times, it's coincidental stuff—say, a suspect description in Indiana matches a suspect description in Arizona, if there's enough similar information. But sometimes the system looks for common links in MOs. Right now, while we sit here and stuff our faces, I'm getting e-mails and texts about any murders that involve keywords like 'fire,' 'immolation,' 'mutilation,' et cetera. It's like having a silent partner that works twenty-four/ seven."

"Who gives it the keywords?"

"I do. Like right now, I'm collecting data for all these matches of murders within the past month that have a fire connection because of the ones I've been looking at this week. The first one was the vic in Homestead, a girl named Wooley, found burned to death in her car. Originally thought to be an accident, but I got very curious when another girl's body was found in Immokalee within the same week. This one was named Suarez and she was burned so bad that I knew someone had to have poured something flammable on her."

I heard her BlackBerry ringing again. "More data?"

"No," she said, red circles forming on her cheeks. She was blushing. "That one was from a friend. But, here, take a look at this file," she said, scrolling through some screens on her Black-Berry. "This is a file I've been putting together with the data I've been getting from all over the nation."

She let me view the screen as she went through her collection. "For instance, I got a mass murderer, a shooter that killed eleven people in a Walmart in Alpharetta, Georgia, a month ago, then set the store on fire and shot himself. Then a mother who drowned all her kids, then set herself on fire in Denton, Texas. An estranged husband in Covino, California, who dressed up like the Easter Bunny, killed eight people, including the wife, then set the house on fire and managed to light himself up by accident. The last one I received described a cop in Pennsylvania who turned out to be a serial killer. Hacked one girl in half, but another one got away. He was chasing her when he got hit and killed by a tractor-trailer. He'd burned the first girl in the woods, and when the investigators went to his house, they found a huge fire pit in the backyard. They started sifting through the char and found what they believe to be the bones of at least seven different girls, including the one in the woods. Pretty creepy, huh?"

As she was talking, I noticed the table of over-coiffed Palm Beach ladies next to us begin to eavesdrop until they could no longer feign disinterest. Each of them stared at us, clutching their Dooney & Bourke handbags as if they contained their life essences, their glossed mouths hanging open, their cell phones dangling from their hands like ornaments on trees after Christmas. Our conversation was not the best one to have at a crowded lunch spot. They saw me looking at them and looked away, gathering their things to leave. I looked back to the waterway. The sunlight kept bouncing off the yachts, flashing in my eyes, and I regretted leaving my sunglasses in the car. The light flashed in my eyes, again and again, like a lighthouse beacon stuck in one spot, flashing, flashing.

And that's when it happened.

I looked back to Rose and she was saying something, but I couldn't hear the words coming out of her mouth. My ears were ringing and I felt pressure as if I were descending, going deeper underwater. A surreal blue aura surrounded Rose's face and shoulders, making her look like an angel, or a ghost, and then my vision seemed to cave in from the perimeter and I lost consciousness.

SEVEN

Journal: Behavioral Studies

It's like "Killer TV." I thought the FBI technology was cool, but the CIA has access to military toys that we never utilized. Spy satellites. Once I've located the subject, I can tune in and watch his or her every move. I can even monitor several of them at once. The technology combined with my peculiar ability to "see" the killer and know what and how they think makes for an entertainment value you just don't get with cable television. Here's a sampling of this week's programming...

• • •

Subject: 56QAH/Lot 117

He watched them from a distance that allowed him to remain invisible but afforded him a clear and constant view. A man, woman, and two children. A father, wife, son, and daughter. A family. A *flock*. In nature, the predator follows the flock until the weakest, or smallest, becomes separated from the rest. The girl was the smallest, perhaps three years old, but she would not stray too far from her father. In fact, she was clingy, almost constantly distracting him while he looked at a tie or coat. The father probably didn't want to be there anyway. A perfectly nice day, he'd rather be at the park with the kids, or riding bikes, or even working in the yard. Save clothes shopping for one of those rainy days. It would be an issue he and his wife would argue about for the rest of their doomed marriage.

The boy, five years old, would stop and look at a new toy—he loved the little Matchbox cars—then catch up with his family. The mother was focused on the incredible sales. One thing about a failing economy, you could get some damn good buys. To die for, really. She noticed her son catch up again with them as they migrated through the store, up one aisle, then down another, blending from one department to another, rejecting offers of help from sales clerks, doubling back to affirm a decision on a garment.

He watched and waited. The perfect time came when the family came close to the exit doors, the ones that led to the parking lot and not back into the mall. The family came so close to the doors that, at first, the watcher thought they might be leaving. They came close enough for the sunlight outside to shine shafts of light that revealed the mother's finely sculpted calf muscles, the father's dark-whiskered jowls, the auburn highlights in the girl's hair, and the spray of freckles on the boy's perfect little nose under his red baseball cap.

The boy was quiet in his musings, not attracting any attention as the family moved away from the exit doors and back down another aisle. He stepped closer to the doors as he watched a cool-looking bright-blue Corvette pass by, mesmerized by its smooth, rocketlike body. He could hear the rumble of its big motor as it flashed by and was gone.

The watcher moved quickly, though he knew he would have at least thirty seconds: the time interval allowed by the mother's instinct to glance back at her children and grant herself the freedom to shop while remaining convinced of her vigilance. The watcher knew that even if she found the boy gone, he would have another minute, perhaps several, while she alerted the father, then the sales clerks, and several more minutes before anyone thought about calling security. Then what would they get? Some fat mall cop armed with a can of pepper spray and low self-esteem over working shopping center security instead of being a real cop.

He moved quickly, a shark through shallow water, easily pushing the boy outside, resolving any hesitancy from the boy with the shiny Matchbox car he'd noted the boy admiring, then shoplifted for him. It was the perfect icebreaker that, along with the lie that he was a policeman whose assignment was to take the boy back to his parents, was enough to dampen the boy's natural defenses. Once they were twenty feet out the door, he swept the boy up and discarded the distinctive red cap by throwing it into the decorative bushes that also helped to obscure the line of sight to the parking lot. He popped the trunk of his car with his remote and, after a quick glance around, tossed the boy in, like a shopping bag of newly bought clothes. He got into his nondescript car, noting that no one gave him any more attention than they did the beautiful blue sky overhead. He started the car and drove away. From time of contact with the boy to having him in the trunk took twenty-six seconds.

A few seconds later, the mother allowed her attention to break away from the dress she was fingering. She did not see her son and felt her heart jump a little before reassuring herself that he was just on the other aisle or that her husband had him. She walked to the end of her aisle and swerved around to the next one, doing a quick scan and seeing nothing. Now her heart began to beat a little faster, her pupils dilated to take in more, the fight-or-flight mechanism ingrained in every parent through a millennium of evolution just beginning to kick in. She saw her husband two aisles over, holding their daughter, and she felt the briefest relief—enjoyed a false sense of security for the last time in her life. She looked down another aisle, then another, now running, acid filling her stomach and adrenaline pumping into her bloodstream like she'd been injected with it. She glanced back to her husband, who saw the look of terror in her face and began to move toward her. They came together quickly.

"Do you have him?" she asked her husband.

"No!" he said, his eyes wide now, his body succumbing to the gut-wrenching fear she was already experiencing. "I thought he was with you!" He handed his wife their daughter, who looked frightened, too, and began sucking her thumb.

The father ran and alerted sales clerks, who called a Code Adam in the store. Security came quickly, though it seemed an eternity to the mother whose husband ran wildly through the store now, screaming his son's name, while she waited at the checkout desk, talking to the clerk, giving a description of her son. From the time she noticed her son was gone until the security guard showed up was less than five minutes, but by then, her son was already five miles away, his pants wet from fear, his world gone from a bright day at the store with his family to a dark and frightening place with no future.

• • •

Subject: 56QAH/Lot 238

He had asked her to help him study for their calculus exam. She'd tried to brush him off at first, but he had been relentless and he was not without a certain boyish charm. She finally relented. She had known him for years; they had been neighbors, actually playing together before time and the teens pulled them in different directions. She went on to become a popular cheerleader, track star, and prom queen. He went on to become the brunt of jokes about his personal hygiene and his fast-paced geeky walk to class, eyes always staring at his own two feet as if he had to watch them to ensure they were going in the right direction. He was labeled a nerd and often bullied.

But a couple years had made a big difference. Now they were in their sophomore year of college. She still had her friends but was more studious, serious about where she wanted to go with her life.

He had finally came out of his shell one summer, his acne cleared and he had his hair cut differently and wore better, hipper clothes and cologne. He was actually handsome, with his dark hair and eyes and ridiculously deep dimples that had turned his smile into a neon sign that young women were very attracted to. He had wasted no time in making up for lost and celibate years. But, inside, there was a pot simmering, longing to boil over, for all those years when he had been the target for jocks who were now already fat and miserable, married to their high school sweethearts, whom they'd impregnated while making passionate, sloppy love in the beer-scented cabs of their pickup trucks. And his problem was not so much with those boys as it was with the girls who had ignored him, giggled at him as he'd traversed the halls, alone, scared, and insecure.

Now they were huddled together, peering into the calculus book that was unfathomable to him but, to her, seemed as easily mastered as elementary school arithmetic. He had worked out earlier that day, scrubbed his skin until it shone pink, and pulled on a tight T-shirt that accented his new, muscular physique. Almost no body fat. She had noticed, too; when she came in, she had said, "Wow! You sure have changed since twelfth grade. You working out?" He told her yes and told her she was as beautiful as ever. She blew off the compliment and plopped her books down on the dining room table, her tone and attitude all business now.

Still, with her so close, it was impossible not to smell the perfume of her hair, feel the heat coming off of her skin, radiating right into his. Twenty minutes into their study time, he couldn't help but bury his nose into her thick, blonde hair, and to his surprise, she didn't pull away. In fact, she brushed her hair back and giggled as his nose came closer to her ear, his lips nibbled at her lobes. His hand, caressing her arms, felt goose bumps pop out. When she looked up at him, he could see her pupils were dilated. She was aroused. He leaned down and kissed her and she kissed him back.

He didn't have to strangle her. He hadn't wanted to. But when she had succumbed to his advances so quickly, then had been so *hungry*, so willing to do…*anything*, he had to take her life. Something clicked in his head and unlocked the memories of when she had been the popular girl in school. She had been kind to him in private, seeing each other across the street from their expansive upper-middle-class homes while fetching the mail or washing the car in the drive or congregating at the occasional neighborhood party. She would smile coyly at him and then ask some innocuous question quietly charged with sexual innuendo for which his face, already scarlet-hued from festering pimples, would turn even redder, and he would stammer incoherently and finally answer inappropriately. At those times, she seemed patient, understanding, even caring.

But other times, when he would see her in school accompanied by other popular teens, she would glance at him, then look away quickly, as if allowing her gaze to linger might invite a salutation from him that she could not, would not, reciprocate. To do so would invite speculation on the part of her perfect friends as to why she would even know such a dweeb as him, and this was something she could not risk.

He would have preferred her consistently cold toward him rather than this two-faced, schizophrenic cunt whose shallow character revealed the true nature of her soul. Each time he saw her and experienced the unpredictable pendulum of her emotions, it confused him, hurt him, and rekindled a burning anger that, initially, he took out on small animals. Neighborhood pets disappeared. He took them for rides away from witnesses and began his self-taught medical school. Using a pocketknife he'd obtained from a failed attempt at fitting into Boy Scouts years earlier, he would open up the chest cavities of the precious Fidos and Mittens and explore what was inside them with an almost insatiable curiosity.

He looked at her, supine on the bed, her eyes open, one pupil enlarged, indicating brain death had begun. His handprints still red on either side of her neck, his thumbprints blurred together over her delicate Adam's apple. Then he saw it: a slight palpation in the hollow of her throat, a shallow beating of a...still... living...heart. *Could it get any better than this?* If he hurried, he could still get her out to his place in the nearby woods where he took the animals. He could still see what was *inside* of her. He might still be able to see her living heart. He wondered if it would look different from some of the others he'd seen. *Would it be black from her lifelong deceptions? Would it be cold to the touch?* He had to find out.

He dressed quickly. Wasting no time, he grabbed her by the most obvious available handle—her hair. He wrapped a hank of it around his fist and pulled her through the house and into the garage where his car was parked. He popped the trunk and placed her inside, quickly checking her pulse to see if it was still there. Yes, faintly.

He ran back into the house and threw her clothes into a plastic grocery bag. He was tempted, very tempted, to keep her lovely underpants, lacy bright-blue things that still smelled like her, but he had been lucky so far and he wanted to keep it that way. She had told him she had not told her parents where she was going—they were both still at work—nor anyone else. Probably, she was still embarrassed to tell anyone she was studying with him; they didn't know the new and improved version, so she would have kept that a secret. *If* someone came to look for her and found some evidence she'd been there, a hair or something, he would say, "Yes, she would stop by now and then to study or swim in our pool." He reminded himself he would vacuum his room and change the bedsheets when he got back; his parents were always complimenting him on being so fastidious, so it would be a normal thing and draw no suspicion. A quick shower and he would be "washing that woman right out of his life…" He hummed the old tune as he locked up the house and went back to the garage. He thought of something else before he left: *should bring a small can of gas and a lighter.* Just in case. He jumped into his car and checked the glove box to ensure his pocketknife was still there. It was.

• • •

Subject: 56QAH/Lot 64

He accepted delivery of the shipment of fertilizer. Not unusual for a man who owned a landscaping service to order large amounts of ammonium nitrate-enriched fertilizer. After the delivery truck drove away, he had a few of the Guatemalans empty the bags into the tanker. Including today's delivery, he would have over five hundred 80-pound bags in the container. Now he just needed to top it off with the diesel fuel and drive the load to its destination. But that was still a few days away. He needed to finalize a few more things.

As his workers toiled away, lugging the heavy bags up a ladder, ripping them open, and dumping them into the tanker one by one, he went back into his office. The office was a converted old house, its Spartan decor holding a desk with a computer and a few peripherals, a chair, a wastebasket, and a wall-banger air conditioner, chugging along, cooling the room enough to make the windows sweat with condensation. There was a small refrigerator, like they use in college dormitories, and from this he withdrew a small bottle of Coca-Cola, opened it, and took a long pull of the sweet, cold liquid. He belched loudly, then went to his desk and unrolled the blueprints of the school.

It was a huge high school that was formed like a squared-off "U." Its open court was filled with some decorative gardens separated by walkways. The only thing closing off the open end of the courtyard was a lightweight aluminum walkway cover that ran the length of the front of the school and allowed students being dropped off to stay relatively dry when it was raining. It would not be a problem to get past that flimsy structure with a tractor tanker filled with thirty tons of nitrate-charged diesel fuel traveling fifty miles per hour.

In the middle of the day, on any weekday, the school was filled to capacity with almost 1,500 students and about 200 teachers and support staff.

He saw himself in the reflection of the computer screen. He was handsome, with thick, dark, curly hair and intensely dark eyes. Looks that belonged more to a magazine model than a land-scape designer. But he enjoyed that work, being outside, the smell of the cut grass and the sun warming his skin. And he made a lot of money for a job that held little stress. Still, for as long as he could remember, he had wanted to *kill* something. His fantasy turned to desire in his teens, then into addiction by the time he was in his twenties.

He had never wanted to get close to the victims; he didn't want to touch them because he had seldom been touched. Not by a father he'd never known, nor by his mother, who had worked two jobs to keep a roof over his head. So he'd killed people from a distance. *Distance* was central to the relationships he'd experienced in life. But shooting lovers in their cars or cuddling on a bench in isolated areas of a public park or lover's lane grew tiresome. Now he needed to do something more. Something bigger.

• • •

Who would have ever thought it would come to this? While they all have, shall we say, obvious talent, it's difficult to determine which ones have exactly what I'm looking for. Sure, they all like to kill people—who doesn't? But none of them seem to have that je ne sais quoi *that will make them useful for our purposes. I'll need to keep looking.*

I know the genetic "trigger" that was morphed in the DNA will allow a five- to ten-year range for the killing behavior to emerge, but having sown that seed over several years and with so many variants from mothers and birthdates, there's no telling when and where they will begin to "ripen." They seem to be doing so exponentially now, though I'm not exactly sure why. I've narrowed my search to Florida, where so many seeds were planted. But I have to say, there are a lot of sociopaths in the Sunshine State and I have found my task to be much more challenging than even I'd suspected. Oh well, like they say, there's no rest for the wicked.

EIGHT

For a brief moment, I was back at the crime site in Broward County. It was like the scene was being played back in my mind but much more vividly, as if it were now on Blu-ray DVD and I could move forward slowly, frame by frame, and see finer detail. Everything happened the way it had happened, but every detail was pronounced: the old man tripping in the pothole, me helping him up and hearing the pop of his knee joints as he stood up, the rustle of his khaki pants, even the sound of his skin brushing against mine as he shook my hand. The sound of my car door as I shut it, the click of my trunk as I opened it to get my evidence collection bag, the feel of the wind on my neck, the scent of burned flesh from across the parking lot. Then, as if it were the reason I was there, the church sign loomed into my sight, now oversized, towering ominously in front of me, blocking my path. I read the words again: *"God's Love Is The Eternal Flame That Will Save Your Soul."*

This time, I reached up to touch the letters, but I couldn't quite grasp them.

"Inspector Gift? Inspector Gift?"

I could hear her voice, but it seemed small, far away, tinny, overwhelmed by the buzzing in my ears. My vision was returning, but I could make no sense of the images; the people moving about me were as unreal as two-dimensional animated figures.

"Inspector Gift?" she tried. "Grey?"

Cold and wet, on my temples and neck. Rose had poured some ice water on a napkin and was dabbing me with it, but it was the scent of her skin as she did so that snapped me out of my daze like an ammonia inhalant. I looked over to the table where the ladies had been, the last thing I remembered before I'd blinked out, but they were gone. I glanced around the restaurant to see if anyone was staring at me, but waiters went about their business, people came and went, sounds of laughter, small talk, and business braggadocio bounced around the restaurant, all completely normal. I felt perspiration drying on my scalp, neck, and lower back.

My hand was extended across the table as if I were reaching for the salt. Our waiter came up to take away our plates. Rose reached up gently and took my hand in hers, entwining our fingers as if we were an old married couple.

"Did you save room for dessert?" asked the waiter.

Rose smiled up at him. "We're good. If we can just get the tab, please?"

The waiter tore off a slip of paper and placed it on the table. In normal mode, I would have pulled out my wallet faster than the eye could follow. But my thinking was slow; I still wasn't quite in the real, tangible world. Rose slipped him a credit card before I could move.

"Whuh," I began. My throat was dry. I used my free hand to pick up my water—Rose still held my other one—and took a long, deep drink. My hand was shaking, ever so slightly but noticeably. "Was I…having a seizure?"

Rose tilted her head quizzically at me. "No. Well, actually, I don't know. You weren't flopping around on the floor, if that's what you mean. But, yeah, something was going on. Your eyes rolled back in your head and your eyelids fluttered. The rest of you was okay but…I was going to call nine-one-one, then I remembered what you said about losing your job. And the whole thing only lasted for half a minute, maybe less."

"I haven't had one that bad for years…" My head was still foggy and it was difficult to find the right words to express myself. "But this one was different. It was as if I were having a dream. I don't usually remember what happens, what is going through my mind, but this time, I do. Sort of."

"You were doing something with your hand, too. Like you were trying to reach for something."

"I…I was *seeing* something. I was back at the Eliathah church, at the Matarese crime scene from this morning. I could see everything, but it was like it was enhanced, like I could see the whole thing happening again through a microscope but…with a wider view…it was…let's talk about this later. Okay?"

She shrugged. "Okay, but what…?"

"I need to call Chief Dugger with the Broward Sheriff's Office."

"What for? He didn't seem like very much help this morning." But I was already calling him.

"Chief Dugger? This is Gift with the fire marshal's office."

"Yeah?" he said, whispering. "What do you got?"

"Do you still have patrolmen over at the church?"

"Not sure. I'm in a meeting. Can I call you back, or is it something important?"

"I think it's important. I need you to get a unit over there and make sure no one touches that sign out front."

"What sign?"

"The church sign. Where they put the spiritual message every week? I don't believe Pastor Wilton put that message up that was there this morning."

"Why not?"

"Because of what it said. It read, 'God's Love Is The Eternal Flame That Will Save Your Soul.' I think the killer might have put that up there. I mean, the 'flame' thing seems awful coincidental."

"I'll get a unit back over there, ASAP. You coming back down?"

"Not sure yet. Just make sure the sign is secured. There might be some prints on it." I ended the call. Rose was looking at me, her lips parted. The frown was back.

"What's wrong?" I asked.

She shook her head. "That's what I was talking about. I've been distracted by all this other crap. I should have seen that message. It didn't register because I focused on that officer's damn cigarette butt. I've been wracking my brain all morning trying to think about what I might be missing. Then you have a seizure and go off to la-la land and see something so obvious it embarrasses me."

"I'm sorry, Rose. I didn't ask to have a seizure. Or the…dream that came with it."

"No," she said, softening a little. "I'm not blaming you. It's my fault. But it's a lesson learned. I need to get past the peripheral stuff and concentrate on what I'm doing, where we're going. How it all fits. That's what I'm supposed to be good at."

"I'm sure you are. Now, what's our next move?"

She thought about it for a moment. "I think you should go to the hospital, or at least your own private physician."

"I'm okay. I don't know what triggered that episode. There was a bunch of bright light coming off the boats out there. It was bothering me. But I'm good now."

"I hope so. I'm not going to try to mother you. But if it happens again, I'm not going to hesitate. I can't be responsible for you going unconscious and swallowing your own tongue, or something. I'll call nine-one-one if it happens again, just so you know."

"Okay. If we get a break in the next couple days, I'll go see my doctor. By the way, that business about swallowing your own tongue—that can't happen. It's attached at the back of your throat."

"Thanks for the correction, Doctor. Now, just try to stay upright so you can help me out."

"You bet."

"I'm going to have to set up a task force. I'll be lead investigator; you'll be co-lead."

"You might want to get someone else. I might be out of your league. Maybe you have a coworker with the FBI you'll want to bring in?"

"Oh, I'll be working with other investigators, from all around the country. Mostly by phone, texting, or teleconference. We're going to need a base of operation. You said the fire marshal's lab is close to Tallahassee. That won't be practical if we collect much evidence. The Palm Beach ME has the bio-bag with what we're assuming is the Matarese girl's organs found here in the canal. That suggests to me that the killer might live up this way. Maybe we can operate out of the ME's office?"

"I'll check with my boss. He can probably get us a space to work out of."

"Good. Didn't I see an airport on our way over here?"

"Yes. On Southern Boulevard. Why?"

"I'm going to call Quantico and get us a helicopter so we can get around quickly when we need to."

"That's cool. Think we're going to have to do some hopping around?"

"Oh yeah. If we're dealing with one killer and he's killed one in Homestead in Dade County, one in Immokalee—I think that was Collier County—one in Tamarac in Broward County, and now we have remains in Palm Beach County, then we're going to be very mobile. This guy's working South Florida with a vengeance. He seems to have a range of about a hundred miles, so we can triangulate his potential kill area. He's been to the south and to the west. If he goes north, he might go as far as St. Lucie or Indian River Counties, and if we go by the assumption, we can make a guess that he lives in Palm Beach County. We haven't heard of any immolation murders here, so maybe he doesn't like to dirty up his own backyard."

Rose thought for a minute before she continued. "He might be on a spree. It's a full moon this week. Maybe he's on a lunar cycle. Who knows? But in any event, we've got to be able to try to predict his next move and be able to get there quickly."

"Did you get much evidence from either of the other two scenes in Homestead or Immokalee?"

"No. Not much." Rose stood up and slung her purse over her shoulder. "Let's go talk to the gardener and then get back to that canal where the bio-bag was found. I'll tell you about the other cases en route."

I stood up and hid the fact that I could still feel my legs trembling.

Rose looked me over behind her sunglasses. "I'm driving," she said.

NINE

As we drove back east, across the bridge that separated the haves from the have-nots, Rose made calls and I served as her navigator through Palm Beach. She was dynamic: with one call, she had a helicopter and a forensic team being scrambled from Quantico. Listening to her, I pieced together that she was part of a special group within the FBI called the Behavioral Analysis Unit.

When she hung up, I told her to keep in the left-hand lane. "That address on Clark Avenue the gardener gave is going to be to the north a few blocks. Used to park my car and surf there when I was a kid, before they prohibited us peasants from parking over here."

"Okay," she said, checking her rearview mirror before nudging over into the turning lane.

"You sure seem like you have some pull with the bigwigs," I said. "Tell me about that unit you mentioned."

"It's actually made up of several units that are a part of the National Center for the Analysis of Violent Crime, or NCAVC, as we call it. The primary unit is our CIRG, or Critical Incident Response Group. I used to be a part of that group until they reassigned me to Miami. We would respond to anywhere in the country they needed us to look into possible serial killings. But Florida was experiencing so many serial murders, they sent me down here as a full-time remote operative for the unit. The CIRG is made up of Behavioral Analysis Units, or BAUs, each with designated, various responsibilities. I was assigned to BAU-4, also known as ViCAP, which stands for Violent Criminal Apprehension Program. You following me so far?"

"Lord. How do you keep up with all the units and acronyms?"

"We feds love our acronyms and nicknames," she said with a laugh. "Anyway, I was in ViCAP until I got my guts cut out. When I got out of the hospital and returned to work, they sent me to Miami. I thought it was their way of putting me out to pasture, but man, I've been busier down here the last couple of years than I was at Quantico."

"Really? I know we've had our share of fun guys down here in the past—Ted Bundy, Gerard Schaefer, Toole and Lucas, Cunanan, Wilder—but I can't say I remember a whole bunch of serial killers down here in recent years."

"That's good. That means we're either doing our job and actually preventing some of these killers from reaching their full potential, or we're at least doing a better job of keeping it out of the media."

"Why would you want to do that? I thought the media helped you, slipping pieces of information out to the killers, secretly talking to them for you..."

"That's in the movies. In real life, the media is a pain in the ass. They get in the way, sometimes destroy or dilute evidence. They report what they think and not what they know and, more often than not, inadvertently help the killer. And if you're not feeding them the information they need to fill the six o'clock hour, they start to raise questions about your agency's competency or look for some sort of conspiracy that makes law enforcement look bad. I promise you, we can do without them."

"I'm surprised they haven't been all over us already."

"I hope we can keep it that way. But the reason they haven't is because no one has put these murders together yet. I'm probably the only person doing that, and I'm not sure even I have enough evidence to prove the murders were all done by one person. Even if I did, I doubt I'd make an announcement to the press unless I was directed to do so by my supervisors."

"You said you were going to fill me in on the other two murders from earlier this week."

"Sure. There's not much to tell other than some peripheral similarities." Rose told me about the two victims. The first one was found in Homestead—a female in her twenties named Shawna Wooley. What was left of her was found in her car and identified from the car's registration. Miami-Dade cops did the initial investigation and ruled it accidental, probably because they weren't aware of any other cases like it. The car was burned from end to end and there wasn't much left of the girl. She'd had the car worked on recently and one of the cops thought the mechanic's shop might have left a fuel line loose.

I asked Rose why she had looked into a fire death in the first place, especially one that seemed like an accident.

"The only reason I looked into Wooley's case was because of the second girl. The one found in Immokalee? That one was definitely a murder. I wasn't called to that one either, but I was scanning for local murders on our computer at the HQ in Miami— part of my fun daily regimen—when I saw it pop up. I looked for others with similarities and found the one from Homestead, so I decided to respond out to Immokalee to see if there were any other similarities. They didn't know who the Immokalee girl was but gave a brief description of what was left of her. Wasn't much, but she did have breast implants. They were going to cremate her remains, but I called and asked them to wait until I could look at them. Her implants, as I suspected, had serial numbers on them, which I traced back to the doctor who installed them and found her identity. A girl named Juanita Suarez.

"I found two glaring commonalities in the two cases: one, both bodies had been burned, of course, and two, both girls were listed on Backpage.com, where they were working, at least part-time, as independent call girls. I found the first girl's cell phone in her car. It was pretty much incinerated, but we were able to pull a couple numbers off the SIM card and made some calls. Naturally, none of the johns were especially eager to talk to us, but when you tell them that they're murder suspects, they start talking pretty quick. That's how I found out about the Backpage.com connection. I contacted the administrators for Backpage.com, told them I was doing an investigation, and had them query their records for the Wooley girl. Sure enough, she was in there, too, under their 'adult services' listing, calling herself Brandy."

"That was all this week?" I asked, incredulous. "You've been a busy lady."

"It's been a busy week. I hate to say it, but I think it's just going to get busier. The Matarese girl, found in the church parking lot in Tamarac this morning, sealed the deal. We're definitely tracking the same killer, or killers."

• • •

We arrived at the employment address Rose had for Jesse Francois, the fisherman who found the bio-bag in the canal. When we got out of the car at the Palm Beach mansion, I looked east toward the ocean and could see a few surfers catching some small but well-formed waves. My heart tugged toward them. After the morning's grim events, nothing could appeal to me more than to be hanging out on a board, sun toasting me, salt baked on my skin, the ocean underneath me, rising and falling slowly—the sensation like being a child napping on his mother's breast.

Gasoline-powered motors buzzed and growled inside the twelve-foot-high, ficus-covered wrought iron fence. We walked through the open gates that allowed access to the driveway leading up to the massive and ornate Mizner-designed estate. Personally, I would have approached the homeowners and informed them we were here to speak to one of their workers. Rose didn't think that was necessary. I could sense her anxiety, her awareness of time passing that she could not regain—and with it, a killer possibly getting away. A woman on a mission, she approached the first gardener we came to and drew a line across her throat, indicating for him to cut the motor on the hedge trimmer he was using. He complied.

He was a short and stocky Guatemalan, his features recalling a time when his ancestors were more Indian than Spanish, their endurance for hard work and industry matched only by the fierceness with which they used to defend their jungle homelands. Now they worked quietly in the Anglo world, adopting a subservient role as if the history of their conquering civilization never existed. He cut the motor and looked up at Rose, sweat dripping from his chin.

"Can you tell us where to find Jesse Francois?" she asked.

He pointed to a lanky black man wearing a floppy canvas hat and black wraparound sunglasses, riding a lawn mower. *"Alla, el hefe,"* he said. Then, without further discussion, he thumbed the *on* button to the trimmer, cranked the pull cord with one quick stroke, and went back to shaping the hedge.

So Jesse Francois was the boss, or "chief" on the job, as indicated by the Guatemalan. As we approached him, I held my hand up to him like an overzealous school crossing guard, wearing a grin. He cut the mower, its spinning blades coming to a halt with a loud *thunk*. Mr. Francois stood up, removing a set of noise-canceling headphones. The scent of oil and gasoline drifted up on a wave of heat. I also thought I smelled a little whiff of something else, maybe some ganja. But the scent was fleeting and, for my purposes, immaterial.

"Allo?" The accent suggested Haitian.

Rose flipped open her badge holder and showed it to him, then introduced us.

"Is dis about da bag I found dis mornin'?"

"Yes," said Rose.

"Let's go talk in da shade." He took a towel he had wrapped around his neck and laid it over the mower's seat, to keep it from getting too hot to sit on when he returned, I supposed. We followed him back around the side of the mansion to an open garage. Inside, a huge hurricane fan whirred and cooled the interior. There was a refrigerator against one wall and the tall Haitian opened it and pulled out a bottle of red Gatorade. "Would you like a drink?"

"Absolutely," I said, just as Rose declined. Then she changed her mind and said, "Well, okay. Water's fine."

"Me, too," I said.

He handed us each a bottle and I downed half of mine in one gulp.

Rose sipped at hers as she got down to business. "The police at the scene told us you were fishing and found the bag?"

"Dat's not entirely correct. I was fishin' and a truck stopped and trew da bag over da side a da bridge. I taught it was jus' someone litterin', but when I saw it was a red bag, da kind dey use at da clinics, I wondered why he be trowin' it in da canal. When I opened it, I knew da remains, dey was human."

Rose looked at me, frowning. Already, something was askew. The sheriff's deputies on scene had not told her about the truck.

"How do you know about biohazard bags?" asked Rose.

"I was a nurse in Haiti. When I come to da States, my license was not good here, so I work as a gardener. But I knew."

"Can you tell us about the truck you saw?"

Jesse Francois removed his glasses. One of his eyes was blue-white, the other filmed by a cataract.

"I was fishin' under da bridge, so I could not see da truck directly. An' he could not see me. But I could see a reflection in da water. It was a big truck wit' da diesel motor. I tink dere was some lights on da top a da truck, and I tink it was white, but as you can see, I have problems wit' my eyes."

Now I could imagine why the deputies at the scene had decided not to tell Rose about Francois "seeing" the truck or looking in the bio-bag. Perhaps they assumed the word of a near-blind, probably stoned Haitian would not serve as a reliable testimony in court, if a suspect was found.

"Mr. Francois," said Rose, "did you tell the deputies at the scene what you saw?"

The gardener smiled broadly, revealing perfect teeth and a smile so warm you could sell it in cold countries for heating purposes.

"When dey first come up, I tol' dem da bag was a biohazard bag wit' da human remains. Dey was…how do I want to say dis? Not very nice. Dey smelled da pot smoke on me. I don't try to hide it. I have glaucoma and it is still da best treatment for dat, even dough it is illegal here. Dey see I'm near blind, and when dey got together to talk, I could here dem sayin' somtin' about da stoned porch monkey and I don' like it. Dey didn't want to hear what I have to say afta dat, anyway, so I tol' dem I have to go to work and dey took my number and I left. Dat's all."

I looked over at Rose and could see the muscles working in her jaw. She'd been frustrated before; now she was furious. I envisioned her squealing out of Palm Beach, the car tires smoking as she sped to the sheriff's office and demanded the deputies be terminated. She cleared her throat to talk but was finding it hard to formulate the words she wanted to say.

I stepped in. "Is that why you couldn't get your nurse's license?"

"Dat's right. Da glaucoma and, of course, da pot. You know you can't use da drug and work as a nurse."

"Yeah. I know."

"Were you a nurse?" he asked me.

"No. I was a paramedic before I went into arson investigation."

"Is dat a good job?"

"Yeah. It was good. A lot like nursing, you know? Helping people."

"I miss dat."

"Yeah. You know, Mr. Francois, you might want to be a little more discreet about the ganja thing. I wouldn't want to see you get into trouble."

"Oh, mon. I'm not worried about dat. You two are not lookin' to bust some ol' Haitian for smokin' de joint. I tink you're lookin' for sometin' a whole lot worse dan me."

We thanked him for the drinks and made sure we had his home address in case we thought of something else later. He put his glasses on and his hat and earmuffs and went back to his mower. As we walked back to the car, I noticed the Guatemalan hedge-trimmer toiling, seemingly oblivious to the opulence surrounding him as he worked his blade back and forth on the hedges like a sculptor.

Salmon-colored bougainvillea petals blew across our path, like ticket stubs to the Broken American Dream.

TEN

By the time we left the ME's office, Rose was fit to be tied. She had wanted to stop by on the way back to the bridge where the bio-bag had been tossed into the canal. But when we got to the coroner's office, the bag—*the evidence*—was not there. They told us they had released it to a man who had identified himself as a CIA agent.

Rose looked at me now, her mouth open slightly, but I knew what she was thinking. "The guy in the suit and sunglasses?" I said.

"Has to be. But CIA? Why would they be here and why would they be interested in a murder, even if it is a serial? You know anybody with Palm Beach County Sheriff's Office?"

"I know a few guys. We work together sometimes."

"Can you see if you can track down those guys from the canal scene and find out our mystery man's name?"

"I'll try, but my boss knows more people than I do at the sheriff's department. Let me see if he can find out something for us."

She handed me her notes with the names of the cops that were on the canal bank. "I have to make some calls, too. This is weird."

I called Bland Sam and gave him the names of the Palm Beach County cops and told him about the CIA guy. He said he'd get back to me in a few. He also confirmed he had requested a designated room for us at the ME's office in which we could work. He'd done one even better than that: he'd requested for the state office to send one of the lab specialists down to work with us, and he was bringing some equipment with him. I hung up and waited. By then, Rose had called her supervisor, too.

"Find out anything?" she asked.

"Not yet. Captain Brandsma is going to call me back. He said he arranged a room for us here. There's a forensics guy coming down from Tallahassee, too."

"That would be nice if we had some, you know, *evidence* to look at."

"We should have some information coming back tonight or tomorrow from the evidence we sent up this morning."

"True. I hope it tells us *something*." She hesitated for a moment, cracking her knuckles. She went on. "I don't know who this 'CIA' agent is, but I don't like that he can come in here and take any evidence we collect anytime he wants. I talked to my supervisor, too. He's checking with some people he knows in the CIA to see what's going on."

"This happen much? The CIA stepping into an FBI investigation?"

"Never. Not with a murder investigation. I mean, we do have some common interests at times. Remember the Critical Incident Response Group I was telling you about? One of the Behavioral Analysis Units, BAU-1, deals with terrorists and counter-terrorist pursuits, as does the CIA. But the relationship is very peripheral—information sharing, mostly. It'd be very unusual for the

CIA to be involved in a murder case unless it was tied to some terrorist activity."

"Could that be a possibility here?"

Rose looked at me, through me, really, her eyes losing focus for a moment, a frown deepening between her brows. "No. This is the work of a serial killer. It's not espionage."

I heard what she was saying, but I could also see her mind working in high gear to try to comprehend a connection. Her phone rang just as mine did. Mine was Bland Sam calling me back.

"I got hold of the shift supervisor over at the Palm Beach County Sheriff's Office. I know the guy from way back. I asked him about those names you gave me and if they told him about a CIA operative showing up at their scene. He said they mentioned it in their report—which is very brief, by the way—and they confirmed a guy had showed up, identified himself as CIA, told them the case was federal, and asked about the evidence. It was already off-scene, taken to the ME's office, and you showed up with the FBI agent. They said there was nothing else of interest at the scene and it appeared the case was out of their hands, so they were done with it."

"Did they get a name from the CIA guy?"

"Oh yeah. Got something to write with?"

I noticed Rose was off the phone and motioned to her with my hand in a scribing gesture. She whipped out her notepad and gave me a nod, ready to write.

"Go ahead," I said, and repeated what Sam told me. "C-e-r-b-e-r-u-s. Got it. How about a first name? Nicholas. Hmm. Sounds Greek. Thanks, Sam. I'll be in touch."

Rose was shaking her head. "That's perfect."

"What? You know him?"

"No. But Cerberus was the name of the three-headed dog that guarded the gates of hell."

• • •

When we got back to the bridge off of Southern Boulevard, the sun was so bright, shadows could not exist. You could peer straight into the depths of the canal and see all the way to the bottom, where stolen bikes and shopping carts served as artificial reefs and fish took refuge among them. I could smell the loamy, fecund scent of the brackish water as it moved under the bridge carrying occasional hyacinth lilies, their purple petals like cotton candy from the state fair.

I found a path that led down to the canal bank where Francois had been fishing, while Rose stayed up on the bridge looking around. I walked high on the bank so as not to disturb any evidence if it were to be found. I could see the prints of Francois's boots closer to the water and a round imprint, which must have been where he'd set his catch bucket. I could even make out the holes in the mud where he'd jammed his cane poles. His tracks led under the bridge and I followed them along to the point where he'd stopped and I could make out the place where he'd sat down in the cool sand, waiting out the fish. He must have been sitting there when the bag was thrown off the bridge above.

I looked up at the bottom of the bridge, doing my best not to let the bats huddled in the cracks here and there freak me out, and tried to imagine the red bio-bag flying over the rail and into the water. It probably would have landed about where a submerged log sat in the stream, its bark long gone, a film of green algae coating the trunk now. An amputated branch stem extended from the trunk, barely piercing the surface of the water. It could have caught a plastic bag easily. I yelled up to Rose. "Rose, can you come over to the rail?"

"Yeah, okay."

"Can you see me from where you're standing?"

"No. Not at all."

But I could see her reflected in the water.

"Okay. That's what I thought. Thank you. See anything up there?"

"Actually, I do. I found a little tire patch where someone skidded their tires. Looks like a wide track like a big truck would leave. Could've come from anywhere, but who knows? Might be worth a shot."

"Sure."

"How about you? Anything down there?"

"Nothing earth-shattering. Might have found the log the bag got caught on. I can see where Francois was fishing and why the driver didn't see him."

Rose didn't say anything back and I could hear her shoes clicking on the surface of the bridge above me and the *whirr* of a camera aperture as she took some pictures. I didn't see anything else other than the detritus of a throwaway society—broken bottles, juice cartons, beer cans, and my personal favorite in the litter category, plastic shopping bags. They're everywhere. They blow across the waves when I'm surfing and across the reefs I dive at a hundred feet like plastic ghosts. Marine animals eat them, languish, and die, but as long as we can tote a few items from the store to our car, we are content and bovinely complacent. I clambered back up the path and into the sunlight, ashamed to be human. Rose was waiting for me.

"Grey, there's a fire station about a block down the street. Think they might know anything?"

"Can't hurt to ask," I said as we walked back to the car. "There's a shopping plaza down the road with a Dunkin' Donuts. Let's swing by there first."

"Donuts, huh? Is that the way to a firefighter's heart?"

"It's a good icebreaker, for sure."

We picked up a dozen assorted donuts and went by the station. There were two units in the station—both vehicles were the traditional red, not white—manned with six guys. One of the men was working, doing reports. One was cooking. One was pumping iron and the other three were sitting in recliners watching television. Greatest job on earth. No doubt about it.

The guy doing the reports had to be the lieutenant, so I asked him if I could talk to him and his crew. He got up from his computer and called over all speakers for the rest of the crew to assemble in the kitchen of the station, where we all sat at the table, the usual meeting spot at most fire stations around the world.

I introduced them to Rose and myself and placed the donuts on the table. The firefighter who'd been cooking, a fresh-faced kid who must have been the squad's newbie, asked me if I wanted some fresh coffee. I looked at Rose and she nodded, so I gave him the go ahead and we sat down, making ourselves comfortable. Every one of them tried to give me their attention, but they were obviously gaga over Rose, who managed to look even more beautiful sitting at the table, her legs crossed and her notepad out, the overhead florescent lights gleaming off her black, luscious hair, the scent of her woman's skin filling their nostrils, winning out over the pot of chili that was on the stove. I was straight with them, telling them about the bio-bag going in the canal.

"I can't imagine any of our guys doing anything like that," the lieutenant said.

"No," I said. "We have a report that indicates the vehicle may have been a white truck with some emergency lights on top. Could be a private ambulance or…"

"Or a wrecker," said the lieutenant.

"Yes, could be," I said.

"The crew we relieved this morning told us the rescue truck broke down early this morning. The tow truck we have to use is oversized. It's a big white truck."

"Would a tow truck carry red bio-bags?" Rose asked.

"Not usually," said the lieutenant. "But some of the tow trucks have them. You know, in case they respond to a wreck and they find…something, after the rescue truck is gone. Or if they are cleaning blood off the road or a vehicle and end up with contaminated rags they need to dispose of. I've had some of the drivers ask me for some on scene."

"Do you know who drives that truck or what company it is?" asked Rose.

"Yes, ma'am. It's called Brother's Towing. I know some of the drivers, but I don't know who was driving last night. Their home base is just down the road, north on Benoist Farms Road at the industrial park between Southern and Belvedere."

Rose looked at me.

I said, "I know where it is."

As we were getting into the car outside the station, Rose said, "Could that have been any easier?"

"I told you those donuts were a good investment."

ELEVEN

A tiny cinder block building—painted like an American flag and barely visible among the numerous giant tow trucks surrounding it—was home to Brother's Towing. Tow trucks of every conceivable size filled the yard. The entire parking lot was shell rock that crunched under the car's tires as I pulled in and stopped.

Rose pulled out her cell phone and brought up the picture of the tire tread pattern from the bridge. She got out of the car, crouched next to one of the big wreckers in the yard, and compared treads. They matched, as did the tires on at least three other trucks. Oh well. At least we were getting warm. A cast and closer scrutiny under a microscope could give us an exact match if we had to do every truck in the yard.

We entered through the front door of the block building and found an elderly woman seated at a desk, the surface of which was covered with piles of paperwork, invoices, and various phones and walkie-talkies. Standing behind her was an obese man, his rolls of fat packed into a stained tank top shirt. Cigarette butts spilled over several ashtrays on his desk and smoke hung down a foot from the ceiling. The funk was terrible, a mix of body odor, cigarettes, and engine oil so noxious it made me long to put on the air pack I keep in the car for when I sort through burn evidence, but that really wasn't an option. Still, it was hard to hide my reaction to the unpleasantness of the room. Rose didn't even try. She scrunched up her nose like she'd stepped in something and looked around the room as if she were trying to find the source of the smell so she could kill it.

The old lady at the first desk lit a cigarette, momentarily illuminating her face, revealing violet-hued bags under her weary eyes that almost matched her unevenly magenta-dyed hair. The lit cigarette seemed to send a signal to the fat man to light one up as well. He did so, inhaling deeply and wheezing audibly. The huge man yawned, stretched his arms over his head, revealing a crop of warts among the sticky bunches of pit hair. His skin was white, translucent with bursts of blue veins spiderwebbing across his shoulders and capillaries like red chrysanthemums in his cheeks and neck. In spite of their drastically different appearances, I grew to believe that the two of them were related, that they were mother and son, underscoring my personal belief that genetics goes beyond simply passing on physical characteristics, that it may extend to habits, rituals, beliefs, and addictions.

I was expecting his voice to boom like a giant's, but when he spoke, his voice was feminine, higher in tone than even Rose's, and had a disgruntled teenager's edge to it.

"Is there something we can help you with?" asked the fat man.

"I hope so," I said, trying not to breathe the same air they were breathing. "I'm Inspector Gift with the state fire marshal's office. This is Special Agent Cleary with the FBI."

"Wow," he said. "Must be somethin' important. You lookin' for a car we impounded, or somethin'?"

"No," said Rose. "We're looking for one of your drivers, possibly."

"What for?" croaked the old lady, her voice sounding like a cracked stereo speaker.

"Just to ask some questions," I said.

"You got a warrant, or something?" she inquired.

"We don't need one," said Rose. "We're not searching your premises."

"You're still on private property," said the fat man.

I'd sensed Rose's irritation growing even before this. She had to be at least as eager as I was to escape the tainted air of this moldy creep-show office. Now, though, her eyes flattened and her voice went dead.

"Look, we just need to ask a couple questions and get out of this shit hole. You can cooperate and we can be gone in five minutes, or you can keep being evasive and I'll have a forensic accountant come in here—with a warrant—and go through your books for the past ten years, and request an IRS audit while they're at it."

"No reason to get hostile," whined the fat man.

"You had a driver pick up a broken-down rescue truck, early this morning. Took it to the fire station just down the road?"

"Ma, you got something on that?"

The old lady rifled through some paperwork on her desk as if she were handling invaluable documents that might disintegrate if handled too roughly. Her hands, twisted with arthritis and knotted with thick green veins, went through each slip of paper, s-l-o-w-l-y, one…at…a…time, the cigarette extending from between her fingers like a lit fuse.

"It was fire station number thirty-four," I said, hoping to God to speed her along. "On Benoist Farms Road."

"It's not where we take it; it's where we pick it up," she said dryly.

Rose couldn't stand it anymore. Quick as a snakebite, she reached over and snatched the papers away from the old lady. "Pick it up or drop it off, who cares? How many rescue trucks did you haul this morning?" She flicked through the invoices quickly and said, "Here it is."

"You're rude," said the fat man.

Rose shot him a look that was so cold I could feel the hair rise on my neck. She held the invoice in front of the fat man's face, as if she were going to make him eat it if he didn't answer her right away. "Who is that? I can't read the signature."

The fat man grinned at her and ran a thick, white tongue over his lower lip. "Whoo, boy. That's one you don't want to mess with."

"Who is it, hon?" asked the old lady.

"It's Devon."

"Ha!" she cackled. "Devilish Devon. You're right. That *is* one they don't want to mess with."

"Is he here?" Rose inquired, tapping her foot now.

"No, he works the night shift," said the old lady. "Got off at eight this morning."

"Last name?"

"Haskell, with two Ls."

"Where does he live?" I asked.

"Loxahatchee."

"That's close to where I live in Wellington. It's a big place. Which street?"

"He's way out there, past Lion Country Safari. On Dellwood Road."

"Would he have made a pickup down in Broward County last night? In Tamarac, maybe?"

"I usually keep two or three drivers on the road at all times," the old lady said. "They listen to police band radios and fire rescue dispatch. If they hear a call for a wrecker, they run for it. This economy makes it a dog-eat-dog world, Officer."

"Why did you say we wouldn't want to 'mess with him'?"

"'Cause he's got a short temper," said the fat man. "Quick with his fists. Wiry dude. Looks kinda like you. Lean. About the same color eyes 'n' hair." He squinted at me, making his own mental comparisons. "But about a half foot taller. Used to be a Navy SEAL. He's a good worker, but we've had some…incidents."

"What kind of incidents?" asked Rose.

"Well, let's jus' say he don't take any guff. Punched out a state trooper that was talkin' down to him last year at an MVA. Witnesses say the cop had it comin' to him, so Devon just got off with probation."

"Married? Single?"

The old lady piped up. "He a ladies' man, fo sure. Good-lookin' fella, like you," she said, leering at me. I had to get out of this room. "Different gal every week. Why you lookin' for him?"

"Does he like to hunt?" I asked, remembering the gutting technique that had been used on the Matarese girl in Tamarac.

"Sho' does," the fat man said. "He got a place out by the lake, in Okeechobee. Don't know the address, though. Summa those places got no address. They just trailers parked on a lot. He hunts hogs alla time. Got some of his sausage in the freezer over there right now."

Rose looked at me and slowly crossed over to the refrigerator that was humming in the corner of the office. She glanced back at me, timidly, I thought, as she opened the freezer door. I could see her swallow as she looked inside.

"We just want to ask him some questions," I said.

"He a suspect?" asked the old lady.

"No," I said. "We just want to talk to him. Does he take a tow truck home?"

"Sometimes," she said. "In case we have to call him out. But he has his own car. One of those fast ones. What's it called? A Grand Am?"

"No, Ma," said the fat man. "A Grand National. A Buick. Fastest six-cylinder production car ever made."

"No kidding," I said. "I used to have one of those, too, about fifteen years ago. It's a collector's item."

"Yeah. He got one uh those souped-up trucks, like a funny car he races, too, at the speedway, or out to the mud flats. 'At's even faster. Uses jet fuel."

Rose gave me a quick glance as she came back from the refrigerator. "I'm going to take this with us," she said. She was holding a plastic bag of frozen meat between her thumb and forefinger, as if she were holding a plague-infected dead rat.

"You got no right to confiscate my food," complained the fat man. "That's good eating there!"

I watched Rose as she headed toward the door, not sure what she was thinking. She nudged me to follow her on the way out.

"Do us a favor and don't call Devon ahead of time," she called back to them. "You might implicate yourselves in some very serious charges. You don't need to know everything yet, but I can say we are looking into some murders involving mutilation-type killings. As for your sausage? I'm just going to have it tested to make sure it's hog meat that Devilish Devon is feeding you. In the meantime, *bon appétit*, sir."

She led the way out, but I looked back at the fat man before I closed the door behind me. He had grown even paler, his mouth sagging open, dumbfounded.

Rose was already in the car, the engine running, the AC blasting away the heat.

"What was all that about?" I asked.

She looked at me with a repressed smile. "Those people probably know more than they are telling. It would've been smart to take them in so they don't call Haskell ahead of time, but we don't have that kind of time. If they believe Haskell's been feeding them people sausage, maybe they'll be too afraid to call and warn him. Why are you looking at me like that?"

TWELVE

Rose had pulled a copy of Haskell's driver's license from the employee file at the tow truck office. She called it in to confirm the address, then punched it into the GPS in my car.

I knew vaguely where Dellwood Road was, but it was way out in the boondocks. Maybe we could have found it with a map, but the GPS got us there expeditiously. We could see a Brother's tow truck in the yard of a small ranch-style home placed smack in the middle of a five-acre plat of land surrounded with cattle-rail fencing and a natural palmetto bush barrier. Huge orange trees shaded the back half of the yard and I could see a small building behind the main house, like a workshop, almost covered with growth. The sun was on the way down. We had maybe another half hour of light, but the dense growth in the yard made it seem like dusk already.

"Why don't you stop here for a second," I said. "I have some Kevlar vests in the trunk."

"Let's see. He's an ex–Navy SEAL and likes to hunt. That's probably a good idea," said Rose. "What else do you have in there? Seems like you come prepared."

"I try to. Never can tell what you'll need. I've got a semiautomatic assault rifle they issued to us last year. Never used it except for target practice, but it is one impressive piece of firepower. There's a short-barreled shotgun back there, too, twelve gauge. Do you want me to call for backup?"

"No. I've already let my people know we were coming here. They can dispatch agents out of the West Palm office probably as fast as the sheriff's office would get someone out. But I don't see the Buick anywhere, so he might not be home. If he isn't here, I don't want the neighbors telling him he had a whole brigade of law officers staking out his place. Let's look around first, see if we even have anything worth our time here."

We helped each other get into the bulletproof vests, making sure we were snugged up, Velcro straps tight, necks covered with the collars—an area often overlooked and often targeted. Rose had to hold her hair up with one hand as I secured the Velcro strap around her neck, a gesture I found powerfully sensuous, even with my nerves on edge as we prepared to enter a possible serial killer's lair.

"Thanks," she said, turning to look up at me. Our eyes locked for a couple of seconds and I thought I saw her soften, just a little. Then she was back to business and as cold as gunmetal. "You ready?"

"Yeah," I said, but as she turned to get back into the car, I took her arm and turned her around. She was the one who had been eviscerated by a madman. "Are you okay?"

Rose finished reholstering her gun around the bulky bulletproof vest. She pulled her weapon out and checked the cylinders, breaking eye contact with me as she did so. She then slid the huge gun back into its holster, ensuring the weapon was loose in its holder so it would come out quickly if she needed it. "I'm fine, Grey. Let's go."

We drove into the driveway and did not try to conceal ourselves. In addition to my holstered weapons, I placed a flashlight in the ring on my belt and brought the shotgun, carrying it in the crook of my arm as we walked toward the house. I used the tow truck fender as cover and took aim at the front door as Rose went to one side of it and knocked.

"Mr. Haskell, are you home?" said Rose. "This is the FBI, Mr. Haskell. We'd like to talk to you."

Nothing.

I could hear cars on a distant highway, a bullfrog in a canal nearby, crickets chirping, and the wind rattling the dried leaves on every tree around us. There was no sound from inside the house.

Rose peeked into the front window. There were no curtains, so you could see straight through the living room. Rose came back to the truck and I lowered my weapon and took a breath.

"I don't need a warrant to go into this house if I think the suspect has a victim inside," she said. "Do you think he has someone inside?"

"I don't think he's here. I wouldn't be surprised if that family of ghouls back at the truck yard called and warned him that we were coming."

Rose looked back at the house; I had never let my eyes leave it. "I don't believe he's here, either. But would you mind doing a three-sixty with me, take a peek and make sure?"

"That's what we're here for. Inside or out?"

"Let's do outside first. You go to the right and I'll go to the left. Take a look in the windows if you can. I'll meet you around back and we'll come in the back door together."

"Sounds like a plan."

A minute later, we met by the back door. Neither of us had seen anyone in the house. Rose tried the knob and found it was open. She led the way in, her cannonlike pistol held in target position. She'd attached a laser sight to the barrel and a dot of red light, like a glowing drop of blood, moved along the walls as she moved forward. I kept the shotgun up against my shoulder, scanning the room in areas I thought Rose might have missed. My heart was beating so hard it was as if it were in my head, pushing out against my eardrums. The vest was tight around my neck. Sweat trickled down my back like insects on the run.

It reminded me of those times when I was crawling through structure fires, smoke so thick I couldn't see more than a foot or two in front of me. Flashlights only make the smoke seem thicker and diminish your depth of view, so I'd turn off the light and peer into the darkness, knowing the fire was in there somewhere, hoping it wasn't in the ceiling. I'd listen to the snaps and crackles of the fire eating the wood studs. On occasion I'd hear cockroaches scurrying within the walls. Sometimes they'd come out, looking for safe haven, find the opening between my bunker pants and turnout boots and come inside. Without a doubt, it's one of the most uncomfortable sensations you can imagine: searching for a fire that might kill you, the heat insufferable, your air supply limited, while a dozen roaches are trapped in your clothing, biting and finding temporary housing among your genitalia or in your ass crack.

All that came back to me as we went through the house, listening to ourselves breathe, the heat of the vests adding to the claustrophobia. I held to the thought of a woman or child being held against their will somewhere on this property, subjected to unthinkable physical and mental torture, until the only release they can hope for is a quick death. I thought of the victim in Tamarac—mutilated, burned, and probably urinated on—and wondered what her last memory on this earth possibly could have been. Those thoughts helped me forget about my physical irritations and push forward to find this creature—if indeed Haskell was the creature we were looking for—and cut him in half with a load of buckshot. The prospect of seeing that fucker blasted apart—being the one who did it, who ended it and him—sent a rush of almost sexual pleasure through me. Was this what had been behind Rose's words when she'd spoken of discharging her duties with such relish?

After clearing the living room, we moved from one room to the next. At each door opening, I found myself holding my breath, my finger tightened on the trigger, trying to prepare myself for the deafening boom the shotgun would make inside a structure, as well as the carnage it would mete out. But each room was empty. The house seemed smaller inside than out. Two small bedrooms, Spartan, with only a chair sitting in the middle of one room occupied by a teddy bear with one button eye missing. For reasons unknown to me, the sight of that bear made goose bumps pop out of my skin, like an adrenaline-fueled rash. The other room was filled with junk: a computer, old baseball and racing trophies, a bicycle with broken spokes and a torn seat, piles and boxes of clothes and magazines, the smell of age and mildew.

I was so keyed up from anticipating running into Haskell in his darkening home that when we did not find him, I felt deflated, almost depressed. But I felt relief, too. My experience as an arresting officer on the hunt was limited, and I wondered about my own abilities. I'd never shot anyone as a law enforcement officer.

Which isn't to say I'd never killed a man.

The events of the short and surreal time I was an Army Ranger in Mogadishu formed the basis for the book and movie *Black Hawk Down*. My killing experience was brief, chaotic, and instinctual. It was shoot, grab cover, shoot some more, try to survive. In a violent kaleidoscope of explosions and unending shots fired, we'd lost eighteen men that day. Another seventy-three were injured, including me, which led to my honorable discharge a few months later. Since then, I had never even pointed a gun at a living target. Oh, I was a terror on the shooting range. I could shoot a full clip into a circle so tight it looked like one big bullet had pierced the target. But that is only a black silhouette of a man and not a three-dimensional, homicidal psychopath staring you down with his own gun locked on you.

After looking into the bathroom, Rose relaxed her attack stance and turned on a light, using the barrel of the gun to flick the switch. The small room was empty, but the bright light revealed its ugliness: a toilet stained with rust from well water and feces, a shower faucet dripping into a scaly tub, the sink smudged with black, perhaps sooty handprints. Dark, curly hair littered the sink, tub, and bath mat. Without a word, Rose loosened her protective collar and pulled a large envelope out of a place inside her vest. Inside the envelope was a foot-long piece of tape with a cellophane backing. She pulled the protective plastic off the tape, bent down, and placed the adhesive side of the tape on the bath mat, then put the cellophane back on the strip and placed it in the envelope. The technique is called "taping" for obvious reasons and has been used by law enforcement agencies since before DNA analysis came into vogue. Spying a toothbrush in the holder next to the sink, she pushed it up from the bottom, judiciously using just the tip of her finger, and let it fall into her envelope as well. Pretty slick.

"Well," she said. "At least if we get some DNA back from the church murder scene, we'll have something to compare it with."

I nodded in agreement, yet I couldn't help but feel I was out of my league. I'm no homicide investigator, but I had seen something that caught my eye when we first got to the house. "How about that outbuilding? You want to have a look out there?"

"Absolutely," said Rose, pushing the evidence envelope back under her vest. "That might be his playhouse."

We went back the way we came in, checking closets and under beds before exiting the rear door. It had grown dark by the time we came out and there was no moon or artificial light. The stars shone brightly without competing lights but did not illuminate the area for us. The small CBS block house in the rear of the property seemed more ominous in the night. The air was warm and moist and seemed to close in on us as we approached the building. I could smell the faint scent of char, as if someone had been cooking some meat on a grill, mixed with the scent of bleach. As a firefighter, I'd been to so many house fires that I could tell from the smell, with reasonable certainty, the cause of the fire we'd find inside a house: the pot of food left on the stove, a wood truss smoldering in the attic, an electrical short in the breaker box. I could tell if flesh had been burned as well. The scent I picked up that night was different, masked somehow, but the mystery of it disturbed me and made me more anxious going into this seemingly empty building than I had been going into the suspect's home.

The windows were blacked out. On one end of the building there was a single garage; on the side was a small door. I covered Rose with the shotgun, holding my flashlight along the barrel as she, once again, led the way into the unknown. She opened the door and slid inside and to the right, hugging the wall. I came in behind her, watching for movement, scanning with my Maglite, the beam elongating the shadows. The scent of char was even stronger on the inside.

Rose found a light switch and turned it on. It appeared to be a small garage or workshop. There was a bench at one end of the room with various tools scattered across its surface. But what was striking was the incongruity of the dilapidated exterior of the building and the apparently newly remodeled interior. The walls were coated with fresh paint and the floor refinished with new indoor-outdoor carpet. The new finish almost diminished the smell of char. Almost.

Rose put her gun back in its holster and put her hand on her hip. "Well, this has been a big bust."

She turned to look at me, perhaps to gauge my thoughts, but I had become distracted. I was looking at the light fixture attached to the wall just above the switch she'd turned on when we'd entered the room. It was just a bare bulb sticking out of a light socket—but one side of it was warped.

"What is it, Grey?" said Rose. "What are you looking at?"

I turned on the flashlight and asked her to hold it. I instinctively licked my fingers before unscrewing the bulb but found it wasn't too hot since we'd just entered the room. I held it in the beam from the flashlight. "Look," I said. "See how the glass on the bulb is warped?"

"Yes. It looks like it's blistered."

"Exactly. See it's only on one side? What happens is that, when there's a fire in a room and the bulbs survive, the glass tends to warp on the side closest to the fire, where it's subjected to the most heat. When a room is burned badly, soot all over the place and we can't quite tell where the fire originated, the bulbs often give us the clue. In this case, I'm thinking there was a fire in this room, an intense fire, and judging from where this bulb was and the side that's warped, the fire was over there, at least in that direction." I pointed toward the back of the room, opposite the tool bench. "And the fire, though hot, was put out relatively quickly, or the bulb would have just popped or melted."

Rose looked around the room. "It doesn't look like there's been a fire in here."

"But it smells like one." I touched the surface of the wall and looked at my fingers. "Someone has painted this room. Today." I put the bulb back in the wall socket so we'd have some light. Then I went over to the edge of the new carpet and pried up a corner from the brand-new tack strip that held it in place. Once I had a purchase, I pulled the carpet up like I was skinning a rabbit.

A strong smell of bleach rose from the floor, which was still damp with the chemical. I pulled the carpet back all the way to the garage door. There in the middle of the floor was a burned spot. It appeared that someone had tried to pressure clean the spot away. Failing that, they tried the bleach, then finally just covered it up. But when a concrete floor is burned with enough intensity, nothing is going to remove the charred area or the outline of what might have been incinerated in that area. In this case, it didn't take much imagination to see a blurred silhouette of what was once a body. It reminded me of some pictures I'd seen in a book about Hiroshima after the *Enola Gay* had dropped its payload. The atom bomb had vaporized people, leaving only a shadow on the ground, a black smear the total remnant of a life.

I looked at Rose, squatting beside me by the burned spot. "Didn't you say the Suarez girl you looked at over in Immokalee earlier this week was completely immolated?"

Rose stood, still looking at the floor, her thoughts hidden to me. But the muscles working in her jaws told me she was angered and saddened at the same time, perhaps considering her kinship with another female, a woman whose fate she might've shared if she hadn't shot the man who'd cut her open. "There wasn't much left of her," she said quietly. "Mostly just blackened bones."

"I think we found our guy, Rose."

THIRTEEN

"Do you have a camera in that trunk of yours?" Rose asked.

"What do you think?"

She turned a tight smile to me, realizing I was trying to break the tension. "I think that, yes, you have a camera in there. Right next to the kitchen sink."

"I'll go get it. I think we can lose these vests, yes?"

"Yes. Hang on, I'll go with you."

As we walked back to the car, we unhinged our armor. Rose was quiet, and I wondered if she was thinking about her attack. We all replay in our minds those significant traumas in our lives: the fall off the horse that snaps a leg, the car accident that breaks a pelvis, the pan of hot grease that scars an arm. But how many times would you feel compelled to reenact something like a man sticking a knife into your abdomen and pulling it open like a zipper on an overnight bag? Could you ever forget what it feels like to peer into someone's eyes as your organs begin to fall out? There would have to have been a horrific intimacy at that moment, a closeness to another human being that you would not, could not, ever experience again.

Back at the car, I opened the trunk to put our vests and the shotgun back in when I heard a car door shut. The sound could have come from one of the home sites nearby, but if it had, I thought I would have heard the car pull into a drive, or a front door open, or some other accompanying sound. Besides, it had sounded like it came from the back of the Haskell property, perhaps from the rear where a tree line and heavy foliage prevented us from seeing all the way through.

"Did you hear that?" I whispered.

"Yes," said Rose, also whispering now.

I held my breath, listening with an intensity that caused a ringing in my ears. Then I got an idea. I took the infrared thermal imager out of the trunk, the device we use to check for hidden fires in the walls of a house. The warmer something is, the whiter it looks next to the cooler objects around it. It was completely dark now, so it would easily show anything warm, if anything was out there. I turned the imager on and waited for the screen to adjust. It flickered through its initial start-up lighting, then the small screen went dark. I held it up to my eyes, the rubber cushion around the screen fitting along my brow snugly, and scanned the horizon along the back of the property. At first, it was all dark, almost black, objects contrasting with other objects in various shades of gray. As images began to focus, I could see the pines contrasting slightly among the other bushes, still holding some of the day's heat in their bark. I continued scanning, looking between the trees and the darker palmetto bushes that ringed the lot. Suddenly, I saw what I was looking for: a stark white silhouette of a man, hunched down behind the natural cover. And I could see he was looking toward us.

I held the imager so that Rose could see through the lens. "See him?" I asked, whispering into her ear.

"Yes," she said. "Can he see us?"

"Not like we're seeing him. He must have seen us walking out to the car. He's probably watching to see if we're leaving."

"What are you thinking?"

"I'm thinking let's let him think we are leaving. Why don't you drive down the road a bit, then cut the engine and double back on foot."

"What are you going to do?"

"I'm going to slip out of the car just as you clear the edge of that property line, over there behind those bushes, where he won't see me circling back. I'll use the imager to find him again. Hopefully, he won't see me and I can get the drop on him."

"Let's do it," she said, an eager tone evident in her voice, but still laced with caution. "But let's put the vests back on."

We got into the car and quickly put our vests back on in the dark. Then Rose cranked the car and backed out of the long drive. I adjusted the car's lights so that when I eased the door open and rolled out of the car, I could do so without the dome light coming on. Rose barely slowed down, and I hoped the impression for our watcher was that we were leaving. She must've been going about twenty miles per hour when I leaped from the car. I didn't have enough height to hit the ground like I would if I were coming down from a HALO jump—foot, knee, hip—to break the momentum of the fall. I hit my hip and then my shoulder, the impact jarring my spinal cord from skull to pelvis and knocking the wind out of me for a few seconds. I rolled under some cover, took a breath, regained my senses, and set a path.

I kept my profile low, log-rolling all the way over to the fence that defined the eastern property line, which was lined with heavy cabbage palm growth and covered with kudzu vine, the nuisance growth that was slowly taking over and smothering everything in its path. Tonight it was helping keep me hidden from whoever, or whatever, was lurking in the back property.

The training I received in the Army half a lifetime ago is still ingrained in my muscles and nerves. I thought all that had vanished along with the nightmares of seeing a guy I was sharing an MRE with a few minutes earlier get vaporized by an RPG. But it came back like riding a bike—or in this case, belly-crawling over roots and thorns, through tenacious vines, and over critters that didn't even hear me coming. The vest helped, serving as a sled, allowing me to glide over the rough ground things easier. I moved quickly but quietly.

I had just cleared an open area when I saw the legs of a man moving out of the cover. I held my breath as I rolled over and watched the man through the imager. I thought he must have heard me, but I could tell by the casual way he began crossing the lawn toward the garage that he was comfortable with the idea that we had left. I moved into a small clearing that would allow me to stand up. Slowly, I placed my legs under myself, squatted, then rose to my feet. I was able to look over the top of a palmetto bush, stay covered, and watch the man as he strode across the yard. I no longer needed the imager to see him; my eyes were accustomed to the dark and he was making no effort to conceal himself. I drew my 9 mm out of its holster and took a bead on his back. He was maybe twenty yards ahead in front of me.

"Hold it right there...sir," I said, and as soon as I said it, I regretted it. I sounded like a complete doofus. Like I said, I don't do this every day. In what I hoped was a bolder voice, I said, "Law officer. Get your hands up, where I can see them." I shone the light on him as I came out of the bushes, my gun hand extended.

The man turned around slowly, almost casually, as if he were bored by my request. He squinted into the light and I recognized him. He was no longer in the black suit, but he was wearing the tortoise-framed glasses, which I now saw had light-gradient lenses, so that his eyes were always shrouded. He wore a dark jumpsuit. Tufts of gray hair stuck out of the neckline that did not match his slicked-back, black-dye-job hair. His skin was bronzed, which helped hide the creases age produced. He exuded a confidence that called to mind politicians or preachers, those persons who can, by the power of their voice, persuade people—strangers—to follow their will.

"'Law officer'?" he said, amused. "What kind of way is that to identify yourself? Aren't you supposed to identify your organization as well?"

"I'm with the state fire marshal's office," I said, moving to within ten feet of him. "I'm investigating a murder case."

The man smiled. "How exciting that must be. Didn't I see you on the canal bank this morning?"

"You're right, Mr. Cerberus. I was there."

"Ah, you've done a little homework," he said. "Where's your girlfriend, the FBI agent?"

There was a click behind him—more than just a click. Like someone cocking back the firing mechanism on a tank cannon.

"I'm right here, motherfucker," said Rose, her Casull Magnum about three feet from his head, the hammer cocked back.

Cerberus turned away from me, disregarding me as if I were a storefront security guard armed with a can of Silly String.

"Good evening, Agent Cleary," he said confidently. "Yes, I caught your name this morning, though you didn't ask me for mine."

"It was easy enough getting it from those tools you were talking to. It's not like you were trying to hide it."

"No, I am not. Let's all be clear here," he said, looking back at me. "I am not who, or what, you are looking for. You can lower your weapons."

"You better talk some more first," said Rose.

"All right. You already know I am associated with the CIA."

"What's *associated* mean?" Rose asked.

"It means I have their absolute highest level of clearance. That can be confirmed with just a phone call."

"Just tell me what you're doing," Rose said, "before I lose my patience, please."

"I'm only going to tell you what I need to, to alleviate this situation. You're making a mistake, but I can understand. You are working a homicide investigation and are not aware of the larger scope of this operation. It's complicated, but you'll understand down the road."

"Educate me now," I said, getting restless and feeling way over my head. A slight breeze came from out of nowhere and pushed his scent toward me. He smelled *green* to me, like freshly printed money and designer cologne made from woodsy ingredients.

Cerberus looked at me as if I were a kindergarten kid who'd wandered onto the scene. He turned back to Rose and addressed only her. I hated him for that.

"My company works for the CIA. We do information management. We...take care of things for them."

"That tells me next to nothing. Why did you take that bio-bag with our evidence?"

"I can't tell you anything more, other than that you must cease what you're doing. You should also stop asking questions you may not want the answers to."

"Let me guess," I said. I felt I had to get my two cents in; pride is a funny thing, even when it's misplaced. "If you're CIA, or one of their hired vendors, you're probably trying to pick up after Haskell. Maybe he's an operative that went rogue or just went nuts. We know he was a Navy SEAL, guys who are trained to kill without worrying about it over their Cheerios the next day. You guys recruit ex-SEALs, offer their battle-cracked minds a promise of money and a future, then point them toward political targets like lemmings with automatic weapons. I met guys like you in Somalia. Guys who worked so deep undercover they forgot who they were and what side they were fighting for, so ended up playing for both."

"You were in Mogadishu, Officer…I don't think I got your name?"

"You don't need it. We're working a homicide case and you're interfering with it. That's obstructing justice, and that's a federal offense, no matter who you work for."

"Okay," said Cerberus with a sigh. "We're done here. I've been patient and less discreet than I should be." He whistled shrilly, and we could hear palmetto bushes parting dryly and branches cracking. It sounded as if we had a whole platoon coming into the clearing toward us.

I turned and held up the thermal imager. I could clearly make out at least three men coming out of the brush, carrying assault weapons: one coming dead on, the other two covering our flanks. When I turned to look at Rose, there were already two more men, all wearing dark jumpsuits, pointing assault weapons at her. All of the men had close-cropped hair, square jaws, and eyes like birds of prey.

"Put your weapons down," said Cerberus. "To the ground, please." When we didn't immediately comply, he added, "These men are on a mission and they will kill you as soon as take another breath."

We set our weapons at our feet. None of the men spoke a word as they picked them up and threw them into the bushes. Whatever they were now, they had been military, probably special ops, at some time in their lives.

Cerberus nodded at one of the men, who darted away. Within a minute, I could smell the fire he'd set to Haskell's abattoir begin to consume the structure. We'd never even taken any pictures, and another key piece of evidence—the shadow that was left on the concrete floor—would be gone, just like the Matarese girl's internal organs, which I was now more convinced than ever held some link to Haskell. Out here, it would take at least twenty minutes for the first fire engine to arrive. By then, it would be too late. Cerberus continued.

"You are working on a case that is complex in ways you cannot know. You will just stand down, go have a drink, and curse the inner workings of your war-mongering, bureaucratic, capitalistic government. By tomorrow, your supervisors will have you in their offices, telling you that you are off this case. Be happy if you are still employed. So long," he said, and walked off into the darkness, balls as big as a bull's.

His voice came back to us one more time before his men slowly moved off after him, not even bothering to point their guns at us as they walked away: "Mr. Fire Marshal! I thought I had seen you before. I *loved* Somalia."

It was silent for a moment and I could hear the distinct squawk of a nighthawk dive-bombing for mosquitoes. They say they can eat one to two thousand of them a night. They're very efficient nocturnal predators. I wondered if Cerberus really had been in Somalia or if he was just trying to get into my head.

We heard their vehicle crank up and they pulled out of the cover that had concealed it. A simple black van, no lettering on the side. The tag light was not illuminated. I was sure it was full of paint and brushes and cleaning equipment, as well as a half dozen men armed with automatic weapons. Men who were just this side of robots, programmed to kill or cause as much havoc in the shortest amount of time possible.

We were lucky to be alive and I knew it. But I also knew convincing Rose of that fact was not going to be easy. I watched the orange light from the burning building flicker across her face, illuminating it and seeming to intensify her anger. Her eyes shone wet and malevolent as a wolf's, her jaw muscles clenching as though she were chewing tough, bitter gum. Ashes began to drift down like smoky snow and I saw one catch on one of her eyelashes. She never flinched.

FOURTEEN

Journal: Breeders

Subject: 56QAH/Lot 454

"Shit," the young mother said after opening the trunk of her car. The little turd had died. She could easily see how, too: the mushy corn and chicken protruding from the turd's nostrils. She must have suffocated.

The young mother, Lacy, removed the duct tape from her daughter's mouth and wrists. In retrospect, she thought, she should have not bound her wrists. But every time she did not bind her, the toddler would wake up and start banging on the inside of the trunk lid. Luckily, no one had ever heard her, but once, Lacy had come out to rest her feet from dancing and get some more cigarettes from her car and heard the kid knocking around back there and crying like a cat stuck in a tree. That was back when she was knocking her out with Benadryl in her bedtime bottle. The timing of the bottle was perfect: about the time the kid wanted to go beddy-bye, Lacy was ready to go dancing, so while the baby had her bottle, she would slip into her too-tight dress that barely covered her "stuff" and accented her assets. "Must be cold in here—my headlights seem to be on," she'd say, plopping behind the bar as though weary of her own sexuality. But the Benadryl didn't last long enough.

One time, she'd picked up this really hot, young Brazilian stud and was riding him like an electric bull in the backseat of the car. The kid woke up and started howling and Lacy had to try to convince him it was a cat in her trunk that she was watching for her out-of-town sister. When, for the third time, he said, "That don't sound like no *gato* to me," she unceremoniously dismounted from him and said, "How would a spick with a green card know a cat from his dong? Now, get the fuck outta my car before I scream rape." He bolted like a greyhound. After that, Lacy started getting Chloroform from a veterinary assistant she was balling, which worked like a charm. No muss, no fuss.

That old Don Henley song said it best. *All she wanted to do was dance.* Have a few drinks. Fuck and have fun. But those things are hard to do when you're dragging a two-year-old around like a house-arrest ankle bracelet. As soon as guys found out about the kid, Lacy could see them look at her differently, like she was damaged goods, and she saw the lust drain out of their eyes like beer from a cup.

Now she'd have to get rid of the body. She hadn't had to bother about that the first time.

She'd killed a friend in high school, once. They were at a keg party and both of them were going after the same guy, a cute surfer dude with curly blond hair and six-pack abs. Lacy had been making out with him but had to tinkle before they got it on. She went to squat behind the bushes, and when she came back, the Big Kahuna was making out with her friend. Funny, though, instead of interrupting them, she watched them from the bushes, and after their heads disappeared below the seats, she watched them through the windows of the car. Watched his butt lift up, then squeeze back down as he rode her cheerleader friend like a wave.

She watched until they were finished, which took maybe five minutes; then, when her friend got out of the car to take a tinkle herself, Lacy followed her into the woods.

"Hey, Mona," she said sweetly. "I'll watch out for you while you go wee-wee."

Mona, startled at first by her friend's appearance out of the shadows, relaxed and crouched on her haunches. "Oh. Hi, Lacy. Scared me." Mona did not replace her panties and kept them balled up in her hand until she could dry off a bit down there.

"How was it?" asked Lacy.

"What? Oh, the surfer boy? He was sweet. He's going to call me tomorrow."

"Yeah?" said Lacy, feeling the angry blood rush to her head and glad that the night hid her face. "Want some toot?"

"Does a slut piss in the woods?" giggled Mona, whose real name was Desdemona but had been abbreviated by Lacy herself, after listening to her bang her boyfriend all night when they shared a sleepover: *Moan-a*. "Hell yes!"

"'Kay," said Lacy. "Let's go down by the lake. We might get caught here and I don't have enough to go around."

"Good thinking."

The two girls made their way through the woods and came out onto a small lake, its still surface reflecting the inky, star-filled sky with perfect stillness. They walked out onto a small, creaky dock, its wood planks twisted and nails sticking up from them like witches' fingers.

"Jack me up, baby," said Mona. "I want to get back to Micky. That coke gets my engine revvin'. You know what I mean?"

"I know," said Lacy. "Here," she said, handing her a small baggie filled with white crystal powder that sparkled in the dim light. "Let me hold your panties."

"Lesbo," said Mona, giggling, then handed her panties to Lacy. She dipped her fingernail in the baggie, stuck it up her nostril, and sniffed, hard and quick. She pointed her nose up to help the coke flush into her brain and left her lovely neck exposed, a new dark-purple hickey revealing itself like a taunt.

Lacy quickly wrapped the panties around her friend's throat, spun around behind her, and twisted them. She kept twisting them until she heard a pop, like squeezing bubble wrap—Mona's larynx bursting, her struggle abating. Lacy eased her body down onto the dock, careful to retrieve her coke from her friend's clenched hand. Then she nudged her body into the lake and dropped the panties on the dock. The panties, with surfer dude Micky James's semen on them, would become the main evidence that led to his conviction for Desdemona Cochran's murder and put him in prison for the rest of his life.

Lacy went on to many more keg parties, dance parties, and sex parties, at one of which she became pregnant from one of a half dozen guys she went through and finally ended up with the little girl she had now killed, somewhat inadvertently, and whose body she had to dispose of.

With as much remorse as one might have over accidentally killing a pet hamster, she tossed the body into a black plastic garbage bag and back into the trunk of her car. She would dispose of it later, maybe after a good Bloody Mary and a nap.

FIFTEEN

We were watching the pyre that was left of the outbuilding behind Haskell's home smolder, pondering our next move, when my cell phone rang and I answered it. It was Chief Dugger with the Broward Sheriff's Office.

"Gift, man, that was a good call."

"Which call is that, sir? I've had a long day."

"The sign in front of the church you told me to check out. The message 'God's Love Is The Eternal Flame That Will Save Your Soul'?"

"Yeah. Okay. Did you find some prints?"

"Well, we found one. It seems clear it must have been put there for us to find."

"Why do you say that?"

"Because every letter is put on the sign individually. Each one was obviously wiped clean except for one, dead in the middle of the phrase. There are forty-five letters in the phrase and we found the print on number twenty-three, the 'a' in 'Flame.' And the print was dead in the middle of that letter on the back, just as clear as if we had been printing him at the jail."

"So he's OCD on top of being a sociopath. Did you get a match yet?"

"Oh yeah. And this is where it gets even weirder: we put the print into the National Fingerprint Database this afternoon, got a hit within an hour. Came up with a con in the federal prison system, up at ADX Florence, in Colorado. The last supermax prison in the system, reserved for special nut bags like Theodore Kaczynski, the Unabomber; Robert Hanssen, the FBI spy who sold secrets to the Russians for years; and Terry Nichols, one of the Oklahoma bombers."

"Doesn't seem like the right place for a serial killer. Wonder why he was there."

"Is there a right place for a serial killer besides six feet under?"

"Good point. What's his name?"

"Gettys. Dr. Harmon Gettys. Ever hear of him?"

I had to think. "I seem to remember reading about a guy named Gettys, maybe in a criminal case study class I was taking. Was he an arson killer?"

"More or less. Serial killer who'd mutilate his victims, then set the scene on fire to hide any forensics evidence. Sound familiar? Worked out for him for a while, too, until he killed this one lady. Worked in a cryogenic lab, sperm bank. Killed her in a car, then set it on fire. The usual. But he left a portfolio in the backseat; I suppose he thought it would burn, but the fire department got there quick and the car wasn't totally consumed. When they found the portfolio and opened it up, it had pictures of another girl he'd killed, and get this, he'd whacked off on them and left some semen on the photos. They identified him through a DNA match, one of the first cases to use DNA in the early eighties. They found some of this guy's semen in the girl he'd tried to burn, too. In her stomach, if you follow me."

"How did they match him? I mean, he wasn't a suspect, right? And there was no DNA database back then."

"Pure luck. One of the investigators got the idea that if the guy killed a girl who worked at a sperm bank, maybe he was a donor. They started going through all the sperm samples collected since the girl worked there and finally found one that matched the sample he'd left in the girl and on the photos."

"So, are we dealing with an escapee?"

"Not exactly. This is where it gets really strange. You ready for this?"

"I'm holding my breath, man."

"He's dead."

"What? How?"

"He died in jail. Managed to set himself on fire in his cell about a year ago. Wrote a message on the wall, doused himself with gas they think he'd siphoned out of some lawn equipment they used for grounds keeping, then turned himself into a Roman candle. Incinerated his sick ass. And here's the best part. You might want to sit down for this. The message he wrote in his cell? It read, 'God's Love Is The Eternal Flame That Will Save Your Soul.' How about them apples?"

"So how did a dead serial killer's fingerprint end up at our scene?"

"I have no idea, but I know where it leaves us."

"Where's that?"

"Dead in the water, end of the trail. Unless your guy gets some new DNA from the urine on the vic's clothing."

I felt strange, like my mind took a moment to leap away, then got sucked back into my head. I thought for a second I might be on the verge of another seizure, things seemed so surreal, but it was just me trying too hard to make sense of things that couldn't make sense. There could be no rational explanation for what Dugger was telling me, other than the bare fact that someone planted that fingerprint at the scene. Why would anyone do that? And what did all this have to do with Haskell?

Rose was frowning deeply as she poked me with her finger, jabbing it into my ribs like a gun barrel, mouthing the words *What? What? What!* I wanted to tell her everything Dugger was telling me, but I had one more question to ask him.

"Chief, would they have Gettys's DNA in the prison records or anywhere else?"

"Hmmm. Good question. Ordinarily, I would say no. Because you're right, he was sent up before the FBI had its DNA database, CODIS, up and running. I suppose the evidence they used to convict him might still be around, though. You want me to ask around?"

"No, sir. That's okay. I'm still here with Agent Cleary. She could probably access that information for us."

"Okay. Do me a favor and keep me in the loop, would you? This is a strange case. I'd like to know where it's going. If it's federal, we'll get shut out anyway, but I'd still like to know."

When I hung up, Rose was fuming at her own phone. "Shit! God damn it!" She held the text message up to my face so I could read it, her eyes wet with anger. Her supervisor had texted her to say she was not to pursue the case anymore. "Fucking wimp! Fucking empty suit couldn't even call and tell me personally?"

When she calmed down a little, I filled her in on what Dugger had told me. Rose clasped her hands together and placed them against her mouth as if she were blowing into them to keep them warm. She lowered her head, contemplating the ground.

"Are you praying?" I asked.

When she looked back at me, I could see fresh fire in her eyes. "I'm *thinking*," she said. "Has your supervisor called you yet?"

"No."

"Can only be a matter of time before you're bumped from the case, too, just like the spook said. We need to think about this. It just doesn't make sense. Why would the CIA pull the plug on a murder investigation? Especially if the killer is still out there, still at it. What are we supposed to tell the parents of these dead girls? Or the parents of the next one he kills? Who is this frigging Haskell? And how does a dead convict, one who lived in the most secure prison in America, tie into this? What in the hell is going on?"

She was asking me questions I couldn't begin to answer. Maybe she was just thinking out loud. Rose pulled up her Black-Berry and began plugging in queries, texting colleagues, searching FBI files. Then her phone began to go dead. I could see the light beginning to dim and it was working v-e-r-y s-l-o-w-l-y. She kept poking at it with her finger like she was trying to do CPR on it.

I placed my hand over hers. "It's getting late."

She looked at me as if she couldn't understand what I was saying.

"C'mon," I said. "We're not going to get the answers here. Let's move out."

She closed her eyes, took a breath, opened them again. "You're right. Where do you want to go?"

"It's about five minutes to my house, a little over an hour back to your car in Broward. I'm pretty decent with a steak and a grill, and tell me you couldn't use a drink right now."

Rose cocked her head and squinted at me, trying to gauge what kind of a man she might be going home with and what the implications might be.

"I'll let you use my computer while I cook."

Even in the dim light, I could see a softness spread across her face. "You do know the way to a woman's heart."

SIXTEEN

Journal: Breeders, continued

Subject: 56QAH/Lot 503

He was staring at her. What in the fuck would a paraplegic—a guy dead from the waist down—want with her? What would he do if she offered him up some, anyway? Stare at *it*, too?

That was the problem with living at a trailer park. You were never more than about fifteen feet from your neighbor, so everyone had their noses up each other's asses all the time. Everyone knew each other's business. She knew, for example, that the cripple was buying skunk weed from the kid—a minor, by the way—three trailers down. He didn't even try to hide it. Sometimes he'd sit right outside her trailer and smoke the shit. When she left her windows open, the stink would come right into her kitchen. Smelled like a fucking rock concert and she sure as shit didn't like rock music. She liked country, where real people sang about real problems: asshole husbands leaving their good wives, like hers did. Wake up one morning and the bastard's gone, along with every dollar in the bank, food from the fridge, and the pickup truck. Life sucked, but it sure sounded good coming from Shania Twain or Rascal Flatts.

She went back into her trailer, turned on Country Music TV, and listened to Kenny Chesney sing a tune. Everyone said he was a queer, but she didn't think so. Just because he broke up with that scrunched-up-faced Renée Zellweger. I mean, who could blame him?

She rummaged around, trying to decide on breakfast, distracted by something, something irritating her and pushing her in a direction she did not want to go. She couldn't help but go back to the window and look out, see the cripple still staring at her trailer. Creepy motherfucker.

She'd had it with him.

In a moment of crystalline clarity, what she needed to do with him came to her as if God himself had put the notion in her head. She picked up the debris in her living room, clothes that had been strewn around, some clean, most dirty; who had time to go to the Laundromat and sit around when she could be home watching her soaps? Besides, she'd gone out on a medical a few years ago—carpal tunnel syndrome from having to type so much—and she was collecting Social Security. She knew people were watching her all the time, so she shouldn't be out in public toting heavy laundry baskets around town. They might get the idea she could go back to work and she sure as shit did not want to do that.

In the back of the trailer was a small utility room. She found a roll of painter's plastic the ex had left in there. Fucking painters and roofers. The kind of men she's always been attracted to who liked the music she liked, and line dancing, and truck pulls, but who always left her high and dry and cleaned out her purse on their way out. It occurred to her that that guy in the wheelchair used to be a drywall hanger before he got his spine snapped from a roadside bomb in Iraq. A drywall hanger is about the same as a painter.

She spread the plastic out, covering the entire living room floor and stuffing the edges under the couch's legs. Then she cut pieces to cover the furniture as well. Back in the utility room, she pulled out some more things: tools and duct tape.

She went into the bathroom and looked at herself in the mirror. A little makeup, like she used to put on when she and the painter were going out on the town. Made her look a little whorey but so fucking hot every beer-bellied redneck in the joint wanted to get it on with her. She'd get them turned on enough to make a move, then shut them down and act offended so the painter would have to duke it out with the guy and there would be blood, lots of blood. She could almost orgasm watching a guy gripping his spurting nose and spitting out teeth. It was cool to have someone fight over you.

The lipstick was as red as the Pope's shoes and she smeared it on thick. Her eyes, their dark-brown color enhanced by the operatic eye shadow with which she surrounded them, the mascara laid on as thick as a tarantula's legs, stared back at her as if she were seeing herself for the first time. There was a little skirt, her tiny come-fuck-me dress, which she pulled over her widening hips, leaving her panties on the ground. Don't ever let it be said she didn't know what bait to use for which fish. Some musky perfume and fluff up her hair—now all she had to do was troll.

He was sitting out there, still watching her trailer, when she came bopping out, stepping heavily so her boobs would bounce with each step. She strutted, slow, to the mailbox, letting her thighs rub together like some insects do when they want to mate, moving her hips like a pendulum...trolling, trolling. Out of the corner of her eye, she saw him place his hands on the chrome wheels and push toward her. She turned back to him. His tongue came out and licked his lips hungrily, his jowls unshaved, his hair uncombed and sticking up from his head like a bug's antennae.

"Watchoo lookin' at, Buddy?" she asked coyly.

"You."

"Oh?" she said, summoning up the little girl's voice that had always worked so well for her. "You wantin' some of this?" Her eyes darted back and forth, checking out the street to see if anyone was watching. Looked like everyone was at work. She raised her little plaid skirt slowly, unveiled her pubes, which she trimmed like an arrowhead so it pointed down there, where the sweet stuff was. She pumped her pelvis forward and back, like a beckoning finger, enticing him to follow. He did. She left the skirt to ride up a little on her butt as she turned and walked back to her trailer. He rolled after her like a dog smelling another dog in heat, then slowed, hesitating.

She turned back to him. "What's wrong, Buddy? Second thoughts? I got some righteous weed inside. Maybe even a little meth."

"Sounds good. No, I was just wondering how I'm going to get up them steps."

"I'm going to help you," she said, making her eyes big and round.

She turned his wheelchair round for him and pulled it over to the steps, then wrapped her arms around his torso and lifted him up. He was light—his lower half was scrawny, anyway—and she pulled him right up, dragged him into her home, and plopped him on the sofa. Then she went back out, folded up his chair, and brought it inside quickly, once again looking up and down the street to see if anyone had seen her. Coast was clear.

"What's with all the plastic?" he asked.

"Oh, I have an exterminator coming later today. I got those tiny cockroaches all over the place. They're going to fog it for me. Said it would be best if I covered the furniture."

"Got a beer?"

"You know I do." She went slinking back into her little kitchen. She withdrew a big quart bottle of Busch beer, icy rivulets running down its sides, a puff of vapor escaping its mouth as she popped it open. She walked back toward him, unbuttoning her blouse, revealing her plump, pale breasts.

He licked his lips again as she drew closer and extended his hand. Instead of handing him the beer, though, she arched her arm back and swung the bottle against the side of his head, shattering the brown glass and spraying blood across the plastic-covered furniture.

When he came to, he was back in his wheelchair with a searing pain in his mouth and his arms duct-taped to the chair's arms, another band of tape around his torso and around the back of the chair, holding him upright. He tasted blood in his mouth, and when he ran his tongue along his gums, he found she had already removed some of his teeth.

"Wha…what the fuck?" he said, spitting. "Whader you doin'?"

She was standing in front of him holding a set of pliers and scrutinizing a tooth, one of its roots shining slick with fresh blood, the other presumably broken off, still in his jaw. Her eyes drifted back to his. Then she was on top of him, grinding her crotch into him like a lap dancer from hell, even as she yanked his head back and shoved the pliers back in, gripping another tooth. When he screamed too much, she simply covered his face with a pillow until he was near suffocation, then reached in again and again, until all his teeth were pulled. She did this all day and into the evening, until he had no teeth left, nor tongue, fingers, or ears, all of which had been removed with kitchen shears, along with his nose and, finally, those eyes that had been staring at her all that time.

He was still alive when she strangled him with a telephone cord, then dumped him into the tub. She used a saw and a paring knife to cut him apart, let his blood drain out, then placed his chunks into doubled plastic yard bags. Tomorrow she would put him in an old metal garbage can she occasionally used to make pit fires when it was cold and incinerate him like the trash he was.

SEVENTEEN

I took some filets mignons out of the freezer, placed them in a ziplock bag with some Dale's marinade, sealed it, and put it in a sink filled with warm water. They would be thawed and ready to grill by the time the charcoals were white hot. I jabbed some holes in a couple of Idaho potatoes with a fork, rubbed coarse ground sea salt on them, and placed them in the microwave. Then I threw together a salad of fresh Bibb lettuce, beefsteak tomatoes, basil, and mozzarella, sprinkled with olive oil and balsamic vinegar. I popped the cork on a bottle of BearBoat pinot noir to let it breathe for a bit, then went in to check on Rose, who had been using the computer in my office.

I found her looking at the walls, the screen saver up on the computer monitor. She was eyeing my old, dusty trophies: a couple from surfing, a few more from jujitsu and kickboxing, all very old and earned by a young man trying to prove something, maybe to himself more than anyone else. Her lovely blue eyes moved across the few photos I kept on the walls: my mother in her nurse's uniform, proudly wearing one of those old nun hats nurses used to wear; another with her sitting on a roan horse, her posture impossibly straight and poised; another with her in her deathbed, about a week before she died, a warm and gentle soul, still smiling at the camera though she no longer knew who I was, the Alzheimer's corroding her brain, like rust eating metal. There was another picture of my sister and me as children, paddling a canoe down a flooded street after a hurricane, and one of my father, a man I never knew, tall and lean, wearing a pressed white shirt, jeans, and western boots, his face shrouded in shadow cast by the flat brim of his Stetson hat. If he was still alive, I would not know him if I bumped into him on the street.

"What'd you find out?" I asked.

"Did you know that the United States proudly produces about three-quarters of the world's serial killers? Europe is a distant second with seventeen percent. Eighty-four percent of our killers are Caucasian and only sixteen percent are black. Ninety percent are male, but sixty-five percent of their victims are female and eighty-nine percent of those vics are white. About half of our killers begin their fun and games while in their twenties and about a fourth of them begin in their teens, while another fourth of them blossom in their thirties. Eighty-six percent are heterosexual."

"You get all that from your agency files?"

"No. It's just crap that floats around in my head."

"Those are dark thoughts to keep with you all day."

"I've got worse."

"Did you find out anything about Haskell or Dr. Gettys?"

"Nothing on Haskell. I found a little bit about Gettys. Only what I could find on Wikipedia and some links to old news stories. Nothing more than what Dugger told you, except some numbers, like they believe he killed some thirty-six women over ten to twelve years."

"FBI files don't have anything more than that?"

"Oh, I'm sure they do, but look at what I found when I tried to get in." Rose had minimized her link to the FBI website on the computer monitor. She touched on it and it widened on the screen and displayed *ACCESS DENIED*.

When I looked back at her face, I could see the anger shining in her eyes to the point of tears, her nostrils flaring. I tried to defuse the situation.

"I've got some nice wine opened up," I said softly. "Ready for some?"

"No, I'll have that with dinner. Do you have anything stronger? Some firewater, Kimosabe?"

"I've got some tequila. I could make a couple predinner margaritas."

"Save your mixer. I want some shots. Got salt and lime?"

"You bet."

We went into the kitchen and I poured us a couple of shots of Patrón. I placed a saltshaker and some lime wedges on the granite countertop that separated the kitchen from the dining area.

"Don't put the bottle away," she said, then licked the web of skin between her thumb and pointer finger and sprinkled some salt on it. "To cooperative federal law enforcement agencies working together." She licked off the salt, downed the tequila with amazing ease, and bit into a lime. She poured another before I had finished my first one. She slammed that down, too, then poured another.

"Whoa, hotshot," I said. "Give me a chance to catch up."

"Don't try this at home, kid. I think I have a lot more experience with this than you do."

"I'll take the challenge, but why don't we eat something first? My mother used to say, 'If you have to drink, then always make a fluffy nest in your belly for the bird to land in.'"

"I hear you. But I want to enjoy the mind-numbing effects of alcohol before I ease into the soul-satisfying luxury of eating a dead cow cooked on an open fire."

"Mmm, mmm, mmm. You sure are a hard case. Suit yourself. I'm going to finish making us dinner. Don't say I didn't warn you."

I placed some sliced Irish cheese and some crackers in front of her, in the hope she wouldn't get too sluiced, and carried the steaks out to the grill. The coals were just right and I plopped the steaks down and heard them begin to sizzle. I went back inside and put some music on; the stereo was wired to play inside or out, or everywhere with the push of a couple of different buttons. I chose a melodic collection by the Cowboy Junkies that I thought might fit Rose's mood, followed by a little Sam Sparro, some contemporary R&B that would make her think I was cool. I don't get to play *cool* very often. Since my last long-term gal pal left me for an ambulance-chaser with a fat wallet and belly to match, I felt I needed some alone time to figure out some things.

"I'm downgrading my octane to wine," I said, "and going to monitor the steaks, if you care to join me."

Rose looked at me and I could tell she was already feeling the tequila. "How are the mosquitoes?"

"They suck," I said, which got her to smile. She slipped out of her shoes and padded out after me. I pulled out some canvas folding chairs, flipped the steaks, then sat down next to her.

"It smells kind of like cows or some sort of livestock live around here," she said.

"Good nose. I've got a little over ten acres, and way in the back, where it's too dark to see right now, I have a small stable with my horse in it."

"Oh, I love horses. What's its name?"

"His name is Sisco. He's a buckskin. He was a racehorse once, but once he got a few years on him, he was put out to pasture. He was going to be sold to the French for hamburger meat. My mother adopted him about ten years ago from an agency that saves unwanted horses." This was my mom's house, I told her. I came to take care of her when she started going downhill from Alzheimer's, and when she died, she left everything to my sister and me. "But my sister moved to California with her family a long time ago, and so, here I am, horse, house, dog, and all."

As if on cue, a small, white rat terrier with a solid black head ran up, all wiggles and paws and tongue.

"Oh, how cute!" said Rose, leaning over to pet her.

"That's Scout."

Rose scratched behind her ears—until they perked up as Scout went into alarm mode and was off to the barn like a shot.

"She's a little hyper," I said.

Rose watched Scout disappear into the night, her smile slowly fading. "Your mother was lucky you were there for her. Where was your father?"

"Probably dead. He was never in the picture much. They were divorced and he moved to Colorado when I was a little kid."

We quit talking after that, just sat, listening to the sounds of the night, the pop and hiss of the steaks on the fire, the frogs in the pond in the back, the wind in the palmetto bushes, a few crickets sounding off to each other. I started it back up.

"Long day, huh?"

"I was on a ViCAP stakeout once for over forty hours," she said, "waiting for a wetworks suspect who liked to keep the hands of his victims in his refrigerator at his apartment. Talk about creepy. We ran out of water after twenty-four hours and couldn't risk coming or going, so our choices were to go thirsty or get a drink from the dude's fridge. The guy I was working with at the time finally broke down and drank a soda he found in there. I couldn't. One of the hands in the icebox had the same color of fingernail polish that I was wearing."

"God." After a minute, I said, "'Wetworks'? What's that?"

"I don't think you want to know if you're going to eat that steak."

When I didn't respond, she answered me. "It's a killer who likes to work up close to his victims. Get their blood on him. Makes him feel like they become a part of him or vice versa. Jack the Ripper was one like that. He was another one that liked to remove the organs, like our boy, Haskell. That kind usually despises women."

"Why? Their moms tortured them?"

"Sometimes, but just as often not. Sometimes they're diagnosed with satyriasis, a hypersexuality to the point of being socially problematic. Think of the term *nympho* but for a man. In any case, they're misogynistic animals that mutilate their victims in lieu of, or in addition to, the actual sex act."

"Good Lord. Makes you wonder how long there's been sickos like that out there."

"My research shows they've been around since man became what we call 'civilized.' In prehistoric times, if a man killed another man, it was over food or shelter. But when people began to live in communities and follow some sort of societal norms, it was as if mankind flipped a switch, and in almost every civilization since, there have been people wanting to kill other people for no reason other than to do it. In medieval times, in my opinion, it's where the myths of werewolves and vampires came from. People didn't understand why other people would want to kill them, or their children, but it happened, so townspeople told their children to stay away from woods or alleys after dark, or nighttime monsters would get them."

"I never thought of it that way, but I suppose you're right. It's scary stuff because it looks like it will never change."

"It won't."

I got up and flipped the steaks, then looked up and watched a meteor shower scratch the sky.

"See that?" We both said it at the same time, then just nodded happily at each other. As Rose watched the sky, she rolled her neck around on her shoulders, trying to get the kinks out. Even after the long day we'd had, her hair was luxurious, its blackness picking up a sheen from the starshine and spilling over her shoulders, contrasting with her pale skin. I was standing up, feeling comfortable, and without putting too much thought into it, I moved behind her and began to rub her neck. I felt her stiffen at first, then relax under my hands. I ran my thumbs down on either side of her neck along the cervical part of her spine, felt the nodules of her vertebrae and marveled how delicate they were, knew from my experience as a medic how fragile they were, how easy to shatter, like a bird's. I moved my fingers down into her shoulders, where I found little knots of tension in the muscles and rubbed them until they felt like they were going away, using a force strong enough to elicit tiny yelps from her, followed by pleasurable moaning.

I noticed some smoke coming out front under the lid of the grill and finished her off with a light chopping motion using the side of my hands. "Sorry, I have to cut it short, or we'll be eating charred wood instead of steaks."

"Mmmm," she said. "That was incredible. Thank you."

"You're welcome," I said, and meant it. A mosquito dive-bombed my face, and when I fanned it away, I could smell Rose's skin on my hand. For some reason, my mouth watered.

"Let's eat," I said. "I'm starving." I pulled the steaks off the grill as flames fueled by melting fat licked at the meat through the grill.

"Me, too," she said, and went to get out of her seat, but maybe because it was too low, or maybe because of the shots of tequila, she struggled a little getting up. I had one hand free and held it out to steady her as she stood.

"Whew!" she said. "Your mother was a smart woman. I should have made that fluffy nest."

"You'll feel better after you eat."

We went inside and devoured the steaks, baked potatoes, and salad, and drank one bottle of wine and opened another. After dinner, Rose picked up the plates and insisted on washing the dishes, but most of them went into the dishwasher and it was an easy cleanup. She was standing at the sink, her hands wet, looking for a towel. I pulled a dishtowel out of the drawer and handed it to her.

"Thanks," she said. "For everything."

"My pleasure."

"Uh, I noticed you have an extra room, or two?"

"Yes, ma'am. There is a guest room. It's well equipped with its own bathroom. The bed has a fat but firm mattress with Egyptian cotton sheets and a fluffy comforter. The rest of the decor is pretty lame, but it's comfortable."

"Welllll," she said. "I hate to ask, but the thought of driving down to Broward to get my car, then me driving to Miami to my apartment...kind of sucks."

"Say no more. *Mi casa es su casa.* I even have an oversized T-shirt that would fit you, and extra toothbrushes."

"Oh, God. I'd love to slip into a nice soft T-shirt, right now. Is it really big?"

"Big enough. Not that that's a good thing," I said, and she laughed at that. She was so pretty when she laughed. Her teeth were perfect and it was nice seeing her eyes crinkle when she smiled. "Follow me." I took her back and showed her the room and the bath and told her to make herself at home, then closed the door behind me on the way out.

Within a couple of minutes, I could hear the shower going. I went into my room, a huge space with an oversized bath in it, covered in marble, floor and walls, and took a quick shower myself, then slipped into some clean sweats and an old fire department T-shirt. I went by Rose's room and could still hear the shower running. I poured myself another glass of wine, sat on the couch, and turned on the television.

The news was just wrapping up and a reporter stood in front of a smoldering house, firefighters moving around in the background, picking up hoses and doing overhaul on the structure. Helicopters soared overhead, lighting up the scene, and I could hear them over my own home. It was Haskell's place.

"...and the owner of the home, luckily, was not home. Fire officials are still investigating the cause of the fire, but are not ruling out arson at this time. They are saying they believe the fire began in the garage, or workshop, in the back of the home, then spread to the house itself..."

"They must have come back to finish the job," said Rose. I turned and saw she was standing behind me, wearing my old University of Florida Gators T-shirt, which came halfway down her thighs. Her hair was wet and combed straight and dampened the shoulders of the shirt.

"Looks like it." She poured herself more wine and came over and sat next to me on the couch. She smelled like soap, simple and clean, which I found incredibly erotic.

"Will they call you to investigate it?"

"No. It's Palm Beach County's fire. They only call the state fire marshal if they have a fatality."

The news wrapped up and I turned it off, started the music again, and poured us more wine.

"I'm a night owl, Rose. If you're tired and want to go to bed…"

"Trying to get rid of me?"

"Not at all. In fact, it's nice to…uh…how shall I say this? I enjoy your company."

"How come you're not married?" she asked, combing her hair with her fingers, occasionally stopping and looking for a split end, her eyes crossed from the proximity.

"Never found the right one, I suppose."

"Oh, c'mon. Girls love firefighters, right?"

"Some do, I guess. Hey, don't get me wrong. I've had some… relationships along the way. One or two kinda serious."

"How about girls at the fire department?"

"Ugh, no. I've got some great friends at the fire department who are ladies. But I've never been attracted to the type."

"Is there a type?"

"To me, there is. The ones who are good with the job tend to be strong and…I don't know…stocky."

Rose giggled at that, then couldn't stop giggling, and I knew she was feeling the wine as much as I was.

"You don't like 'em stocky?" she asked, grinning mischievously.

"Nah. I tend to stay away from any gal who can beat me at arm wrestling."

Rose busted out laughing, snorting a little as she tried to stop. It wasn't that funny, but I loved hearing her laugh.

Then she was brushing my cheek with the backs of her fingers, leaning close to me. Her face came up to mine, so close it drifted out of focus.

I put my hand against the side of her face and pushed her wet hair back. It felt cool against her warm skin. I leaned forward and kissed the spot where her hair had been and inhaled the scent and felt the small, fine hair in front of her ear on my lips. I nibbled lightly there, then moved around to her mouth. I could smell the wine on her breath and I licked her lips, sipping, before I drank deeply from her mouth with a kiss that began as tender, then grew into something stronger. My tongue found hers and they glided over each other like eels moving in and out of a reef, smoothly but hungrily, looking for…something.

We didn't try to slow down. I suppose a nobler man might've stopped things before they progressed, blamed the passion on the alcohol, and at least negotiated an appropriate waiting time before moving on with something that might interfere with our professional relationship. But I am not that man.

There had been a mutual attraction from the beginning and a long day filled with hard work and trials, not only to her patience, but to both of our sensibilities. She was a very smart lady whose tolerance for working in a man's profession had worn so thin it was changing her psyche, adding disillusion to a job that, on its best days, was psychologically torturous. I had been thrust into a world that I'd known existed, but whose ugliness and pure evil I couldn't have imagined. And we'd been thrown together as each other's lone ally against a powerful, shadowy intelligence agency clearly doing something morally wrong, if not illegal. There is no stronger aphrodisiac than to realize a sudden trust with someone you've known for such a short time.

We were illuminated by the flickering blue light of the television. I managed to hit the mute button on the remote, but did not want to turn the lights off. I wanted to see her. Her mouth moved from my neck up to my ear and her warm breath pushed into my brain, reached my spinal column, extended into every nerve in my body. I could feel her heart beating through her chest wall as we embraced each other and my hand found the edge of the T-shirt and pulled it up and over her head and threw it across the room. I pushed her back on the couch and looked into her face, then down to her body, arched up at me with anticipation. I fed on her breasts, then moved lower toward the dark, triangular area of her pelvis. On the way down, I found the scar—a reddish-purple welt—where the maniac had opened her up, traversing her abdomen like a hysterectomy scar. It looked like a giant night crawler and appeared painful, still. I kissed around it and on it and I felt her belly vibrate and her hand shot down as if to push me away from it, but I would not allow it. She brushed at my head, gently trying to pull me back up and away, but I wanted to pay homage to her sacrifice and let her know that it did not detract from her beauty. I moved down farther and tasted her, found her so wet that I was tempted to stop what I was doing and enter her then, but I did not. I took my time and worked on her, letting her overcome her inhibitions, then move into the act and enjoy the moment. Within minutes, she began rocking her hips, pushing against my face, then cried out and shuddered convulsively.

I moved back up along her long, lovely sides and softly kissed as much of her as I could while trying to slow down my approach and abate my own need. She opened her legs up underneath me and guided me into her with her hand and I felt an incredible heat around and inside me, as if I were overcome with a fever that built in my loins and moved its infection up through my body, into my head, where it blinded me, so that all I could see was her. The fever grew until I could feel my breath coming in gasps and my eyes burned from the heat we generated, and when I came, it felt like this cosmic explosion that threatened to suck the air from my lungs and left me collapsed on top of her, our hearts beating against each other's, separated only by our flesh and the thin bones of our sternums.

Eventually, our hearts and breathing slowed and I slid into the space between Rose and the back of the couch and stroked her breasts, feeling my sweat on them and quietly enjoying the reaction of her nipples as they alternately scrunched up, then softened, then scrunched up again as my hands moved over them. Her mouth opened and her breath began to come in little clicks, the slightest of snores as she fell into a deep sleep. I allowed myself to follow.

I don't know how long we were lying there. What woke me up was the movement of her breath catching and a trembling in her abdomen, and as I woke, I realized she was crying.

"What's wrong?" I asked, confused, as I had not felt so content in so long that I had forgotten how nice the physical act could be. In the dim blue light, I could see tears streaming down her face and wondered how long she'd been awake and what had triggered her tears.

She rolled into me so I couldn't see her face, curled into a fetal position, and through muffled sobs, said, "I'm sorry. I was just lying here feeling sorry for myself."

I could feel her hand stroking her abdomen and knew she was feeling her scar.

"I…I…won't…c…can't…they…*he*…ripped out my g…guts! I…lost my…womb. I'll….never…I'll never…" She sobbed silently after that, as if her heart had been ripped out, too, and I just held her, not knowing what to say. Our relationship was so new that I didn't yet know what she needed to be comforted. So I held her and stroked her hair and back until she stopped crying and her breathing became slow again and I knew she was sleeping. Then I extricated myself from her embrace and stood over her, looking at her sleep.

I felt an anger build in me toward the man who had done this to her and toward a world that had allowed such a creature to exist and to harm one as beautiful, as good, as this woman. The anger pushed me into an epiphany: these people were aberrancies in nature that should not exist, that should be "terminated with extreme prejudice," as we used to say on military missions. I began to imagine what I could do with a knife...

When my thoughts had gone so dark they began to scare me, I steered myself away from them and tried to ponder other matters.

I couldn't help but wonder what the fuck was wrong with her husband to have wanted to discard her. They'd apparently had a good thing going, a promising future and company on the rise, and he'd had her. She'd had the fortitude to pick herself up and start all over in a new career, but now it was coming apart. A brutal attack by a madman had taken away the one thing that most women feel is an essential part of being a woman, the ability to bear children. This exquisite woman, whose natural ability was to analyze things, see how they come apart and go back together, wasn't able to apply those same principles to herself. That confidence and toughness I had seen earlier in the day was what she displayed to the world, but it was all a facade.

I picked her up, surprised at how light she was, and carried her not into the guest room but into my own bed, where I could watch over her in the night and wake up with her next to me in the morning.

• • •

That night I dreamed of my father. He was leaning against one of his horses, a big red roan that supported my father's weight as if it were nothing. My father wore a white long-sleeved shirt, its creases sharp, on top of blue jeans, an ornate tooled belt, and snakeskin boots. He hand-rolled a cigarette, his head down, the brim of his Stetson Silverbelly hat forever guarding his features from my view. Through the shade on his face, I saw the tip of his tongue stick out and run along the length of the twisted paper. When he finished, he pulled out a blue-tipped kitchen match and flicked it with his thumbnail. A sulfurous light flared up and I could see his face, his dark eyes locking on mine. In that brief instant, I saw his eyes go from shining with pleasant warmth, almost happy, to a dull sadness, and then he looked away. He turned to the horse, put one boot into the stirrup, then swung his other long leg up and over the horse and settled into the saddle, its leather creaking under his weight, his comfort on the roan as obvious and natural as if he had been born there. He began to ride off.

I felt a surge of fear that I would not see him again, so I began to run after him. The horse kicked up small clouds of dust as it pulled away, its heavy haunches flexing. My father sat impassively, rocking to and fro in the saddle as he rode away. Knowing I would lose him, I began to yell, then screamed for him to come back, if only to give me one last hug or even to just say good-bye before abandoning me, but nothing came out of my mouth. At least, I didn't think it did.

Suddenly, he stopped as if he'd heard my silent scream and slowly turned the horse around. He sat up there, and though I could not see his face, I saw the shine in his dark eyes staring back at me. I started to run toward him as he reached up and took off his Stetson hat. I stopped, horrified by what I saw. It was the face of the man I'd seen burned in the pawnshop fire when I was a rookie firefighter: the eyelids burned off, the eyes burned white, the blackened skin sloughing off his cheeks like torn taffeta.

His face morphed again; this time it turned into a young black man's face, a Somalian soldier who had come to kill me as I tried to rescue some of the downed Black Hawk survivors. He had flecks of blood on his face because I had shot him, unloading a full clip from my assault rifle into his chest. He was staring at me, his eyes wide, blinking in wonder, as if contemplating this man, this boy, really, like himself, who had just taken his life. He was waiting to fall, his own rifle gripped impotently in his hands. It was the last thing he saw before his vision turned dark and his soul left the earth.

But what scared me most of all about the dream was the sense of elation it left within me.

EIGHTEEN

Journal

Subjects: 56QAH/Lots 488 and 1115

It was early morning, the sun coming up from the horizon as yellow as an egg yolk, surrounded by a blue sky so clear it was the very picture of hope and gave even the most callous observer the sense that life could go on forever.

The men parked the car in a state park just above a freeway, the parking area bordered with thick foliage: old oaks interspersed with palms and pines skirted by mulberry bushes and tiny wildflowers that swayed violently back and forth as cars whooshed by on the interstate below. The men, one tall, the other slightly shorter but showing an obvious family resemblance—uncle and nephew, respectively—talked sporadically, chitchatting. Just a couple guys on the way to work. The tall one opened the trunk of the car and the shorter one reached in and took out a duffel bag as if it were a sport bag filled with baseball bats, balls, and gloves.

They wore khaki instead of camouflage, which tended to draw attention, particularly when worn in a suburban setting outside of hunting season. In their nondescript uniforms, they could have been park attendants or mechanics or any of those people who are invisible simply because they are seen so often they become a part of the landscape. The men strode into the tree line and found a nice flat area that afforded ample cover along with a perfect view of the interstate.

The road already held the speeding cars of early-morning risers, seven o'clockers racing to their places of work to sit on their asses in uncomfortable chairs, in loathsome, artificially lit offices, to brown-nose bosses they detested and work long days for paychecks that were, inevitably, too small. People who, in truth, hated themselves so much that they deserved to be hated by others. Or so our khaki companions had convinced themselves. Could it ever have been God's plan for people to live such an existence?

The nephew dropped the duffel to the ground and opened it up. He pulled out a blanket for them to lie on, then withdrew his choice of firearms for the day: a beautifully polished walnut-stock, .30-06 Springfield into which he loaded M2 light armor-piercing cartridges, their black tips gleaming dully in the dawn light. The kid was a traditionalist, typically using the same rifle he hunted with, which was fine. "One needs to be comfortable with one's chosen weapon," his uncle had counseled him.

The uncle carefully chose his firearm from the collection in the duffel: a Winchester Model 70 Extreme Weather SS, .270 caliber, with a dulled-down black stock and a perfectly tuned ergonomic triggering mechanism, with zero creep, zero over-travel, and zero take-up, no mechanical backlash or pull. So flawless in its form and operation it was like all that was between him and the bullet coming out of his gun was his finger, just point and shoot.

Both men used the Leopold Mark 2 tactical rifle scope, the same used by many police snipers. The same used by the uncle himself, when he'd served as an Army sharpshooter years before, when he'd been the best he could be, though that hadn't been good enough.

The men put on their yellow-tinted shooter's glasses, and rather than ear muffs, they put iPod earbuds in their ears with their own individual choices of music. The nephew enjoyed new rock with a message, such as Filter's "Hey Man, Nice Shot," and "Youth of the Nation" by P.O.D., while the uncle favored classic rock, the Beatles' "Happiness Is a Warm Gun" and Pat Benatar's "Hit Me With Your Best Shot." Never let it be said that serial killers don't have a sense of humor.

The men moved into prone positions and began their waiting game. Each was eager to be the first to shoot, but the action had some ground rules: If you fired first and did not make a great shot, you were a putz. Better to fire second and make the shot, rather than blow your wad trying to be first and screw up the morning. Often, they fired simultaneously, and just as often, they scored perfect shots. The only other rule was they could not fire at the same target.

On this day, the uncle chose an innocuous-looking Dodge Caravan, driven by a doughy middle-aged soccer mom, hair askew, yakking away on her cell phone, her double chin shaking, while she should have been paying attention to her driving, especially seeing that she was chauffeuring a busload of kids to school. The nephew chose a sports car driven by a middle-aged man, obviously trying to appear young, even as his gray comb-over waved in the wind like a tattered old flag.

They both scored head shots. The nephew's sports car driver went first, hit so cleanly that, even with the top of his head blown off like a cap lost to the wind, he seemed to drive almost a quarter mile before he realized he was dead and then swerved wildly, clipping other cars, running them off the road with him and adding to the carnage. The uncle's soccer mom was a bit of a disappointment. Instantly as dead as a frigid Catholic on her wedding night—which in fact she had been, so many years before—she maintained, even in death, some preternatural maternal instinct that allowed her to pull the van off the side of the road, slowly, then come to a complete and safe stop, the kids howling in the back, her brains sprayed across the inside of the windshield like red Windex.

Uncle and nephew looked at each other and the uncle gave a resigned shrug—you can't win them all. Then a smile spread across his face as they high-fived each other and marveled at the success of the sports car mayhem, as car after car piled into the path of its wreck and added to the body count.

Before they left, they each dropped a tarot card. One was the Emperor; the other was the Psychic.

● ● ●

Promising candidates, to be sure. The uncle's military training offers clear advantages for our needs. The nephew is cool as he goes about his business, though a little young, and that concerns me. But would they be willing to work independently? Would their unusual bond become a hindrance? Only time will tell.

NINETEEN

I awoke to the sound of Rose screaming.

Adrenaline coursing through my body and jump-starting my heart like a defibrillator, I jumped out of bed in a fighter's stance and looked around the room for an opponent.

Rose was thrashing at something slithering under the sheets, moving purposefully but blindly, until, finally, it came to the edge of the sheet and stuck its head out. It was Scout.

I laughed so hard I sank to the floor by the bed.

"What? Oh, it's Scout. She scared the hell out of me." Rose reached for Scout and pulled her close. "I didn't know you were a tunnel rat! Where did you get the name *Scout*?"

"Named after the girl in *To Kill a Mockingbird*. Also known as 'Rat Dog.' Another one of my mother's orphans. She kind of likes to crawl into tight spots."

"No kidding. She was trying to tunnel up my butt! Thank God I had a blanket tucked around me." Scout licked Rose's face. "She's adorable. Where was she last night?"

"Oh, she comes and goes as she pleases. There's a doggie door in the garage. She likes to go out to the stable and keep Sisco company at night."

"That's sweet."

"Yeah. So, how about some coffee?"

"Oh, yes, please. I'm a little hungover. And I'm starving, too."

"No kidding. You were putting away that tequila last night like a pro."

"I know. It's a bad habit I succumb to when I'm pissed off, which I was pretty much all day yesterday."

"How's the mood today?"

"Do you mean did our hooking up put me in a better mood?"

"Something like that."

"It took the edge off."

"Glad I could be of some use."

Rose smiled at me, her hair tousled across her face, the sun coming through a crack in the curtain and lighting her up. She was gorgeous. She rolled across the bed and took my hand and kissed it. "You were very sweet. I'm sorry I got so emotional. I guess I still have some posttraumatic stress issues I'm dealing with. And booze makes the emotions all the more powerful."

I leaned down and kissed her forehead, then threw on a robe and went to the restroom to freshen up. When I came out, Rose was already dressed, hair and teeth brushed, and looking well rested, though a little puffy around the eyes, probably from crying.

"Damn, you're pretty," I said.

She smiled and said, "Don't get mushy on me. I'm a lot of work right now."

"I don't mind work."

I made us some coffee and some omelets with salsa; nothing like a spicy breakfast to chase away the tequila cobwebs. While I was cooking, Rose played with Scout. They looked happy together.

My phone rang. It was Cecil Button, forensic investigator for the Bureau of Forensic Fire and Explosives Analysis, an old friend and one of the most intelligent, and strange, men I have ever known. He talks fast in a high-pitched voice, mixing humor with obscure references that can take me days to figure out.

"Grey, it's the Button Man. What the hell you sending me something that needs bio-forensics for?"

"Good morning to you, too, Cecil. I'm here with Special Agent Rose Cleary of the FBI and I'm going to put us on speaker phone."

"Oh, hi, Agent Cleary, nice to meet you. Wow, you guys get started early—or maybe you stayed up all night with our Mr. Gift?"

Rose's cheeks flushed. "Nice to meet you, too, Dr. Button. I've read some of your papers on explosives."

"Well, thank God Gift is hanging out with someone who has some class. When I saw your name on the evidence submission form, Grey, I said to myself, 'Button, you know he's going to be asking a favor,' and you know I don't mind, but damn, I had to stay up all night with a buddy of mine over at FSU's lab to look at your 'Other Requests' sample. You know, the one you marked 'urine' next to, so discreetly, by the 'O' on the form, when you know we don't do bio-forensics here at the lab? And didn't I tell you to quit calling me Cecil?"

"You sound a little wired, Button Man."

"Wired? Are you kidding? I've been eating my Concerta—you know, the amphetamine I take for my ADHD? I've been dropping that shit like frickin' M&Ms, man, and chasing it with Red Bull."

"I know I'm going to owe you…"

"Owe me, Gift? Your right arm and firstborn child wouldn't even be a down payment."

"Think of something and I'll get it to you. Maybe a new tie-dyed lab coat or a subscription to Geek magazine?"

"Okay, funny man, just remember who is always there for you."

"I know you are, bud. Now, what do you have for me?"

"Well, I'm going to need a couple more hours for the mass spectral detector to complete the analysis of the gas chromatography, but the cool thing is we have a new machine up here. Still takes sixteen hours to break the chemical down, but the new detector starts giving us a graph of chemicals as it does the breakdown. Pretty cool, huh?"

"Yeah. Pretty cool."

"Anyway, I saw you made a note about the first sample possibly being gasoline, and all I got to say is, you must be losing your nose, Gift. I could tell, just by sniffing it, it was something stronger. I mean, the gas chromatography has already shown the stuff has a weight of over fifty-seven atomic mass units, which is indicative of an organic chemical compound like alkane, and we all know that means a petroleum distillate, but the other components are way off from gasoline. I mean, I'm seeing peak spreads of the n-alkane numbers *starting* at C-fifteen and going up, up, up—"

"Cecil! Cecil!" Rose and I had started laughing in the middle of Cecil's rant. "Can you come down to my IQ, Cecil, and just tell me what you think it is?"

"A heavy petroleum distillate, you know, like Jet A aviation fuel, you tool. God, what has happened to you, Gift? You on crack or have another head injury?"

"No, still dealing with the last one. How about the sample with the urine? Was I way off on that one, too?"

"No, you were right. It is urine. I could have told you that with a piece of litmus paper, but you wanted to know more than that, didn't you? You wanted to know if I could get DNA from it, right? Well, any of my other colleagues would have told you to go pound sand and sent it back to you, but you know you get the extra mile with me. I got with Amy Pogue over at the university lab last night—you remember Amy, don't you, that really hot research babe who owns the biotech company that gave FSU a grant to build one of the best research labs in the country? I mean, who would mind spending the night with her, anyway? Rich, brainy, and beautiful, my God. Anyway, we started the DNA analysis. And the really cool thing is that Amy has developed a patented process that actually *speeds up* the analysis, so we can have a reading in a couple hours."

"And?"

"And I can tell you this: it is male urine."

"That's it?"

"No. We knew that right from the get-go because there were so few epithelial cells in the sample. Women have a lot more epithelial cells in their urine, obviously because of the vaginal cells' contribution, and there wasn't many in this sample. But Amy, God bless her, that clever girl—who I will marry one day—she was able to *amplify* the sample. At first she used all the stuff you'd usually use to identify DNA—the Elmer AmpF/STR Profiler Plus and Cofiler PCR Kits—but nothing, right? Because those kits work better on *female* samples. Then Amy showed me how brilliant she really is: she did a procedure amplifying the mitochondrial DNA using the Fastype mtDNA System that uses a polymerase chain reaction, and focused on regions of the mitochondrial genome, and she was able to produce enough clean template DNA to put in a search of CODIS through a connection I have with the FLDE up here."

Rose and I were laughing again. "Okay, Button. Take another pill. I'm standing here, holding my breath."

"Okay, okay. Keep in mind, we did not get a great sample, and that's probably why we're getting the readings we're getting, but either we're way out of orbit here, or your killer…you did indicate this was a homicide case, right? Your killer had dozens of possible matches."

Rose and I weren't laughing anymore. We just stared at each other. "How could that be? I thought DNA was supposed to be more conclusive."

"Amy says the sample just wasn't good enough, even after the amplification, so it's not conclusive. But we can certainly narrow it down to a few dozen suspects, and that's got to be better than the three hundred million–plus people in the US alone, right? Amy was simply looking for VNTRs, variable number tandem repeats, and there were dozens of possible matches because we didn't have a particular suspect to compare to a specific evidence sample—CODIS only gives you a list of *possible* matches, those names with the most matches in base pairs of specific loci and type of nucleotides in the DNA strands."

"Oh my God, Button. I have no idea what the hell you are talking about. But I guess I am going to say thank you."

"I guess I'm going to say you're welcome, you ingrate. Do you have any idea how much work it was to get this far? See, Sherlock, the way it's supposed to work is that you *have* a suspect *and* their DNA, *then* you compare that to what you've found at the crime scene. Now, because of our hard work, you at least have a starting point for correlation if you have a particular suspect you are looking at."

"We do. Sort of."

"If you can get that suspect's DNA, we can see if it matches what we have so far. Remember this, though: CODIS only contains samples of *criminals*, people they have samples from because it was found at a crime scene or they were arrested and convicted. Still, we have a list of names and case numbers of possible matches from open *and cold* cases for identification purposes. Amy and I wanted to introduce your nonspecific sample into CODIS, in case it pops up in another crime—kind of doing a proactive anticipatory investigation—but as of July of oh-nine, you can't introduce samples into CODIS unless you have been audited by the FBI, and quite simply, this rule is so new a lot of research labs haven't been audited yet, including Dr. Pogue's. In the future, this is going to really clean up the database, but in the meantime, it's a pain in the ass."

"Is there another system we can access to get those so-called noncriminal samples?"

"I don't know. Why don't you ask Agent Cleary there? Now, I have to go. I need to take a nap."

"Ok, Button, enjoy your nappy time. Catch you later."

"Yep. Like tomorrow."

"What?"

"Yeah. Didn't you know? Your Captain Brandsma requested a lab tech to work with you down there, and when I heard, how could I resist? I'm hoping Amy can come with me. Maybe we can turn it into a working vacation with some time spent on the beaches; can't imagine what she looks like in a skimpy bathing suit. Later, Gator."

I hung up. Rose was deep in thought as she watched Scout chase a ball she'd thrown for her.

"So, what are you thinking?"

"The military has started collecting DNA from all its personnel. I don't know how far back they go, but it's possible Haskell's could be in their system. The high-grade aviation fuel Cecil mentioned could tie the Matarese girl from the church scene to Haskell and his race cars. The question is whether or not my supervisor is going to let me continue on this case. While you were saying good-bye to Cecil, he sent me a text saying he's flying into Miami this morning and wants to meet with me." Something about the way she spoke of her supervisor pushed my thoughts in a weird direction. I hoped I was not getting jealous after just one night with her, but I had to wonder why a supervisor who would not even call her when he pulled her off the case and shut down her FBI file access would now be making a special trip to come see her.

"Okay," I told her, "I'll take you back to your car. But I need to feed and water the horse real quick. I've got a girl who stops over and brushes her down and walks her and rides her, but she won't come over until later. Right now, she's in church."

I thought Rose might ask me about "the girl" I'd mentioned, but she seemed lost in thought and started texting again on her recharged BlackBerry. I shrugged and went out to take care of Sisco.

Sisco was in his stall and started waving his head, saying good morning to me. He was excited, thinking I was going to take him for a ride. Emily would have to do that, though.

I'd met Emily through a therapeutic organization I'd lent Sisco to called Vinceremos, which partners horses with children with special needs as a form of therapy. Emily is classified as retarded. I'm not sure I agree with that assessment. I think she just doesn't like to talk a lot, probably because she comes from an abusive family. She doesn't possess mongoloid features; she's just a girl who is "slow," as they say, but animals don't care. They just know when someone loves them, and Emily loves Sisco as if he were her own horse, which is a big help to me. She's been taking care of Sisco for two years, since she was sixteen years old, and it's been a big relief for me. I get called in to work and have to be gone for a couple of days and I know Emily is there to care for Sisco. They have a symbiotic relationship: Sisco gives her an excuse to get out of her house and away from her alcoholic parents who sit smoking cigarettes and watching television, wondering what they did to have produced a retarded child and doing little to hide their resentment of her; Sisco and the barn are a refuge for her, a safe place, and she comes by every afternoon.

Scout had followed me out to the stable and was nipping at Sisco's feet and generally trying to get some attention. The morning was warm but offered a gentle breeze on which a bright-red cardinal came floating by. I watched him dart through the window, then bent over to fill a trough with fresh water. The sun shone through the slats in the stable wall and reflected on the water's surface. The light glinted, turning as red as the cardinal, and suddenly my head began to hurt again. Dizzy, I looked back up to the blood-red cardinal and past him, right into the morning sun.

The trough was overflowing and the water pouring onto my feet and pant leg when I came out of the seizure. I was still standing, holding the hose, my ears ringing like I'd just come out of an AC/DC concert. Both Scout and Sisco were looking at me. It was Scout I couldn't take my eyes off of as I tried to reorientate myself. She was biting at a flea. The word *flea* was stuck in my head, as was a crazy notion. I finished putting down some hay for Sisco and hurried back up to the house to tell Rose.

She was in the house, just tucking away a notebook she had been jotting thoughts in when I came in. "All set," she said, rather businesslike, I thought.

"I was watching Scout—I think she has a couple fleas—and I got to thinking about the Matarese girl we looked at in Tamarac.

In her purse, there was a picture of her with a small dog. I wonder if the dog is still at her apartment."

"Probably. Good thought. We should call animal control or her family to come pick it up."

"We should, but that's not what I'm saying. You told me her ad on Backpage.com said she did in-calls, which means she was probably hooking at her home to keep costs down. I was thinking, if Haskell was at her home, and she has a dog, we might get something from that."

"Such as?"

"Well, if her dog has fleas and some chewed on Haskell, they might have his DNA. And you've still got his toothbrush. It's a long shot…"

"Wow. That's…clever," she said, her eyes lighting up with new life. "You're right about being a long shot, but it's worth a try."

"Great," I said, longing to recapture the closeness I felt we'd molded the night before. I walked over to her and lifted her chin, but there was nothing in her eyes but an intensity that said she wasn't going to give up on this case until she had Haskell behind bars or laid out on a slab. I stroked her face, like a man trying to rub a genie back out of a magic lamp, but the magic was gone. Still, I was lost in the surreal blue of her eyes.

"Grey," she said. "Don't fall in love with me. Okay? Last night was…what it was. You're a good man, very good man. But I'm not…I'm not ready for…anything like that."

I nodded and backed away from her, a wave of nausea washing through my stomach. Scout sat at my feet in the awkward silence that followed, wagging her tail, looking up at me, dying for me to pet her.

TWENTY

The apartment was like a million others in Broward County, one of four on a floor accessed by climbing offset stairs to each landing. All of the other apartments on the second floor were empty, the residents' names removed from the mailboxes downstairs— another sign of the economic downturn of South Florida. Haskell could have killed the Matarese girl here and no one would have heard a thing.

The door to the girl's place had bands of yellow plastic crime scene tape over it in an X pattern, along with a *DO NOT ENTER* notice from the Broward County Sheriff's Office. There was graphite dust all over the doorknob where they had checked for fingerprints. I was quietly pleased that there were other people working on the case. Whether Haskell was the perpetrator or not, there was still a serial killer roaming around out there, and from what I'd learned already, they typically don't take too many days off when they're on a spree. With Rose evidently removed from the case, at least temporarily, it was of paramount importance that someone keep the heat turned up.

I used a K-tool to open the door to the apartment. Just about every fire engine in America has one; it's a flat piece of steel about three inches by three inches, with a K-shaped notch in one side.

You place the notch on a door's deadbolt lock cylinder and give it a smack with the flat side of an ax. It breaks the cylinder and you just slip it out and open the door. That business you see on TV where the canny investigator pulls out a couple of dental tools and fiddles with the lock for a few seconds and *voila* it opens is bullshit. It takes too long, and just the right tools, and it does not always work on every lock. When you really want to get past a door using the least amount of time, the K-tool is the way to go.

With BSO having already been there, I thought the dog would have been removed already, but before we gained entry, I could hear it whining inside. It didn't bark, which surprised me until I went inside and saw the animal, a small, timid cocker spaniel. Its huge, watery, brown eyes looked like they belonged on one of those velvet paintings they sell on the side of the road. It was pitiful. The cops who had been there probably couldn't get animal control to come out over the weekend, but they'd left it with some water and food. It was in a cage with its own mess, vibrating with fear—and contorting back on itself now and then to chew on an itch. A good sign.

I opened the cage and the Spaniel crept out sheepishly, its hindquarters tucked down. I let it smell my hand and picked it up. I turned it over and immediately saw fleas, like pepper flakes, swarming all over its belly. A few of them sprang onto my wrist. I brushed some into a ziplock bag and sealed it before they could get out. I put the dog down and it scurried back into its cage.

The rest of the place was typical for a twentysomething-year-old woman: secondhand furniture, utilitarian housewares, a lamp with no shade, laundry waiting to be folded, a few old pictures on the wall and stuck to the refrigerator with magnets. A good investigator can pinpoint the age of an occupant in a home by counting the pictures on the walls: the fewer photos, the younger the occupant. In the not-too-distant future, people will no longer have photos of family and friends on their walls and appliances. Digitized images on cameras and cell phones are replacing them, sometimes downloaded to computers or digital frames, but just as often, just stored on a device's memory card until they're deleted or replaced by newer images, one party or event replacing the last.

Rose had drifted into the back room. I heard her opening drawers and cabinets and going through the closet. I was going to check on her when my phone rang. I answered it without looking to see who it was.

"Gift."

"Hey, G." It was Leonard Cotton. "Do I need to worry about you stealing my position?"

It cheered me to hear his voice. It seemed like a month since I'd done so, though it had only been the morning before. "Leonard. Hey, bud. Next time you ask me to cover your shift, I'm going to say some not very nice things to you."

"I know, I know. I heard. Talked to my boss and Chief Dugger already. I'm sorry, bro. Who'da thunk it? I go out of town for a short weekend, thinking it might be quiet for you, and you get stuck with a serial killer. It's nuts."

"You have no idea."

"On the upside, though, I heard you been keeping company with some foxy FBI lady."

"Yeah. We're working on the case together. But—"

"But what—you can't keep your mind on your work?"

"No, I'm doing okay there, but there's some weird shit going on."

"You mean with the killer?"

"No. I mean, that part's freaky enough, but there's something else going on. Some CIA connection, military special ops spooks, and Rose—I mean, Agent Cleary—suddenly got pulled off the case last night."

"Holy crap."

"When you getting back? I want to bend your ear."

"I'm back now. Kids had enough of Mickey yesterday. Which means you don't have to cover my shift anymore."

"I don't know, bud. I'm knee-deep in this mess. Gotta go where it takes me."

"Sounds like it's not our deal anyway. If the CIA is pulling rank on the FBI, where do we fit in? Why don't you come over this afternoon and fill me in? It's the twins' birthday. We're hangin' by the pool, and I'm cookin' ribs."

"God, that sounds good. Pencil me in. I'll let you know in a little while after I see what our next step is going to be."

"I'll hold you to it, man."

"Tell Vanessa I said hello."

"Tell her yourself when you come over."

I looked down after I hung up with Leonard. My pant legs were covered with the pepper flakes. The moving kind. Rose came running out of the bedroom.

"Yuck!" she said, slapping at her long, shapely legs. "Grey, I think we have enough samples. This place is gross."

"Anything of interest back there?"

"Nope. The cops pretty much ransacked the place. Maybe they found something; I'll check with them. But the carpet is *moving* with fleas. I don't know what made you think of that, but you hit the nail on the head. If Haskell was in here, you'd think he'd have fed at least some of these fleas. I know I have. Let's grab some and get out of here before I freak out."

"Sounds like you're already there."

She smiled at that, and it was good to see that elusive feature again. "You're right. I am uptight."

"About?"

"Meeting David—uh, my boss."

"Is he that much of a prick?"

"No. He's actually a good guy. Very dedicated to the department and to the country. I don't like letting him down, I suppose. He's…it's complicated."

"How so?"

"Well, remember when I told you I had a research company and did some contracting for the government?"

"Yeah?"

"I told you someone I met suggested I apply with the FBI?"

"Sure."

"It was him. David. My supervisor."

"I see." And I did. Something in the way she said *my supervisor*, along with her reaction the night before when she'd found out he had shut her down. The fact he was personally coming down to meet with her. It all seemed more personal than professional.

"We used to work together in the field. He was part of the BAU and he brought me in right after I finished school in Quantico. We used to be closer…until he was promoted."

"How long ago was that?"

It took a while for Rose to answer that, for some reason. She seemed to be rewinding a movie in her mind to recall. Then she snapped out of it.

"It was right after the time I was attacked."

"Tough year. Getting hurt and losing your partner to a promotion at the same time. Is he married?"

Rose frowned at me. "What's that got to do with anything?"

"You tell me."

Her eyes locked on mine as if searching for something, a flash of anger in them. I saw her heart beating in her throat.

"He *is* married." She paused, then added, "We better be going."

"Sure," I said. We hadn't known each other long enough for me to ask any more questions, in spite of the intimacy of the night before. We'd moved too fast as it was. Besides, I thought I knew the answers to those questions already.

We were still standing in the living room, just about to leave, when I heard a shoe shuffle on the landing outside. Rose heard it, too, and we flanked the front door, our guns drawn. I was on the hinged side of the door, so wouldn't be the first to see whoever was at the door if they came into the room. Another shuffle and I saw Rose set her hips into a slight crouch, readying herself to either fire her weapon or grab the intruder. I got myself ready as well, realizing we were in each other's crossfire if either of us fired. I put my gun back in my holster and flexed my hands, wishing suddenly that I'd spent more time on my days off sparring in the dojo than hanging at the beach.

The door began to inch open. I could see Rose's eyes, pupils dilated with anticipation. I couldn't take the suspense anymore. I grabbed the door handle and yanked the door open as Rose dropped back into a firing stance. The force of me jerking the door open pulled the man into the room and he stumbled forward, doing a two-step, trying to right himself. He was carrying a small pry bar, so I grabbed his wrist and twisted, then moved his arm up and locked him into a submission hold—my old martial arts training coming back as effortlessly as if I'd just been practicing the day before. I pushed him to the floor.

Rose had handcuffs on the man so fast I didn't even see her take them out. She put her knee in his lower back, her gun to his head, her movements as vicious as a lifer in a state penal system, or perhaps as calculated as a person who's had her guts handed to her by a maniac she'd underestimated.

But her voice was as cool as an assassin's and disturbed me as much or more than her feral attack. "FBI. What's your business here?"

The man went limp but turned his flushed face to the side in an attempt to look at her as he spoke. "Jolie Matarese is...was my daughter," he said, and though he did not sob, a tear ran down his nose as he tried to catch his breath.

Rose pulled his wallet out of his pants without hesitation and flipped it open, then handed it to me and helped the man to his feet, though she left him cuffed. I glanced at the driver's license and saw he was Clarence Matarese and had a Ft. Lauderdale address.

"Why are you here?" Rose asked him. "Didn't you see the crime scene tape outside?"

The man just nodded. He had black curly hair, streaked heavily with gray and apparently unwashed. His whiskers were white and he smelled sour, with a scent of engine oil, like he had not bathed in a couple of days after working on a car. His huge, dark eyes were underscored with dark circles. I noticed grease under his fingernails and figured him for a mechanic.

"I think we can uncuff him, Rose," I said.

She looked at me and I saw her soften a little as she gave me a small nod. She took the cuffs off.

"You here just to get some things, Mr. Matarese?" she asked him.

"Yes, ma'am," he said, his voice deep and ragged. "Maybe just some pictures. Have you all had any luck finding who...did... who killed my little girl?"

"We haven't made an arrest yet, sir. But we're following some leads."

Rose glanced at me and I could tell even she wasn't comfortable with this part. How could she ever tell him we felt we knew who his daughter's killer was, but were being forced to stand down? How could that possibly make sense to any parent? His "little girl" had been moonlighting as a hooker, but I had met very few parents who could dismiss their children because of their faults, or addictions, or poor decisions. I had met even fewer who could accept the deaths of their children. We simply aren't wired to imagine our offspring's demise before our own. Some species of monkeys carry their dead babies around with them for weeks, like luggage filled with grief, before letting them go. Most parents never can.

"I talked to the cops yesterday. Said they're not handling the investigation. If that's so, who is?"

Rose looked to me briefly, then lowered her eyes to the ground before looking back to the distraught father. "I am."

He started to say something, then seemed to rethink his words. He stumbled toward the kitchen, his legs unsure beneath him, and gently plucked the photos from the refrigerator as if pulling petals from a flower, his hands trembling.

Watching him, I couldn't help but feel he was experiencing regret as much or more than remorse.

"Sir," I said, "maybe you'd like to take her dog with you."

He turned and looked at me with haunted eyes and shook his head. "I lost my job four months ago. Just working as a shade tree mechanic now and then for a church. Priest lets me sleep there sometimes. I can't use a dog."

I nodded my head. "I'll take care of it."

"I'd be obliged, sir." He shuffled past me on his way out and stopped, framing himself in the doorway. "You're not a cop, are you?"

"No, not really," I said. "I'm just a fire marshal. But I'm going to help find the man who took your daughter."

He smiled wanly at me, then turned and drifted off, a man with nothing left and nothing to lose.

I took the dog in the cage with me, making a few calls along the way. I called Chief Dugger to ensure there were no other family members who wanted the dog, then called the Peggy Adams Animal Shelter in West Palm, a no-kill refuge for homeless dogs and cats, which agreed to take it. Rose thought I was being a softy, but I couldn't see letting the spaniel sit there and suffer until someone came to pick it up and take it to animal control, where it would wait out its days and finally have to be euthanized to make more room for others.

When I dropped Rose off at her car in Tamarac, there was a tall, blond-haired man waiting for her. A big man in a great-looking gray suit, his beefy shoulders filling out the jacket as though he'd played some football or at least pushed some heavy weights along the way. Rose seemed surprised to see him, but didn't say anything.

"We'll talk later, all right?" she said to me, gathering her purse and coat, her fingers on the door handle.

"Sure," I said, and instinctively leaned over to give her a kiss on the cheek. It was stupid, probably—I wasn't thinking about the waiting man as her supervisor—but we'd slept together the night before and it seemed the gentlemanly thing to do. To cover up the move, Rose nodded her head as if I had told her something and she was responding to it, then she bolted out the door.

"Thank you for the ride and hospitality, Inspector Gift," she called back in to me. "I'll be in touch. The bureau appreciates your help." Then she slammed the door. She'd been so quick to leave, she'd forgotten to take the evidence we'd collected at Haskell's home, not to mention the "people sausage" we'd taken to analyze. I'd give it all to Cecil Button when I saw him. We had Haskell's toothbrush and some hair samples. If Cecil and Dr. Pogue could match Haskell's DNA to the sample they'd already analyzed for us, we'd have enough to make an arrest, if we could find him.

My suspicions of Rose and her supervisor—David Rasmussen was his name, I'd learned along the way—were confirmed by their body language with each other. His deep frown softened as she approached, and her strong, confident stride faltered. He cupped her elbow in his hand and they fell instantly into animated conversation. It was obvious to me that they were at least former lovers.

Some things made sense to me then. Perhaps having the investigation taken out of her hands wasn't the only cause of her seething anger. Self-loathing could play a part in it as well. She was, after all, doing the same thing to another woman that had been done to her.

TWENTY-ONE

Journal

Subject: 56QAH/Lot 704

It was dry as a popcorn fart, as his stepfather used to say. He never knew his real father. His mother, an independent, driven business owner who owned several McDonald's franchises, had told him that, when she wanted a child, she had simply gone to a sperm bank, and after choosing the qualities she thought would be admirable in a man, she'd "gone through a procedure" and had a baby. Him.

Later, she'd married a man—she needed help raising a boy, as she was too busy to do it herself—and that man became his stepfather. He also became the teenage boy's first victim. After the stepfather had grounded him for skipping classes in ninth grade and punctuated the moment with a fist that swelled his lip and loosened some teeth, the boy stabbed him through the eye while he was napping, using a common ballpoint pen. He used the same pen, after it was cleaned up, of course, to write a "Dear Jane" letter to his mother, in the stepfather's hand, saying he was leaving her for a younger woman. Then he hauled the stepfather's body out to the woods, laid it in a shallow grave he'd dug, doused it with gasoline, and incinerated it. He covered it with some dirt; it was never found, and he'd gotten away with his first murder.

He'd also introduced himself to the joy of setting fire. He'd always been mesmerized by flames, staring into the huge stone fireplace in their mountain vacation home, sometimes for hours. But to actually watch it consume a body…Well, now, that was a thrill. If only he could do that on a grander scale. Wildland fires had been breaking out regularly and becoming more problematic as they moved into urban Central Florida. One more would not be a surprise to anyone.

He chose an area that used to be thickly wooded, an evergreen place he'd explored as a child, creating solitary adventures and fantasies. Now it was a zero lot line housing project called Olympia, surrounded by a few remaining and very dry pine trees, palmetto bushes, and sparse grass. Pine trees can actually explode when they catch fire—a magnificent sight.

He poured gasoline in a thin swath from a five-gallon jerry can. He did it in a series of dots and dashes, like a flammable Morse code he was writing, then began igniting the line using a long barbecue lighter. He'd light up an area, then drive to another spot on the perimeter of the residential area, do the Morse code thing again, then drive to another area and repeat the process. Within twenty minutes, he had completely surrounded the area with a wall of flame and had not heard the first fire truck responding. Within half an hour, the fire had grown so intense it was beginning to create its own weather, actually making turbulent winds that grew into fiery tornadoes and pushed the fire at incredible speeds.

Residents had begun to notice smoke and even flames in some areas, but confident their local fire departments would handle the matter, many waited too long to try to get out. The fire raced through the area like a dragster from hell, consuming cookie-cutter homes and their white picket fences, SUVs, playgrounds, and walking paths. It jumped highways and even canals and moved into commercial areas and school grounds.

By the time the fire was brought under control it had destroyed over five hundred homes, a shopping plaza, an elementary school, and even a fire station. Twenty-three people were killed, including five firefighters and a family trying to flee, whose car was overtaken by a giant wave of explosive flame. What an accomplishment!

The fire starter was so pleased with his work that he planned on doing it again to a community a few miles away. He stopped at a filling station along the way and began refilling his gas cans. He wondered why so many people were worried about terrorism from Islamic groups and the government poured money into security at any and every port of transportation when all anyone had to do to create chaos, terror, and death was to light a fire in the right place.

• • •

Not sure about this one. He's another distance killer, and while that has its place, what we really need is someone who can work up close. Someone who can infiltrate. He's obviously a sociopath and can kill without remorse, but it's almost an afterthought to him and not a goal, as with some of the other subjects. That, and he's just so damn blond and fair! Couldn't blend in where they're going to need them.

Of course, he might still be useful as a donor.

TWENTY-TWO

I could see smoke curling up from behind Leonard's house. He was cooking his famous ribs. Just smelling the hickory burning on the low fire, the rib fat dripping down into the coals, made my mouth water as I pulled into the drive.

When the kids saw me rounding the house, they jumped out of the pool and rushed to me, clamoring over me like crazed, dripping seals. "Uncle Grey!" they screamed, their hands darting through my pockets, looking for the treats—M&Ms for the twins, Skittles for the "baby."

Then they saw the dog. Big mistake.

I had stopped at home and given the dog a bath, with Scout watching me to make sure I was doing it right, I suppose. I scrounged for and saved more fleas. She was fluffed up and ready, but the animal shelter was already closed by the time I got there, so I just brought her with me to hang out. I felt sorry for her; she was alone now.

"You brought us a dog for our birthday? Yayyyyy!"

"Uh, well, no. I'm just looking after her for the weekend."

"Can we keep her? It's our birthday."

Now I was in trouble.

Vanessa was sitting by the pool, grinning at me, watching her kids maul me, and shaking her head about the dog, but I could tell she was going to give in quick. Leonard might not be so easy. Vanessa set down the large salt-rimmed margarita she was sipping and stood up. She glided over to me, the long, sleek muscles of her thighs flexing. Vanessa was a great woman, totally devoted to her family, a churchgoing, God-fearing, Bible-thumping Southern Baptist with the face of an angel and a body like the devil's mistress, in spite of, or perhaps because of, having three kids and a full-time job as a legal secretary.

The kids scattered as she got to me, momentarily forgetting their treats as they began playing with the dog.

"Hey, Grey," Vanessa said. "Thanks for covering Leonard's shift so we could go to Disney."

"No problem. Sorry about the dog." I told her the dog's story. "I'll take her to the homeless shelter tomorrow."

Vanessa smiled. "Still looking out for all the helpless creatures in the world?" She leaned in and hugged me, her bathing suit still cool and damp from the pool, but her smooth, graphite skin held the warmth of the sun and I could feel it through my shirt.

This one was a keeper—a great mother and partner, a big-boned beauty and healthy lover. Smart, beautiful, classy, and strong. She held a lot of the same philosophical beliefs that Leonard did but never backed away from a healthy debate if her opinion differed. I loved and respected Vanessa as much as Leonard, partly because she was my best friend's soul mate and partly because she accepted me as I was: a damaged former firefighter her husband had brought home like a stray cat. She gave me a kiss on the cheek and gave the back of my neck a comforting squeeze. I wished they made more like her.

"How you doing, Grey? I heard you've had a tough weekend."

I nodded. "I've seen some ugly things."

She shook her head. "Let's go get you a drink, my friend. And don't worry about the dog. The kids have been asking for one for months now. You just saved us an inevitable trip to the shelter to adopt one. Margarita sound good?"

"Like heaven."

I joined Leonard at the grill while Vanessa went to fetch the drinks. He put down the barbecue tongs and gave me a giant hug. Often, I forget how big Leonard is, until we are in close proximity. He can be quite menacing, too; that shaved head gleaming like a polished bowling ball sitting on top of a neck like a tree stump that flowed into a linebacker's muscled torso. Leonard had been a cop before he'd become a fire marshal, and he could still turn on that icy bad-assed cop stare—and then back it up by actually being a badass, if the situation warranted it. His arms wrapped around me like a bear grasping a child, picking me up as if I weighed nothing.

"G-man! How are you, bro?"

"Don't hurt me."

"Ah, man, you're such a candy-ass. I didn't think you'd show. You see the kids?"

"Yeah. God, they're getting big."

"You mean from two weeks ago?"

"You bet. Every time I see them they look like they sprouted another inch. Must take after their daddy. Sorry about the dog. I don't think they'll let me take it back."

"No worries, G," he sighed. "They wanted a dog; now they got one. Besides, the price is right. Right?"

Vanessa came back with the drinks, but the children had disappeared with the dog, so she left to check on them. "They might be painting that puppy's toenails, for all I know."

I watched Leonard admiring his wife as she walked away, even after fifteen years of marriage. King Kong with the heart of Mother Teresa, and Vanessa held that heart. I held the loyalty of his friendship and there wasn't a better one anywhere on the planet. Still, I liked to play with him when I could.

"You see the way she looked at me when she handed me that drink?" I said. "Mmmm-mm."

"Careful, white bread, you're outta your league. You don't have the stamina, and unless I willed you my pecker for a postmortem transplant, you wouldn't have the right tools for it, either."

"I can hold my own."

"Well, hell yeah. Who else would?" We laughed until we saw the flames coming out of the grill and jumped into emergency grill action. After containing a small blaze with a cold beer, we settled into some loungers.

I filled Leonard in on the murder scene I'd visited and the possible connections with the other two murders, on Haskell, and on the CIA connection and the investigation being put on hold. I told him about Rose and the mysterious Cerberus and about the return of my seizures after so many years and their strange, new, almost clairvoyant quality.

"All that shit happened in one day while you were watching my shift? Man, all I can say is that I'm glad it was you and not me. I'm sorry you got stuck with that dirty, but at least it's over now. I mean, your part is done, right?"

"Uh, not really."

"What do you mean? Thought you said they shut you guys down."

"They shut down the FBI."

"But not you? C'mon, Grey. You're not a homicide detective."

"No, I'm not. But I got pulled into this and it must be for a reason."

"Well, pull yourself out. You only got called in to determine fire cause and site investigation. Why would you want to go further with it and put yourself out there?"

I had to think about that one. What were my reasons? Was it because of Rose? Was it because of what I was seeing when I lost myself to the absence seizures? Was it because of the forlorn look of Clarence Matarese, a man who had nothing more than the love for his daughter and now she'd been taken away from him? Was it because some spook, one who may have shared a particularly dark segment of my past in Mogadishu, had taunted me (*"You are working on a case that is complex in ways you cannot know..."*)? But I did want to know now. I might be out of my league, might have no experience as a homicide detective, but I knew my way around a crime scene and criminal thinking.

I finally answered Leonard's inquiry. "Because I've seen what this guy does and I don't want him to do it anymore."

Leonard looked me in the eyes as he thought about it. "All right. Then you gotta do what you gotta do, but I'm in on this, too. If I hadn't traded you the shift, then this would have been my problem."

"This one's got stink on it, Leonard. We might be dealing with a killer backed up by some group subcontracted by the CIA. We might not be able to get to him, even if we can find him, which by now seems pretty improbable. He's probably five thousand miles away by now. Plus, you've got a family; I don't. You've got vulnerabilities that these guys could exploit."

"It's your problem, it's my problem. I don't like that they held a gun on my friend, the G-man. We'll cover each other's back.

'Nuff said about that. I'm in. Now, you want some coleslaw and beans with those ribs, or are you gonna go primal and just eat the baby backs?"

"Put me in for the whole enchilada."

Leonard stood up and called for Vanessa and the kids, then started making plates for me to pass around. When he finally handed me one, he said, "Vulnerabilities. Kiss my leg, tiny man. You see the guns on this bitch? I'll show you vulnerabilities."

I laughed as Vanessa and kids and the dog came scrambling to us, then I dug into the food, eating ravenously, as if I hadn't eaten in days.

While his wife and kids chattered, Leonard frowned and cocked his head, looking at me. "Did you say the church they found that girl by was the Eliathah in Tamarac?"

"Yeah. Know it?"

"I do. Remote spot. But, hey, do you know what Eliathah is— or more accurately, who he was?"

"If it's from the Bible, I'm afraid not."

"Hedonist. Well, I'll tell you, seeing's how I'm a saved soul."

"Do tell, Father Cotton."

"Eliathah is from the Chronicles in the Bible. Chapter twenty-five. You know all those people had sons, who had sons, who had more sons. Musta been a buncha horny bastards back then…or they didn't have big-screen TVs to pass the time. Anyway, it goes like this: David meets this dude named Asaph and he becomes a musician in his choir. There were some other dudes, too, all musicians, and God gave them all sons. Lots of sons, and daughters, too. Let's see how those verses go…'The first lot came for Asaph and Joseph, the second to Gedaliah, who with his brethren'— that's what they called the brothers back then—'and the sons were twelve. The third to Zaccur, he and his sons and brethren were twelve.' See they had them by the dozen in those days, you know, like eggs, I guess. Then it's, 'The fourth to Izri, and his sons and brethren were twelve,' and so on, I don't remember all the names, until we get to the *twentieth* child, who was Eliathah, and his sons and brethren were twelve. It goes on and on, sons and brothers of sons and brothers. Don't remember what was so special about Eliathah, though. But that's how it goes, in case you're interested."

Leonard wrapped up his sermon and dived into his food with reckless abandon. He didn't give it another thought. But I did. I began to think of sons and brothers, of offspring. That was the word that got stuck in my head. *Offspring.* A stupid little word, almost silly sounding, really. But for the rest of the day, I couldn't get it out of my mind.

TWENTY-THREE

Journal: The Chosen One

Subject: 56QAH/Lot 656

The turbulence from the chopper blades pushed the saw grass down like a giant's invisible foot. They had landed, in military-speak, about a half klick from the target site. Stealth and surprise would be the only special tactics used here tonight. Sure, they could have launched a couple of RPGs into the building and blown it to hell, but this was a test of the man, not a siege on the target.

The target site was a CBS block building about one hundred feet long and about half as wide, not unlike the prison barracks the detainees came from. There was a makeshift boundary of concertina wire around the compound, perfunctory, which existed only to lend the site more realism. There was a smaller building to the west of the prison in which its officers and guards would reside between shifts guarding the men.

The men, or prisoners, were a dozen from Guantanamo, scheduled to be repositioned in the United States in various federal penitentiaries. This site was designed, according to federal records, to be a detention site only, not for long-term residence, security minimal due to its isolated location in the middle of the Everglades. These were the hardest of the prisoners, those who would not break under any method of torture; waterboarding to them was like their daily bath, and they often laughed as their interrogators tried to use the technique to extract information from them. Sometimes they would feign defeat and offer up insider information that would lead their torturers directly to Osama Bin Laden—information that, once translated, would actually prove to be the recipe for *qaboli palao*, the national dish of Afghanistan. When beaten on the soles of their feet or having their genitals electrocuted, they would often ask for more. Every one of them had tried to escape at least once, some many times, and several of them had killed either other inmates whom they deemed to be infidels or the occasional hapless guard who had grown careless around them.

The squad that exited the helicopter double-stepped it to the location and the test subject prepared himself for entry. The rest of them were there for observation. Given the distance from any city lights, the starlight was bright, and the approach would be the most dangerous part of the mission. The test subject was allowed to choose his weapons and picked his favorite combat knife with a hand-guard, a standard-issue .45 handgun, and two incendiary grenades.

"Any gasoline or fuel nearby?" asked the test subject.

"There are some Hummers parked next to the building. They could have some jerry cans on board."

"Hope you ain't thinking about driving out of here with one of them Hummers," said one of the squad, the one with his head shaved, his slightly tilted, almond-shaped eyes lending him an almost Asian appearance, though he actually hailed from the Carolinas—in fact, Wolf Mountain, where generations of inbreeding had produced some rather bizarre physical and behavioral tendencies.

The test subject ignored him.

"They've already killed the guards in there. Brave Marines who knew what they were getting into and still made the ultimate sacrifice."

The test subject smeared swatches of green and black camo paint on his face so it would not shine in the starlight.

"This ain't gonna be as easy as guttin' a few unsuspectin' whores in a controlled environment," said the Carolina man.

The test subject ignored him and took off running, first along the edge of the saw grass, then flattening himself onto the ground and into the long shadow cast by the building itself. In the shadow he became invisible, so that the squad could only see him through infrared goggles.

Watching under cover of the saw grass, the squad saw him enter the building. A few of them held their breath, waiting for the gunfire that would surely come from the test subject or from the al-Qaeda fighters inside who had already overpowered the guards, taken their weapons, and skinned them alive.

There was no gunfire, however, only isolated screams that sounded as though they came from men who had been disemboweled and had time to bemoan their demise before bleeding to death. For each of those waiting outside, a squad of men who excelled at killing and endured little regret, the quiet brought out a primordial fear, and each of them, to the last one, felt a chunk of ice form in his belly.

Inside, the test subject moved like a ghost. He knew that each of the al-Qaeda fighters would be using the cover provided by their environment—in this case, the dark and shadows—as a tool of war, because that was what they were trained to do. In their native land, it was the harsh landscape, the outcropping of brush-covered rock ledges on mountains, the naturally occurring caves in which they could take refuge after a quick sniper attack or from which they could launch a surprise attack. Their skillful use of their environment was why they had won a war against Russia, though they had been outnumbered and outgunned by exponential amounts. It was why they were winning the war against the United States now. They were the ultimate guerilla warriors, fervently dedicated, not only to a cause, but to God, Allah, himself. Still, they were no match for him.

He did not hesitate as he moved through the building. It was as if he *knew* where each one of them would be. He took a round or two into his Kevlar vest from those few who were not frozen with fear. Allah or not, it's easier for a man to make a martyr of himself if he does so witnessed, encouraged, and acknowledged by his compatriots. Bravery and martyrdom are just words when you're in the dark, alone, and listening to the sounds of your own racing heart, or the rattling, dying breath of a comrade as an unseen killer stalks you.

He never fired his own weapon but dispatched all twelve of them with his knife and hands, slicing some of their throats, stabbing some in their chests, slicing lungs or major blood vessels, always going for the death stroke on the first strike. He stabbed one of them directly in his head, through a fright-filled eye he saw gleaming up at him from the dark. His blade became stuck and one of the Afghans took advantage of the moment and attacked him. The subject could have shot him, but chose instead to rip his throat out with his viselike fingers.

On his way out to get the gas cans from the Hummer outside, he found one of the guards who had been overcome by the prisoners. He had been beaten and tied up with an electrical cord, saved for use as a possible hostage.

"Thank God!" the guard said as the test subject moved over to him. "How many are you? Where's the rest of your outfit?"

The test subject looked at him by the dim starlight illuminating the room in which the guard had been held captive, his head cocked to the side, like a dog trying to understand the incomprehensible words of its master.

"It's just me," the test subject said quietly, wiping some blood that had sprayed into his face with the sleeve of his shirt. He took out his knife and the guard audibly sighed with relief, believing his savior was going to cut the cords that bound him. Instead, his savior lashed across his abdomen with the knife and began pulling out his intestines. The guard was alive long enough to ask him what he was doing, but the killer did not answer as he wrapped the man's intestines around his neck, several times, and strangled him with his own organs.

The test subject retrieved the gasoline and spread the liquid through the building, pausing in each room to douse the bodies of each dead soldier. Departing the prison, now a death-filled offal house, he lobbed an incendiary grenade inside and watched it burn white for a second, then ignite the building with a roar.

Walking back to the mercenary squad, listening to some of them applaud his actions, he removed his knife from its sheath once more, wiping the blade on his sleeve, as if an afterthought of caring for his weapon. Then he plunged the blade into the throat of the Carolina soldier.

"You're right, Carolina, that wasn't as easy as killing those whores," said Haskell. Then he turned to the rest of the group and asked, "Any more comments from the peanut gallery?"

• • •

This is the one, then. This one, while crude, is my near equal in skill, cunning, and boldness, if I must say so myself. This was what I'd pictured could be done if my DNA was weaponized. That had been the intent of my project, the one they came to call the "Armageddon Project." The one they pulled me away from, so to speak. The one Cerberus has exploited and from which he is obviously profiting. Why have they waited so long to put it in place? What is the urgency now, with the current administration wanting to pull out of the war?

Cerberus is the man who holds all the answers, but he is too insulated from me. He's constantly surrounded by his special ops soldiers and keeps me at a distance, feeding me information from afar. He arranged for my freedom and has given me access to my old research, to my old files, and to incredible technology and databases so that I could locate my "experiments." But there is something he is not telling me. Perhaps a closer look at some of the "candidates" will yield the answers I need.

I must find out. And if I do not like what I find, a lot of people are going to die. I found these offspring, even helped this test subject transform into what they are looking for, gave him knowledge and guidance. (Never leave your DNA in the victim!)

But if what I am beginning to sense is true, I will kill him. I will kill them all.

TWENTY-FOUR

Journal: Corruption

Miami
　　Subject: 56QAH/Lot 836
　　Up to now, all of those in the 56QAH lineage had been Americans. Imagine my surprise and dismay as I began to discover foreign recipients...

• • •

I was having some unsettling suspicions, so I watched this one closely for several days. He was different from the others, though I knew he shared some of their—some of *our*—unique traits. He still had the gray temples, but the rest of his hair was as thick as a bear's and as black as pitch, the product of his Arabic lineage. The eyes were dark but not particularly penetrating, perhaps because of his brainwashing; it diminished his intensity somehow. And, of course, he was dark-skinned, with heavily whiskered jowls, lacking the fine skin and bone structure of the other subjects.

　　I followed him from a nightclub in which he had picked up a drunken American girl, a trollop with bottle-blonde hair and abundant belly fat. He fixed that roly-poly problem by opening her up with a knife and dissecting her in an alley behind the nightclub.

Whether he was disgusted by the taste of her tongue in his mouth, or because he had wanted to further illustrate his hatred of Americans, he spit on the ground on the way out of the alley, leaving his victim in a bloody heap in a dumpster, covered by a discarded cardboard appliance box. Of course, I collected his spit and analyzed it. The DNA was positive for the trait, and so I knew.

Now, I had the proof of my suspicions. I knew what had to have happened. Cerberus had found a way to make money from both the US government and from the Afghans. Who else could do it? Who else had his access to the leaders who would see the potential in his schemes? He had sold all of my seed, and now the demand was back up and he didn't have any "product." Thus, my freedom. Release me to find those subjects that had matured— aged like fine wine—and determine if they were useful and/or able to produce more profitable product. Motherfucker.

I had been in this subject's home and found his plans; he wasn't very careful, and once again, I found myself wondering about the capabilities of Homeland Security to uphold what it was formed for in the first place. I found out where he was taking his flight lessons: Ft. Lauderdale Executive Airport, the same one where Mohamed Atta, one of the terrorist pilots from 9/11, took his lessons, for God's sake! I had even found his planned target, the Sun Life Stadium where the Miami Dolphins play football. It appeared he was going to fly a crop duster over the stadium and disperse atomized ricin, a poison of which five hundred micro-grams—about the size of half a grain of sand—is lethal when inhaled. The irony was that by killing this one, I was probably saving hundreds, if not thousands, of lives.

Damn me.

I followed him again a few days later. This time he went into a gay bar and emerged with a hunky young man wearing a leather jacket, no shirt, and tight cutoff jeans. They ducked into a car, and when I saw it rocking with their, shall we say, physical exertions, I was almost nauseated. While they were locked up like two dogs in heat, I approached the car and smashed out the rear window. They could not extricate themselves quickly enough, their pants down around their ankles acting as self-imposed shackles. I poured a container of gas on them, then tossed in a flash-bang grenade, which further disoriented them just as it set them afire.

I'm not particularly homophobic, but for a number of reasons, their screams were music to my ears. Perhaps, for once, I was actually angry because I now had proof of my suspicions.

● ● ●

The problem with outsourcing government services is that while you can assign a task, you cannot assign loyalty, patriotism, or fidelity. The very clear logic of outsourcing, in itself, should be clear to those who seek it: if someone will do something for money, then they will surely do the same thing for someone else, for more money.

I am a serial killer, but I am not a terrorist.

It's time to stop this project, this abomination.

TWENTY-FIVE

The next morning's sky was brushed with pastel shades of lavender, yellow, and rose, and offered promise as much as beauty. Maybe that was just the perspective I wanted to put on it and a good night's rest had helped persuade me to do it.

I had not talked to Rose since I'd dropped her off, and myriad and conflicting thoughts of her in trouble with her job, in danger for her life because of this case, or in bed with her supervisor ran through my head like the chaotic thoughts of a true psychotic. *Let it go, Grey. She's a big girl, smart one, too. She's not looking for an armored knight to come to her rescue; much as you'd like to be that knight, she might not even want you at the castle. Either way, whether she continues with the case or not, you have your teeth into it and your own motivations. Let the rubber hit the road and quit thinking about the drive.*

I walked out onto the deck in the backyard to drink my coffee and saw Emily was already in the stable, brushing down Sisco and preparing for a ride. She was wearing her riding pants and boots and a tight white T-shirt, her body in full young-woman bloom. Her hair was strawberry blonde, long and straight, her pale skin flushed in the cheeks. Her blue eyes matched the sky and were full of hope. My heart ached for her. She was such a good person, and

189

those are the ones who are so easily and often hurt by the callous majority of people on this planet. I wished it wasn't that way, but it was.

"Hey," I called down to her, "what're you doing to that horse out there?"

Emily turned to look at me and waved like a person stranded on an island waving to a rescue helicopter. "Hi, Grey! What do you think I'm doing to this horse? I'm getting ready to ride him. No one else does," she said, giving me a friendly jab back, and added, "He looooooves me. Doncha, Sisco?"

Sisco nodded his big head up and down as if agreeing with her, then began to sniff at her pockets, which were always filled with chunks of carrots. Watching the two of them lifted my heart and made me think good thoughts about the world again, but it was a momentary contentment. As I watched Emily mount Sisco, I saw his flank quiver, trying to shake off a horsefly or some other pest—a completely normal thing for a horse to do. But later, the image of that movement would come back to me in one of my seizure-addled dreams and signify something evil aborning, a coming pestilence, a dark and malevolent harbinger whose presence and actions would forever change the course of all of our lives. But at that moment, I could not see that darkness, and I watched the two of them trot around the perimeter of my ten-acre plot, then head out onto the rider's path that meandered through the equestrian home sites of Wellington, Emily's hair and Sisco's mane catching the wind and lifting gracefully like angel's wings.

I thought I heard the doorbell ring, and Scout started barking. I snapped back to reality. My initial thought was that it was Rose, coming to pick me up and continue with the investigation. I yelled to Emily to have a good ride and be safe, but she was already beyond the sound of my voice. I turned and went in to answer my door.

I was a little disappointed when I opened the door and did not find Rose. Instead, I found a woman with tousled red hair and emerald-green framed glasses at my door, wearing jeans and a pressed white button-down shirt with dramatically pointed lapels. She wore too much perfume, a designer fragrance that I could not quite identify, though I knew it was expensive. Her lips and fingernails were matching ruby red, her skin flawless. She wore emerald studs for earrings and a heart-shaped emerald necklace. She looked like the leprechaun queen.

Behind her was a white van, its double back doors hanging wide open. I heard someone rummaging around in the vehicle.

"Can I help you?" I asked the leprechaun lady.

"Why, yes, Mis-tuh Gift, or shall I call you Grey?" she said with a Dixieland drawl, then jerked her thumb over her shoulder in the direction of the van. "You can help me greatly, if you do not give that man any more coffee. But I'll have some! Oh, by the way, I'm Dr. Pogue. You and I actually met once, a few years ago, at a conference. Call me Amy."

"I think I would remember if we had met…"

She stepped past me into my home. "I look a lot different in a white lab coat with my hair up. But I remember you. May I use your restroom to freshen up?"

"Sure. Down the…uh…hall to the right." She was already halfway down the hall. "Coffee's in the kitchen over there."

"You might check on Cecil," she called back. "He probably needs help carrying in the equipment."

"Oh…okay."

I went out to the van, and sure enough, there was Cecil, tugging at a black box, roughly the size of a big carry-on.

"Morning, Cecil."

He jerked around and looked at me, a crazed look in his eyes. Cecil is nothing to look at, physically. His curly, dishwater-blond hair is swiftly receding from his forehead, and he's skinny and slightly hunched over, maybe about five foot eight, with absolutely no muscle tone. His eyes are wide, seemingly out of focus most of the time, and kind of buggy. If he died and were reincarnated as an animal tomorrow, it would be as a bush baby.

"Yes," he said. "Yes, it is morning." Then, in a conspiratorial tone, he said, "Hey, you met Amy, right? Is she hot, or what?"

"She's...uh...pretty."

"I told you so. And listen, man, it is *on* with us. You know what I mean?"

"I...think so."

He looked back toward the house. "You have no idea," he whispered. "She's brilliant, which is a turn-on to me in the first place. And rich, which is nice. And *insatiable* in bed. Do you have any Viagra, Grey? I'll buy some from you. Just a couple to get through this week."

"Sorry, bud. I'm still going natural."

"Damn. Oh well, maybe she'll slow down once she tires of me. Maybe she's like a cat with a toy, you know? Here, give me a hand with this."

He had been pulling on the case with all his weight. I grabbed it by its handle and picked it up with one hand. It weighed maybe thirty to forty pounds.

"Can you carry that yourself?" asked Cecil.

"I'll manage, Samson. Good to see you, by the way. What's in here?"

"The future, my friend. Truly, the future."

"Well, let's get the future into the house. Want some…" I caught myself, remembering the caution about the coffee. "Breakfast?"

"Sure, got any coffee?"

"Uh, I just finished the high octane, but I think I have some decaf in there."

"Decaf? Yuck. Thank God, I have some Red Bulls in the cooler."

"When did you guys get in?"

"Late yesterday afternoon. I was going to call you, but when we got to the hotel room and Amy said there was no need to get two rooms…well, let's just say my attentions were drawn elsewhere."

"Still want to marry her?"

"If you were a notary, I'd put you to work right now. You know I'm as attracted to her mind as much as her body."

"Riiiight."

"Wait till you see this little baby," he said, pointing to the black case. "I hope you don't mind us using your house to set up our temp lab."

"Not at all. Plenty of room if you guys want to stay here, too."

Cecil looked at me with a very serious expression on his face. "We'd keep you awake all night."

"Animals!"

Cecil pointed at the case again and shook his head in disbelief. "The *future*."

We took the case into the house, where we found Amy in the kitchen, just finishing off the pot of coffee.

"All right, kids," I said, laying the case on the counter. "Tell me what you brought me."

Cecil looked to Amy. "May I?"

"Of course, sweetie. Show him your new toy."

Cecil trembled with glee as he popped open the latches on the case, and pronounced, "*Voila!*"

Cecil pulled out a black box, roughly thirty inches by thirty inches and maybe ten inches tall. It had dials, gauges, inputs, out- puts, and a hole in the top with a myriad of wires sticking out.

"You brought me a new stereo amplifier?"

"Tool," said Cecil. "You tell him, Amy. It's your invention. I'm not sure I could do it justice."

Amy smiled at him, came over, and stroked his wild hair out of his face and ran her fingers down his cheek. "You're so sweet." She carried her smile over to me as she began her dissertation.

"This, Grey, is a portable DNA detector."

"Cool. But how fast can it give us a reading?"

She moved around the object like Vanna White showcasing a new car. "We put a DNA sample in here, which is then replicated by the unit's one-hundred-sixty-nanoliters-polymerase chain reactor, or PCR, as we call it. The PCR is coupled with an on-chip heater and temperature sensor. The PCR reagents are exposed to three distinct temperatures for a certain amount of time and use a separation channel to analyze the DNA with capillary electro- phoresis."

"You had me through portable DNA detector—after that, I was lost. How long does it take to make a positive match?"

"As little as two hours," she said, grinning ear to ear. "We can get a complete analysis as good as any full-size lab in six."

"Incredible."

Cecil could not contain himself. "Amy took Dr. Mathies's research—you know, the professor from Berkeley?"

"Uh, no."

"Well, she took some of his research and, shall we say, enhanced it, utilizing microphotolithographic CE systems—uh, basically computer chips, if you will, that can do the analysis a hundred times faster than conventional methods. Want me to blow your mind? Get this, the little redheaded girl here has actually developed ultra-high-gain cascaded PCR reactors that use chip-based logic circuits with the *DNA acting as the information carriers* to microfluidic wires within the system. You know, this might be insider trade information, but you really ought to buy some stock in Amy's company."

"Sounds like it," I said, not having the vaguest clue what either one of them was talking about. "Can we use it now?"

Amy shrugged. "That's what we're here for, isn't it? Do you have some samples?"

"I sure do. I've got some hair and a toothbrush from a suspect's home. I also have some sausage I'd like you to look at, and some fleas."

"Fleas?" asked Cecil.

"The sausage is odd," said Amy, sticking one of her ruby fingernails into her tangerine hair and scratching her scalp. "But fleas make sense, Cecil. They're blood suckers. If they hold a little blood from one of their hosts, it can be extracted."

"That's what I was hoping you would say," I said. "Did you bring the urine sample I sent up for analysis?"

"Yes, and we can use it for a comparison, but as I believe Cecil told you, I had to amplify the sample, which is fine if it's a good sample—say, from blood or saliva—but urine doesn't produce the best samples to begin with, doesn't have enough of the cells we need, so it wasn't a great barometer for us. Still, if you have additional samples, we can cross-match and see where that takes us."

"Sounds good."

Amy turned to Cecil. "Cecil, would you be a good boy and go get that chem box I had you lug out to the van? We'll have to do some chemical breakdowns with the hair, for sure, probably the fleas and the sausage…hmmm…that's going to need to be broken way down, for sure."

"If the sausage is a problem, don't worry about it," I said. "I just need to know if it's…uh…well, if it's from an animal or human."

"Oh, why didn't you say so? I can tell that pretty quick."

"Oh, how?" I asked.

"By the taste, silly."

I'm not sure what the look on my face was, but I could see that even Cecil, as nutty as he could be, was taken aback.

Amy looked back and forth between us, with a stunned and hurt look on her face. "I was just joking, boys. Geez. Lighten up."

TWENTY-SIX

Journal: Betrayal

*Using my access to his own top-secret database—did he think I was
too stupid to learn this new technology?—I was able to access Cerberus's files and track his "sales" from some thirty years ago. What
I found was that, after I was removed from the project, Cerberus
must have had a fire sale.*

*His mistake? Thinking that I would not care what happened to
my "seeds."*

• • •

Afghanistan

Subjects: 56QAH/Lots 1244–1303

Orange light flickered from a small campfire inside the cave.
The shrouded man spoke softly, but with a fevered gleam in his
eyes. He was tall, even seated, and projected saintliness and oth-
erworldliness. This was his gift and strength. It is what drew his
followers to him. That, and his endless supply of oil- and opiate-
earned money.

He addressed this new group of followers. These were special men. The ones his predecessors had "ordered." The ones who
would do anything he wanted them to do, not so much because

of their religious convictions and allegiance to Allah, but because they *wanted* to do it.

These were the men who would place explosives on their bodies and walk into crowded markets in order to see that briefest look of terror in their victims' eyes before they exploded themselves and killed dozens of others. They were the men who would gleefully fly a commercial airliner full of Western infidels into a skyscraper in a metropolis that was the very symbol of the gross eccentricities of the American dogs. These men could devise ways to torture, disrupt, infect, murder, and terrorize the enemy in ways that he could not imagine, because he was not one of them. His actions were for his ideals. Their actions were for their own enjoyment.

They were perfect for what he needed. They only needed to be guided, shown the way. He might suggest some level of depravity in which they could dispatch their enemies. But just as often, he found that they exceeded even his rich imagination. When working in unison, they could be particularly malevolent. He recalled when two of them working together had surprised and disarmed a group of Coalition fighters outside the village of Nishagam. There, in front of all the villagers, they had skinned the men down to their muscles. The torture took the entire day. Of course, some were disemboweled, and they forced some of the others to eat their friends' intestines while they were still alive, even as they cried out in pain and disbelief. When some of the soldiers had squeezed their eyes shut in order to save themselves from this additional visual torture, the two men had simply cut their eyelids off. Finally, they burned them all, and many were still alive, so that the whole village would remember not only the sight but the sound of being an infidel.

The rebel leader shivered, thinking about the sheer evil inherent in these men. He reassured himself by touching the automatic weapon he kept under his robes. He would never be in the same space with these particular soldiers without having a weapon, because the other thing he knew about them was that they were completely unpredictable. While they had pledged their allegiance to him and al-Qaeda, their own motivations could take over at any time. Their need to witness, cause, or exacerbate the pain and suffering of other human beings was insatiable, unstoppable, and insane. Simply, they could not help themselves. It was in their genes.

TWENTY-SEVEN

I had a couple of hours to kill until the portable DNA analysis spit out whatever information it was going to, so I drove to my office in West Palm Beach to check in with Captain Brandsma. Driving out of Wellington, eyeing some of the palatial equestrian estates, I had to marvel, once again, at my mother's tenacity and business savvy. She had been a nurse, raising two kids on her own, but once she could begin to save two nickels, she did, then began to invest them in the then-lucrative Florida real estate market. These investments were often our homes. We'd pick up and move every few years—not far, and not to the point where we had to abandon all our friends, because once you were a friend of Nurse "Mo" Gift, as she came to be known by nurses, patients, and doctors in area hospitals and clinics, you were a friend for life. But with each one of these moves, Mo would turn a profit, then put a chunk of it into the next home, and the next, and so on.

Raised on a farm in Missouri, her ultimate goal was to have a home with some land around it where she could keep some horses and have some breathing room. She managed to find that in Wellington just as the area was coming out of the ground, when land and construction were affordable. Before Merv Griffith and Zsa Zsa Gabor and, later, Madonna and Bruce Springsteen moved into the neighborhood. Where, on any given day, you can look out your window and see flocks of white-feathered ibis hunched over manicured lawns, pecking through the grass like addicts looking for crack rocks in the carpet, while purebred horses worth hundreds of thousands of dollars prance in the polo fields in front of a backdrop of Ferraris, Porsches, and Maybachs.

Mo did all right for herself. Shrewd as a Scotsman, she quietly managed to tuck some money away and keep her family fed and clothed and content. It was a lesson she drilled into her children's heads, and one of the first things I did when I began my career with the fire service was to buy a condo on the beach so I could watch the sun set and rise, along with the equity in my home. I still own the condo, but when Mo grew too frail to care for herself, I ended up staying with her so much that it was smarter to just rent out my place. After she passed, I found I cared too much for her other tenants—Scout and Sisco—to move back.

Bland Sam was eating out of a box of glazed donuts when I came into the office. He looked up from his computer screen and licked the sugar off of his fingers with obvious content, his ruddy countenance aglow with a sugar high.

"Don't look at me like that," he said. "Want one?"

"I wouldn't think of depriving you. Besides, look at that body," I teased, eyeing his girth.

"Fag. Hey, glad you're here, though. You know a guy named Rasmussen?"

"I know who he is. Bigwig with the FBI. Southeast regional supervisor, or something?"

"Yeah, something like that. You have words with him?"

"Not at all. Why?"

"I got a call from Chief Dugger at BSO this morning. He told me this Rasmussen guy called him and asked him about his involvement in that arson homicide in Tamarac. Dugger told him he was support on that case only because that FBI gal you were hanging with the other day took the case away from him and *she* was the lead on it. He asked about your involvement and Dugger told him that you were called in as a burn expert only, to investigate cause of fire, et cetera. That about right?"

"As far as anyone has to know."

Brandsma squinted his eyes at me for a long moment. "Talk to me, 'cause I have a feeling I'm going to be getting a call pretty soon telling us to butt out."

"What you don't know can't hurt you."

"Yeah, I hear you, but I don't want to be caught off guard."

"Okay. Tell them I picked up some samples, sent it in, and we found out the accelerant used on the Matarese girl was gasoline. Case closed for us."

"Was it gasoline?"

"No. Cecil Button tells me it was jet fuel."

"And why do we want to lie to the federal government?"

"There's a lot of weird stuff going on, Sam. They're not wanting to play in my sandbox, so I don't want to play in theirs."

"C'mon. Don't make me beg. What the hell is going on?"

So I filled him in, just as I had Leonard. I told him about Haskell, and Cerberus showing up and telling us to lay off the case, and the fingerprint found at the murder scene that belonged to the dead prisoner, Gettys. I included the part about me wanting to continue with the investigation, even if the Feds didn't want me to.

"Kid," he said, "you haven't been around here long enough to realize the repercussions of doing something like this. The Feds call you off, you're off."

"I was hoping you wouldn't say that."

"Of course, if you wanted to take a couple days vacation, what you do is up to you."

"Can I keep Cecil?"

"Who?" he said, then added, "See you in a couple days, and don't tell me how you spent your vacation. And be safe. You're a wackadoo sometimes, but you're pretty good at your job, if I never told you."

"Uh, thanks, I think. Nice to know you care…Dad."

"Ah, get out of here," he said, picking up a donut as though he were going to throw it at me. Of course, I knew he would rather throw me the deed to his home than lose that donut. "You know that's why I don't tell people those things. They make fun."

TWENTY-EIGHT

When I got back home, I found Cecil and Dr. Pogue flushed with excitement, their lab coats askew.

"You two been fogging the windows in here?" I joked.

They looked at each other as if they were kids caught doing something they weren't supposed to be doing.

"Of course not, Mr. Gift," said Amy, trying to act as if her dignity were bruised, then busting out laughing.

"Actually, no, Grey, we weren't fornicating all over your house…yet," said Cecil, giving his new girl a wink. "But we are very excited about what we found." He jumped up and dragged me over to the computer screen next to the portable DNA machine they'd been using. They had completed their analysis of the hair and toothbrush samples from Haskell's home, as well as an animated comparison of those samples against the urine sample from the Tamarac scene. They had also analyzed the sausage sample and found it to be…pork.

"See the similarities between the samples, Grey?" asked Cecil.

"I do. They're very close, but they don't seem to be *exact* matches."

"You're right," said Amy. "Which means, if this went to a court of law and your suspect had a good attorney, he probably wouldn't get convicted using these samples, even though they are so close. The difference in the variable number tandem repeats, or VNTRs, in the strands are less than one-tenth of a percent. But when we looked at the sample taken from the fleas, we got three distinct VNTRs."

Cecil pointed to the screen now that showed three vividly different strands and their VNTR counts and variances in percentages at the bottom of the screen. "This first one on the left is the dog—easily discernable. The other two are human, of course, one being the girl, we assume, as it contains female components and was identified in most of the fleas you collected, though we did not have a sample from the victim for exact comparison. But now, this one on the right is...well, just watch."

Amy tapped a couple of the keys on the computer, discarding the dog and the girl's samples, and floated in the screen with Haskell's sample, then overlapped it with the one remaining sample's image. They were exact, with the percentage number on the bottom of the screen racing up in number until it read, *100%*, then blinking the words *POSITIVE MATCH.*

I had to think about what the evidence was telling us, though. It would appear that Haskell had been at the Matarese girl's apartment but that either someone else had been at the scene in the church parking lot or we had managed to screw up the sample I'd taken from the victim's clothing. This last possibility seemed to be the most justifiable, in that the samples were so close that if it wasn't Haskell's DNA, slightly altered from the amplification process Cecil had explained to me previously, then there had to have been a second person at the murder site, and that person was so close to Haskell's DNA that they would almost have to be related. I shared my thoughts with Cecil and Dr. Pogue.

"Well, duh," said Cecil. "We thought that was rather obvious."

"Maybe to you two nerds. I'm still just trying to learn the vocabulary here."

"Sorry," said Amy. "You're right. I do this all the time. But your conclusions are the same as ours. Those samples are so close, the donors almost have to be related."

It was something about the way she said *donors* that caused a sensation in my head, like what I imagine hypoglycemic people feel when they haven't eaten. I felt dizzy, and the memory of what I'd seen during my seizure at lunch the day before drifted into my head and held me there, like seeing the image of a lightbulb even after the light is turned off. But it was only the old man again as he stumbled and I went to pick him up, and he touched my wrist...

"Grey? Hey, dude. You okay?" asked Cecil, his face inches from mine.

I looked down at my arm and Amy was holding my wrist, checking my pulse. "You just had a seizure, Mr. Gift," she said.

"I did?"

"Yes," she said. "Your eyelids fluttered, then you sat down. Good thing you had a chair behind you."

I looked from her to Cecil and back again.

"It didn't last long, Grey," said Cecil. "Only a few seconds. You feel okay? I thought you were over those."

"I thought so, too," I said, trying to regather my wits.

"I'll get you some water," said Amy.

"Thank you," I said as she walked away briskly.

"You okay, man?" Cecil asked.

"Yeah. I've been getting these absence seizures again, just lately. Maybe it's stress. I'm kind of over my head with this case, you know?"

"You seem to be holding your own...for a fire guy. You talk to a doctor yet?"

"No."

"Well," he said, but did not belabor the speech. "We have something else to show you, if you feel up to it. It's in your office."

Amy brought the water into my office just as Cecil sat me down facing the computer. I took a sip of water, feeling its coolness spread through my throat and all the way down to my stomach as they began to explain their next discovery.

"We were going to do a search for some other genetic information because the laptop was working up to its capacity with the DNA analysis, and we found this. What's really cool," said Cecil, wiggling his eyebrows like a perverted Groucho Marx, "is that you have a new *friend* in the FBI who logged on to your computer but never logged off."

"But her access was denied," I said.

"We saw that, but Amy used to be quite the hacker and was able to get into Agent Cleary's departmental access."

"Yeah," said Amy. "It took all of my computer savvy and technical know-how. I hit the refresh button and it let me in."

"They must have restored her access," I said, but inwardly wondered what deal, or compromise, Rose had to make to get her access back.

"What we did was access their bio-research files and did a search to see if they had any similar DNA chains like those we had found. This list popped up."

They showed me a file of similar hits in a document that was filled with brief descriptions of crimes and included geographic location, time of murder, victims' names, if available (there were a few Jane Does), and the suspects' names, again, if available. Very few suspects with this particular DNA sequence had been apprehended. Most were marked *UNSOLVED*.

I scrolled down and kept scrolling. There were dozens, if not hundreds.

"Wow. Can this be right? Could that many people have similar DNA?"

Cecil looked to Amy to answer, as she was the expert in that field.

"In a word," she said, "no."

"So what does it mean?"

"It means that either we have one killer who has been working for years and years or we have someone at least related to your suspect who is doing these killings. And it would appear he or she has been working a long time, too."

"Could that be possible?"

"You're the detective," said Cecil. "We're just the genius sidekicks. The only other explanation is there has been a bunch of DNA wrongly analyzed, or the data was entered wrong into their file system. And that, to me, is as hard to believe as a family of serial killers working for years without getting caught."

I continued looking at the data. Many of them were very recent, up to and including the day before. As I read them, I remembered Rose getting a bunch of text messages while we were at lunch on Saturday. She had described some of them to me and I looked to see if they might be on the list. I did not have names, so I couldn't be sure, but I found the incidents, or some so similar it would be foolish to think they weren't the same ones.

And I got an idea.

I was about to make a suggestion to my fellow researchers when I heard the doorbell ring. My office has a window that allows me to look outside and, if I crane my head around to the right, see who is at the front door. It was Rose Cleary and her "boss," David Rasmussen.

"Shit," I said.

"What?" said Cecil and Amy simultaneously.

"It's the FBI."

"So?"

"So, they might not like us going through their files, for one major thing. Also, if they kicked one of their own agents off of the Haskell case and denied her access, they sure as hell don't want me or a couple of my egghead friends poking around in it."

"I'll start breaking down the machine," said Amy.

"I'll start hiding it," said Cecil.

"That only leaves me one thing to do."

"What?" asked Cecil.

"Stall."

TWENTY-NINE

I opened the door and greeted Rose. She played it all business, giving me a handshake, but I noticed a slight, knowing Mona Lisa smile and her eyes shone.

Rasmussen stood a few feet behind her. With his square jaw, steely gray eyes, and fresh haircut, he looked like Captain America in a Hugo Boss suit.

Rose started to speak, but Rasmussen interrupted her. "Inspector Gift? I'm Branch Director David Rasmussen. May we talk for a few minutes?" He shoved his hand in my direction. I took it, noting the firm, dry, manicured grip of a politician.

I glanced at Rose, but now her face was blank. No help there.

"Sure," I said. I was going to ask them in and hope like hell that my overachieving friends had hidden their gadgets and logged out of Rose's file access, but Rasmussen nodded for me to follow him back down the drive.

It was a warm morning, but we walked in shade provided by the huge royal poinciana trees that lined the drive, their huge, gnarly roots gripping the earth like giant arthritic fingers.

"Agent Cleary tells me you were a lot of help to her on this case," Rasmussen said without looking at me. "The FBI is grateful."

"I needed to hear that from you?"

Now Rasmussen turned those steely eyes on me and made them go hard. When people do that, it makes me want to slap the shit out of them.

"Well," he said, "Mueller is not going to come down, so you'll have to accept my gratitude."

"And where are you on the food chain?"

"National Security Branch. I head the Counterintelligence Division."

"Wow."

"Yeah. Wow." He stopped walking, and we faced each other. He pursed his lips and squinted his eyes as if deciding how much he wanted to, or could, tell me. "Look, I know you are aware that I had to halt this investigation, and—"

"Is that normal? I mean, the nation's premier law enforcement agency stopping an investigation of a possible serial killer?"

All of us are capable of juvenile behavior, particularly those of us who think we've outgrown those elements that produce such behavior: jealousy, rejection in love or career, public ostracism, plain old one-upmanship. But none of us is more than a heartbeat away from name-calling, or gossiping, or in the worst of us, fisticuffs. Sometimes my own thoughts embarrass me.

The branch director narrowed his eyes. "It is when the Department of Justice, by directive of the Department of Defense, tells us to and invokes the Patriot Act when they do."

I had a million questions, starting with if he thought Clarence Matarese, an out-of-luck, homeless mechanic whose only daughter was gutted and cooked like a pig at a Cuban barbecue, gave a fuck about the Patriot Act. But I kept my thoughts and my words to myself. I'm sure Rose didn't need the heat, and I wanted to defuse his interest in me, anyway.

"Well," I said, "you guys know best. My part was just to determine what accelerant was used at the murder site. But I'm sure Agent Cleary is frustrated with the dead end."

"She'll be fine," he said confidently, glancing back at her. "*She's* a professional. Besides, there are a dozen other cases we need her on."

"I bet. If there's nothing else, then, I need to get to work."

Rasmussen continued staring at me for a long moment, then said, "Look, I'm not elated with this, either. But this Nicholas Cerberus has connections all the way to the top, and has for over thirty years. He's made millions—hundreds of millions—contracting with the Defense Department. He has as high a security clearance as any US senator. The man dines with world leaders."

"Yeah? Saddam Hussein used to do that as well. These people only have as much power as we give them."

The branch director's face went dark. He turned away and took a deep breath, the muscles in his jaw working. At last, he turned back to me. "I shouldn't be telling you this, but Cerberus has a vested interest in Devon Haskell. And whatever he is, whatever he's done, the Department of Defense has told us hands off. Rose told me the things he might have done. It's sickening but… my hands are tied."

I nodded. I understood he was just following orders; I'd been there, too. But I wasn't going to look the other way while a sadistic killer was on a rampage. That was one thing I knew for certain. "Like I said, I have to get to work."

"Understood. I need to get going, too. Thanks again," he said, as though we'd come to some kind of agreement. He touched the screen on his cell phone on the way back to Rose and the car. By the time we got to her, a sleek jet helicopter whooshed in like the first of the Valkyries coming to the battleground.

"After it drops me off, the chopper will be at your disposal when you need it," Rasmussen told Rose. "I can't send in the rest of the CIRG right now, for obvious reasons, but you've got enough work to keep you busy for a while. We'll talk later."

Rose nodded and Rasmussen strode to the helicopter, a man in charge. The chopper lifted and pulled away, Rasmussen looking out the window and giving us a slight nod. Rose's face remained as emotionless as a statue's as she watched her boss—and possibly, lover—fly away out of sight.

The juvenile set in again. "How much does the devil charge for a soul these days?" I asked.

When she looked at me, her face was a mixing bowl of emotions: she was scowling, but her eyes filled with tears and her lips quivered. She sniffed once and said, "Shut the fuck up." Then she moved into my arms and kissed me. When she pulled away, she said, "I did what I had to do."

"Sorry."

"He says he's protecting me. That's why he pulled me off the case. He had orders and he wouldn't give me specific details. Maybe even he doesn't know it all."

"So, where does that leave you?"

"Well, I guess I have the chopper at my disposal for this pile of other cases. His little guilt payoff for yanking the case, I suppose. But I was told to leave the Haskell case alone, so I have to do that."

"I don't."

"You're right. But I'm not going to beat around the bush: if someone rattled Rasmussen enough for him to shut me down, whatever is behind all this is big and it's dangerous. You're going to have to be very careful and I can only help peripherally. As soon as they think I'm looking into Haskell again, and I'm sure they're monitoring my file access, they'll arrest me and charge me with obstruction."

I cringed; Amy and Cecil had just been in her files. If someone was monitoring Rose's computer, she could be in hot water already. But I couldn't think of a way to tell her without destroying what I felt we'd just gotten back.

"What about me?" I asked her.

"Please don't think I'm being melodramatic here, because this is serious. You could end up dead. There are government-contracted mercenaries involved here, and they don't follow the same rules we have to."

"So we make our own rules. What exactly is Cerberus's business, anyway?"

"He runs a small but elite organization called SEE. It stands for Scorched Earth Enterprises. They are vaguely referred to as 'information control and security.' Think of the upper echelon of Blackwater on special missions."

"If he's so high up the food chain, why is he still out in the field, dirtying his hands and trying to rein in a guy like Haskell?"

"I don't know, but he must see a profit in it."

I rubbed my palm, hard, over my face. "Jesus, am I in over my head."

Rose smiled and wrapped her arm in mine. We headed back toward the house.

"I missed you," I said.

She looked at me and said, "Me, too."

I stopped and took her into my arms then, my hands moving across her back. She felt thinner than she had a couple of days ago. She slid her hand around my neck and pulled my face to hers. Our mouths met and we consumed each other's kiss. She smelled wonderful, her hair a bouquet of flowers, her skin like powder—

"Are we safe?" Cecil had cracked open the front door and was peeking out.

Rose drew back and looked quizzically from Cecil to me.

"Cecil, meet FBI Agent Rose Cleary. Rose, this is Cecil."

"The lab rat?" she said, her smile brightening the morning.

"We prefer lab *weasels* these days, Agent Cleary. Are we cool, Grey?"

"I think we're cool." I looked at Rose and held her at arm's length. "We have something we need to show you."

"Okay," she said, looking puzzled. "But let's be quick. I don't know how long I'm going to get the use of that helicopter."

THIRTY

Journal: Cases Closed

I could not take any chances. If any of them were left alive, Cerberus would find them and exploit them for his own ends. They were mine, God damn it. I would dictate how they were used. No one else!

• • •

South Florida, Miami Gardens
    Subject: 56QAH/Lot 117
    The cop had eaten about half of his BMT sub at Subway when he heard the screech of the car's brakes locking up. He looked out the window, saw the car careening wildly, thick blue smoke pluming off its tires. His eyes darted around, looking for the other car that had perhaps hit this car or pulled in front of it to cause the sudden braking, but there wasn't one. The car was completely sideways in the lane now but stopped, the car and driver rocking back and forth as if they'd hit an invisible wall. Then the cop saw what had caused the incident. A small boy was standing in the middle of the road, covered in blood from head to toe. *

    The cop dropped his sandwich and ran into the street, his hand held high to stop any other oncoming traffic. More brakes locked up and he heard the inevitable sound of metal crunching into metal, the sound growing into a deafening clatter. The boy did not seem to notice.

When the cop got to the boy, he looked him over. He was maybe five years old. The blood that covered him had to have come from another source. The cop could find no wounds. "Are you okay?" he asked the boy over and over, but the boy would not respond. He would only point across the street. When the cop looked to where the boy was pointing, he saw a house much like the other houses on the street, a simple ranch-style home on what used to be a residential street, but had devolved into a mixed-use occupancy area before succumbing to the declining economy. Now, between homes on the street were empty gas stations and convenience stores bearing Hispanic names, their windows covered with *cerveza* and *leche especiale* posters.

Smoke billowed from the house as tongues of flames reached out and licked the eaves. The cop called it in on his handheld radio.

"Are your parents home?" the cop asked the boy. The boy did not answer. "Are your parents okay?" The boy still did not answer, but continued to point at the house. The cop decided to move to a safer place than the middle of the street and picked up the boy. As he carried the boy toward the house, the boy began to scream and kick his feet wildly.

"It's okay," the cop told the boy. "I'm a policeman." But this only seemed to make the boy scream and fight more.

When the cop got the boy to the other side of the street, he put him down. "There, there, now. You're okay." The cop looked into the boy's eyes; they were wild with fear. "Okay, now. Can you tell me who is in the house?" The boy did not respond. The cop was torn between staying with the boy or running into the house to see if he could help anyone who might still be in the home. He looked back and forth between the boy and the house, the smoke coming from the front door growing thicker and blacker. He had to do something.

The cop picked up the boy again and the boy began screaming again. But the cop had to keep going. Gripping the boy under his arm, he made it to the front door of the house next door and set the boy down. The cop pounded on the door, but no one appeared to be home. Four-by-four wood pillars held up the front porch roof, and the boy had grabbed one and was holding on so he could not be picked up and carried off again.

"Okay," said the cop. "Stay here. The firemen will be here soon. I'll be right back. I need to go check on your parents." The boy seemed to understand this, but began shaking his head no.

"I'll be right back," said the cop. "I have to go." The boy stared at him, wide-eyed, his face a mask of horror. The cop turned and sprinted across the lawn to the burning house and through its open front door. Close to the floor, he could find fresh air, so he inched along, calling out to anyone who might be able to hear him.

"Anyone here? Police! Anyone—"

The cop had made it into the living room, where he found the couch ablaze. Fire leaped off the couch as if it had been doused with gasoline—which, in fact, it had been—and flames moved across the carpet with a voracious appetite. But the fire was not what transfixed the cop's gaze. It was a television set, its plastic housing just beginning to buckle from the heat. On top of the TV was a man's head. Its eyes were open and slightly crossed, the tongue sticking out, giving the face a rather dumb look, in spite of its aristocratic gray temples. Blood poured from its severed neck, down the front of the viewing screen, and puddled on the floor. The cop felt his lunch began to emerge and ran outside.

Once outside, the cop retched and tried to regain his breath, the scent of smoke and his own vomit suffocating him. He could hear the sirens of the fire engines and the sound gave him some reassurance. He wiped his mouth with the back of his hand and looked to the boy. He wondered why he had been covered with blood, and as he scrutinized the red mess, he saw it wasn't just slopped on the boy randomly, but *painted* on, and there were letters and numbers written on the boy's shirt that read, *56QAH/Lot 117*. That's when he noticed the boy was gripping something in his hand. It was a small Matchbox car. A metallic blue Corvette.

• • •

Palm Beach Gardens, Florida
Subject: 56QAH/Lot 238

He drove her out to his favorite place in the woods. His secret place where he had taken the neighborhood pets when he'd begun his experiments. The place where he'd brought his friend who came over to study. She was still there, under just three feet of dirt, sans her flesh. He thought he would stop after doing her. Just do the thing one time. It had always been on his mind, and when she had offered herself up to him so willingly—practically begging him for it—he just went with it, like a horny virgin finally giving it up. But soon, within a couple of days, he wanted, needed, to do it again.

Now he had "Friend #2," as he was already referring to her in his mind, wrapped and ready, so to speak. Wrists and ankles bound with thin but strong polyester rope. Duct tape over her mouth and eyes. Right in his backseat. And this one was so young!

She'd come to his house selling magazines for a school fund-raiser, of all things. *Were his parents home?* He could see her blush; she was embarrassed having to try to sell something to someone so close to her own age—well, a little older, which only made it harder. Someone she might want to go out with in another year or two. She did think he was attractive. And he could see all that in her eyes before she dipped her head and let her hair help cover her face and her shyness. Her submissiveness was what had compelled him. It was so overwhelming; she could have pulled her tight little tank top off and revealed her budding, puffy-nippled breasts and it wouldn't have enticed him any more. She dug her hands into the pockets of her jeans that hung so low he could imagine some pubes might show if she pulled them down another half inch or so. She crossed her legs, standing uncertainly, and licked at her lips. Could it be his imagination, or did she actually smell like candy?

No, his parents weren't home, but he could use some mags, maybe renew his scrip to Details *or* Rolling Stone. *Did she want to step in out of the sun while he fetched his wallet, maybe have a glass of water, or something?* Sure she would.

As soon as the door was closed behind her, he looked around for something to hit her with. Seeing nothing handy, he just punched her in the back of her neck so hard she crumpled unconscious. Just like that. He picked her up—she was so much lighter than the last one—but she should be at, what, fourteen? Bet she was still a virgin, too. He'd find out soon enough.

He was sitting in his car, cooling with the AC on, listening to music, working himself into the perfect state, relishing these moments. This was *the time*, the best part, the anticipation of toying with her, then taking her life, because after it was over, there was the inevitable deflation. It must be what postpartum depression was like, like you couldn't get the glow back. Although, a couple of times he'd almost felt the elation again, when he'd driven out here and, thinking about the moment again, jacked off on Friend #1's grave.

Now Friend #2 was awake and he could smell her fear. He turned to her and watched her—she was beginning to squirm—and he grew hard. What exactly did he want to do with her? There were so many possibilities. He had his knife. He had the tank of gasoline in the trunk. What else? The shovel—he could do something with that. There was a jack handle in the trunk, too. Maybe stick that into her. Suddenly, he remembered some jumper cables he had back there. *Oh my God!* That presented some very chill opportunities.

He heard the tap on his window and I knew he felt ice run through his veins. He was caught! But when he looked out his window, he saw only me, smiling, benevolent, wearing what appeared to be a zipped-up coverall, like a janitor's outfit. It was paper, disposable, like the suits firefighters wear when they do hazmat cleanup. I'm a harmless-looking man, these days. My age has, alas, disempowered me to the casual observer—except for my eyes. Some say my eyes are still unnerving. I don't know, but I could see the young man's confidence swell. He could handle this. He hit the button for the window and cracked it a bit.

"Yeah? What can I do for you?"

"Could you please get out of the car?" I said.

"Fuck you," said the young killer and snapped up his window. I'd asked nicely. He was reaching for the ignition as the butt of my gun exploded the window, the glass spraying like droplets of hard water throughout the interior of the car. Then I held the gun to the young man's head and pulled the trigger.

The girl in the backseat screamed as brains and blood were slung onto her like cat shit.

I got into the passenger side of the car and removed the young man's knife from his glove box, then leaned over and ripped open his button-down shirt, revealing his hairless chest. Meticulously, I carved into the boy's chest, deeply but deftly, the identifying numbers and letters: *56QAH/Lot 238.*

I looked adoringly at the girl in the backseat and shook my head; she was scrumptious, but too young. A couple more mango seasons, a little more ripening, and she might appeal to me. "Another time," I said, before getting out of the car and trudging my way back through the sand, removing the paper suit I'd used to keep the splatter off of my clothes and setting it on fire. The flame, my friend that always gave me that warm glow inside, that feeling of completion. Then I walked calmly through the shady pines of the woods, enjoying the evergreen scent, and back to my car.

• • •

Lake Worth, Florida
Subject: 56QAH/Lot 64

What the fuck is that guy doing out there? he asked himself, looking out the window of his small office. It was lunchtime and everyone was gone. The landscaping business had been slow lately because of the shitty economy, so he must have told them all to take the rest of the day off. He might have been thinking today would be *the day* to go by the school with the truck and *just do it*, like the Nike ad kept telling him to do. The truck was loaded as full as it was going to get with the fuel and the fertilizer. But he'd been undecided. Was it the right day? He hadn't really heard the call, had he? Hadn't heard the voices he usually heard that told him to do the things he did. But the more he thought about it—just swinging by the school, leaving the truck, and walking away, then coming back to the office to watch it all, over and over, on all the network and cable news channels—the more appealing it became.

I know. I know how he must have felt. The temptation is arousing when you get a taste for it. But now, here I was, this odd fellow who had wandered in and was sniffing around his truck.

He belted down the last of his Coca-Cola, stood and adjusted his jeans, and walked out of his office and into the heat, his high-heeled cowboy boots projecting him that much closer to the sky, to heaven. I was sitting in his truck, fiddling with the device in the cab, the driver's door hanging open. I heard him grinding his heels through the shell-rock parking lot, so confident he didn't worry that I might hear him.

He approached me and leaned against the open door. "The hell you doin' in there?" he asked.

I sat up. It was too warm for me to have my long-sleeved shirt buttoned up all the way to the top, and circles of sweat grew from under my armpits and around my neck. But one must be careful about getting too much sun. Skin cancer is insidious, and it does, unfortunately, run in my family.

"Just making some adjustments to your detonation device," I said.

"What? What are you talkin' about?"

I looked at him, my eyes fixed on his, finding myself slightly perturbed for some reason. Perhaps because he thought he was so smart and I knew he was not. "You know what I'm talking about." I slid out of the driver's seat and stood before him, taking in the Florida cowboy look he had given himself. I noted the color he'd added to his hair to hide the gray temples, which took away from any distinguished look he might've lent himself. "Good thing you let everyone go this afternoon. That way, no one else will get hurt."

"What?" he said, squinting and trying to make himself look tougher than he really was. He was wearing a knife in a leather case on a hand-tooled Western belt that matched his cheap cowboy boots. He slid his hand up to the case and unsnapped the cover.

Once again, I moved quicker than people think I am capable of moving. A snake could not strike faster. I slid the metal pry bar out of my long sleeve and struck the trucker cowboy in the temple with it, not enough to crack his skull, but enough to take any fight out of him. I caught his bulk before he hit the ground. Good thing I keep myself in perfect physical shape, even now. He was tall and lanky but heavy, especially unconscious. I hoisted him into the driver's seat of the truck. Then I fastened the man's hands to the steering wheel with some handcuffs I'd recently acquired.

Before I could walk away and listen to the fireworks, I took the can of orange construction paint I'd brought with me and sprayed *56QAH/Lot 64* on the front wall of the office building, like some macabre graffiti. Give them all something to think about. Could I make it any easier? Then I found some cold water in the tiny office and brought it back to the truck, unable to resist my own delirious desires. I reached over the man and set the timer for three minutes, then began to pour the water over the would-be bomber's neck and shoulders. He awoke in a daze.

"We're a little different, aren't we?" I said to him.

"Don't...know what...you're talking about..."

"I mean that we're *different*, not only from other people, so-called normal people, but from each other. I've always enjoyed working up close, while you're a distance killer." I nodded toward the dash of the truck where the detonation device was moving through its countdown. "Blowing things up from a distance. Tsk, tsk, tsk."

The man's eyes widened, tried to focus on what was happening to him.

"That's so…pussy," I said, then hopped down from the truck. "I'm disappointed in you, son."

I walked quickly to my car, listening to the shouts of the man in the truck, hearing him trying to wrestle his hands away from the cuffs that bound him to death's chariot.

I was about a quarter mile away, watching in my rearview mirror with more than a little excitement, I should say, when the impact jolted the car. I saw a huge fireball, like a miniature reenactment of Hiroshima going off, unfolding into the sky.

I had stopped a school from being blown up and saved hundreds of lives. Some people would call me a hero. "What a guy," I said to myself, and continued driving to my next destination. It had been a busy day, but I was just getting started.

THIRTY-ONE

After brief introductions all around, Cecil served as emcee.

"So, Agent Cleary, I'll just get this out in the open...We've been looking through your FBI files."

Rose looked at me and I cringed, then scrunched up my shoulders in an attempt to convey my guilt and apology through one clumsy use of body language.

Cecil continued. "Before you shoot Grey, you should know he had no part of this. He left us unattended and it is the natural tendency of the research scientist to...uh...well, look into things. And we did not hack your account. You...uh...well, you left it open on Grey's PC."

"Get to the point," said Rose, the words coming out covered in frost.

"Okay. The point is we have a portable, experimental DNA analyzer here with us. We've been analyzing evidence you and Grey collected over the past few days. We collated the info, put it into a common language file with animated diagrams of various DNA profiles we're looking at. We are aware of the sensitivity of the subject Haskell, so we stayed away from direct queries utilizing his name, specifically. However, we did put in our DNA profiles for comparisons to those in CODIS."

"And?" asked Rose.

"And," replied Cecil, squirming with excitement, "out of several million DNA profiles in your system, we found a few dozen profiles, scattered around the country, that share enough VNTRs that we think there is some common denominator."

"Are you saying we have other perps who may be related somehow?"

"Yes and no. Yes, it appears that there are some relations, but what is significant is this: not all of the samples are from criminals; some are from the victims."

"How can that be?"

"We don't know. We're just the lab weasels. You guys are the criminologists."

Rose looked out the window, her brow creasing.

"So, are you pissed at us for using your access to look into the FBI's files?" I asked Rose.

She turned and shook her head. "I got over it. You weren't looking into anything personal about me. You were trying to keep this investigation going, just like we agreed the other night. You're doing what is right, what should be done. I wish I could do the same."

"You can. We'll just come at it from a different way."

"It's going to have to be very different. David said I could use the agency's chopper, but he's not going to let me assemble the CIRG unit. Bringing in a Critical Incident Response Group would risk more people coming in and finding out about Haskell, and any link back to him is definitely forbidden."

"That's okay. We have our own unit right here," I said, nodding at Cecil and Amy.

"You're willing to do that?" Rose asked them. "I'm not going to bullshit you, it could get dangerous. Even if you're in the background, doing the research, and not out in front with us, which is, by the way, the only way I could allow your help."

Cecil looked at Amy, then turned back to Rose. "This is *exciting*," said Cecil, like a kid going on his first trip to Disney World. "We're yours and we'll do whatever you tell us to do."

Amy spoke up. "I hate to state the obvious, but if we keep following the DNA link, it seems sooner or later we'll come back to Haskell."

I watched Rose to see her reaction. She was in a tight spot, and ultimately, it would be her responsibility, and her career, if we got caught investigating something she had been expressly forbidden to look into. Moreover, it would be her fault if Cecil or Amy, two civilians, came to harm. She chewed on the inside of her cheek until I thought she would gnaw right through it.

"Then we'll deal with it then."

We could hear the helicopter coming back, hovering over a landing zone outside.

"What now?" I asked.

Rose held up her cell phone and showed me an FBI alert that had come through as a text. It was another mutilation murder, with an arson involved, in Miami.

"These are popping up all over the state. Let's follow the pattern, the behavior. Maybe it'll take us where we need to go."

"Even if it's a place we're not supposed to be?"

"It's a risk I'm willing to take."

"But how will we know if we're getting too close to Haskell?"

Rose didn't hesitate. "Well, if we get too close, we know they'll shut down my file access again."

"Then what? What happens to you?"

"I don't know. If they kick me out because I was doing the job I was hired to do, then I can live with that. Maybe I can go to someone higher up. Maybe I go to the media if I have to. Right now, they're saying Haskell is contained, whatever that means, so someone else is responsible for these new killings. Let's find him."

"Or them?"

"Good point. Now, how portable is that little DNA gizmo, Dr. Pogue?"

"It's practically a clutch purse, Agent Cleary. And call me Amy, please."

"Okay. And it's Rose for me. Let's grab the equipment and go."

We'd picked up the laptop and the portable DNA analyzer when a thought occurred to me. "Hey, can we call this thing something other than a portable DNA analyzer? I mean, that's kind of a mouthful if I ask you to go grab it out of the chopper."

Cecil looked at Amy.

Amy looked at me and shrugged. "Its actual name is much longer than that, but I don't have a nickname for it. Do you have something in mind?"

"Not me. I'm just the dumb fire inspector."

"I got it," said Cecil. "Why don't we call it the *Sanguinaut*? You know, sanguine is, like, blood, and naut is an explorer, you know, like astronaut or the argonauts…"

No one said anything for a moment. It seemed like everyone was holding their breath. Then Amy began shaking her head slowly, from side to side.

"You hate it, don't you?" said Cecil.

"No," said Amy. "I love it. It's perfect." She walked over and grabbed Cecil and mashed her lips into his. "God, you're so clever," she said heatedly. "You have no idea how much that turns me on."

Rose looked at me and arched an eyebrow. "Shall we go?"

Amy, still nibbling on the now blushing Cecil, said, "We're going to need a few minutes. Can we meet you in the helicopter?"

"Okay. But don't be too long."

I looked at Rose and laughed for what was going to be the last time in a long while, though I couldn't have known that at the time.

We gathered up the *Sanguinaut* and the rest of the equipment and headed out the door. There was just one other problem. I hate helicopters.

THIRTY-TWO

Journal: More Cases Closed

Central Florida, Lakeland
> Subject: 56QAH/Lot 454

I watched this one through the windshield of my car and, in spite of my colorful past, felt like a pervert. Like a peeping Tom. It was not my usual MO. I used to like to engage them, get to know them, seduce them. But this one would have none of that. This one was clever. Impetuous, lusty, and irresponsible, but clever nonetheless. It was in her genes, after all.

A few days earlier, I had watched her belt down a Bloody Mary to take the edge off of a hangover, then calmly drive out to a low traffic highway, park along the side of the road, and discard a garbage bag that held her only child, with no more thought than someone dumping some household refuse. Perhaps her only hesitation was that of anyone who might be caught littering.

I observed her impatiently set up a lawn chair in the sunlight that lit up her front yard like a theatrical spotlight. Most young ladies would be too modest to lie in their front yards to work on their tans, would wait until the sun moved around back so as not to entice the heated glares of the mailmen or the utilities workers in the area. Not this one. This one wanted the attention, craved it.

She stretched, going up on her long legs, pawing at the sky like a big cat, her tiny swimsuit tied loosely on her pelvis and around her neck. She rolled onto the chaise as lithely as a cat. I ran my eyes down the length of her body, noted the oddly sensual site of her armpit stubble that gave way to the curve of her breasts. Nice hips, I thought—good childbearing hips. Almost no body fat upon her sleek form. Physically, she might have been a target for my own desires, but she lacked the one ingredient that I find to be most magnetic—innocence. It wasn't just the taking of sexual innocence, as with a rape—that wasn't my bag—but that loss of the innocence that comes with the extinction of trust in their fellow man when they realize they are going to lose their lives. And in a most terrifying way. It's exquisite.

I wondered if this one might actually enjoy the anticipation of her own death, and knew regrettably that I would not get the same pleasure from this conquest. Still, she had to go, especially this one, because she was a proven breeder and this all has to cease. I walked up to her, carrying the plastic bag I'd picked up along the way.

She didn't hear me approach, but my shadow fell over her and blocked her sun, and after a few minutes of me standing there, she cracked open her sleepy eyelids. She held her hand up over her eyes and looked up at me. Her top was untied and fell down a notch; a nipple peeked out.

"Whatcha want?" she said, not bothering to cover up.

"I'm with the Division of Children and Families," I said, a silly little improvisation, just to see her reaction. "Do you have a daughter?"

"I do," she said. If she'd been innocent, she would have asked for some identification or demanded to know what business it was of mine if she had a daughter. She would have jumped up and run in the house, or covered herself up, or done any number of things other than what she did. I saw her stomach muscles tighten and she straightened in the lawn chair. Now one boob was completely exposed. Rivulets of sweat ran down her abdomen and soaked into her bikini bottom. I wondered if she shaved down there like most of the young women do now or if she retained a little hair, a Hitler moustache, or a heart, or a "landing strip," as they call it, which guides the plane into the hangar, so to speak.

"Where is she?" I asked.

"Babysitter's."

"For five days?"

And she knew I knew. She threw a leg out, spreading open her crotch, reached over, and found a glass of iced tea sitting next to her and took a long drink, her throat working the liquid down, like a snake swallowing a mouse.

"Is this her?" I asked and plopped the black garbage bag between her legs. The top of the bag had loosened and the smell of death seeped out of the bag like a noxious cloud.

She looked at the bag, then back up at me.

I looked around to see if anyone was passing by on this rural road in Bumfuck, Central Florida, and saw all was quiet and we were alone. I moved quickly, again, grabbing that long throat of hers within my hands and beginning to squeeze, surprised at my own feelings, the quick flash of rage.

She grabbed my arms at first. She was strong and obviously a fighter—probably from working out with weights, keeping that lusty body near perfection. But there was something that made her give in easily and quit, a personal debt, perhaps, an acceptance of what should happen to her, for her grievous sin, and she stopped struggling. As I tightened my grip, closing off the blood supply to her brain and the sweet, life-sustaining oxygen, a serenity overcame her. The veins stuck out on her forehead and a blood vessel popped in her right eye, but I knew she felt a peace she hadn't felt since she was a child, an innocent child, so long ago.

"Good-bye, Lacy," I said, and crushed her larynx with my thumbs, feeling it pop like an eggshell, much as she had done to her high school friend years earlier.

Before I left, I stuffed a piece of paper in her mouth. On the paper, scribed with letters cut from various magazines, was her identifier: *56QAH/Lot 454.*

• • •

Eustis, Florida
Subject: 56QAH/Lot 503
They jokingly sell T-shirts in the convenience stores and gas stations along Highway 19 that read, "Take a bite out of Eustis, Home of the Vampires," or "Vampire Crossing Ahead," or some other idiotic saying intended to lend a good-natured, down-home quality to this town in the middle of Florida. Its nearby rival, Mount Dora, had long ago established an identity for itself as a town with frequent antiques shows and festivals: the Antique Boat Show, the Antique Car Show, the Antique Furniture Festival, and so on. But Eustis was famous for naught but the grisly murders that were committed some time ago by a group of kids who believed themselves to be vampires. Bored, lackadaisical Goth kids with their tribe's standard affinity for black clothing, black lipstick, and black-painted fingernails whose leader prompted them all to help him kill his parents and transform themselves into real, true-life vampires. The town was aghast, briefly, until after the onslaught of press that pumped media money into this dead place began to subside, and then they realized they could

continue their salad days if they set good taste aside and allowed the harmless exploitation of the "Vampire Crimes," as the case came to be known. Plastic fangs and bats and black capes lined the counters, and tourists who could not get a room, or did not care to spend the money, in nearby Mount Dora, came to Eustis and purchased the made-in-China culture.

And they called me a monster? I'll show them a fucking vampire.

I approached her trailer, wondering if anyone had missed the crippled veteran she had tortured, then dismembered, and finally burned in her garbage can outside her mobile home. I wondered, too, why they called them mobile homes when most residents in these aluminum cans sold the axles out from under their homes to junk dealers, who in turn sold them to boat trailer manufacturers, thus creating a significant underground trade of small-time criminals who bought, sold, and stole trailer axles from each other. Oh, the glamour of it all!

I stopped at her mailbox and noted her name for the first time: Joanne Swanson. *Well, Joanne Swanson, today is your swan song.* I wondered briefly if that was her maiden name or one she had obtained from one of her husbands along the way. Her mailbox door was hanging from a broken hinge, the box full of magazines and junk mail and overdue bills. I noted the *Last Notice* bill from Florida Power and Light, one of the most unethical power companies in the world and a very good argument for all Floridians to go to solar or wind power, but for today, they could assist me.

I let myself into the screened front porch and knocked on her door. I was wearing another white-paper gown because I knew this one was going to be messy.

I heard her shuffle to the door and I imagined her wearing cheap terry cloth bath slippers, the kind decorated with animal heads where the toes stick out. I would have bet my life that she had some of those vampire T-shirts in her closet, too, probably the tank top model with a bat flying over each boob, saying, "Suck on these!"

She opened the door. I had the slippers right. She was also wearing an open button-down shirt with a purple bra and dingy yellow panties, through which I could see her dark pubic area, in the aforementioned arrowhead design. She was smoking a cigarette and made no effort to conceal herself. Unlike Lacy, who, in spite of being a matricidal killer, retained some femininity, Joanne was mannish. Her thick shoulders were rounded, like a brick mason's who had worked too many years. Her hands were worn and rough, and a layer of beer fat covered her body.

Obviously, most of my *children* had received my genes that dictated our unique homicidal behavior, but not all of them had received the gift of my physicality. This one's mother must have been a cow.

"Whatchoo want?" she said, her voice raspy from the smoke. "And why you wearin' that space suit?" When she spoke, her tongue came out of her mouth as if it had to, to help her add emphasis to her words. It was pointed and had a blue tint to it, like a predatory bird's. There was fine but abundant hair above her upper lip and along her chin. I noted the premature gray of her temples, but could not recognize any other physical traits of her heritage. She looked like she should be cooking lizards and bat wings over a boiling cauldron.

"I'm with FPL, ma'am. Here to turn off your power, I'm afraid."

She softened and I knew I was going to get the whore act, along with an invitation. "Oh, I'm sorry," she said, that blue tongue working like a witch's finger. "I got a check for you right here. Why 'oncha *come* inside while I go get that for you?"

"Well, okay," I said, arching an eyebrow as if I'd picked up on her sexual entendre and held an interest.

"Let me slip into somethin' more presentable," she said, shuffling down the hall toward her bedroom, taking off her shirt.

"May I get a glass of water, ma'am?" I asked humbly.

She glanced back over her shoulder and pulled the bra strap down. "Help yourself," she said slyly, and disappeared into the wood-paneled hallway and the dark back of her trailer.

I opened a kitchen drawer and found the biggest knife available. It wasn't particularly sharp, but it had a good point and a thick blade I wouldn't have to worry about breaking if I hit a bone. Up the sleeve it went. I found a bottle of water in the refrigerator and pulled it out. I turned around and was startled. It takes a lot to startle me, to be sure, but the image of her standing in the gloom of her hallway, nude, pale as some ghostly apparition, staring at me like her next meal, was unnerving.

She crooked one arm up and beckoned me toward her in a manner I guessed she imagined to be seductive. The other arm she kept behind her. I suspected it held a weapon.

I gave an "awe shucks" grin like a boy about to lose his virginity and trotted right over to her. When I got within her reach, she struck out with her own weapon—a stun gun. But I was practiced in taking weapons away from people, and much more skilled at wielding them than she. I caught her wrist and we became locked in a struggling, but quiet, embrace. She was as strong as I suspected and our breathing grew labored as we wrestled for control of the weapon. I did not want to stab her yet, so I did not use the knife. I could smell her musky, cheap perfume, and a sour woman's body scent wafted into my nozzles like fumes from acid. I saw some dandruff in the roots of her oily scalp and, for one of the few times in my life, was slightly nauseated.

I broke her wrist and turned the stun gun back on her, mashing it into her neck and squeezing the trigger, using her own, now limp, fingers. The gun crackled and she fell limp and pissed herself. I took her considerable weight and dragged her into the bathroom. I slung her into the tub, her head hitting its porcelain side with enough force to shake the trailer. I pulled the plastic shower curtain down, tore it into strips, and tied her wrists with it. Then I cut off her breasts and stuffed one into her mouth so she wouldn't scream when she came to, which she most certainly would do when she discovered the mess from my impromptu surgical procedure. I looked around her bathroom and found some items I would use on her: a curling iron, a toilet plunger, some spare light bulbs, and various cleaning solvents.

I woke her up using some ammonia, and for the next hour or so, I tortured her with the bathroom implements until she finally lost consciousness. Then I set fire to her trailer.

A guy's gotta have *some* fun.

Before leaving, I placed one of her breasts—I couldn't help myself—in her mailbox with her identification written with a Magic Marker on the nipple in block letters: *56QAH/LOT 503*.

• • •

Ocala

Subject: 56QAH/Lot 704

Ocala is at once a very rural area and a haven for ultra-rich horse people. On one side, it has the state fire college, which draws eager young men from all over the state whose only desire is to get a job in the fire service and—while they are going through training there—get laid by the cowgirls who frequent the nearby Painted Horse lounge. On the other side, John Travolta parks his jet, a full-size Boeing 707B, right next to his house and awaits his next Hollywood project while surrounded by his neighbors, oil-rich Saudis who fill their multi-acre ranches with the finest genetic lineage of equine flesh on the earth.

This is where the fire-starter lives.

This man intrigued me, unlike the Lake Worth landscaping business owner who dreamed of blowing up a high school. I don't fully understand the motivations of such anonymous distance killers, beyond the stupid thrill they experience in witnessing mass destruction. But this one already had a truly impressive score, though that has more to do with poor law enforcement than his own prowess, I'm afraid. He wasn't even on a suspect list yet, in spite of killing almost two dozen people, including several firefighters, and destroying a school, a shopping center, and a fire station, as well as hundreds of acres of national forest land.

I hated to see the forest destroyed. It was really quite beautiful. Unlike much of Florida, which is flat and dreadfully dull, the Ocala National Forest has rolling hills and lakes and moss-covered oaks that lend hikers shade from the relentless Sunshine State heat. Years ago, I liked to go hiking, occasionally happening upon lone female hikers easy victims, as often no one knew where they were or noticed if they were even missing, sometimes for days. I would walk with them for a ways before dispatching them in some creative fashion and placing them in their, forgive the cliché, *shallow graves*. I didn't need an excuse to kill the fire-starter, but preserving these naturally beautiful woodlands would certainly be a fine auxiliary reason.

I didn't want to take a lot of time with him, either. Not that he didn't deserve it; I'm sure the families of those people who were incinerated by his last feat would love to have him for hours and pick away at him with some sharp instruments. But I still had several stops to make and had to keep on schedule to fulfill my agenda. Besides, I've always preferred killing women to men. Call it a weakness.

I approached him directly. His face was like that of a young boy, but he was so lean he looked older, and of course, I could already see a couple of gray hairs in his temples, as well as the dark, penetrating eyes. He was home alone and I told him I knew who he was and what he'd done. I showed him the aerial video on my tiny digital camera I'd taken of him several days earlier igniting various fires throughout the community. When he asked what I wanted, I said I admired his work and wanted to do another one with him. He grinned from ear to ear and said, "Really? That's all?" I assured him it was.

We took my car, which would really slow the investigation into his disappearance, if indeed there ever was one. He suggested we start in an area at the edge of the national forest; it had been dry lately, and this area had not been undercut for some time, he explained. It was like kindling waiting to be ignited. We parked and I gave him the can that said *Gasoline* on the side, though it was mostly water. I told him to get started as I got more accelerant from my trunk. I had placed some jet fuel I'd obtained earlier in a yard pesticide pump sprayer.

He was bent over trying to ignite the liquid he had just poured in an uneven line around the edge of some fallen and dried-out trees. He didn't hear me when I came up behind him and almost jumped off the ground when I began to soak him with the jet fuel, which, truthfully, is so volatile that it actually burns your skin if you leave it on too long. He had the torch in one hand, and when he jumped, he accidently caught his own clothes on fire. He began patting wildly at the flames, but that jet fuel is particularly flammable; it burns hot and fast, hence its facility in airplanes and drag-racing "funny cars." I hastened his fiery demise by spraying more on him.

At first he tried to think his way through it, throwing himself to the ground and trying to snuff it out by thrashing about. I guess somewhere along the line he had heard that old "stop, drop, and roll" line, perhaps from one of the firefighters he had killed recently. Who knows? Sometimes karma works likes that—if you believe in that kind of thing. I'm not much of a believer myself. If bad karma is coming my way for the many, many bad things I've done to so many people, it's very slow in coming. I suspect nothing that could happen to me would begin to compensate for my misdeeds. At least I can be truthful about that.

When his rolling about did nothing for him, he leaped to his feet and made a run toward a small pond nearby. I gave him another dousing as he ran past, noting the painful-looking blisters popping out of his skin like oversized zits. I was mesmerized by his doomed plight, his suffering, his physical transformation from a young, confident, and virile male to smoldering, bursting, and sloughing flesh. I have burned a number of my victims, but always after they were dead and typically to conceal evidence. But this was different, and I must admit, I did enjoy the event more than I had expected I would.

He made it to the pond, but as it was just a shallow, muddy refuge for frogs, lacking anywhere near the depth required to smother the flames, he continued to burn. I helped him along by dumping the rest of the caustic fuel on him. He tried mouthing something at me through the flames, but I couldn't make it out. I think he was saying he was sorry. Oh well. So am I.

But not that much.

• • •

Orlando, Florida

56QAH/Lots 488 and 1115

These fellows moved around the state working their magic but were living, appropriately, in Orlando, a place of superficiality, where tens of thousands of acres of natural Florida wildland had been replaced with landscapes made of plaster-covered chicken wire and plastic plants in place of real flora. A pair who works as a construction superintendent and a Home Depot clerk—the uncle and nephew, respectively—but who are really serial killers, fit right into the artificial world that is Orlando.

They were easy to find and easy to follow, believing themselves to be invisible and invincible at this point. Who could blame them? Law enforcement assigned to the case, including several local police and sheriff departments, the Bureau of Alcohol, Tobacco, and Firearms, and the FBI, had no clue who the shooters were, in spite of the bullet cases and cryptic tarot cards left behind as evidence. Theories ranged from a single shooter acting out an antiwar campaign to a gang of deranged motorcyclists roaming the beltway in an attempt to initiate some anarchist revolution.

People who watch those shows that feature forensic investigators as heroes are the same people who believe in Santa Claus, unicorns, and that one day everything will be all right, peachy keen. There is no one coming to the rescue, no Sherlock Holmeses, or Hercule Poirots, or even Horatio Caines from *CSI: Miami*—thank God. (With a name that stupid, would you really want him on your case?) Serial killers are caught because they *want to be*, because they long to bask in the glory of having fooled so many people—cops, family, media—or because they make a stupid mistake. They leave clues, sometimes on purpose, sometimes inadvertently, perhaps subconsciously, in order to get caught. They are pulled over because of a burned-out taillight or because they're parked in front of a fire hydrant, and when the cop shines the beam of his Maglite into the car and looks in the backseat, he sees a body covered up with a bloody tarp. It unfolds from there, and the media, always looking for a hero, makes one of the flatfoot cop who was only making his rounds and would have written the killer a warning ticket if the perp would have been clever enough to conceal the body in the trunk of the car.

They all get caught sooner or later. Even me.

I thought it would be fun to try my hand at their particular bent. I had always been keen at sharpshooting, though I had never dispatched any of my victims with that method. As I've mentioned before, it is too remote and does not afford the intimate satisfactions of hearing, feeling, a victim's last breath against my cheek, watching the pulse die in the hollow of their quivering throats, seeing the shine in their eyes turn dull.

I chose a Bushmaster .223 with a Burris full-field tactical scope, similar to the one another set of snipers used in highway shootings in the Washington, DC, area a few years back. Not a particularly large-caliber weapon, but the bullet goes where you send it, with little to no deterrence in its trajectory.

I had decided this would be the way to go with these two because surely Cerberus's mercenary group would have realized by now what I was doing and would be, at this point, looking for me. Even if they were not, they would certainly be looking for these two, so distance was imperative to me, at least for these targets. A safety precaution. These men were armed and dangerous, after all.

They were having lunch together at a patio diner near the Home Depot where the nephew worked. Perhaps they were planning their next "hunting trip." I could see their mouths clearly through my scope and watched their lips, trying to make out what they were talking about. But I was only so-so at lipreading, so I gave up and then wrestled for the next five minutes with the decision of which I should kill first.

The uncle had some military experience and might therefore be warier, might possibly make a run for it if I shot his nephew first. Of course, the nephew was younger, with quicker reflexes, and might jump and run quicker than the uncle would. It was an interesting dilemma. I watched them for a while, contemplating my decision, and could not help but notice that, in spite of having two different mothers, they shared a striking family resemblance. As I put the crosshairs on the uncle, I was surprised to find my heart quickening. I noted his gray temples and his lean form, echoed in his nephew, and marveled at the tenacity of those physical traits. I actually felt a little tinge of regret—foolish, I know—like a parent who fears the empty nest one day, but this was quickly replaced by my own eagerness to kill.

I was lying prone, some three hundred yards away, so this represented a bit of a test of my abilities. I slowed my breathing, then held my breath while slowly squeezing the trigger. The rifle jumped a bit, but I refocused quickly, in perhaps a half second, looking through the scope in time to see the delayed arrival of my faraway shot as it exploded the uncle's head. He sat for a second before toppling over, and I resisted the temptation to continue watching him, to see how he collapsed or what effect his sudden and savage demise might have on the surrounding diner patrons. I simply moved over an inch and lined up the crosshairs on the nephew, who, sure enough, was already beginning to stand, preparing to flee. I caught him right between the shoulder blades and he arched his spine backward as if he'd been hit by an invisible buffalo. I wanted to get them both in the heads to make clean and sure kills, but he was on the move, so I took the shot I could get. He reached back with one of his hands as if to pluck the bullet out with his fingers and I fired another round. This one hit him in the neck and snapped his head forward so violently that it had to have broken his spinal cord. He fell as if his legs had been cut out from underneath him.

I looked at my watch. Three shots in about six seconds. Of course, I was using a semiautomatic weapon, but I was also at least a hundred yards farther away than the world's most famous sniper had been, and I could not help but ask myself, *Lee Harvey who?*

The highway killers had been leaving tarot cards at their shooting sites. I felt obliged to leave something. I left two bullet casings; I didn't care if they traced them back to the weapon. It wasn't in my name and would soon be at the bottom of a black-water canal, guarded over by alligators and water moccasins. On the casings, I had, as carefully as I possibly could, written their identification numbers using a Dremel engraving tool: *56QAH/ Lots 488 and 1115*. Such an easy thing to do, but some poor investigator would probably spend days, maybe weeks, trying to trace the origins of the bullets, hamstringing their investigation, which I found extremely entertaining.

I am reminded of a clever saying I once heard: "If you can't dazzle them with your brilliance, baffle them with your bullshit."

THIRTY-THREE

It was the chopper blades that did it this time. The flight was quieter than my previous experience in Somalia, but once you've taken fire from fifty-caliber weapons and RPGs in a low-flying helicopter, you tend to be a little edgy around them the rest of your life.

As we zoomed toward Miami, our chatty conversation came to a halt as the chopper's barnstormer pilot zipped us east toward the ocean, electing to follow the coast down but leaving our stomachs back west in Wellington. While contemplating the gyroscopic ride, I looked up through the windows at the huge fan blades that kept us aloft.

Thwick, thwick, thwick…thwick…thwick…thwick…

And I was in my own private Idaho again.

This time, I saw my mother right after she'd had her first electroshock therapy. I'd come back home after basic training. When I got there, my sister greeted me and told me that my mother had been at work when it happened. She had complained to coworkers that she was tired, then sat down and began to cry and couldn't stop. That she'd been suffering from depression and anxiety was understandable, having to raise two kids by herself, then shouldering the added responsibilities of two full-time nursing

246

jobs and dabbling in real estate investment. Having to move her home and family every couple of years to take advantage of the escalating real estate market had to add some stress as well.

My sister and I were aware of her condition, but because she was in the medical field and knew so many doctors, she was able to easily obtain whatever she needed to get her through the day, the week, the year, and so it went until she was popping Valium to control her anxiety, which added to her depression, then taking Prozac to fight the depression. Mix that with a couple of beers when she did have some downtime, and her body and mind were on a collision course with reality. My going off to play Army probably didn't help.

My mother was a kind woman and never let her personal demons or self-imposed exile keep her from anything that was good or pleasurable for herself or alter her love for her children. We knew she was stressed sometimes; it would come out in her taut instructions to us to stay in school, keep trying, you'll never get anywhere if you don't push yourselves, you can be anything you want, etc. It was as if she were trying to make up for lost time, for those leisurely days when she and my father were taking life easy, working and building a family at a sure but slow pace. After he left, and before I got to know him well enough to know his side of the story, she was a juggernaut, pushing us to always do better, but pushing herself even more. It was not a question of if it would happen, but when.

I remember looking at her lying in bed, crumpled and worn, like a bird that has been flying against a strong headwind for too long and has fallen to the ground. Her jaw was slack, a thin, clear line of saliva escaping the corner of her flaccid lips. I could see the red marks on the sides of her temples from the electrodes they'd placed on her head to give her the blast that would scramble her brains but allow her to come back to some measure of normalcy.

Later, I would think of that time, standing by her bed, looking at the pattern in the curtains of her hospital room. I thought of it when we looked over our tactical field maps for our planned invasion of Mogadishu to hold the peace and, later, to rescue our fellow soldiers. Grid maps. Always grids. I could see another one now, on the laptop, as Cecil showed me the DNA comparisons, and something began to jell in my mind. But there was an element missing and I could not quite put it all together. Grids. Maps. Maps with grids.

That's what was in my mind—those grids—when Rose, sitting close to my side, began pushing and whispering my name.

"Grey." Then, more urgently, "*Grey*. Are you okay?" It was not what she was saying but the way she was saying it that shocked me back to consciousness. She reached into her purse and pulled out a tissue and wiped the corner of my mouth. When she saw the pilot looking at me, she said, "He's so comfortable in your chopper, he fell asleep and was drooling." The pilot turned back to his instrument panel and the windshield that held the bright sky like an aquarium. I couldn't tell his thoughts behind his aviator sunglasses.

I saw the looks on Cecil's and Amy's faces, and knew they did not buy that story. Amy reached over and took my pulse.

I cleared my throat and said, "I'm okay."

Amy said, "Okay," and, thankfully, did not push the matter.

Cecil followed suit, but I could see him steal a glance my way now and then.

"I swear to God," Rose said in a harsh whisper, "you're going to see a doctor, if I have to drag you there myself."

"I'm okay, doll," I said, sounding, or thinking I sounded, confident. "I told you I have these now and then."

"You told me you haven't had one in years and now you're having them every couple of days…that I know of. Something's not right," she scolded me. "You know it, too."

She was right; something was not right with me. Because these were not like my old seizures. First, I could remember I'd just had one, and second, I could remember what I'd dreamed, or envisioned, or whatever you want to call it. These seizures were like minimovies, snippets of things I'd seen or intuited that while still in that semiconscious state made sense to me, though when I was fully conscious, they did not. Still, these visions seemed to be giving me some direction. This time, it was *grids*. I did not share this new information with anyone, but reminded myself, *Keep an eye out for something indicating grids or grid patterns.*

We were in Miami in minutes. The pilot radioed ahead and was patched through to the Miami-Dade Sheriff's Office that held command of the scene. Fire engines were still there and one of them was assigned to securing a landing zone for us. We ducked our heads beneath the slowing blades of the chopper and scrambled toward the still-smoldering house, hauling the evidence kits with us.

We were met by a homicide detective. "Agent Cleary?" he asked, and Rose acknowledged him. He began to fill her in, but I let my attention drift into the house, where I could see clear evidence of burn patterns, indicating that this was an arson and that an accelerant had been used. I could also see the severed and slightly cooked head of a man sitting on top of the television in the living room.

I turned to Cecil and stopped him and Amy from coming closer. "Not to be disrespectful, bud, but you and Amy might want to wait in the chopper for us."

"Ah, come on," he said. "We want to play, too."

I told him what I'd seen in the house and that we might find worse. He looked at Amy and nodded. "We'll...uh...just stay back, then. You let us know if you want us to collect any samples or...anything."

Rose brought the detective over and introduced us. "This is Detective Santos with the sheriff's office. Detective, this is Fire Marshal Gift and our research team, Dr. Cecil Button and Dr. Amy Pogue. We've been working on some similar cases."

"That's what I've heard. Good to meet all of you." Santos was polite and wore a superbly tailored suit. His Cuban heritage was evident in his dark, suave looks and the slightly pronounced *S* sounds he put on certain words. "Just so you know, my men went in as soon as the fire department told us it was safe to do so. Everyone was careful not to destroy any evidence. Even the fire department was pretty good about it, other than some windows they broke out in the back to help get the smoke out."

"That head sitting on the television in there might have something to do with their good behavior," I said. Firefighters are funny like that. In a way, they're kind of like kids—fascinated by the bizarre, but unlike investigators, they don't want to get too close to it.

"I think you're right," Santos said, flashing a set of perfect ivories. I bet every woman in this guy's department had a crush on this guy. He looked like an actor from the old swashbuckling films, a young Anthony Quinn or Tyrone Power.

"We believe the guy whose head you saw was actually the man who kidnapped a five-year-old boy from the Dadeland Mall a few days ago. He's a convicted sex offender named Jeffrey Wasslink."

"The boy," said Rose. "Was he...did he...?"

"The boy is alive, but traumatized. There's no telling what he's seen in the past few days."

"How did you find them?"

"The boy ran into the street and a patrolman eating lunch over there saw him and went to help him. Then he saw the house on fire."

"Did anyone see anybody leaving the scene?"

"Nope. We already canvassed the block. Not a single witness. It's like whoever did this was a ghost."

"Maybe we'll find something inside."

"It's pretty burned up in there. Maybe you can find something, Inspector Gift. I'll warn you guys, though, it's pretty gruesome in there. Bloodstains all over the living room and some... pieces...you know, of the victim."

"Understood," said Rose.

We entered the house—Cecil and Amy stayed back—and the scent of burned carpet and furniture mixed with a broiled meat smell brought our hands to our mouths and noses. I was used to it, but the visual was disturbing enough on its own.

Wasslink's head sat on top of the TV, his yellowish-green eyes open, hemorrhaged from whatever indecencies he'd been subjected to. His tongue hung out obscenely, probably given extra length by being severed from its ties in the neck. The rest of his body sat in a dining chair, blood dripping down from the severed neck like wax from a red candle. His hands were bound behind his back, the fingers cut off. His toes appeared to have been smashed with a hammer. There were burn marks all over his torso, obviously from an iron. Blood was splashed on the walls like a macabre Jackson Pollock painting.

I took careful notes, jotting down my initial impressions as well as statements from Detective Santos and some of the firefighters who were still on scene. Impressions based on a fire investigator's experience are admissible in court—some of the few that are. Because arson destroys so much physical evidence, a fire investigation is very often based on the investigator's opinions as much as anything else. Of course, it can't be something off the wall, like you think a burn pattern might have been left by an alien spacecraft. It has to be based on your findings and should be able to withstand a standard peer review that includes proven methodologies, theories, and time-tested techniques. It has to conform to proven methodologies as dictated in the *NFPA 921 Guide for Fire and Explosion Investigations*. Every fire investigator from Alaska to Alabama who is worth his salt spins those criteria through his head before he even gets to the crime scene, because if he doesn't, his testimony will not be admissible in court. It's as simple as that.

"Looks like the perp was one angry dude," said Santos. "Hacked the guy to pieces, probably in front of the boy, then set the place on fire."

"How do you know he did it in front of the boy?" asked Rose. "Did he talk to you?"

"Not a word. But the boy was covered in blood. In fact, his shirt has some writing on it we are trying to figure out. Some numbers or letters—like a code or something. I've got some guys working on it now, but so far, we've got nada. The shirt's in an evidence bag in my car if you want to see it."

"Of course," said Rose. "Grey, you good here?"

"Yeah. I see the accelerant patterns. If you like, I'll take some samples from the carpet to see what was used to spread the fire." I had the origin of the fire determined, which I have to do as an essential part of my investigation. Simply put, if you don't have an *origin*, you can't determine *cause*. If you can't determine cause, you can't convict. It's similar to the challenge of *motive* for prosecutors. Without motive, you can't always convict, even if you know the guy is guilty as hell.

"Not necessary. Why don't we let the local teams do the forensics here? We'll take the boy's shirt and get what we need from that. If Wasslink was a convicted sex offender, he'll be in the database already."

We walked over to the detective's car, Cecil and Amy plodding along with us. If they were thinking they weren't going to be of much use to the investigation, that feeling would not last long.

Detective Santos pulled a clear plastic bag out of his car and handed it to Rose. "The blood has seeped through the cloth a little. I put it in the cooler to try to keep it from moving through the fabric so quickly."

"Good idea," said Rose.

The detective nodded. "Thanks. Not sure if you can still make it out, but the numbers were fifty-six, Q-A-H, lot one seventeen, all written in blood, which had to have come from Wasslink. Like I said, the boy didn't have any visible marks on him."

Rose turned the package over in her hands. "So the killer's leaving us a message, obviously."

"Yeah," said Santos. "But I feel like I'm walking into a movie and missed the beginning. I was hoping you might know something about it."

Rose looked at me, then back to Amy and Cecil. "Any clues, gang?"

Cecil shrugged. "Doesn't ring a bell with me, but we can do the DNA on it."

"We'll have Wasslink's in our files by tonight," said Santos. "Tomorrow morning at the latest."

"We'll have it in ours in a few hours," Cecil bragged.

"Let's do it, then," said Rose. "Just to be sure the blood is the victim's."

Santos and Rose exchanged some paperwork, the boy's address and contact information, some printouts on Wasslink he had run off from the laptop in his car.

"E-mail me some photos, too, when your CSI guys are done, Detective."

"You got it."

Now we had a direction to follow and we all began to move back toward the house—everyone but Amy, who stayed behind. I doubled back to where she stood rubbing a knuckle across her lips.

"Penny for your thoughts, Dr. Pogue."

"The number on that shirt seems familiar."

"How so?" Rose had joined us.

"It's like a reference number I've seen before in my research. I'm trying to think. It was a few years back when we started constructing the portable DNA machine." Amy began to chew on that knuckle. "We were working with various test samples. Blood, hair...and semen." She snapped up straight, animated again. "That's it! It was a code they were giving the samples. Same kind of code, a combination of letters and numbers."

"For what?" I asked, already knowing the answer.

Amy turned to me as if she knew I knew. "For sperm samples. We got them from a sperm bank."

It all began to come to me then: the sperm samples, the DNA, combinations of letters and numbers, like mapping, like *grids*. I almost could put it all together, but did not want to risk sounding like a nutcase—not yet, anyway.

"I hope I'm not out of line here, folks. But, Rose, is it okay if Amy and Cecil do that DNA analysis right now?"

"Of course. That's why they're here. Why?"

"You said the other day you had some similar cases the computer program was throwing at you with combination arson-homicide scenes?"

"I still have them in my messages," said Rose, thumbing through her e-mails.

"Can you get any DNA analysis from those?"

"Should be able to. What are you thinking?"

"I'll let you know when we find out more about the analysis, but I have a theory…Cecil, you were showing me some patterns of similar DNA before we left the house. Can you map those for me? In other words, put them on a grid, showing me where each sample was taken from?"

"Like crime mapping? Use a GIS to display where the crimes took place? Piece of cake, I should think. Agent Cleary, the COMPSTAT program can give us the crime data, right?"

"It should. It's updated weekly. But it's only as good as the data that goes into it."

"Okay, then," I said. "Let's see what we find out. I've got an idea. It might be I'm way off the wall with it, but we'll see soon enough."

"Better think fast, then. We have another one, Grey," said Rose, bent over her phone.

"Another arson-homicide?"

"Not so much an arson, unless you consider the coveralls the killer burned after he killed the vic. But it's the numbers, or code, like those on the shirt again."

"You're kidding me."

"No. But this time they were carved in the victim's chest."

THIRTY-FOUR

I thought about it for a moment before asking because I knew it would be taking us into shaky territory.

"Think it's Haskell?"

"No. I don't know. I don't think so. This one left a survivor. A young girl. If it was Haskell, I think he would have killed the girl."

"Who *was* killed?"

"A young man named Cummings. Not an innocent victim, either, evidently. He had abducted the girl. Had her bound and gagged and took her out to a spot in the woods where they've found the remains of another girl they think Cummings killed, maybe last week."

"Oh my God," said Amy. We were back at the helicopter, and she and Cecil had isolated and treated a blood sample from the boy's shirt and had it running through the *Sanguinaut* as Rose and I climbed in.

"What's going on, Rose?" I asked. "An epidemic of serial killings? Is that…possible?"

"There have been sprees, you know that. But it's usually the same person doing them. I don't think that's the case here. I want to go have a look, though. You guys ready to go?"

I said I was ready, though my mind was reeling from the enormity as well as the inexplicable nature of these murders. I was a long way from doing fire cause investigations at this point.

Amy and Cecil nodded they were ready to go. They were already running off the chopper's power, so Amy said she saw no reason that they couldn't do the analysis on the go.

"Then let's go," said Rose.

My phone rang. It was Leonard. "Hey, man. You busy?"

"Kind of, pal."

"This'll only take a minute. I told you I had your back on this, so here you go. I called the investigator assigned to the Haskell house fire and talked to him about a few things. Guess what?"

"What?"

"When you and the lovely FBI agent creeped Haskell's house, did you miss the computer?"

"No, we saw it and would have grabbed it, but like I told you, we kind of got run out of there, and not in a nice way. You ever had a half dozen guys holding assault rifles to your head?"

"Let me think…can't say I have. I get you. So, anyway, here's the good news. The computer Haskell had in his house got fried. But the hard drive was saved. I remembered you said he was finding his victims from Backpage.com."

"Yeah?"

"Well, I had our lab techs check it out and they were able to piece together all the sites Haskell visited over the past few months. One of our guys is a forensics accountant, but he does computer and data research, too. Haskell was all over Backpage.com. We got some phone numbers, too. I think we can definitely tie him to that Matarese girl."

"Good job, buddy. While he's in the hard drive, have him look up some other names. There were two girls killed and burned a few days before the Matarese girl, one in Homestead named Shawna Wooley and one near Immokalee named Juanita Suarez. He may have met them through Backpage.com, so they probably weren't using their real names, but see if your guy can link any of Haskell's e-mails back to them. Can I call you back in a minute?"

"I'm here for you, man. One other thing."

"Yeah?"

"Haskell ran his e-mail through Yahoo. We got his account number."

"And?"

"And he's online now."

"What?"

"Yeah, man. Our guys are trying to find where he's operating from. He's got DSL, so they think they can trace him through his phone line. We're working on it."

"Wow. That's cool. But, Leonard, let's keep this on the down-low. We've been ordered hands off of Haskell."

"And you give a shit about that?"

"No. I want to catch the sick fuck. But I want to keep Rose out of trouble, too, if we can. If we could get another agency looking at Haskell, it would be good—they can't tell everyone to back off."

"One last thing and I'll let you go," Leonard said.

"Okay, be quick, we're on our way to another murder right now."

"Jesus. The world is upside down and it's taking a dump right here in sunny South Florida. I just wanted to see if you heard about the explosion in Lake Worth; it would be your call if you were here right now, so they're sending me to it. Payback's a bitch."

"Hadn't heard. What kind of explosion are we talking about? Casualties?"

"Just one. I'll fill you in after I get there, but from what I've gathered already, this guy was planning on blowing up a high school with a tractor-trailer full of high-grade ammonium nitrate fertilizer and a diesel fuel mix, but managed to blow himself off the map. They found blueprints of the school and some manifesto he was writing about his plan."

"Geez. Sorry I'm going to miss it."

"No, you're not. You can imagine the red tape this is going to generate. ATF is already on scene."

"Perfect. ATF might be who you can direct your hints to. Maybe you could suggest the landscaper was friends with Haskell. Get them looking for him. Maybe they raced cars together and played with some explosives on the side—I don't know. But ATF is a big agency. If you can get them to take the bait, that would solve our hands-off problem. I mean, I don't care who gets the collar as long as we stop this whacko."

"You white guys are so smart."

"You mean, like George W. Bush smart?"

"Okay. I take it back. Let me work my magic."

"Cool. I'll call you later. *Hasta*."

Everyone was loaded into the helicopter when I got off the phone. I climbed into the seat next to Rose and buckled up.

"Anything important?" she asked.

"I'd say so," I said, raising my voice over the noise of the chopper blades kicking into gear. I told them about Leonard's nut who'd been planning to blow up a school but managed to kill himself.

Rose was looking at me strangely. She'd gotten a text message while I was talking to Leonard and now she took her phone out to peer at it again. Attached to the text was a JPEG photo file sent out from the ATF to the FBI. It was a picture of a landscaping business, obviously the same one that Leonard had just told me about. There was a huge black explosion mark and the smoldering remains of a tractor-trailer. The blast mark extended to a small office building near the blast site, its windows blown out and one of its sides pocked with holes from the blast fragments. But it was what was written on the front of the building in bright-orange construction spray paint that made my blood run cold: *56QAH/Lot 64.*

THIRTY-FIVE

That day, we stopped at the Palm Beach Gardens murder site before getting notice of four other homicides in Central Florida. The murders themselves all had very different MOs, but they all had two commonalities: all the victims had been given an identification number, and all of the victims were suspected of being killers themselves.

The young man in Palm Beach Gardens named Phillip Cummings had had sex with a young girl who lived in his neighborhood—we did not know if it was consensual or not—then strangled her, took her body out to the woods, and after dissecting her chest cavity, burned her remains and buried her in a shallow grave. Investigators found skeletal remains of small animals in the same area, indicating that Cummings had taken the common road among developing serial killers, practicing on neighborhood pets before graduating to humans. He had undoubtedly been planning on repeating his graduation ceremony with a second young girl he had abducted and who was in the backseat when he, himself, was murdered.

The girl, though shaken, was able to talk to us. As she had had her eyes covered with duct tape, she could not describe the man who killed Cummings, but said he sounded "older," which to her generation meant anything over thirty. His voice sounded like it came from "higher up" when he first spoke to Cummings outside the car, but it was impossible to determine height. She said he was well spoken and did not have a Southern accent, which, to my mind, further removed Haskell as the killer. I concluded if Haskell drove a tow truck and raced cars at the Palm Beach International Speedway on weekends and had grown up in South Florida, he likely had at least a slight Southern drawl. The girl said this man spoke "almost, like, ya know, an actor, sort of English, certainly not from down here." She said he "smelled nice," which, in my mind, further excluded Haskell. She also said that, while she was glad he'd shown up when he had, just before he left he'd brushed her cheek with his fingers and said, "Another time," and her "heart stopped beating for, like, ya know, a minute." He was also kind enough to leave the car running with the air-conditioning on.

The day had taken on a surreal quality, all of us jumping from murder site to murder site as casually as Captain Kirk and Spock transported from the *Enterprise* to some new planet on which we would surely find something new and strange. We were definitely, and boldly, going where no man had gone before. Later, when I would think about it, it would all seem like a dream; at times, I would actually be able to make myself believe that it did not happen. One thing that *did* happen that day was the promise I made to myself that, while these cases were certainly not without interest, especially to someone who enjoys investigative work, this was not the way I wanted to spend my life.

I don't know how long it takes a homicide detective to get burned-out, but at the end of that day, I was there. Give me a burned-down warehouse or even a guy who's fallen asleep while smoking and burned to death rather than this endless series of obviously premeditated executions of other murderers. I felt caught in a constant loop of a *Twilight Zone* episode—one in which I would, as the final frame came into view, find myself a victim. Which would mean, of course, that I was one of the murderers as well.

I was creeping myself out and wondering how Rose could do this type of work, week after week, and keep her sanity. I looked over to Cecil and Amy, and while they were happily breaking down DNA samples on the *Sanguinaut*, I was nonetheless regretting bringing them along. They were research people, not case-hardened field investigators equipped with psycho-mechanisms that helped shield them from all this sickness and bizarre taking of one life after another.

We were flying to yet another site in Central Florida, having just left a young mother who had been strangled herself but who had also probably killed her own child. Investigators said they found evidence from the scene that indicated the child was regularly kept in the trunk of her mother's car, perhaps while she was out dancing and carousing, and that the baby had probably aspirated and suffocated on her vomit.

Particularly nauseated by this case, I had to ask Rose if this young mother—her name was Lacy—was a murderer who would fit into the group of other killers we'd already seen or just one of the worst mothers in recorded history.

Rose looked at me, deadpan. "Well, I haven't told you every subtle nuance I've gotten through my BlackBerry. But if it will make you feel better, I'll tell you this about the young and once-beautiful Miss Lacy. While she was in high school, her best friend was murdered. Strangled at a keg party. Lacy had been there with her, but it was a young surfer dude who took the fall. He's been sitting in jail, swearing he was innocent, for over seven years now. That puts a slightly different spin on it, doesn't it?"

I shook my head in disbelief. "How can so many people be so...evil? How can there be *so many* of them out there?"

"I think I mentioned it before. In the past thirty years, serial-type killings have been increasing exponentially. And in the past twenty years, the phenomenon has become almost pandemic. We, as a nation, are so used to it we see it on the evening news and barely even stop between bites of our take-home Macaroni Grill dinners."

Rose went back to reading her BlackBerry again. I had come to hate that fucking thing.

"See if you like this," she said, almost nonchalantly. "In the yard behind the house where they found the abducted boy, they found the remains of at least four other children. Jeffrey Wasslink, the sex offender, had been a serial killer of both young boys and young girls."

"Oh my God."

She went on. "The site we're going to now, in Eustis, is a trailer park. They found the remains of a woman inside who was mutilated before she was burned. Sound familiar?"

"Uh, yeah. Sounds like Haskell again."

"Wish it were that easy, but I don't think so. And before you get to feeling too bad for this...uh...what's her name?" She scrolled through her BlackBerry for a second. "Joanne Swanson. It seems Joanne had some bad habits, too. They found remains of a man who's been missing for a few days in her garbage can—a crippled veteran. They found his dog tags. Looks like he'd been tortured, maybe for days, before he was killed."

"Shit. So everyone is victim *and* perpetrator. Hmmm. Makes you wonder who the good guys are."

Rose slid her hand into mine, intertwined our fingers, and whispered, "Just us, baby." She smiled, almost coyly, and added, "Maybe just you."

THIRTY-SIX

An hour later, we were in Eustis.

The woman in the trailer was not completely burned, which only made her that much harder to look at. The killer had done horrible things to her with a hot curling iron, a toilet plunger, and various household solvents. Her skin was browned and taut, as if she'd been smoked from the heat in the trailer. The worst part was the soot I found in her nostrils, which meant she'd still been breathing when the place was set on fire. But by then, she was probably praying for the flames to consume her.

"I think our killer is getting angrier with each victim," said Rose. "That might be good."

"How could that possibly be *good*, Rose?" What would we find next—a slaughterhouse filled with mutilated bodies?

"It could mean he's getting more emotionally unhinged, and if he is, we'll catch him. He'll slip up or just offer himself up. We can't be far behind him now."

"We still don't know who he is."

Cecil piped in. "The samples of Wasslink's blood show the same DNA similarities we saw in the urine sample from the Matarese girl's clothing, which is also very much like the others we mapped out. Also I have that COMPSTAT mapping info whenever you want, Grey. Maybe that'll help. What was that idea you wanted to share with us?"

I felt some heat enter my face because I felt like I was going out on a ledge, but my thinking had gone down a path and my "seizure movies," as Rose had begun calling them, were pushing me in the same direction. "You can look up businesses with COMPSTAT, too, right?"

Cecil peered at Rose with a quizzical look.

"Sure," said Rose. "Cities use it to look at demographics, civil engineering, site planning, almost anything you can think of. What did you want to find? Butcher shops? Smoked meat catering?"

"Not funny, lady," I said, shaking my head, though at least she was getting back to her former wise-assed self. "Cecil, see if you can find cities that have sperm banks, fertility clinics, or cryogenic depositories. Anything along those lines."

"Feeling an urge to make a deposit?" chimed Amy.

Everyone was a comedian, though I knew, again, it was just gallows humor emerging as a coping mechanism. Me? I guess I just have seizures to help me cope.

"No, smart-ass. Aren't you following me?"

"Sorry, no," said Amy. "To tell the truth, I'm a little overwhelmed."

"What I'd like to see," I said weakly, clearing my throat, "is if we can lay them out—the locations of the sperm banks—on a grid and superimpose that over a grid that shows where the murders with that similar strand of DNA took place."

I saw Rose nodding out of the corner of my eye and turned to her.

"Because Harmon Gettys met his victims at sperm banks?" she asked.

"Yeah."

"But he's dead, Grey."

"I know. But it's his DNA, or at least a similar thread of it, that seems to be the common link."

"So...are you saying you think someone is leaving *his* DNA at these crime scenes?"

"I...don't know. I don't know what is possible or really what's going on. But, to me, it keeps coming back to Gettys, and I'm just wondering, if he killed a girl he met at a fertility clinic at which he'd...left his seed, so to speak, then I would just like to know, did he go to other clinics or sperm banks? Say he did. Say he went to lots of them. How many offspring could've resulted from those deposits?"

When I stopped talking, everyone was looking at me with their mouths hanging open. It would have been comical if what we were doing hadn't been so deadly serious.

"Grey," said Amy. "First, let me say, that's insane. But so is everything we've seen today. All that aside, if what you're thinking is true, it would certainly explain that identification number, or whatever you want to call it, we've been seeing. But if we are to accept that, then...oh my God...the number of offspring would be...could be exponentially *staggering*."

The cops had been canvassing the neighborhood talking to residents, and some of the personnel from the coroner's office were standing just outside the yellow plastic crime scene tape, watching us. A single fire engine and its crew stood idly by, waiting to see if we, or the cops, would need them to search any further through the charred wreckage.

Rose walked away from the blackened ruin and the tortured body we'd been looking at. One of the men from the ME's office came up and asked her if they could go ahead and take the remains. I saw her nod, then put her hand on her forehead and begin kneading it as if she were trying to wring something from it. The man who had approached her went over to another man, and they both came over with a long, black, zippered bag and a shovel.

"You guys probably don't want to watch this," I said to Cecil and Amy.

They both nodded and scurried back to the chopper, along with a tissue sample from the victim's breast that had been found in the mailbox.

I went to Rose, who was still working that forehead. I gently lifted her hand and peeked under it. Her face was blanched, a light patina of sweat on her brow and upper lip. "Are you okay?"

She looked up at me, blinking her eyes slowly, as if trying to find the words that would best express what she wanted to say. "Have you...do you ever watch *Sixty Minutes*?"

"I catch it after the football games sometimes."

"Did you ever see the segment about behavioral tendencies being passed on to offspring?"

"I'm not sure. I don't recall offhand."

"There was this student who had donated sperm to a cryogenics lab while he was in med school. He was what they considered a perfect candidate. High IQ. Going to be a surgeon. Little to no significant illness in his family medical history. Nice looking, decent build."

"Okay."

"So, years later, this man, now a successful doctor for many years, is contacted by a young man who thinks he may be his son and he wants to meet him. The doctor thinks about it for a while and says, *Why not?* He meets him and they have a pleasant reunion and there are some physical similarities and that is kind of cool, but that is not the point of the story. What is really remarkable is that the young man has also become a doctor."

"So, the point is that behaviors can be passed on as well as physical traits?"

"Exactly. But the high point of the story was that some of his other children began to contact him as well. I don't remember the exact numbers, but I want to say it turned out he had fathered some seventy children, and fiftysomething had become doctors."

"That's pretty wild."

"No matter how they were raised, the various social strata, financial well-being of their families, religious beliefs, political standing, whether they had siblings or were single children, or even their gender, most of them became doctors."

"So the obvious question is, what if he was a serial killer?"

"It's something we need to consider, if what you're thinking is true."

"You think it's possible?"

"It's your idea."

"Maybe it's a dumb one."

"No. At the end of the day, it might not be the answer, but it is certainly not a dumb idea. And if it is true, we're in big trouble. If one man, at one fertility clinic, could produce seventy-something children, and most of them became what he was, then what if Gettys visited several of these sperm banks? Can you imagine how many twisted people could be out there? Jesus, it could very well explain why, and how, we have had so many serial killers popping up in recent years."

Just then, a shriek came from the helicopter, followed by squeals of delight. I turned to find Cecil and Amy running at us, as best they could carrying an open laptop. They reached us, panting, nearly out of breath.

"L…look," said Cecil, thrusting the screen at me.

I saw only a map overlaid with a yellow grid featuring a few illuminated yellow points.

Amy added breathlessly, "I…think…you…were…right. Cecil did the GIS for the fertility clinics, then made a grid. It's the one in yellow." Cecil hit a key, and another gridded map, a red one, appeared beside the first one. "The one in red is where this DNA has turned up at crime sites. Watch when we merge them."

I felt my heart hammering and glanced over at Rose. I could see her pulse beating as fast as a rabbit's in the hollow of her neck.

Cecil hit another key and the two grids—one yellow and one red—overlapped.

They were almost identical.

Each city that had a fertility clinic or sperm bank also held at least one DNA identification number found at a crime scene. There was an abundance of them in Florida's larger cities: Miami, Orlando, Tampa.

But there was more. Much more.

Cecil had expanded the data fields and matched the grids nationally. We could all see clearly now, on the yellow grid, fertility clinics in some of the biggest cities in the nation: Atlanta and New York on the Eastern Seaboard; Chicago, St. Louis, and Denver in the Midwest; San Francisco and LA on the West Coast. Aligned with these were, in red, dozens of murder sites at which the distinctive DNA pattern had been found in the apprehended perps themselves or the genetic material left behind by killers still at large. These red dots were clustered heaviest in the urban areas, but sprinkled out from the nuclei of those cities, speckling the countryside with little red dots, like tiny drops of blood.

THIRTY-SEVEN

Journal: Help Needed

I could not do this one by myself. Not without getting caught or killed. I did not mind dying so much, but my work was not complete. I would take help on this one, then, and would also take the opportunity to expose this whole bastardized facade.

I could see Haskell roaming around in his trailer, restless, like a tiger in its cage. It was almost night now and he'd been in there most of the day. His bloodlust was at its peak now. He was an arrow notched and ready to fly. I wondered why he was still here, why they had not deployed him, but knowing his director, his commander, I knew it was a matter of timing. Perhaps he was waiting to up the ante, bargain for more money, or create some other scenario that would give him better control over the situation, or the money to be made from it. He was a slick mother-fucker, I had to give him that.

But what was this? An unexpected visitor. I focused my binoculars and almost fell out of my hiding place. It was an FBI agent—but why was he by himself way out here? Could he possibly have no idea who, or what, he was dealing with? Perhaps he had some backup agents hidden in the woods, sneaking up from behind even now. I did a 360 with my binoculars, moving very slowly, searching for anything. I had chosen a perfect hiding spot. There was nothing.

This was turning out to be very interesting.

I watched as this lone agent moved through the protective edge of the woods and into the clearing before the house. He wasn't even in SWAT gear. Perhaps he was just doing a preliminary investigation before he launched a full field force. Maybe he thought he was a badass who could take care of whatever he found. Up to now, perhaps, he had been. But he was not going to be able to take care of this one.

I looked back to the trailer and saw Haskell had already spied him. He stood still as stone behind the blinds through which I had been watching him. He slowly closed them.

The FBI agent approached the front door and I saw him loosen his gun in its holster. He knocked on the door and waited. It was dusk now and the fading light would not be his friend, inhibiting his range of vision as well as his peripheral. Didn't he know that? He should have waited until it was dark, then moved in when his eyes had adjusted.

Haskell sure as hell knew that. I watched him as he crept under the trailer, flattening himself like some malevolent toad trained in covert operations. He moved without sound as the FBI agent continued to knock and glance at his watch. Finally, he moved away from the front door and began to peek into windows, moving right into harm's way. He tried to see through the blinds, even calling out to the occupant of the doublewide. He moved around the perimeter until he was directly in front of Haskell.

Haskell reached out and grabbed the man's ankles and pulled, downing the agent and moving his own body out and atop him with reptilian quickness. He chopped the agent in the throat with his elbow, then smashed his fists into his face, repeatedly, until the agent no longer struggled. Haskell slid back under the trailer. A moment later, the agent, unconscious, began to be drawn under the trailer as well, inch by inch, until only his extended hands were still sticking out, limp and useless.

Like I said.

I wonder what my boy had in mind for him.

THIRTY-EIGHT

We stopped in Orlando, where two men had been shot, their DNA already placed on CODIS because, as it turned out, they, too, were killer/victims. The men—an uncle, 37, and a nephew, 23—had been shooting people on the interstates around Orlando. They had killed twelve people that law enforcement knew about, so they put their DNA out to see if it matched any other pending, open, or closed cases.

It matched ours, the ones we were now referring to as the "Gettys strain."

The shooters had been leaving messages at their sites. Whoever had killed them obviously knew this detail, though police had been careful not to include it when leaking information to the press. Their killer had also left some bullet casings with similar identification numbers engraved upon them: *56QAH/Lots 488 and 1115.*

We now knew there was no doubt that we were looking at people who had been products of in vitro fertilization. All of the identification numbers began with the 56QAH prefix, and the following numbers we took to mean they were from various lots, either from donations split and stored separately or perhaps donated on different dates or locations.

Rose had been quietly chewing the inside of her cheek for about a half hour as we flew to yet another destination, this one in Ocala, where a young man's body was found burned. Authorities there believed he was the suspect who had set a brush fire and ran it into a community where almost two dozen people were killed, including several firefighters. Someone had sent a DVD showing the man setting fire to the woods and fueling it with gasoline into an unstoppable firestorm. On the DVD was a title printed from a computerized label maker. It read, simply, *56QAH/Lot 704.*

"You said Chief Dugger told you that when Gettys was caught, the cop who caught him found him by going to the sperm bank and discovering Gettys had been making donations there," Rose shouted over the chopper's racket.

"Yeah. One of his victims worked in a fertility clinic, I think it was, and the cop thought maybe Gettys had been a donor there," I said. "He checked and confirmed that he was."

"Do you know the name of the cop or what department he was with?"

"No, I didn't get that."

"I can find out," she said, diving back into the world of her BlackBerry and playing the keyboard like a mad pianist on speed.

While she worked on that, I turned my attention to Amy and Cecil, who were still hard at work pushing samples into their *Sanguinaut.* Over the din of the helicopter engine, I called, "How's it going, you two?"

They looked at each other, then at me, their eyes burning with elation. Was it for being part of an active homicide case or getting the opportunity to give Amy's new toy a really good trial run? I got a big thumbs-up from both of them, though I could see fatigue settling in.

I was tired, too. It was late in the afternoon and we'd been all over the state, looking at mutilated, burned, strangled, and gunshot bodies—victims who garnered very little sympathy as we looked into their recent and distant pasts and found that they were probably as heinous and unremorseful as the killer, or killers, we were seeking. I could smell my own gamey scent. The muscles in my neck and shoulders were as tight as guitar strings, and there was a dull throbbing in my head. I hoped I would not have another seizure. If this ever ended, I would have to get checked out by my doctor and see what was happening to me.

I leaned back and found a comfortable spot against the vibrating wall of the chopper and closed my eyes for a second. I breathed deeply and tried to think of pleasant things: lying on a private beach, the sun toasting my skin, the waves lapping rhythmically at the shore. I fantasized about Rose lying next to me in a thong, her top off, her white breasts turning pink, tan lines diminishing as she browned all over, a light patina of sweat covering her body, forming rivulets that ran down her abdomen...

I was getting myself aroused when Rose said, "Grey, look at this."

I opened my eyes and found her damn BlackBerry two inches from my face.

"I looked up the Gettys file. It wasn't a cop who busted him. It was the FBI, which I found to be very curious. But take a look at the name of the agent who brought him in."

I took Rose's wrist and pulled it back from my face so I could read her BlackBerry's screen. I read an abbreviated version of the case, then focused on the line that named the agent in charge of the case. It read, *Special Agent Nicholas Cerberus.*

"No shit" were the words that came out of my mouth.

I looked at Rose and could see her struggling to work through the implications of the connection when my phone rang once, indicating I had a text message. I figured it must be Leonard getting back to me, but I went through my phone menu and followed the prompts to where my IM messages are stored. The number associated with the new message wasn't Leonard's, or anyone else's I knew. The message said, *Quit fucking around fly to the lake and look for the race cars he is there now.*

I showed it to Rose. "What do you think?"

"It says 'the lake.' I can only assume it means Lake Okeechobee. Isn't that where that blob at the towing company said Haskell hides out and hunts?"

"Yeah. That's what he said."

"Who would be sending you that information?"

"I don't know, but if it is Haskell, are you willing to throw your orders to the wind and go after him?"

She thought about it for a good five-count. "Does a bear poop in the woods?"

I smiled, remembering her saying that the first day we met, and because I could see something else in her face. This was her chance to redeem herself, to herself. She had not felt in control of the investigation from the beginning, and then she was ordered to leave it alone—and then the bodies had piled up exponentially. It all had to stop, and we all knew Haskell was the key to it. His connection to the CIA and Cerberus was almost immaterial. We might be able to find more killers by tracking the Gettys strain, but right now, we might have one in our grasp. He might even be the one who was killing all these other killers—for what reason, only he could tell us, which made it all the more imperative that we go after him.

I looked at Rose and knew she was thinking along the same path. "So?" I said.

She turned to Amy and Cecil. "Do you guys mind making one more stop this evening? It could get a little hairy."

The two lab weasels looked at each other, then nodded.

"We like hairy," said Amy.

"Let's go," said Cecil.

Rose leaned forward and lifted the helicopter pilot's headset from his ear. She said something to him, he nodded, and the chopper took a quick, stomach-churning turn to the right.

I called Leonard to check in with him. He apologized for not getting back with me but had been busy with the explosion at the landscaper's business. He also confirmed that he had "dropped the dime" on Haskell to the ATF. They were all over it like a dog on a bone, he said, and had thanked him for the tip. Sometimes just the tiniest fib can really help things along.

I told him we were on our way to try to find Haskell now, based on an anonymous tip. He didn't like that. "You might be walking into a trap, Grey."

"Set by who?"

"I don't know. Like you said, this thing has spooks all over it. I just don't like it. Let me see if I can clear this scene and I'll head out that way."

"Don't put yourself out, Leonard. We'll be there pretty soon anyway and we still don't have an address. We're going to see if we can find his place by finding his cars. I don't know how many trailers we'll have to buzz, but this could take a while."

"I hear you. Still going to try to make it."

"Let your conscience be your guide, but if you're coming, do me a favor and don't come alone."

• • •

Within an hour, we could see the vast expanse of Lake Okeechobee open up beneath us, its surface lit by the moon and preternaturally calm, the reflection of our helicopter rippling along under us like the shadow of a pterodactyl. The pilot hugged the perimeter of the lake and the spotlight on the bottom of the chopper lit the shoreline like daylight. We all took places at the windows and started looking for cars, anything that looked like a race car, or in particular, a black Buick Grand National, a car that had not been made in over twenty years and that I knew very well, having owned one so many years ago, when the world seemed to be a simpler place, when tuning your street rod, greasing the tires, driving by the beach, and flirting with tanned surfer girls looking for a ride home was the edgiest thing you could think of. Before you came to realize that all those horror movies and the monsters in them were, as Rose had said, symbols of creatures that were real. But now they are more frightening because they are not as obvious as a werewolf or a creature from the Black Lagoon. They are hidden by their day-to-day anonymity and we call them neighbor, or coworker, or friend.

THIRTY-NINE

Lake Okeechobee gets its name from a Seminole Indian word meaning "big water." It is over a thousand square miles. It was formed in a shell-rock depression over six thousand years ago, when the ocean receded and Florida came out of the sea like a phallus with a big hole in it. The only other freshwater lake bigger than Okeechobee in the continental United States is Lake Michigan. It's only about fourteen feet in its deepest areas when the South Florida Management District is not fucking around trying to adjust levels so that levies don't break or the lake-bottom weeds can grow better or when they're trying to placate the hundreds of farmers who need water for drought-stricken crops. I wouldn't mind the farming so much if it weren't so corporate driven now by sugar giants who take from the land and give back by letting the nitrogen-fueled runoff water flow back into the canal system and into the sea, where it has wiped out the reefs like a liquid-hydrogen bomb.

We would only have to search the perimeter, but that still represented hundreds of miles, even if we knew were to begin. I made the case for us to begin searching in Clewiston because it is, as the crow flies, the closest town to Immokalee, where one of the victims was found, but it was still going to be like looking for the needle in the haystack. We flew low and, I'm sure, terrified every resident along the southern coast of the lake.

Rose had been working on a laptop trying to find an address for Haskell anywhere around the lake but was not having any luck. Then we got a call from Leonard on my cell.

"Grey," he said, almost whispering. "It worked. ATF is running with the story I gave them about Haskell and the school bomber being buddies, and they want to question him. They went to his employers, that weird family who owns the trucking company, and put pressure on them. They say they don't have an address for his place on the lake, but they went there once with him and remembered it was in a tiny place called Lakeport. Ever hear of it?"

I sorted through my memories of the many trips I took with my mother and sister around the lake, fishing or picking fresh strawberries or tomatoes, stopping on the way to break off a piece of sugarcane to chew on. It came to me. "Yeah," I said. "It's just south of the Brighton Indian Reservation. Not much out there but—"

"Farmers and serial killers?"

"Something like that. At least it should make finding Haskell's place easier. This is a big lake, man."

"Don't fall in it. I'm coming with the ATF guys. We're leaving now. How long do you think it'll take us to get out there?"

"Driving? Maybe an hour."

"'Kay. We'll meet you out there. Are you going to wait until we get there to check it out?"

I looked at Rose, who was looking very anxious. "I don't think so, bud. Who knows, this guy might have someone else he's doing something to right now."

"Be careful, Grey. You're no killer and this dude is. Stay safe. The cavalry is coming."

I filled Rose in and told the pilot to fly north along the shoreline. He plotted Lakeport on his GPS and kicked in the throttle. We shot ahead, the force of acceleration pushing us back into our seats. Rose insisted on us putting on the bulletproof vests again, including Amy and Cecil, now finally beginning to look worried. I couldn't blame them.

There weren't many homes on the shoreline in Lakeport, but there was a lot of growth, thick oaks and Washingtonia palms that served well as camouflage. At times, we had to circle a trailer to see what was parked around it.

I saw the race car first. I'd seen a few here and there as we searched, usually stock cars sitting on trailers, blowers sticking out of their hoods. But this one was a bright-red souped-up Mercury with a rebel flag painted on its roof and doors. It appeared to have been placed on a truck chassis and was sticking up off the ground like a giant locust preparing to launch. I didn't get too excited until I saw another car, its black sides barely catching our lights, gleaming from behind some palmettos in spite of being partially covered by a tarp. I knew from the squareness of the car's body that it was a Buick Grand National, like the one I used to own. It was a rare collector's car; the likelihood of there being more than one way out here was remote. I pointed it out to Rose and the pilot and told him to keep moving; maybe Haskell would think we were just a mosquito-control chopper spraying for bugs. The pilot marked the spot on his GPS and we sped off, then circled back partway. We found an open field about a half mile west, put the chopper down, and killed the motor.

It was so quiet and dark one could imagine being at the bottom of the ocean or perhaps marooned in space. Then the bugs and night birds got comfortable with us and began chirping, buzzing, and clicking.

Rose and I would do recon while the others stayed with the chopper until Leonard arrived with the ATF. There was some talk about us waiting until we had backup, but Rose wouldn't have it. She'd grown so intense once we'd sighted the car, there was no talking with her. It was as if Haskell had assaulted her himself, and she was bent on revenge.

"No one else is going to have done to them what this man did to those girls," she said as we unloaded from the helicopter.

She moved forward quickly, but with the stealth of a Florida panther on the hunt. I could barely keep up with her. We used a flashlight to make sure we weren't wandering into a gator hole or frog pond until we could see the lights of the trailer. Then we turned off the lights and switched to the thermal imager I'd brought along. We could see clearly without exposing ourselves; the only visible light on us now was the imager's small red LED power light. As we hastily made a plan of approach, I could smell Rose's skin and feel the heat of her breath against my face. When she was ready to push off into the blackness, I grabbed her arm and pulled her back into a crouch with me.

"What?" she said testily.

"I just wanted to tell you something before we go in," I said. But I didn't have anything to say. I placed my hand along the side of her face and pushed a few loose strands behind her ear. I could barely see her, even though our eyes had adjusted to the dark as much as they were going to at that point. The words I wanted to say were there, but it was not the time. "Just be careful," I said. "Stay close."

She nodded, her jaw muscles flexing. I heard her take the safety off of her gun, and then she was gone.

She ran about ten yards ahead of me, a tactical move we had agreed upon to ensure we wouldn't both appear in the same view of Haskell's rifle scope if he was watching us. I wanted to go first, but she wouldn't have any of it and I knew her well enough now to know not to argue with her. We covered the perimeter of the trailer, doing a quick 360, just as we had done at Haskell's home in Loxahatchee, then meeting in the back.

There was a slight but haunting sound like the mournful wail of a peacock.

"Did you hear anything?" Rose asked.

"Yes," I whispered back. "But it sounds distant. Doesn't sound like it's coming from inside."

"Ready for a look?"

Just then, we heard a moan that chilled my blood and sent goose bumps racing over my skin.

"He's got someone in there," said Rose. "We have to move."

Heart pounding, I crept behind Rose, up the rickety aluminum stairs to the trailer's back door. She turned the handle slowly and cracked the door open.

There was no light behind us, so our silhouettes wouldn't stand out in the doorway. Still, once the door was open, we moved in quickly, staying crouched. Our eyes were used to the dark and we led with our guns pointing the way. The trailer's tiny living room was empty. The trailer creaked with every step we made, making stealth impossible.

I turned on my thermal imager and saw nothing but sparse furnishings. The cramped kitchen was just to the left of us; I skirted in quickly to glance under the counter but found nothing and came back to Rose.

"Bedroom," Rose whispered, though if anyone was there, they had to know we were there. The hallway was so narrow we would have to go single file. I was closest, and Rose did not protest this time when I went first. I inched forward, peering through the imager, my free hand on the butt of my gun. We moved past a bathroom, also empty, and crept into the bedroom, which turned out to be empty as well. We stopped and took a breath.

Still whispering, I asked, "Where the hell did that sound come from?"

Just as I did so, we heard the moaning again. This time, it sounded like it was coming from *under* the trailer, but back toward the living room.

We inched back along the way we had come. The moans had now turned to wails and I thought I could hear someone sniffling, perhaps crying. It did not sound like a woman. Once again, the living room was empty. The sounds stopped.

"I don't get it," Rose whispered.

Sweat ran out of my scalp, down my back, and into my butt crack as I slowly scanned the room with the thermal imager. The pounding of my heartbeat in my ears was distracting and I tried, foolishly, to will my heart to stop so I could concentrate on what I was doing. I was straining so intently to detect any body warmth behind the furniture that I almost missed a small spot on the wall that indicated a temperature difference. It was just a small spot, easily missed, and as I scrutinized it more closely, I could see it was a handprint, or part of a handprint. When I moved forward to get a better look, a whole body came into view. I gasped and ducked away, only to realize I was looking at a full-length mirror and actually seeing myself, my own body's warmth. Fool.

Still, that wasn't my handprint.

"What is it, Grey?"

"Not sure," I said, moving closer to the spot. I was maybe a foot away now, so close that I could clearly see the fingers and thumb making up the white "warm" spot of the handprint.

Suddenly, the mirror flew toward me in a flash of dim light and smashed the imager into my face. I fell back and down to the floor, dropping the imager, half blinded by the blood pouring into my eye. I could hear Rose's clothing swish in the darkness as she pulled her gun up to draw on the shadow that had emerged from behind the mirror.

I got to my knees and tried to stand but was bowled over by a flurry of kicks, elbows, and twisting, straining limbs powered by a pure force whose efficiency was exacerbated by my imbalance. I could see the glint of sweat over hard-packed muscle and sinew, and smell the sharp, hot stink of an enraged animal.

"Stay down!" Rose yelled.

Then the room exploded as her huge gun went off and I saw for the briefest of moments a hole cut in the living room wall, within which the man had been hiding. He lunged from me toward Rose and tripped over my sprawled legs. The scent of gunpowder hung in the room like a sulfurous, choking gas, and my ears were ringing so badly from the concussion that I could barely hear the sounds of the struggle around me.

I was running my hands over the floor trying to recover my gun when Haskell threw Rose into me as if she were a rag doll. I heard the breath get knocked out of her lungs and scrambled over her to shield her with my body, sure the man would press his attack. But it did not come. I sensed him moving away. I felt for Rose and found an arm, running my hands up it, then fear gripped my soul as my thumb found a sticky, spurting laceration. Her sleeve was torn, the flesh beneath it ripped open and bleeding. My own blood dripped from my eye, over my lips, and off my chin, and a shameful feeling of weakness and stupidity overcame me. What brazen arrogance had allowed me to think the two of us could take on this psychopathic killer in his domain, in the dark, in the middle of a saw grass field miles away from the near-est help?

From the corner of my eye, I saw the dark shape of our attacker and I jumped up into a fighting stance, my legs quivering. I could see him more clearly now, at least his height and a flash of his eyes in the darkness, my horror amplified by his relentless silence. He was standing near a small pantry in the kitchen, his hand inside it. He was wearing Army fatigues and a black sleeveless tank top. Light creeping in through the trailer's windows illuminated a blanket of hair that sprouted, like the pelt of a predatory animal, on his muscled shoulders and neck.

Figuring he was going for his own gun, I was preparing to lunge at him when he made a quick movement and suddenly the floor was no longer beneath us. I heard Rose emit a small yelp as she fell with me, and my bent knee met a flat, hard surface with a loud crack and a bolt of pain shooting through my core. I was briefly aware of coming to rest flat on my face on a dusty con-crete floor—enveloped in the sharp scent of urine and fecal mat-ter and the coppery smell of blood—before losing consciousness and continuing the sensation of falling and spinning and being consumed by blackness.

FORTY

I may have been conscious for a while. My eyes may have been open, but in the absolute blackness, I didn't know for sure until I heard the moaning begin again. I rolled to one side and began to catalog my injuries, moving from pain to pain. My kneecap felt shattered, the merest touch of the area eliciting pain, the crunchy broken patella feeling like broken china in a baggie under the swelling flesh.

My own grunts had joined those of the moaner. Realizing the sounds were not coming from Rose—they were too deep, too masculine sounding—relief and fear hit me at the same time. If she was not making the sounds, it meant she was hurt so badly she still had not gained consciousness—or worse, she was not there with me. That frightened and frustrated me more than anything I'd ever felt, so I pushed myself into a sitting position and tried to begin searching the floor for her in total darkness, but the excruciating pain in my knee stopped me.

I managed to quell my growing panic. I used to do confined-space rescue in the fire department, and some of the old training came back to me, most of which prepares the rescuer to manage their emotions and try to complete one task at a time. I took off my bulletproof vest and my belt and managed to improvise a makeshift splint around my leg that allowed me to drag myself around like a cat with its hindquarters broken. My hands found sticky puddles of unknown substances. I breathed through my mouth, unwilling to smell what I was getting into; though I was sure, whatever it was, it had come from another human being. I had been raking the floor with my hands for what seemed like an eternity, though it was probably only a few minutes, when I fumbled onto a foot covered with what felt like a tactical combat shoe. My fingers found an ankle, then moved up the leg. The ankle was thin, the legs shaved—Rose. I worked my way up the body, the curve of her wonderful hips, the slender waist. She still had her Kevlar vest on, but it seemed pushed up around her neck and against her throat. I could hear her labored, slow breathing, so I unstrapped the vest as I performed a blind but thorough assessment of her physical wellness. She seemed to be breathing better as I ran my finger along her neck, checking the rate of her pulse, then for any broken cervical bones or crepitus. There were none, but when I got to her head, I found a huge throbbing egg on the back of her skull and knew why she was still out. I prayed she didn't have a subdural hematoma or a cracked skull—wouldn't last long if she did.

I needed a light. Keeping one hand on her body so I wouldn't lose her in the darkness, I began sweeping the floor again. As I groped around, I came across a strap and clutched desperately at it, pulling it to me until I found the object at the end of the strap— my thermal imager. I snatched it up as if I'd found Aladdin's lamp. When I looked through the screen, I could see the imager had been left on. The battery was nearly dead, the glass lens cracked, but it was still working.

I went back to Rose and looked her over. I could not see great detail, but I could see her body was warm, her limbs all intact. I rolled her onto her side in a standard recovery position and used her vest to support her head. The effort required by my modest emergency field care exhausted me, so I stopped for a breather.

The moaning began again and startled me. It sounded very close. I looked around the room for the first time using the imager and was sorry I did.

Across the room, maybe fifteen feet away, was a chair with a man strapped into it. He was nude. I could see his ghostly outline, his breathing making his shoulders rise and fall as he methodically lifted his head and groaned. I watched without saying anything until I was sure no one else was in the room with us, then inched toward him. As I got closer I could make out some of his features. The imager works off of relative heat; the thickness of skin holds heat, and lines and depressions in facial features show up as darker areas. Eyes usually just look like white orbs, as they are connected to a blood supply and are therefore warm. You can't see color, or the details of the irises or the pupils, but you can see the eyes through the imager—that is, if they're present. Those of the man in the chair were not. Where his eyes should have been were two dark holes.

As I moved very close to him, I saw other parts of his body were missing, too. He opened his mouth to cry out again and I could see the tip of his tongue inch out of his mouth to lick his lips and then, finding no liquid to slake his need, snake back into his mouth impotently, running over dark areas in his gums where teeth had been. I'd never been witness to such human agony in my life. The fact that I was doing so in complete blackness, in a hole that undoubtedly held many terrible secrets, made watching him that much more moving and horrifying. While I still had some power left in the imager, I wanted to free him, not knowing if his injuries were too severe to sustain life, or if he even wanted to live again.

"Sir," I said. "My name is Greymon Gift. I'm going to untie you, okay?"

His head jerked up and I could see him trying to look at me, his eyeless sockets, frankly, scaring the shit out of me. He began to sob, his head bobbing up and down as I found the buckles on the leather straps that held him captive to the chair. I felt stiff areas of what I assumed was dried blood on his skin. When he had the use of his arms again, he brought them up and ran them gently over his face as if assessing the damage done to him. It was pitiful. Then he stood shakily and reached toward me. I took his flailing hand and put my hand in it to give him what comfort I could.

He immediately pulled me toward him and embraced me with a strength I would not have thought was left in him. Still holding me, he whispered into my ear as best he could with his tortured mouth. "It's me, Gift. It's…Rasmussen."

I could not believe it. This was what was left of the confident, strong branch director who I had just talked to—had it been just that morning? It seemed like a lifetime ago. I did not want him to hear the astonishment in my voice, so I summoned up one that sounded as if the situation was in hand, when nothing could have been farther from the truth.

"Hang in there, David. Help's coming," I said.

I watched him sit back down in the chair, his strength ebbing out of him like a tub of hope draining to emptiness. That's when I noticed his penis was gone and there was a gaping wound in his abdomen. His entrails were hanging out, like the umbilical cord that had once attached him to his mother. The organs were dark through the lens of the imager, which meant they were cold and dead.

He shook his head and said, "I'm dead, anyway. Are we still in the…room?"

"Yes, sir. Rose is here, too. She's unconscious, but I think she is okay. Did you see...uh...do you know if there's a way out of here?"

"Rose?" he said, then lowered his head again, the pain of my words as palpable on him as if I'd stabbed him with another knife. "Yes," he said, trying to gather himself. "There is another entrance. Do you have a light?"

"I haven't found one. I'm using a thermal imager; it's like infrared goggles. I can see some things. I see you and Rose from your body warmth."

Once again, his head bobbed up and down, this time as if he were acknowledging the situation. "Thank God she can't see me...what he did to me."

"Yes, sir," I said. "But we'll get you some help. I don't know how long we've been down here, but a friend of mine, another fire marshal, is coming with the ATF."

"I told you two to stay away from Haskell. You don't know what you've gotten into. The Defense Department is running this show and they tried to get the Justice Department to...uh... arrrgh." He stopped to spit, but to no avail. The dehydration from his open abdomen and the enormous loss of blood was killing him. I couldn't imagine the pain he must have been enduring; what a tough bastard he was. "I was trying to protect her," he said weakly.

"You had to know she wouldn't give up. We had to keep following the evidence and the murders, and there've been a shit-load of them. And every one of them had DNA that led back to Haskell. One way or another we were all going to end up here." I didn't want to beat the man while he was down, but I was also angry. Rose might be dying right now while we sat around, helpless, hoping we might get rescued. "Maybe if you'd been more up front with us, we could have worked together and—"

293

He turned his sightless gaze at me. "I couldn't tell her… everything. She was…God help me. She became a part of it and she doesn't even know. She was…used. It's…it's why she was attacked."

"What? What do you mean?"

"No…time for…that."

It would be a long time before I'd get an answer to that question, but I wasn't getting it from Rasmussen that day. I watched him through the imager as he shook his head from side to side, his mouth opening to wail but no sound coming from it, nor tears from his eyeless sockets, though what he was telling me seemed to be causing him more pain than his physical injuries. I could see he was near the end—of his capacity to withstand what had been done to him and of his time on earth.

"Listen," he said. "If you do get out of here, there's a file on my laptop. It's called *Armageddon*. My password is… *ROSE*, all caps…If…you make it…tell her. It might explain… to her what happened. It's a…journal. I think whoever wrote it was…tracking serial killers. It's from a man named Gettys…"

"Harmon Gettys?" My mind was swimming.

"Yes, yes," Rasmussen said, exhausted, his life slipping away. "Gettys's journal will…help you understand. He's…I…I don't think he's dead."

"But he killed himself in jail."

"I started looking into his…case. The…same day…he supposedly killed himself, one of the prison guards went missing. The body in Gettys's cell was assumed to be him, but it was never autopsied. I…think he's alive."

"But why would he be in league with Cerberus? He's the one that busted Gettys in the first place."

"I...don't know...but I think he sent me the file." He arched his back against a fresh wave of pain. "G...Gift. You have to...help me. Finish me. Finish me."

I knew what he was asking me, just as sure as I knew I was going to do it. But before I could do it, I felt a hand on my shoulder. It brushed me softly at first, as if to let me know she was there without startling me; then her grip grew stronger. She took the imager from my hands, and in the darkness, I saw her put it to her face, lighting up her eyes for a second before she peered into the viewfinder. Rasmussen continued to plead with me.

"Please, Gift!" he cried. "You were a firefighter, a *medic*. You guys can't stand to watch people suffering, right? You have to... end this for me. Ple—"

Suddenly, the room lit up as if a strobe light had flashed and a deafening boom reverberated in the small room, percussing my ears so fiercely that I was left dizzy and disoriented. It had been only a brief moment, but it would be one I would never forget: Rose pointing her Casull Magnum at Rasmussen and firing. Just before everything went dark again, the image repeated for me: Rose holding her gun as if she were at a firing range, calmly, even coldly, leveling the pistol at his face and blowing his head off. He never even knew she was there.

Even with my ears still ringing and the noxious scent of the gunpowder filling the room with its burning stench, I could hear Rose exhale as if releasing a sigh of relief. But the flash of the gunfire had done its job; my vertigo continued, and had I been able to see, I'm sure the room would have been spinning. I sank to the floor and even the pain of falling on my injured kneecap could not stave off the seizure. I lay on my back, hoping a brief respite would steady me and I could hold on to reality until the seizure passed, but I was falling into that deep well.

Suddenly, a blinding light filled the room, and Rose, now fully enveloped in the harsh brightness, was holding her gun and squinting at the light, ready to fire. But she wasn't looking in the right direction. She wasn't looking behind her where Devon Haskell was standing, his eyes gleaming in anticipation in his otherwise expressionless face.

I tried to call out and warn her, but I was already slipping into my other world, the one where the electrical activity of my brain misfires and produces an incorporeal world in which I have no control over body or mind. As I drifted away from the horror of this tangible reality, I held Haskell's face in my mind and remembered what the fat man at the towing company had said. *"Wiry dude. Looks kinda like you..."* Those were my last thoughts. A man who looked like me, but "about a foot taller," who had already killed several people in ways that even the most demented mind could not imagine, standing behind the woman I loved. Then his arms shot out as fast as a snakebite and he had her.

FORTY-ONE

In my dream state, I envisioned Rose drawing down on me with that monstrous gun of hers. When I tried to talk to her, ask her why she was aiming at me, no words came out. She fired the gun, but instead of a bullet hitting me in the chest or taking off my head, there was a small popping sound, like a cap gun. I looked myself over, seeking a gunshot wound, and when I didn't find one, I started to laugh, and that's when I burst into flames.

I didn't know how long I had been awake. My eyes were open, but the room was black again, so I had the eerie sensation that I now knew what Rasmussen must have felt, staring through empty eye sockets. The sensation of my eyes blinking repeatedly finally kick-started my brain into realizing I was conscious.

"Rose," I whispered, my voice softened by the dryness in my throat. Clearing it, I said louder, "Rose?" But there was no answer.

I rolled onto my side and attempted to get to my knees. The broken kneecap once again announced its presence by firing a jolt of pain through me, pulling my breath away but sending a rush of adrenaline that served to fully awaken me. It was better for me to stand and inch my way around, and I did so. I wandered around the dark room, my arm extended until I could find a wall, then began a perimeter search, just as I would if I were searching for a body in a smoke-filled house fire. Within a few feet, I stumbled across a body.

It was as if my thudding heart came up my throat and filled my mouth. As I reached down, I hoped, on the one hand, that it was Rose and I'd at least know what had happened to her and, on the other hand, hoped it was not.

It was not.

Running my hands over the body, I found the naked form of a man, his hairy chest still slick with what I had to assume was blood. Groping further, I found the neck and the remaining lower jaw of what had been Rasmussen's head. I pulled my hands away as if I'd been fondling a tarantula in the dark and wiped the sticky, wet residue on my pants. The scent of his body in death filled my nostrils and my stomach heaved, but did not release its contents. I fumbled along farther, found another part of a skull, some hair still attached to it. I felt the hair to ensure it was Rasmussen's short-cropped hair and not Rose's long, dark tresses.

I thought about Rose ending Rasmussen's life. In fact, the image consumed me, the brief image flashing in my mind over and over again. Would I have killed him? I think the answer was yes, given his pain and unsalvageable condition. But could I have? And how could she have done it so…easily? Without saying a word, she had looked at him and made the quick decision to end his life. Did she do that because they had been former lovers and it was the most humane thing to do, or was it something else that had allowed her to pull the trigger? Did she harbor some resentment toward him for turning her into the thing she most despised, a mistress stealing the affections of another woman's husband, just as some other woman had done to her? And what did Rasmussen mean when he said Rose was a part of this thing, this conspiracy that was evidently sponsored and overseen by some of the nation's most powerful forces? Could she have known that? And how did the attack on her figure into this bizarre and terrifying plot? Where did Harmon Gettys fit in? There were too many questions and I wasn't going to find the answer holed up in this dank and dark crypt.

I continued my perimeter search, one hand on the wall and one feeling outward toward the center of the room, like a cockroach investigating with its antennae, crawling through a horror-filled abattoir. I hoped I could find a gun, radio, or flashlight that had been left behind, but had no such luck. I checked for my backup gun on my ankle and found it was gone, so it was safe to assume all the guns had been picked up. I cursed myself for being so confident in my own physical strength as to ignore the seizures that had been occurring more and more frequently. This is why they don't let people who have seizures carry on in my field of work. I'd thought I could deal with them and had, in the end, placed myself and another person in harm's way, perhaps sealing our dismal fates.

My hands brushed something hard and cold, and I grasped at it, thankful that it was not another piece of a body. I turned it over in my hands. It was the thermal imager. It had been left on and the battery was almost dead, the pale LED power light flickering. Quickly, I held it to my face and looked around the room. As I had searched, I had felt the walls, trying to find a door or an opening. Rasmussen had said there was another entrance. Was that how Haskell had slipped into the room while our attention was turned toward the dying branch director?

The imager's picture was pale and kept going black, but I kept the device to my eyes, praying I could see something that would indicate a way out and trying not to think what Haskell might be doing to Rose, if she was even still alive. I thought I saw something, a small white blotch, just before the picture went black again. I moved toward that white mark, that small image that indicated heat, hoping beyond hope the imager would kick on one last time and lead me out of there.

It did.

I had managed to get right next to where I'd seen the white splotch when the imager came back on. I could clearly see the image now, so well, in fact, that I was able to make out what it was: it was a handprint, and much more. It was hope.

I held the imager within a few inches of the handprint so I could see it clearly. It was small, too small for Haskell to have left it. It had to be Rose's, and it had to have been left within the past few minutes, the image still holding some residual heat, or the imager would not have been able to find it. Then I saw another, then another, each one slightly brighter than the last. It had to be Rose leaving her handprints. She would know that if I found the imager, I would use it and had somehow managed to conceal it from Haskell. If this were so, I had to believe she was leaving me indicators, like trail markers leading through a forest.

I followed the handprints eagerly now, hope building in me like a small fire, but the trail suddenly ended with a print that was cut in half, as if some of the hand were now missing. That thought sent fear into my belly and I had to shake off the images that began pouring into my head. Then the imager went dead. I tried to get it to come back to life, but it was dead now, along with it my source of light and direction.

The fear began to well up in me again, so I pushed myself to keep busy. I tried to feel the last print, the half print, running my fingers over the steel walls. Pinching my eyes shut, I tried to recall exactly where that print had been in relation to my body, then reached out and touched the cold steel surface. I found a crack, a very tight seam running vertically up the wall. I let my fingers run up its length, found a corner, and then ran back horizontally, then down again, vertically. I found a hinge, kept going down and found another. A door! But I could not find a door handle or clasp—it must have been on the other side, fitted tight into this chamber of horrors that Haskell kept for torturing his victims.

I concentrated on putting all of my sense of touch into my fingertips and felt the hinges. I could feel the hinge pin, its head slightly above the body of the hinge, and the fire of hope within me turned into a blaze. If I could get the hinge pins out, I might be able to remove the door. But I would have to do so in complete darkness. And what could I use for tools?

I fumbled for the imager and felt the edge of its screen. There was a small metal lip surrounding the screen to help protect it if it was dropped. It was narrow, but it might work. I fingered the hinge again and placed the lip of the imager up underneath the head of the pin. Then I smacked the butt of my palm against the hinge. The imager slipped off and I almost dropped it. I tried again, changing the imager's angle against the pin and smacking it again. This time, I felt the pin give a half inch or so. I did it again, and again, until it gave all at once and I dropped the imager as it did so. I heard the pin fall to the floor with a liberating *ting*.

I felt the floor for the imager again, found it, and began on the middle hinge. When I had removed its pin, I did the same to the bottom hinge, careful not to pull it out until I moved myself to the side in case the door came loose and fell after the pins were out. But the door was wedged tightly into its opening and did not fall. I used one of the pins to find a purchase in the door's edge and picked and pried until the door crack began to widen, then widened yet more. I inched it out enough for me to get my fingers on the door and pulled with all the strength I had left. The door was solid and heavy, but came loose with a rusty groan and fell with a heavy thud.

The opening led into a hall—actually, a tunnel carved through the Florida dirt and mud, its sides lined with plank wood to keep the muddy walls from crumbling. I felt along the rough-hewn wood, picking up splinters along the way but feeling the freedom, or the thought of freedom, giving me renewed strength and purpose. The tunnel seemed to go on forever. It had to be at least a hundred yards long. As my eyes adjusted to the new space, I could make out light, ever so pale, at the end of the tunnel. I moved toward it quickly but cautiously.

When I came to the end, I found a handcrafted ladder leading up. I put my foot on the lowest rung and began to climb up, my heart racing again with anticipation, my injured leg protesting with each vertical ascent, the knee so swollen it threatened to burst through my pants seam. It was a short climb and I found the exit to the tunnel covered with another heavy door or panel. This one was made of heavy planks of thick, splintered wood that allowed some dim light to eke into the shaft. I prayed it was not locked as I fingered its edge, looking for a clasp or handle. Again, there didn't seem to be one, and after considering my options and finding them very limited, I placed my shoulder up against the tunnel lid and heaved. The top came up and flipped over with a *plop*, the sound deadened by thick saw grass that surrounded the opening.

The lights of the stars had never seemed so bright. I felt truly nocturnal now, my eyes as sharp and focused as an owl's after being in the blackness for so long. My hearing felt just as acute. There was no one around, but I could hear car doors opening and closing, and what I thought was some scuffling and a small, almost imperceptible protestation from Rose. Then I heard the sound of flesh striking flesh, followed by an unnerving silence. The sound terrified and energized me, and I came out of the hole, trying to forget about my stiff, wounded leg and searching wildly for something to use as a weapon. Nothing.

I inched through the tall, dry saw grass, its sharp edges ripping at my clothing and exposed skin. I moved as quietly as I could, dragging my bad leg behind me like a piece of heavy timber. I made my way to the edge of a clearing, where I encountered a strong fuel smell, like gasoline but stronger. Jet fuel, just like the fuel used on Jolie Matarese, the hooker whose body was found in Tamarac, gutted and burned. Acid poured into my stomach as my mind conjured an image of Rose lying mutilated somewhere nearby and Haskell dousing her with fuel before he set fire to her. I tried to restrain the sense of urgency I felt so that I could formulate a plan of attack, but it was nearly impossible to keep my head straight.

I inched closer and could clearly see Haskell's trailer ahead. The "race car," which I could now see was more swamp buggy than NASCAR racer, was sitting in front. Suddenly, its huge motor cranked to life, idling unevenly, smoke puffing out of its mufflers like the nostrils of a fire-breathing dragon.

Haskell jumped from the cab of the buggy and approached the mobile home, a huge fuel container in his hand. He was splashing fuel around the base of the trailer and up onto its sides. I forced myself to think it through: he was cornered, and with a pit below his house full of evidence that would undoubtedly earn him multiple life sentences, he was setting it all ablaze, along with the dumbass fire marshal sleeping off a seizure down below. Fucker.

But where was Rose? I looked around the clearing but couldn't see her. I prayed she was not in the house. Hadn't I just heard her a few moments before? I had no choice; I had to find her if she was still alive. I got up and hobbled over to the area where the Buick Grand National was sitting under a tarp. I approached the car, noting the containers of fuel stored around it. I hefted one and found it to be full. I inched up the tarp, hoping if the car was open, I could get in, pop the trunk, and at least arm myself with a tire iron, or something. I pushed my thumb against the door button and popped open the door, sending a wash of light flooding over me from the overhead bulb. I slid as quickly and quietly as I could into the driver's seat and pulled the door shut, but the floor of the car was full of beer bottles and they rattled a warning.

There was a rip in the tarp covering the car and I saw Haskell stop what he was doing and look toward the Buick. I lay down flat on the console and hoped he had not seen me or the flash of the dome light. I stayed down for what seemed like a half hour but was probably only a minute. When I mustered the nerve to look up again, Haskell was about ten feet away from the car, approaching with a flashlight and a pistol. I was trapped.

To the well-documented fight-or-flight responses we share with all animals when faced with danger, I would add one more: find a weapon. What I did was out of desperation and employed two other survival mechanisms: stealth and cunning. I grabbed one of the bottles off the floor, and after disabling the dome light, I slipped out of the car and shut the door as quietly as I could.

I had to squat down, which meant I had to bend that broken knee, and the pain was so severe it brought tears to my eyes and pumped adrenaline through me like a load of epinephrine, increasing my heart rate and respirations as if I'd been running for several miles. I had to ignore it. I knew I was screwed and there was nothing left to lose. I peered over the edge of the trunk and saw Haskell reach over and tear the tarp off the car, using the hand that was holding the gun. I would never have another chance. I drew back as far as I could with the hand that held the beer bottle and let it fly.

Hoping it would hit him at least hard enough to startle him and give me a chance to jump him, I was already running at him as fast as a person with one bum leg can run, but fate was with me. Haskell had looked up and turned his face toward me, already dropping the tarp and coming around with the pistol, just as the bottle struck him squarely in the face. Shards of brown glass and a spray of blood exploded from his face like an overripe melon hitting a window.

Haskell was off balance and I took advantage of that momentary disadvantage to fly into him. The first thing I had to do was get that gun away from him. Fighting technique and training went out the window in my desperation. I bit down on his hand until I tasted his blood spurting into my mouth. He howled in pain but came around with the flashlight and hit me in the face with it, reopening the wound I'd received earlier when he'd come at us from behind the mirror in his living room. But he'd dropped the gun and we were now on more or less equal footing, if you didn't take into account my broken knee or the fact that he was both a trained and psychotic killer.

He had wrapped one arm around my chest and I saw the flashlight go up again. He was going to bash my brains out if he couldn't shoot me, so I snapped my head back as fast as I could, head-butting him hard enough that I could hear teeth break, and his grip loosened. Amazingly, we were still standing, but I knew I couldn't count on my bad leg to see me through a stand-up fist-fight. I could feel his imbalance and, using my old but retained skills in jujitsu, managed to lever him into a move that allowed me to flip him, and he hit the ground hard.

I saw the gun in the grass and went for it, but Haskell saw what I was doing and grabbed my leg and took me down with him.

It was assholes and elbows then as we struggled, trying desperately to kill each other. He was powerful and seemed to anticipate my every move. At last, we fell into a grappling embrace, rolling around and careening into fuel containers, dousing ourselves with jet fuel, his intent to smash my head into the ground, mine to survive until help came, if it was coming.

I managed to get my arms locked around his neck as he pummeled my sides with his fists, each punch feeling as though a horse were kicking my ribs in. I managed to catch one of my own sleeves with one hand, then my other sleeve with the other hand. This left my sides open to his blows and he took full advantage of it, his heavily muscled shoulders driving his punches like pneumatic hammers. I felt one rib after another crack as he pressed his attack. But I knew the technique I wanted to deploy and had no choice to but to stick to my plan.

Using my sleeves as a sort of corkscrew, I began to twist their fabric, one forearm against the back of his neck, the other against his throat, scissoring his neck like a vise. I hooked my one good leg around his torso and began to bear against his kidneys and lower vertebrae with it. It is a submissive technique that ends up with one of two things happening: your opponent concedes or is strangled to death. Haskell did not concede. I watched his face contort, inches from mine, his eyes and neck veins bulging as he tried to tighten his neck muscles against my grip. I could hear the air whistling through his constricted windpipe and smell his breath escaping in short gasps, the scent sharp, like pickled pigs' feet or sausage. He sputtered and spit, then tried to gulp some air but could not get enough. Finally, he quit fighting and his head slowly slumped forward.

I rolled over and just lay there, trying to catch my own breath. I could feel the caustic jet fuel begin to burn my skin and knew I had to rinse it off. At last, I rolled to one side, the one I felt had the least amount of ribs broken, and managed to crawl over to the gun and pick it up. It was Rose's Casull Magnum. Now she was back in my mind, and I switched from survival mode into search mode. I had to find her.

I was creeping my way back toward the trailer, wheezing, my skin blistering, and wondering if I hadn't punctured a lung, when a movement caught the corner of my eye. It was coming from the souped-up swamp buggy. It was Rose. Her head bobbed up into the steamed-up window of the vehicle and she looked my way, her eyes wide with desperation. She had tape over her mouth, but even over the buggy's engine, I could hear her trying to call to me. I gimped my way over to her and opened the door. She managed to squirm out of the car, though her wrists and ankles were bound. I pulled the tape from her mouth and kissed her, then looked for something to cut her bonds. I looked in the backseat of the vehicle and saw all of Haskell's guns, rifles, and some knives piled in there, as if he'd been on his way to fight a war. I knew I was probably soiling evidence but grabbed one of the knives anyway and freed Rose.

"Here's your gun back," I said, handing her the small cannon. She took it and hefted it in her palm.

"God, Grey," she said in her cool, methodical way, "you smell horrible. Like maybe you could ignite."

"I know," I said weakly. "Need to rinse off."

Rose helped me over to the side of the house, where we found a hose. She turned the spigot and took a sip of water, then began to rinse me off. I peeled off my shirt and rinsed myself thoroughly just as we heard the distant but familiar sound of chopper blades cutting the air.

"Here comes the cavalry," I said.

"Better late than never, I suppose."

We both smiled weakly at that, but immediately lost our grins when we heard the swamp buggy's engine accelerate, its loud mufflers roaring like a blast furnace. Haskell had regained consciousness and made his way to the vehicle. Remembering the weapons in the backseat, I considered grabbing Rose and taking cover. But Haskell wasn't watching us. He was staring out the windshield at the bright light of the approaching helicopter. In the distance, we could hear sirens and see flashing blue lights as well. He looked back at us with an angry sneer, then gunned the motor. The back tires spun, spraying dirt and mud as he rooster-tailed the vehicle away from us, toward a nearby sugarcane field.

I stood there, spent, unable, or perhaps, unwilling, to move. "He can't get too far," I said weakly.

Rose looked at me as if I were the biggest tool in the world. "Fuck that," she said, and began to run after the truck.

I yelled after her, but it was like screaming "stop" at a bull running through the streets of Pamplona. It just wasn't going to happen.

She stopped and fired at him, then ran again. I was amazed at how fast she could run. Maybe Haskell was spinning the wheels too much to get good traction and get out of there, but for a moment, it looked like she was actually gaining ground on him. Then he began to pull away and I could just imagine the stream of profanity coming for her mouth. As he neared the edge of the cane fields, she finally stopped, but she wasn't giving up. She placed herself into a shooter's stance, took a deep breath, steadied her aim, and fired once, the huge gun recoiling, then again. She had used one shot on Rasmussen, and now three more at the fleeing Haskell. The Casull only held five. She must have known that, because she took her time aiming before firing her last round.

I saw the flame erupt in the rear of the swamp buggy before I heard the explosion. She must have hit the jet-fuel-filled tank in the rear of truck. There was another explosion, then a series of smaller ones as the vehicle slowly rolled into the sugarcane, immediately setting fire to the dry brush before coming to a complete stop, its tires aflame, black smoke billowing from its burning hulk.

I saw Haskell leap from the cab of the buggy, fully engulfed in fire. He ran around like a Hollywood stunt man, wildly waving his arms, trying, like all of his victims had, to live. Just live.

Watching him burn, then fall to the ground, I could muster no sympathy for him, though I could think of no worse way to die.

Rose made her way back to me, barely concealing a mad grin. "That's one cooked killer," she said, then sat back flat on her butt, laughing uncontrollably at first, before that dissolved into crying, her wails increasing like those of a man on fire.

I went over, awkwardly sat down next to her, and placed my arm around her shoulders. But I could not help but think of the vision I'd had earlier, when I was trapped in that dark place beneath the trailer, coming out of a seizure: Rose firing her gun at me and setting me on fire.

FORTY-TWO

One week later, I was home recovering on the patio in the back-yard. Emily was out in the barn tending to Sisco. I had watched them trot around in the backyard, an inseparable duo, each incomplete without the other and both happy as clams. I saw Emily walk Sisco back to the barn and brush him and love him, letting him gently pull carrots from her mouth. Another, almost unbearably tender world compared to what I'd experienced over the past few weeks.

My leg was in a cast, the stitches in my head itched, and my ribs were tender but healing. But my heart was aching. I missed Rose. She was under house arrest, but still being shuttled back and forth between Quantico and Miami, undergoing an internal investigation into the killing of David Rasmussen.

Rose and I had talked about what to tell the ATF and the soon-to-follow FBI agents who swarmed Haskell's hideaway and found Rasmussen in the crude basement/torture chamber under the trailer. It would have been easy to blame Haskell—we could even find his prints on her gun—and I tried to persuade Rose to go along with that idea, but she wouldn't have it. So I tried to take the heat for killing Rasmussen, saying I'd done it out of mercy—he had been tortured to the point of death and pleaded with me to kill him. But again, Rose wouldn't have it and told the investigating agents she had been the one to put Rasmussen out of his agony. No one who'd been at the scene or studied the evidence held malice toward her; they could see what Rasmussen had been through. I overheard more than one conversation between agents saying they would hope someone would do them the same favor under the same horrific circumstances.

Still, it was the killing of a high-ranking FBI official and Rose had included every detail in her report, including their previous relationship, the fact of which did not sit at all well with their superiors. There was little doubt Rasmussen would have died from his injuries, but no matter the circumstances, mercy killing is not a legal option in conservative America, and the leading law agency of this country could not just let it go.

I was going to have to testify in a few weeks as part of the investigation and I intended to tell them what I'd seen and do all I could to paint a picture that would place them in the scene and realize what had to be done. But because I was subpoenaed to testify, Rose and I were not allowed to have personal contact or discussions about the case, and I was finding that extremely difficult to endure.

Our last discussion was a couple days after that unholy event, before her agency gave us the bad news that she was, more or less, under arrest. She had come back home with me after I was released from the hospital and made gentle but passionate love to me, trying not to aggravate my injuries, but both of us had been so consumed with lust for each other that we almost broke my cast as we went at each other like it was the first time again. It was, I came to realize, a cathartic thing for her. When we spoke of it later, she told me she would never again have a relationship that was not open, honest, and exclusive and that, indeed, she held so much self-loathing for her relationship with Rasmussen that she felt the need to bear some suffering for it. I understood that she, having been raised a Catholic, expected to pay such a penance. But should I have to pay for that sin, too?

Years later, I would still wonder to myself if Rose had killed Rasmussen purely to ease his suffering or if, indeed, it was at least in part her way of cleaning the slate—of subconsciously trying to wipe away their sins by performing the ultimate sacrifice for both of them.

Rasmussen's laptop was of no use to us. He had parked his car in that same field where Haskell had driven his jet-fueled monster truck, and thirty acres of sugarcane burned along with Rasmussen's car and personal effects. Nor did we find the Gettys journal he had referred to. If it was on his laptop in the car, it had been consumed by flames. If the FBI had access to his files, they were not telling us.

We were still trying to decipher exactly what had been happening. We knew, with reasonable certainty, that the man named Harmon Gettys had spread his serial killer DNA through fertility clinics across America a generation before. We knew Cerberus used to work at the FBI and that he was the man responsible for capturing Gettys those many years ago. Beyond this, though, it got real fuzzy.

Shortly after Gettys went to jail, Cerberus left the FBI and formed his own intelligence and security consulting firm—SEE, Scorched Earth Enterprises. He subcontracted services for intelligence and consulting for years to the CIA as well as numerous other agencies, both in and out of the United States. He had worked behind the scenes in every geopolitical hot spot in the world since the late 1970s and early 1980s, including the Soviet-Afghan war in which, we were able to find out from the FBI, he had dealt in "conventional and experimental weaponry" and "intelligence security." But Cerberus was so deep undercover and his work so top secret that no one knew anything beyond that, including his present whereabouts.

Rose and I speculated that Haskell must have been one of his operatives, a trained killer who also happened to be a serial killer, and that Cerberus had been trying to protect him. We could not have known then how wrong we were at that time. We made assumptions about all of those killers with Gettys's DNA who were also killed, blaming their deaths on Haskell because we felt he was the only one with the skills and ruthlessness to execute them, though we could not come up with his motive. We made a lot of false assumptions because we did not have all the information, and we did not have all the information because so much of it was classified as top secret. In truth, we'd come to realize that no one in their right mind, even armed with all of the facts, would have been able to piece together all that had transpired.

It was late in the day and I was sipping a glass of chardonnay—nothing else in the house—like some old retired Broadway queen, trying to relax, and watching the sky begin to change. It went from brilliant blue to that greenish color near the horizon that precedes the yellows and tangerines and pinks and purples of the Florida sunset.

I was doing a lot of self-analysis, too. Maybe too much. One item I was seriously debating was whether or not I was going to stay employed as a working state fire marshal. I could lie to others about my seizures, but I could not lie to myself. I was a danger, not only to myself, but to others. People had to depend on me and could not do so if I was off in "la-la land," as Rose had called it, when I was needed. It was nothing short of miraculous that I had come to and managed to escape from that dark hellhole under Haskell's hideout and that I had not had more "episodes," as my doctor referred to them. Again and again, I asked myself, what if I would have had a seizure when I was fighting Haskell? The answer was always the same: Rose and I would both be dead. Every time I thought about it, I came back to the same conclusion: it was damned irresponsible for me to continue in my line of work. I felt empty and purposeless and I was probably going to need some counseling or a good antidepressant before I got to where I was feeling "normal" again.

My phone rang. It was Cecil.

"Hey, Grey, you sitting down?"

"No, Cecil, I'm doing wind sprints and hurdles in the backyard with my cast on."

"Okay, smart-ass. I know you have some boo-boos and you're feeling sorry for yourself, but I called because I have some important information for you."

"You're engaged to Amy?"

"Well, yeah, that's coming. But really, pal, you need to hear this."

I wasn't used to this serious tone from Cecil and I felt a chill going up the nape of my neck. "Okay, Cecil. What is it?"

"You know they asked Amy and me to collect some samples at Haskell's trailer while we were there that night, because we told them we had been collecting DNA samples for a string of serial killings? Our buddy Leonard Cotton helped clear some red tape for us after you were taken to the hospital."

"I heard."

"Well, Amy and I took samples from several areas in the house, including the living room where you said you first encountered Haskell before he sent you through the trapdoor and into the basement. Now, think very hard. You said you got your head

314

cut open in the living room, and Rose sustained a laceration to her arm, right?"

"That's right."

"And you said you bit Haskell on the hand, right?"

"I'm sure, Cecil. He got the jump on us. He had a secret hiding spot cut into the wall where he could hide behind a mirror. Guy was a covert special ops nut who took his work way seriously, on top of being a psychopath. But, yeah, I managed to bite him and he bled just like the rest of us."

"Well, omitting his blood type, which we've already identified, and assuming no one else was in the trailer, then I have something very disturbing, or at least as weird as shit, to tell you."

"Get to it. Please."

"Okay, okay. We analyzed three blood samples from that room. They were fresh—that is, they had not been there prior to the night you guys took him down. Two of them have DNA that matches the Gettys strain."

"Rasmussen's?"

"Nope. We checked that. Unless someone else was bleeding in that room, one was Haskell's and the other is either yours or Rose's."

I didn't know what to say. The implications were horrifying. Of course, my natural response was to assure myself it was not mine. I mean, it couldn't be, right?

As if he were reading my mind, Cecil said, "Grey, even if it is yours, it doesn't mean that all people who have a strain similar to Gettys's are serial killers."

"No," I said, my head swimming. "But every one of the serial killers we looked at last week had that same DNA. I heard the FBI did further analysis on all of those sites we visited that day and they confirmed that."

"Yeah, we heard that, too. I suppose the good news is that we know the *Sanguinaut* functions well in the field. Amy's probably going to make millions from it. You still there?"

I sipped my wine and looked up into the sky again. "Yeah, Cecil, I'm still here. Just thinking."

"Sorry, Grey. I know you have a lot to think about these days. How are the seizures?"

"Haven't had one since that night at Haskell's. Thanks for asking."

"That's good. Are you still thinking about quitting the fire marshal's office?"

"Thinking about it."

"Well, keep me in mind. We could get Leonard to come in with us and open a private investigations business. 'Button, Cotton, and Gift'—how's that sound?"

"I don't think so, Cecil. Sounds like Bed, Bath, and Beyond."

Cecil snorted at that. "Hey, Amy's calling on the other line. Can I get back to you later?"

"Sure."

And we hung up.

Powered by this new information, my mind was racing with scenarios and possibilities, all of which led to more confusion. And I couldn't help but think about what Rasmussen had said before Rose had shot him: *She became a part of it and she doesn't even know. She was...used. It's...it's why she was attacked.*

I had not discussed that conversation with Rose, but surely she had heard it. What had he meant by *she was used*, and what could the attack on her have had to do with these murders? Was it possible she did know she was a part of some conspiracy and that's why she shot Rasmussen?

I needed to talk to Rose, and even though I knew her phone might be tapped, I called it anyway. I had done nothing wrong, and as far as I knew, she hadn't, either. So what if we talked? Would I get my wrist slapped? I needed some answers, some closure to this crazed mess. Maybe she could make sense of this new information. I had, at the very least, an obligation to tell her about it. But there was no answer at her home or on her cell. I got her voice mail but could not begin to think of the appropriate message to leave her, so I hung up, disconsolate.

The dark blue of twilight had begun to seep up from the horizon, replacing the collage of color in the sky, and I realized Emily had not emerged from the barn after she'd put Sisco up. While I'd been on the phone, I'd heard Scout yapping and assumed she was just carrying on, annoying Sisco in her affectionate way, but Scout had grown silent, too. I knew Emily had to be home before dark, so I called out to her. There was no answer. I called out to Sisco. If he were not tied up in his stall, he would come running out, but he did not appear. I called for Scout, who certainly would have come running, but again, there was silence.

A couple of sandhill cranes flew in and landed in the pasture behind my place, their scarlet-topped heads making them appear as though they had been scalped. At four feet tall, their fierce, predatory yellow eyes make them seem like atavistic throwbacks to a prehistoric and savage time. They began screeching as I watched them, like pterodactyls going in for a kill, and their presence at that time, at that particular moment, made them seem like ominous harbingers of doom.

Listening for Emily, Sisco, or Scout, I looked down the trail that led out of my backyard and into the equestrian community. Maybe they'd slipped by and I'd just missed them. But they weren't there, either, so I yelled again, louder this time, but my shout was again met with silence. It was so quiet my ears began to ring. I was just beginning to stand to hobble my way out there when I noticed a man emerge from the barn. He waved to me as if we knew each other from long ago.

FORTY-THREE

He strode toward me comfortably, like an old friend. He was an older man, but everything about him suggested strength and self-assurance. He was lean and tall, handsome and poised, with dark, penetrating eyes and coiffed and aristocratic gray hair. His clothes were pressed and his shirt buttoned up to his neck. His hands appeared wet and he shook them in the air to dry them. As he came closer, I thought I recognized him, but couldn't place him.

"Good evening, Mr. Gift," he said.

"Do I know you, sir?"

He smiled and looked at me benevolently. "We've met before. I think I told you, and rightly so, that you are a gentleman and a scholar."

His words twisted my mind so severely that I felt on the brink of another seizure. The memory of our meeting hit me like a train: he was the old man I had seen in Tamarac. The one who had tripped and who I'd stopped to help to his feet. Some instinctive animal awareness kicked in and I felt my scalp rise up and a sheen of sweat form on my lower back.

"I don't believe I caught your name," I said. A lump had formed in my throat and I swallowed, feeling as though I had just eaten a cup of peanut butter.

He came up on the patio and took a chair next to me. I could smell his aftershave. He was impeccably groomed, with perfectly manicured nails and iridescently white teeth, like china. But I smelled something else, too—a trace of some other scent I could not place—and an inexplicable fear crept into my stomach.

His smile showed those immaculate teeth as he said, in a self-deprecating manner, "I think you may know me as Harmon Gettys."

I stood up, not really knowing where I was going, but feeling I needed to go somewhere, do something.

"Please sit down, Mr. Gift. We need to talk. I think I can help you."

"Where's Emily?"

"The girl who tends your horse?"

"Yes. I called for her, but she didn't answer."

He looked at me almost sheepishly, then down to the ground as if he were embarrassed. He shrugged his shoulders and I knew.

I started to run to the barn, but he shot his long leg under my compromised one and tripped me. I rolled to my side and was trying to push myself up when he walked up nonchalantly and kicked me in the ribs. My vision turned red as white-hot pain seared through me. I heard shards of bone rubbing together in my chest and I could not catch my breath.

"Please," I pleaded. "If you want to kill me, please let the girl go. She's...innocent."

"Oh, I understand," he said, rolling me over and sitting on top of my chest. He produced a small automatic pistol, a chrome-plated .32, and a pair of handcuffs, which he slipped onto my wrist and his as quickly as a magician. He held the gun in front of my face. "Don't worry about the retarded girl, or your horse, just now. We have a few minutes, but you will have to listen to me and do as I say if you want them to live, Mr. Gift. There will be no deals, no compromises."

"What did you do?" I gasped through clenched teeth, trying to breathe.

His expression went from benevolent to cold in the blink of an eye. His Adam's apple worked up and down as he spoke, undulating like the insatiable pumping of some ancient reptile as it swallows a rodent. "I will tell you, but you have to listen to me first. If you refuse or continue to struggle, I will kill you. Come now, you are in no shape to fight even an older gentleman like me."

With that, he stood up and grabbed my hand. "Up with you now," he said in a commanding tone. "You're wasting valuable time." He kept his gun hand back away from me, but the gun's barrel never strayed from me. I let him help me to my feet. "Sit back down, if you want to see Emily alive again."

I did as I was told.

"I need to tell you some things, and I hope my telling you will instill in you a sense of urgency and need. I need you to be committed and willing to complete the task I am going to obligate you to."

"What the fuck are you talking about, Gettys?"

"Please, let's not get crude. I know you are angry, and that is good. It is what I need. But first let me say, my name is not Gettys. That is a name they gave me when they staged my arrest and conviction. I think that was Mr. Cerberus's idea. Don't you see how ridiculous it is? Harmon Gettys? Arma-geddon?"

It made an awful kind of sense to me. Such playful, hideous men. "Go on," I said.

"I was a scientist working for the R&D sector of the FBI in the late seventies and early eighties. Research and development, you know?"

"I know what R&D means."

"Of course you do. You're hampered by some emotional weaknesses, but you are a very intelligent man, Mr. Gift. I've done my homework. Anyway, Armageddon was the name of a project I started. Nicholas Cerberus was an assistant, actually a field agent, assigned to work with me as part of his thesis project. I was an anthropologist studying criminal behavior. I had developed a theory that behavioral traits could be passed on to offspring just as easily as, perhaps more easily than, physical traits."

The realization of what he was saying had already fallen into place in my mind, though it seemed incredible, surreal, like some crazed sci-fi movie come to life.

"The FBI had just begun toying with the idea of a behavior analysis unit and I was setting the groundwork, establishing the core of knowledge that is required to further any field of study that is worth pursuing. But when I presented my theories to my supervisors, they were not interested—at least not then. You see where this is going, don't you? I know you are the one who figured out the fertility clinic connection."

How could he know that? "Yes, I put it together."

"Of course. Simple, really, wasn't it?" When I didn't answer him, he said again, his voice like ice, "Wasn't it?"

"Yes," I said.

"But that's the thing. Sometimes things are so simple people overlook them." He seemed to drift off for a moment, but his eyes shifted back to the barn before coming back to me.

"We don't have much time, so I'll have to give you the *Reader's Digest* condensed version. I'm sure you won't mind. If you want to know more, you'll just have to do your own homework. The short of it is that I decided to do some experimenting on my own. Fertility clinics were just coming into vogue and opening in most big cities. I traveled to many of them and made my deposits, as you have discovered by tracking so many of my offspring. What can I say? It worked."

He said this last part as though he were bragging about his sublime theory or his virility, or perhaps both. I did not know or care. I had begun to smell smoke, and though I could not see it yet, I knew it must have been coming from the barn. I looked at the wooden structure, then back at him. When I did, I found he had scooted forward, his face only inches from mine, as if he were observing me. It was one of the eeriest moments of my life. He was so close I could smell his breath and see the whisker pores in his throat. I had a sudden urge to sink my teeth into his jugular vein and rip his throat out, but I held back, waiting for him to finish.

"Uh-huh," he said triumphantly, but did not explain himself.

"What went wrong?" I asked him, trying to hurry him, just as I saw the first wisp of smoke coming from the cockloft of the barn.

"Wrong? Nothing went wrong. The only thing wrong was that I am, at no fault of my own, a serial killer," he said, as if it were as much a surprise to him as to anyone. "I was born that way. Just as some people are born to be fat, or short, or geniuses, or cops, or doctors, or even...firemen. Dark eyes, dimples, good teeth, somewhat pointy ears, lean body mass, musical abilities, the artist's eye, premature gray hair—these are all inheritable traits, of course, but behavior? That was a new spin. More is known about it now, but it was new back then, and Cerberus knew I was on to something. He also found out about my...weakness, shall I say. So he exploited it. He turned me in, but the heads of the FBI at that time decided they could not allow the public to find out that one of their own researchers was not only a serial killer but one who may have spread his *disease*, if you will, throughout the nation. They made up a name for me and quickly convicted me and put me away. If you dig deep enough, somewhere you will find reference to the Armageddon Project, as they were calling it for a while.

"Meanwhile, Cerberus quit the FBI and began his consulting firm. One of the first things he did was to approach the Afghans, who were our allies at the time and fighting a war with the Russians, about some *experimental weaponry*. It involved making supersoldiers, not unlike the Nazis tried to do in World War II."

"Are you telling me…?"

"Yes! Now you've got it. He sold my seed to the Afghans to be implanted in their women. You have to understand, these are patient people, Islamic extremists who have been fighting the Western infidels for almost two thousand years. They could wait and see, and they did. Let me tell you, when you take the seed of a serial killer and mix it genetically with people who have evolved into religious fanatics, you get some *very* dangerous people. Do you think I'm making this up?"

"I wish you were."

He was silent for a moment, as if contemplating, then continued. "Why do you think the incidents of serial killings and terrorism have increased equally and exponentially in the past thirty years? It's because of *me*," he said, and I watched his face transition from gleeful boasting to almost tragic disillusion. He was without a doubt the most insane person I'd ever encountered.

"You don't seemed pleased with your *experiment*," I said.

He sighed heavily. "You're right. It was not the legacy I wanted to leave. I am a serial killer, but I am also a patriot. That's why I was working for the FBI in the first place. I love my country. But Cerberus ruined my vision by selling my seed—selling *me*, actually—to the very people we're now fighting! Worse, Cerberus has found a way to double-dip, so to speak. Now he is selling the services of some of my people, my children, back to the US government to go fight these terrorists. It would almost be comical if it wasn't so…*wrong.*"

"So now you're trying to erase what you've done? Is that what you're telling me? Is that why you've been killing these other killers? They're your offspring, aren't they?"

"Yes. And Haskell was the first one Cerberus was selling back to the US. He was to be the ultimate soldier, a serial killer assigned by our government to help kill a nation of serial killer offspring."

"Oh my God," I said. "You tried to tell us, didn't you? That's why you urinated on the Matarese girl, then put your fingerprint on the church sign." The incredible scope of this madness had hit me as if I'd run into a wall. "You're the one who sent me the text message that Haskell was at his trailer at Lake Okeechobee."

"And the identification numbers at the crime scenes of the other killers. Yes, all mine and a righteous service to the public, too, if I have to say it myself. These were really awful people, you know." He paused as if waiting for my appreciation of his efforts. I could think of nothing to say. He went on while I just listened to him, contemplating my options and feeling the panic of time running out. "I was hoping my clues would tell the right investigator what was happening, but you know, cops are so dumb. Who knew a fire investigator would be the smartest one in the group?"

"I had help."

"Yes, you did," he said, almost proudly. "You had my genes, after all."

I stood up again now. The smoke was coming heavily from the roof of the barn, and I could not ignore it anymore.

"You're wrong," I told him. "I know who my parents were."

He grinned at me like a Cheshire cat. "Do you really? I think not, but I will not quibble with you. I see you've noted the barn is burning and you'll want to save your friend. But rest assured, I know my own offspring when I see them, and you're one of them. Don't tell me you didn't notice some family resemblance when you encountered Haskell?"

"That's what you came to tell me?"

"Yes, and to give you a task. You see, I am through. My time on this earth has reached its end. I want you to kill me. Make me pay for my transgressions."

I stared at him for a long moment. "Okay. Gladly. But why not just kill yourself? You have the gun."

"Because I needed to set you on a path. One which you will pursue until you have eliminated my progeny—your brothers, sisters, and cousins."

"I'm not a killer. Why me?"

"Ah, but you *are* a killer, you just haven't realized it yet. You have the perfect blend of genes. But you also have the gift, too, yes? You can see things, right? You see these killers sometimes before they even act. Just like your mother and me."

"My mother?"

I heard wood popping now and turned to see flames beginning to come from the eaves of the barn's roof. It was full of hay, and once that caught, the whole place would ignite like kindling. I had to get out there and try to save Emily, if she was still alive.

"Yes, but we're out of time." He took the gun and handed it to me. "I'm afraid it's not loaded. You're going to have to do something more…primal. So, *do it.*"

Now it was up to me. I did not have all the answers I needed from him and I certainly wanted to know more, especially that bullshit about my mother. I wanted to know how he had escaped from jail and what Rasmussen had meant when he said, *Rose was a part of it and didn't even know*...But there was no time. He had timed it all perfectly.

I tried pulling him with me as I pushed toward the barn. He grabbed hold of a rail on the patio and would not let go.

"I killed one of my daughters a couple of weeks ago," he said, his breathing becoming labored as he struggled to stay anchored as I yanked on him, my own breath ragged, my aching ribs burning inside my chest. "She had...killed her own child. But...when I came to kill her and I...placed my hands on her throat...it was beautiful. She *wanted* me to do it."

I stopped pulling on him now, went forward, and began smashing him in the head with my elbows. Images of my boot camp training when I was becoming a Special Ops Airborne Ranger—a trained killer—popped into my head: *Never use your fists if you're serious about maiming or killing someone. Use your elbows.* I pummeled him until he was almost unconscious and let go of the rail. Once he let go, I did not hesitate. I fumbled through his pockets trying to find keys to the handcuffs, but there were none. If I tried to drag him to the barn with me, it would take too long.

I looked around the patio and remembered my grill. I had left some barbecue tongs and a knife out there when I had cooked for Rose a week ago. I dragged Gettys with me to the grill. It was a struggle just getting that far with him, but it confirmed for me what I had to do. I grabbed the knife and began hacking at his wrist. It was a sharp knife, but did not have a chopping blade. But it was a boning knife, and I maneuvered its edges through the bones in his wrist. Gettys screamed in agony until he vomited and passed out from the pain. His hand fell off as his wrist spurted blood all over me and the handcuff pulled away.

I turned and began to run as fast as I could with my useless leg, the cast riding up and biting into my groin with each step. I brought the knife with me, my years as a firefighter telling me to bring a tool, any tool, with me into a fire. Finally, I reached the barn, thick, black smoke roiling out of it like an old coal-burning engine. There was a garden hose on the side of the wooden structure, but it was far too late for that. The sides of the barn were burning now and I would be lucky if I could even make my way in. I swung open the barn doors and was pushed back by the heat and smoke. I went down to my belly and began to crawl, calling for Emily as I went. I did not know where she was and my fear was that I would make it to one end of the barn only to find she was not there, but it was a chance I had to take. I went to the right, toward Sisco's stall. Smoke was hanging low and as thick as wool blankets just over my head. I could hear the wood groaning and popping above my head and knew I had only minutes, maybe less, before it all came tumbling in.

I found the stall and Emily and Sisco were there. They were alive, but both of them were unconscious, saliva dripping from their mouths, obviously drugged.

I grabbed Emily and shook her and she began to flutter her eyes and moan.

"Emily! Emily!" I shouted. "The barn's on fire!"

Emily woke up groggily and shook off the narcotic as best she could. She had lived in this equestrian community her whole life. Barns catching on fire were nothing new and she did not seem surprised. She got to her knees quickly, found Sisco's lead rope, and began pulling on him. I got behind his neck and tried to push up on him, but he was too far under from the narcotics and was not moving on his own. We pushed and pulled on his legs and his neck but could not move him more than a couple of inches.

A heavy timber cracked and fell, fully aflame, into the center of the barn, sending out showers of sparks, spreading the fire into our stall. The rest of the building would be right behind it. I kicked out the flames with my one good foot and turned to Emily, who was still trying to move Sisco.

"We...we have to leave him, Emily," I said, the words catching in my throat.

"No!" she yelled back at me. She would not let go of Sisco's reins, though she was choking now from the smoke, her face scarlet from her exertions, tears streaking the soot on her face.

"We *have* to," I said. I leaned down and kissed Sisco's face and smelled his wonderful horse smell one last time. I could hear him breathing slowly, so drugged he would never wake up and, I prayed, never feel anything.

Emily was crying uncontrollably now and holding onto Sisco's reins. It was now or never. I wrenched her hands free even as she fought me as though I were her attacker, a killer, and not someone trying to save both of us. I managed to avoid her flailing hands and fingernails, swooped her up, and threw her out the open window through which, in gentler days, Sisco would have been peeking his head out, waiting for me to bring him a carrot or a lump of sugar.

I smelled meat cooking, like someone was in there with us grilling a tenderloin. I looked back and saw the straw burning under Sisco's legs. He was being cooked alive and a desperate urgency filled my chest until I thought I would burst. I went back to Sisco, quickly found the knife I had dropped in the straw littering the floor of his stall and began to feel his skull. I placed the knife at its base, where I believed the medulla oblongata, the organ that regulates breathing at the top of the spine, would be. With shaking hands, I put the point against the crease between skull and spine and drove it home with the palm of my hand.

I watched Sisco's body shake violently, then his respirations stopped. His eyes glazed over almost instantly. Then I dived out the window, my cast-stiffened leg hitting the ground with a loud snap. I did not care about the pain as I got to my feet and made Emily get up under my arms and help me back toward the house. She protested leaving Sisco behind, but took my weight anyway. We did not get ten feet from the barn when there was a final groan and a loud crack and the entire roof tumbled into the barn, the walls falling in after it, flames shooting into the sky as if from a funeral pyre and a wave of heat hitting us so hard it almost pushed us over.

Emily sobbed but helped me to the house, both of us coughing as if to spit up a lung. Gettys was there, sitting on the patio like he had just stopped by for an evening cocktail. He was holding pressure on the stump of where his severed hand had been; the bleeding had slowed significantly.

"Bravo!" he said. "You made it. I *knew* you could. I would applaud…" he said, shrugging his shoulders and holding up the stump. It was all one big joke to him. But it was not to me.

"That's the man that poked me and Sisco with a needle and hit Scout with a shovel," whispered Emily, as if telling me a secret.

"I know, Emily," I said, and pulled her to me. I kissed her dirt-smudged face tenderly and hugged her. "Would you do me a favor and go call nine-one-one?"

She looked at me, worried.

"Go on," I said as gently as I could, trying to hide the rage that burned as hot in me now as the fire that was consuming my barn. "Tell them there's been a fire and someone is hurt."

She looked at me and nodded. Then, keeping her eye on Gettys as she walked past him, she waved her finger in childish admonition at him and went inside my home to make the call.

Once I knew she was in the house and could not see me, I went to where Gettys was sitting. He looked up at me and said, "Do it."

I grabbed his skull with both of my hands, placing my thumbs over his eyes, then began to push. I stuck my thumbs all the way in past the sockets, his eyes popping like gelatin balls, and kept going, pushing past the thin bones at the back of his eye sockets and digging into his brain. He screamed at first, then began to convulse as I twisted my fingers inside his sick brain until he was dead.

He was right. I am a killer.

FORTY-FOUR

They let Rose visit me in the hospital. They had allowed her to plead to manslaughter and she was going to have to do some jail time at a federal facility, but she remained free until her sentence began in the fall. When she came in, she looked more at peace than I had ever seen her. Her black hair gleamed blue in the florescent light of the hospital room, her smile was wide, her skin full and hydrated and smelling like vanilla. No more nervous tics or dark circles or worry lines in her face. She didn't seem like the tough law enforcement officer anymore, but simply a woman, innocently alluring, sensual, but fragile at the same time. She seemed so at ease I could never bring myself to tell her what Cecil had told me about the blood samples, nor did I have him take my blood to match against what they found that day in Haskell's trailer. I believed I knew what the sample would tell us, but what good could it possibly do to confirm anyone's relation to a family such as this?

When she left that day, she told me she loved me. The admission did not help make things easier. I was not sure when I'd see her again, and as the door closed behind her, I felt that subtle but steady pain of longing begin. I didn't know when it would end, if it ever would.

I had breathed in too much smoke in the burning barn and developed a touch of pneumonia. My kneecap had to be rebuilt again and my doctor thought it best for me if I stayed in the hospital and recuperated for a few weeks. When he found out about the seizures I'd been having, he insisted on running a battery of tests, none of which suggested a physiological cause for the seizures. I was mentally and physically exhausted and deeply depressed. No one should have to find in himself the awful things I uncovered within me the day I killed Gettys. It opened my mind to too many pitch-black thoughts and a soul-sickening uncertainty about not only who I was but what I was capable of doing.

I had seen some possessors of the Gettys strain, so I knew I did not share their most commonly held physical attributes— the dark eyes, the gray temples, the dimpled chin. Though, the night I had fought with Haskell, I could not help but notice some physical similarities between us. But all of Gettys's progeny had different mothers, and their maternal gene pools were surely as capable of influencing their children as much as Gettys's had. They wouldn't all look like him, nor would they necessarily have to be homicidal killers.

Yes, I had killed a man, so I was by definition a killer. But what kind of killer was I? I wondered if the desire to kill had always been there in me without my being aware of it and if it was something I would do again, and if so, when. Maybe Gettys killing Sisco and almost killing Emily had flicked the switch that allowed me to kill that which I hated. If so, that rationalization did not lessen the guilt I felt, nor did it offer any validation or solace. And it only deepened my fear of discovering I was indeed one of Gettys's godless seedlings. It made me not only wonder who and what I am, but dread the answers to those questions.

It did not help when I later found out Gettys had had terminal melanoma. He knew he was going to die and passed on his twisted quest to me. And I knew I would take it on, too. Knowing what I knew now, how could I ignore the fact that there were dozens, perhaps hundreds, of potential and realized killers out there, stalking other people's loved ones, and still others training to become terrorists under the watch of clandestine and unconscionable mercenaries subsidized by unknowing or uncaring governments?

On the positive side, Scout was alive. She came wandering up to me after my last business with Gettys that day, covered in soot, a gashed bump on her head. I attribute her tiny dog kisses with bringing me back to the real world and out of my mad, homicidal rage.

My sister Grace came to see me, too. Leonard had called her and told her about the fire at the barn and that I was in the hospital. We had grown distant in the past few years. Her family responsibilities in California and my involvement with the state fire marshal's office had consumed us. But when she walked into the room, that distance vanished, and after a few awkward moments, we were recollecting funny times from our youth, the love and closeness we once shared with each other and our hardworking, dedicated mother.

Finally, I just came out and asked her. "Grace, you were six when Dad left," I said. "You had to have had a better inkling about what made him go. Do you remember what happened?"

Her smile faded; the crinkles around her eyes flattened. Her chest rose and fell with several deep breaths before she answered. "Why are you asking now?"

"I don't know," I lied. "Maybe when you see your own mortality, it makes you wonder about where you came from as much as where you're going."

"So the fireman becomes the philosopher?" she said, her smile edging out again. "What did Mom tell you?"

"She was always vague about it. Said it just didn't work out. And yet, when I see old pictures of them together, they looked like a happy couple."

"They were," she said thoughtfully. "But you remember how driven Mom was."

"Sure. She was brassy."

"I don't know if I should even be telling you this, but what the hell. We're grown up now, right?" She looked out the hospital window, her eyes a little glassy. "Mom always wanted another child. She wanted me to have a sibling I could play with and grow up with. But Dad wasn't keen on the idea. And anyway, when they did try again, I found out later, nothing happened. I don't know exactly what the problem was. All I know is that she told me once, right after my Charlie was born, that she had wanted a bigger family, but that it 'couldn't happen.'"

My pulse had quickened and a lump had formed in my throat. My skin grew itchy, and though they kept it freezing in the hospital, I began to perspire. "So how did I come about?"

Grace took my hand with one of hers, then ran her other hand up my arm, as if trying to flush circulation back into my skin. Then she stopped, got up, and paced the room for a minute, pulling at the neck of her sweater, before coming to rest by the window, the sun lighting her up like a Madonna statue. "Mom worked in all the area hospitals and knew a lot of doctors. One of them was a fertility doctor who she became good friends with. She talked him into giving her artificial insemination without Dad knowing about it. It wasn't exactly new back then, but it wasn't common, either. She was always ahead of her time."

A ringing had risen into my ears. "So you're saying I was a… test tube baby?"

"That's not a very nice way of putting it, but yes. She had herself impregnated. And once Dad found out she was pregnant—I guess somehow he knew you couldn't be his child. He accused her of messing around, began to drink more, and they had horrible fights. Then he was gone."

"Why didn't she ever tell me that?"

"Maybe she didn't tell you for a reason."

"Such as?"

"Because she didn't want you to think you were the reason they split up." She took another deep breath, then forced herself to look at me. "When I was a young, self-centered girl, I used to blame their splitting up on you. I'm sorry. It really had nothing to do with you. You didn't ask to be born and were nothing but a good son to Mom. And a great brother to me."

Her arms were clutched across her chest and she rubbed them briskly with her hands like the room had grown colder. After a minute, she came back to sit on the edge of my bed.

"I hope you're not mad at me for not telling you before now, but I didn't know until a few years ago. I was sort of surprised, but it didn't really matter. You were and are still my brother. I love you, Grey. I'm sorry we've let distance keep us from getting together more often, but the boys are a little older now and are becoming who they are going to be. I feel like I'm starting to get some of my old self back. We should plan something. Why don't you come to Cali when you get out of the hospital? The summer's beautiful in San Francisco. We could take a trip to Napa or out to the coast."

I smiled at her. "Sure, sis," I replied. "That sounds great."

Cecil and Amy called to tell me that they were engaged. No surprise there. I summoned some false bravado and told him I'd be up soon for a visit and we could celebrate then. I'd bring the bubbly. When I asked him to keep our secret about the possible origins of those blood samples under his hat, Cecil just said, "What samples?"

Emily called to see how I was doing and tell me she was doing fine. In fact, since she had almost been killed, her parents had "turned nice," she told me. She didn't know why, but I could hear a lightness in her voice I'd never heard before. She said her daddy was building me a new barn. When I told her I didn't have a horse anymore, she informed me that a new horse had come into the Vinceremos School. It had been mistreated and orphaned by some "bad people," but she was fattening it up. It was going to need a new home, and would I consider it? I said I'd think about it and thanked her for calling. "Thank *you*, silly," she said, and I heard her giggling as she hung up the phone. For some reason, I thought of the light spray of freckles that spread across her nose and cheeks, and that made me feel a little better for a while.

Of course, Leonard came by with Vanessa and they tried to pull me out of my funk. Shaking my hand, dwarfing it with his huge paw, Leonard said, "I heard your blood pressure was a little low, so I brought my gorgeous woman along to fix that." He nodded toward his wife. "Take a look at this fine wine."

"Oh, good Lord, Leonard," Vanessa said, giving him a playful slap. She leaned over and gave me a big kiss on the cheek. "How you doing, baby? You gonna man up and crawl outta here sometime this year? You're missing a lot of barbecues at the Cotton home." She was dressed in tight jeans, little black pumps, and a cream-colored spandex top, her ample breasts threatening to pop out at any moment. She was an angel, I knew, but she sure didn't look like it.

"You are one lucky bastard, Mr. Cotton," I said.

"Language, Grey!" said Vanessa, her eyes getting big, round, and serious. Then she softened again. "We brought you a surprise."

"An oversexed personal nurse from Sweden?"

She turned down the corners of her mouth and shook her head, feigning displeasure of my crass ways.

"You better get out of here, and soon. You need a soul-saving visit to my church."

"Hallelujah."

She laughed, then placed her hands over my eyes.

"Make sure he can't see," said Leonard. I heard him move across the room and open the door.

Vanessa whipped her hands away from my eyes and said, "Surprise!"

When I opened my eyes, I found a young man sitting in a wheelchair. He was maybe seventeen or eighteen years old. He looked vaguely familiar, but I couldn't quite get there. He stared at me intently and a huge grin appeared on his face.

Then he stood up from the chair.

He was a little wobbly and Vanessa moved to help stabilize him, but he shooed her away. "I got it, Mrs. Cotton."

Vanessa backed away, her big brown eyes pooling with tears.

Leonard looked at her, crossed the room, and took her in his arms. "Don't start, baby, or you'll get me going, too," he said, and kissed her forehead. But it was too late and tears ran down their cheeks even as they smiled at me.

The young man made his way over to me, slowly, with increased confidence in each step. He made it to my bed and took my hand and squeezed it with a strong, firm grip. "You probably don't remember me," he said, his eyes shining. "But when you were a firefighter and I was a little boy, you pulled me out of an attic just as the roof caved in on both of us."

And all at once, I could see that terrified, trapped boy in his face and could see the relief in his eyes when he saw I'd come to rescue him. But then the roof had collapsed, crushing his spine and my head. The last time I'd seen him was when he was in the hospital getting the news he would never walk again.

But now he was walking.

"My name is Michael," he said.

"I remember," I said. Then we were all crying. For once, it was for something good.

• • •

Restless, I checked out a few days later and went home, my leg in a new cast, a cane assisting me as I limped into my house. The place seemed larger than I remembered, too big for one person, and I began to think about moving back to my cozier condo on the beach. The Wellington house had never seemed so empty as it did at that moment. The loss of Sisco and the absence of Emily tending to him underscored my loneliness. I roamed around as if I were looking for something but could not remember just what.

I wandered out to the patio and saw the stain of blood where I had killed Gettys. My boss, Sam Brandsma, had stopped by and tried to clean it up after the investigators were done with their inquiries, but I could still see the outline in the rough surface of the paver stones. The one time we'd talked since then, Bland Sam had mentioned, *unofficially*, that perhaps I might want to look into some anger-management counseling. I think I needed something more than that.

I tried to plant other, more positive information in my mind: memories of citrus-scented drinks, sleek and tanned bikini beauties partying poolside after a day of kitesurfing, ska music drifting on the air, a peaceful kaleidoscopic blend of wine, women, and song. But all that dissipated quickly when I looked at the stark remnants of the murder scene in my own backyard.

When I turned away, something caught my eye over where the grill hunched like a giant metallic frog with something sticking out of its mouth. A piece of paper was jutting out from under the lid. The crime scene investigators must have disregarded it as just paper used as fire starter, but I knew it wasn't supposed to be there. I limped over and opened the grill. There was a dog-eared journal on the grate. I picked it up and began to read.

It was a hard copy of the journal Rasmussen had referred to just before Rose shot him. Evidently, Gettys had been recording his activities as he first searched for his offspring, then began to kill them.

There were dozens of entries from all over the country detailing the lives of the Gettys strain. The entries were detailed, no doubt due to Gettys's memory of where he'd sown his seeds, aided by new technology and by his inherent ability to "see" his progeny as they carried out their various horrors. Gettys knew all the sample numbers from the 56QAH lots and where he had made the deposits, information Cerberus evidently did not have, or he would have acted on it on his own, recruiting these killers for his own nefarious plans. Cerberus gave him top-secret computer access that enabled him to track them. A deal was struck. Gettys would get out of jail and be paid lots of money, and Cerberus would get more "super-soldier" candidates, as well as potential seed donors. But when Gettys found out Cerberus was working all the angles, betraying the United States while reaping millions, Gettys decided to put an end to Cerberus's scheme.

But he had not killed them all. As I read, I tried to wrap my mind around who and what he was. If he was a monster for having created these sociopathic progeny who had taken so many lives, had he achieved some measure of redemption for, having realized his terrible mistake, fighting to stop their spread?

I went inside to my laptop and looked at the models Cecil and Amy had constructed showing the fertility clinics littered across the nation and, blooming around them like human petri dishes, the grisly murder site evidence of the spread of Gettys's DNA. The sites correlated exactly with his journal. Now it was all inescapably real to me, and the horror and enormity of the problem overwhelmed me. It was something that was not going to go away, and realizing that allowed me to begin to accept the dark burden that had been placed upon my shoulders.

I had a lot of work to do.

• • •

That night, I dreamed of the day my mother died. At first, she was in her bed, withered to a flesh-covered skeleton, cheeks and eyes sunken, bedsores beginning to develop no matter how often I turned her. Her body already showing signs of decorticate posturing as she began to move into a fetal position. Her breathing was rapid, and when I put my fingers on her wrist to check her pulse, I found she was cool and clammy and her heart was racing at 180 beats a minute, and I knew she would not last much longer. The realization that I was about to lose her caused fear to well up in me one moment, then relief the next.

Hospice had been caring for her for months. The last few times they'd been there, they'd given me the same instructions: give her as much morphine as she wants when she has pain. Knowing that an overdose of morphine can cause respiratory failure, I said I didn't want to give her too much. Finally, one of the hospice nurses looked at me and said, "Why not?"

I knew what she was saying, and when the time came, I gave my mother as much morphine as she needed.

A breeze came in through her open windows, stirring the room's gauzy curtains and rippling the flame of the candle I had placed on her nightstand next to the small porcelain statue of the Virgin Mary that she favored. The breeze stopped, like a final exhalation, and as the flame stood tall again and the curtains lay back against the window screens, I felt her pulse stop, like a switch had been turned off. I saw her eyes fix and her pupils dilate, and I heard her last breath go out, as if it were following that gentle breeze.

Then, in my mind, I could see her again as a young girl, running through a field of alfalfa in Missouri, her auburn hair curled and bouncing and reflecting the sunlight as a small dapple-gray pony, her favorite, ran behind her, tossing its mane and kicking up its rear legs, the very embodiment of youth and hope, of renewed life and eternal spring.

THE END

EPILOGUE

"I know, Senator," said the man into the phone. "We had the operative ready to go. But there were…complications. A security breach. I thought we had the Justice Department on board, but evidently they've got some freelancing going on in their organization that compromised our mission."

The man removed his light-gradient glasses and wiped the lenses with a silk handkerchief he kept in his breast pocket, then replaced his glasses and gazed upon his reflection in the glass of his office window, superimposed like a ghost over the window's magnificent view of the streets of Athens and, in the distance, the Acropolis. The man's black eyes looked tired. They were unsettling eyes to look at. He knew this; it was the reason he wore the darkened lenses. He didn't want to unsettle his clients, many of whom were funny about people's eyes. "Windows to the soul" was not just some cliché in the Arab world in which he did 90 percent of his business.

"No, Senator, you didn't make a mistake. We're already looking at other operatives, as well as more donors. This is just the beginning. Most of our subjects are only now reaching their useful prime. We'll have what the United States needs to turn this war around."

The man smiled.

"Yes, sir. That's precisely right. We're going to be fighting fire with fire. I'll be in touch when we are ready for the next deployment."

He hung up the phone and it immediately rang again. Sometimes he wished he had three heads so he could conduct his business more efficiently. This time it was the tribal chieftain he'd been doing business with for years.

"*Aasalaamu Aleikum, Haafiz,*" the man said warmly. "*Kayf Halak?*" Nicholas Cerberus enjoyed speaking Arabic. It came from the gut, up the esophagus, and propelled itself out from the back of the throat. He had said, "Hello, Haafiz," a name that meant *guardian*, or *preserver*, appropriately, and "How are you?"

Haafiz tried to respond in his broken English, upon which Cerberus complimented him, but continued using Arabic. After thirty years, he was quite proficient with it.

"Yes, Haafiz, everything is in order. We have several of our operatives in place now. In fact, you should be hearing about one very soon in your country. We have another deeply embedded in the United States Army. He's ready, too. This very day, we will strike into the heart of the infidels. No, sir. No need for that bank transfer. No. I have decided that more of the Saudi oil shares would be beneficial to me right now. Not for you to worry about. I've worked it out with your business office. Thank you, sir. Allah be praised."

• • •

A secret CIA base in Afghanistan
Subject: 56QAH/Lot 1711

The group of high-level CIA handlers and their Afghan counterparts had assembled at an Army field base in an obscure area just outside Pakistan. Their number one operative, a man named Kabullah Khan, had called with an urgent message: he could give them the leader of the rebel movement, a man the world knew only as Mohamed, Osama Bin Laden's successor.

There was nervous energy and excitement, so much so that the handlers were going to call in General Petraeus, but decided to talk with Khan first. They wanted to see what Khan had to say, even though this was the closest they had come to capturing or killing Mohamed and they were all bursting to move ahead.

No one had ever told them, evidently, that if something sounds too good to be true, it probably is.

They had called in the highest-ranking intelligence officials in the area and they were now all huddled in a single large tent, smoking cigars and sipping precelebratory brandy. None of them could believe their good fortune in having recruited Khan, who had only a year before been an al-Qaeda operative. Khan, a Jordanian doctor who had been pursuing the roots of his Islamic heritage when he was captured and "turned" by the insurgency group, was rescued by allied forces and "turned" again, this time for the "right" side.

The phone rang and one of the CIA agents picked it up. After a moment, he placed the phone back down and, unable to fully suppress a grin, said, "He's here."

A few minutes later, Khan was escorted into the tent by a soldier who was dismissed so that the top-secret conversation could begin.

"Greetings, Dr. Khan," said the senior operative. "We're so glad you could make it and are eager to hear what you have to say." He added, "I'm not supposed to say this, but even the president has heard of this meeting and wants to be briefed as soon as we conclude here."

Khan smiled widely at them, his dark-brown, nearly black eyes gleaming in the dim light of the tent. He ran his fingers along the sides of his head, brushing back the windswept gray hair at his temples. He breathed deeply and looked around at each man who was there with him. He swallowed, cleared his throat, and looked up to the top of the tent—and, for him, beyond, to heaven.

"Allah be praised!" he said, then reached down to the detonator on the explosive belt he wore and ignited the bomb. The tent and all who were inside it became an expanding ball of fire that ascended up into the sky, into the heavens, where all good martyrs go to collect their promised seventy-two virgins.

• • •

Columbus, Georgia, Fort Benning, US Army Base
Subject: 56QAH/Lot 1432

Major Alan Bashir thanked the driver of the transport vehicle that had dropped him off at his new quarters. He declined the offer to help him with his luggage—a single, heavy, military-issued duffel bag and a laptop case—and entered his Spartan housing.

The major, Ashouk Al-Bashir Hussim—his Islamic given name, legally changed prior to his indoctrination into the US Army over twelve years before—thoroughly scrutinized his new but very temporary home. He removed all light bulbs and looked under all moveable objects—lamps, toaster, soap dishes, wastebaskets, and so forth—to confirm there were no electronic listening devices present. He removed all electrical outlet covers, looked into all overhead light fixtures and phone jacks to ensure that there were no hidden video recording devices. He spent his first four hours on base assuring himself that his quarters were not being secretly monitored, and worked up a sweat doing it.

The major looked at himself in the mirror as he freshened up over the bathroom sink. At thirty-two years old, he already had some premature gray in his hair in the temporal area of his head, but otherwise looked ten years younger than most soldiers his age. His body was hardened muscle and lean, with less than 3 percent body fat. His eyes were dark, focused, and intense. His teeth were like luminous porcelain over his dimpled chin. He was handsome, but not particularly vain; his religious beliefs did not allow that. While in the restroom, he also took time to look into the toilet tank and peered into the cabinet mirror to assure he was not being covertly observed. Why should he be? He was a major in this man's Army, as well as a respected doctor of internal medicine, having gone to med school on the Army's dime.

Confident his quarters were "clean," he laid his duffel bag on his bed, opened it up, and began to remove the automatic and fully loaded weapons that were inside. If he hurried, he could still make it to lunch. The base's mess hall would be open for the midday meal and full of unsuspecting fellow soldiers: shallow, capitalist, American infidels who did not deserve to live.

He would kill them all.

About the Author

Photograph by Cooper Kendrick

Patrick Kendrick spent thirty years in the fire service, working every rank from firefighter to chief fire officer, before retiring to burn up the pages as a full-time mystery writer. *Extended Family* is his second novel. His first, *Papa's Problem*, won a 2009 Florida Book Award. Patrick lives in South Florida, where he enjoys the ocean and spending time with his family.

www.talesofpatrickkendrick.com

BAYVILLE FREE LIBRARY

3 6639 00047 1089

FIC
KEN

Kendrick, Patrick.
Extended family/

14.95   7/2/12
B&T

Bayville Free Library
34 School Street
Bayville, New York 11709

Telephone 628-2765

BV